Angel Manor

Lucifer Falls Trilogy Book 1

Chantal Noordeloos

First published in 2014 by
Horrific Tales Publishing
This edition published March 2015
http://www.horrifictales.co.uk
Copyright © 2014 Chantal Noordeloos

A CIP catalogue record for this book is available from
the British Library

ISBN: 1-910283-02-9
ISBN-13: 978-1-910283-02-8

Angel Manor

"[Chantal's] writing pins you in place and delves deep into your soul to find those things you'd rather keep hidden. It is sharp, focused, and direct. It strikes when you least expect it and burrows into your soft, unprotected places. The heart. The brain. The guts. The soul."

JG Faherty, Bram Stoker and ITW Thriller nominated author of *Carnival of Fear, Legacy,* and *Fatal Consequences.* jgfaherty@jgfaherty.com

ACKNOWLEDGMENTS

Ahhh, the acknowledgments... my moment to thank everyone who has helped me through the insanity of publishing a book. This is the moment where I get to dazzle everyone with beautiful words that will make those special people feel invaluable. In truth this actually the moment where I sit in front of a blank screen for hours, feeling the train of blind panic approaching the station, because I want to get it right... but I don't know what to say.

cracks knuckles So... here goes nothing.

This is to all of you who believe in me. Who take the time to pick up this book, or any other work written by me, and read me. To those of you who take the time to write a review (I love you for it)

I have to wave my pom-poms for the very awesome Stephen Bryant who made my cover. He took my ideas and made something so stunning that the first time I saw it, I may have gotten a little teary eyed.

A great big thank you to my editors, Lisa Jenkins and Simon Marshall Jones, who have made this manuscript into a real book. Who have hunted down all my mistakes and beaten them in submission.

A hug and a kiss to my awesome beta readers, Vix Kirkpatrick and Kerri Patterson, who read the manuscript when it was still far too big and messy. They gave me their time, critical eye and honest opinion... what more could a writer want? You girls are amazing.

And finally all the love to the people who got me through the rough moments. A special shout out to my loving husband, Daan Noordeloos, and to my very dear friend Jim McLeod, who both have my back when I need them to.

I am very fortunate to have so many great people who support me. Even if I didn't mention you by name in this acknowledgment, know that you mean the world to me. Thank you all.

To Graeme, who is the Statler to my Waldorff

To my nun-fearing Jim, who will forever haunt my pages,

And to Chris, whose voice will forever chase my demons away.

Prologue

Summer Solstice 1822

The blood trickled over the sagging breasts of the Mother Superior, staining her white skin crimson. The limp body of a five-year-old boy hung slack in her arms.

"Reverend Mother..." Sister Agatha's voice trembled. "There must be a kinder way to kill the child, one not so... inhumane?"

The nun looked up at her, her wrinkled face a canvas of red splatter framing pale-blue eyes which almost seemed to glow. The older woman straightened herself, letting the child drop with a wet smack, her wrinkled hand still wrapped around one of his arms as the lower part of his body hung slack against her ankle. He looked like a limp doll, a toy she hadn't quite finished playing with.

The nun's lips curled into a sneer, and her eyes narrowed. "Sister Agatha, I know you are new to the order, but when you took your holy vows, you were instructed in the rules of the convent. This is your first solstice, and I understand that our methods may seem harsh to a newcomer, but we have a sacred duty." The woman dropped the arm and stepped over the young boy. Trails of blood trickled down her torso and across her legs, covering them in a slick red layer. "Do you think I enjoy this?"

"Yes," Sister Agatha wanted to scream, *"You've lived too long in this world of torment and murder, and it has turned you into a monster."*

"No, Reverend Mother." Agatha lowered her eyes, focusing on the blood pooling around the young boy's body.

"I know this isn't easy, Sister." Calloused hands grasped

her cheek and chin, forcing her to look into those terrible eyes. "But we follow God's will. If we don't, the consequences will be disastrous, and for more than just a handful of unwanted children. No one cares for these wretched souls."

I do, Sister Agatha thought, but she held her tongue. The screams of dying children reverberated through the stone convent. Her eyes pleaded with the Mother Superior.

"Have you considered the ritual that I found? It would save so many of them. There would be no need for all this bloodshed."

"You would ask us to make such a great personal sacrifice for a ritual that might not work?" The older woman shook her head, a condescending smile playing on her wrinkled lips. "Sister Agatha, we've discussed this. There is only one way to ensure the safety of the seal, and we can't take any risks. This is not a game." The blood-stained hand moved down Sister Agatha's neck, passing over her shoulder, and gripped her bare arm, squeezing the flesh. "We thought you were ready for this when you made your vows. You are no stranger to death. You were especially chosen for the blood already on your hands."

Agatha's voice was barely above a whimper. "I am indeed no stranger to blood and death, but I killed sick and deformed children, not healthy ones. I've never seen such gratuitous torment as I have here." Her eyes darted around the chapel to the naked figures of the other Sisters. The sound of lashes drew her eyes to the stout figure of Sister Helene, who cracked a long bullwhip across the backs of a trio of bound children, each no older than seven. Their fragile skin tore as the leather thong licked across their flesh, spilling crimson tears.

In the centre of the chapel hung a twelve-year-old boy, suspended upside down from black ropes. The blade of a large rust-covered saw sliced through the flesh of his groin, a red waterfall gushing from the wound, spraying across his chest and face. The agonised screams the boy made sounded otherworldly, every morbid vibrato note hammering against Agatha's mind. A wave of nausea hit the back of her throat.

The bodies of fallen children lay scattered around the room, their blood coagulating in a pool covering over half the chapel floor. The whimpers coming from the survivors were little more than a pitiful hum.

Agatha had thought her mission noble when she'd first joined the order, but this suffering overwhelmed her with nausea and regret. There was a better way than this needless waste of young life; Agatha was sure of it.

"We could save thousands of lives by sacrificing but a few. Sister Anne and I have studied the texts, and we're pretty confident we can do it... tonight even. We've made all the preparations, just in case you changed your mind. The sacrifice required is relatively small compared—"

The Reverend Mother's hand lashed out, connecting with Agatha's cheek with a loud crack. Pain spread out in tiny pinpricks across her face. Shocked, she clutched her face and looked at the Mother Superior.

"Enough of this!" Spittle flew from the Reverend Mother's lips. "Your rituals are pagan. We serve our Lord here as we were instructed. You had best mind what blasphemous words you utter here, Sister Agatha. The Lord does not look kindly upon heathens." The older woman's face relaxed slightly, and her expression turned from angry to stern. "We will never speak of this again. Now go and make the sacrifices required of us." The old woman shoved her forward with a force that belied her frail appearance. Agatha slipped on a puddle of blood, her legs sprawling under her like an awkward doe's. She fell to the ground, her wrists and elbow hitting the floor hard. Pain shot up through her arms, her naked body shivering on the cold stones. She looked up to see the Mother Superior walk away, leaving bloody footsteps in her wake. Agatha's eyes followed her until she passed the body of little Margaret. The young girl lay with her neck twisted at an impossible angle, eyes staring lifelessly at the horror within the chapel.

I must find Anne. Sister Agatha scrambled to her feet, her hands and legs stained with cold, sticky blood. She glanced at the carnage around her and then she ran, the soles of her feet slapping against stone, the impact rattling her teeth.

She ran from the chapel, through the narrow passages, and across the great cloister. The Sister felt the cold eyes of the twelve stone angels lining the walls of the large open area look down on her. Slowing her pace, she glanced up at the imposing statues. Even knowing stone couldn't judge her, she found it difficult not to imagine God peering down through those blank eyes. A shudder ran through her spine, and she picked up her pace, not stopping until she reached the library.

"Anne..." Her voice reverberated off the high walls, echoing parts of her words back at her. "Sister Anne?"

A voice came from behind her. "Sister Agatha..."

Agatha turned to face her ally. Anne was dressed in a long, white chemise, her red hair loose and flowing like liquid fire over her shoulders. Anne ran down the stairs, the white nightgown fluttering behind her.

"Did you inform the Reverend Mother that we are ready to perform the ritual?"

"I tried." Agatha bit her lip, tasting the salt of her own sweat. "She won't listen to me. She thinks the ritual is too pagan, that it would be an insult to God. And she believes that the risk is too great."

Anne's face fell and she shook her head. "I cannot believe that the sacrifice we make during the solstice and the equinox is God's will. It would be foolish not to at least try. Think of all the lives we could save... I don't understand why..."

A thought formed in Agatha's mind. "Can we perform the ritual ourselves?"

"What?"

"Can we perform the ritual ourselves? Without the help of the order."

"We... we could, but the sacrifice would be much greater. The Sisters might share the children's fate. And we still need a willing sacrifice along with the victims."

The light of the fading sun streamed through the stained glass window, illuminating the picture of an angel. His wings were spread, and he covered his face in an expression of shame. The light danced off Agatha's blonde locks as she straightened herself.

"I will be the willing sacrifice."

Anne gasped, putting her delicate fingers in front of her mouth.

"But it was your task to act as Guardian. To ensure the spell stays in place... to teach future generations how to keep the seal from breaking."

"That task will be yours. There is no one else. Anne, if we want this bloodshed to stop, if we want these to be the last victims, we have no other choice."

Faint screams echoed through the convent. The candles flickered as an unfelt wind blew past them, casting dark elongated shadows across the bookshelves.

Anne sighed. "I agree, as you said... there is no other choice. Very well, I shall take on the task of Guardianship. But if this doesn't work..." Sister Anne clutched her chemise tightly around her neck and shuddered at the thought.

"Then you must continue what the order of the Angels started, Anne. You must create a new order."

11

"I don't know if I can... not on my own."

"Do you have any other choice?"

Anne's shoulders sagged. "That's what it all boils down to now, isn't it? Choice." The two women stared at each other, the tension apparent on their young faces, until a nearby scream broke their eye contact. Anne looked up to the last hints of sunlight glimmering through the window.

"We must act quickly. The sun is setting, and I will need the last of the daylight to perform the ritual. We need the power of the solstice."

"What must I do?" Sister Agatha's voice and body trembled. She'd seen plenty of death, but facing her own was different. Her mortality weighed heavily on her, but the thought of those children's faces was too much for her to bear. Sister Anne grabbed a book that lay open on one of the rough oak tables, the thin paper threatening to fall apart in her hands.

"I need you to draw this symbol on the floor." Sister Anne's finger pressed down so hard on the page that the tip went white. "It needs to be large enough for you to lie in the middle." She handed the book to Agatha, who was surprised by the weight of it. The leather felt smooth in her hand, and the pages smelled of time long past and a little of mildew. Sister Agatha stared at the symbol. To her relief it was no more complicated than a circle with a triangle on the inside.

"I think that shouldn't be too hard a task, as long as you don't expect the circle to be perfectly round. What do I draw with?" She looked over the top of the book, and the expression on the other woman's face made her heart sink. "What?"

"You need to draw it in the blood of a virgin."

"All the children are virgins." Agatha thought about the bodies in the chapel.

"Taking the blood of the dead children isn't enough, Sister Agatha. That won't make it a sacrifice. You must find a living victim for the blood circle; otherwise, you will interfere with the magic of the spell."

Agatha nodded, her face a mask of conviction, and turned on her heel. The slow, heavy drumbeat of determination pounded in her chest as she strode back towards the chapel. A movement caught her eye, and she turned to see Beth, the youngest of the children, slip past one of the stone angels. Beth was only four years old, and she was Sister Agatha's favourite. The girl was exceptionally smart for her age.

"Beth?" Her voice quavered when she spoke. The girl looked at her with big, grey eyes from under blood-matted black curls, her bottom lip trembling.

"Come here, child." Sister Agatha squatted and held her arms open. The girl's face was filled with doubt, but after a few seconds she ran into Agatha's bare arms. The small limbs wrapped around her, the tiny face nestled in the crook of her neck, and Agatha felt how cold the child's skin was. She slid her hand over the girl's shoulder and tangled her fingers in the mass of curls at the back of her head. Her slender fingers closed around a tuft of hair and she yanked the child away from her. Her mouth was a thin line, her eyes hard. Sister Agatha scrambled to her feet, her fingers still clinging on to the little girl's hair. She wanted to say something comforting, but the words stuck in her throat. Instead, she pulled Beth along while the angels looked down on her. Beth struggled, but the child's strength was no match for hers, and the nun could tell that the little girl was exhausted. *It has been a long day.*

Agatha stopped at the large wooden doors, throwing the girl to the ground before them with more force than she intended. A sense of urgency coursed through her body as she fumbled with the latch, and after a brief struggle, she managed to open the door. The scent of fresh grass, intermingled with the faint smell of wild flowers, greeted her, and Sister Agatha felt the last lingering warmth of the setting summer sun on her naked body. She beckoned for the child to come closer.

"Beth..." Her words were no more than an urgent hiss, and she pointed her finger at the floor next to her. "Beth, I don't have time for this, come here." The girl blinked at her and crawled closer. Sister Agatha grabbed the child again and hoisted her to her feet.

"I'm afraid." The girl's voice was sharp with panic.

"As well you should be. I need you to do something, Beth. I need you to run far away from here. Don't look back. Don't tell anyone what you have seen here or where you came from. Can you do that, Beth?"

The little girl nodded, tears pouring down her face, and she wiped the snot from her nose with the back of her hand. The only garment she had on was an off-white shift, but at least she wasn't naked like most of the other children.

"Don't send people to the convent, Beth. This is a bad place. You have to keep our secret." The girl nodded again, her face filled with hesitation, and after a small pause, she pressed her body against Agatha's in a brief hug.

"Go now."

The nun watched the girl run from the convent, towards the valley the locals called 'Lucifer Falls'. Then, as quickly as she could, she closed the door and replaced the latch. An overwhelming sob rose in her throat. Sister Agatha walked away from the door, but fell to her knees only a few steps further. She looked at the stone angel standing only a few feet away, its finger pointing as if it were condemning her actions.

"Forgive me, Lord. I had to save one..." Tears ran past her cheeks and trickled in lukewarm paths down her neck. "Just one." The rays of the sun slowly retreated across the floor and she remembered Sister Anne's warning that time was running short. Without any further hesitation, she ran to the kitchen and found what she needed. Her hand wrapped around the handle of a large knife, and she turned to run again.

"Sister Agatha..."

Agatha froze, her shoulders tense, as she looked up into the face of the Mother Superior. The nun's voice was harsh and demanding. Agatha hid the knife behind her back.

"Why are you here? I instructed you to do your sacred duty." The older woman took a few steps forward, her aging, blue-veined breasts moving like soft, flabby pendulums. A cat o'nine tails, studded with metal barbs, hung next to her leg, the end of the handle tapping against the folds of skin. There was madness in the old crone's eyes; bloodlust. Agatha realised that the Mother Superior would not take her insubordination lightly, and she suddenly understood why the older woman had followed her into the kitchen.

"Reverend Mother." Her hand clutched the knife behind her back tighter, her eyes fixed on the woman's pale blue ones. She was aware of the gentle swaying motion of the whip. "I was just on my way..."

"You don't understand, do you? You don't grasp the importance of what we do here?" The whip dragged across the floor, the metal spikes scraping against stone. "We suffer in our own way, Sister Agatha. We are the Angels sent by God Almighty to keep the world safe. We torment these children out of love. One day you will understand this, but today you must be punished for your heresy."

Agatha straightened her shoulders and lifted her chin.

"Very well. If that is what God demands of me, I shall take my punishment." She inhaled and held her breath as she walked towards the greying nun. Her hand moved from her back to her side, still hiding the knife from view, her arm stiff with tension. The elder woman's blood-streaked face stayed on her, but Sister Agatha didn't think she'd spotted any suspicion in the Reverend Mother's eyes. The other woman's arm twitched, and the whip made another rustling sound. Agatha waited until she was close enough, then lowered her head in a false sign of submission. The older nun took a step aside, allowing her to pass by on the way out of the kitchen, but instead of walking to the door, Agatha turned and slid the knife into the Mother Superior's kidney. The woman let out a wet gasp and toppled forward. The whip clattered to the ground. Agatha was aware of its existence, as if it was a poisonous snake that could still be a threat. With one foot, she tried to kick it away, but the barbs caught and tore her skin. She pulled the knife free with one swift motion, flipped the Mother Superior around, and clutched her neck, pressing the sharp edge of the blade against the folds of skin under her chin. Her body was tough and hot, blood and sweat making the Reverend Mother slippery. The wound must have taken the old woman by surprise because she barely struggled as Agatha pushed her towards the kitchen doors. The Reverend Mother's body pushed against Agatha's breasts, twitching and gurgling as they walked.

"I've decided I will try this ritual after all, Reverend Mother." Agatha's voice was a low hiss, and a guilty pleasure in feeling the older woman tremble filled her mind. "I need the blood of a virgin. Initially I thought I would have to use one of the children, but then I saw you..."

The Mother Superior moaned and struggled to get loose, but Agatha pressed the knife harder against her neck, and the woman stopped moving. She pushed the reluctant figure towards the library.

"God will punish you for this." Defeat resonated in the older woman's voice, and Agatha realised that the Mother Superior was a coward. She appeared strong and merciless in the face of those who were weaker, as Agatha herself had been, but fear ruled this woman as much as it did the children.

"What are you doing?" Sister Anne stood in the centre of the library, her long, rosy face a mask of incomprehension. "I thought Mother Superior didn't agree to our ritual, and yet you bring her..." The words died on her pale lips as her eyes moved down Agatha's face to the way her arm was wrapped around the older nun's throat, then further still to the cut in the abdomen, from which blood poured in languid trickles.

"You said we needed blood from a virgin." Agatha moved the knife against the puffy skin right beneath the Reverend Mother's eye. "I would stake my life on the Mother never having felt the pleasure of a man between her thighs." The metal point pierced her skin and a red drop welled from the wound. Agatha met Sister Anne's eyes, and for a moment, the world appeared to stand still.

"Sister Anne, please..." The gnarled hands reached up towards the younger woman. "Help me stop this insanity. You of all people must know why it is so important we do what we do. You are one of us."

The expression on Sister Anne's face changed from shock to determination, her eyes hard and filled with hate.

"She'll do," the Sister finally agreed, and she turned back to her ritual. "Just hurry." Agatha brought the knife to the soft flabby wattle beneath the Mother Superior's chin and drew the sharp end of the blade across it with all her strength. The flesh gave way to the pressure, metal sliced through skin, muscle and larynx. Hot, sticky blood gushed over Agatha's arm, and she took a step back, releasing her victim. The Mother clutched her neck and fell to the ground with a wet, meaty thud. A rattle escaped from her creased lips, and her eyes rolled up into her head. Her body twitched, and blood pooled around the dying woman as Agatha grabbed her ankles. The Mother Superior didn't struggle as the younger nun dragged her around the library floor, her gushing blood creating a smeared circle on the stones, and by the time the triangle was halfway done, she had stopped twitching altogether. The final markings on the sign were fainter, but the symbol was complete. Agatha discarded the body to one side.

"It's not perfect." She eyed her handiwork and tapped her blood-covered hand to her chin.

"It'll have to do," Anne said, and she pointed towards the triangle. "Now it's your sacrifice that I'll be needing. Hurry, the sun is almost set. This won't work in the moonlight." Agatha nodded, not giving herself time to think about her imminent death. The floor kissed her skin with icy cold stone, and Agatha couldn't stop shivering.

"Are you prepared?" Anne loomed over her, a lit candle dripping hot wax on her face. Agatha flinched, but fought the urge to protect herself, allowing the hot drops to slide down her cheeks in a scalding path.

"I'm ready."

"I'm not quite sure what the side-effects of this spell will be. It's very dark magic, you... you might suffer." Anne's eyes shone with guilt.

"I told you, I'm prepared."

Anne nodded and took a deep breath, her chest swelling in her chemise, pressing the lightly freckled skin to the white fabric.

"In order to activate the spell, I have to crack the seal."

"What... no, you never told me... you can't..." Agatha sat up, but a bare foot pushed her back in her place.

"It is the only way to keep the dead bound to this place. It is the only way to make their suffering eternal."

"But, if you do it wrong, you may break the seal completely."

A flash of irritation flickered across Anne's face. "Then I must not do it wrong."

Sister Anne held the tome that Agatha had copied the

symbol from, her eyes hazy with concentration. Then she began to read.

"Nunc mei mano fati facio.

Astrum et Infernum abdicabo.

Meus spiritus diu aeternitem since pace an redempte sufferbo, finalam hostiam mundo numero.

Cum amor et tormentum adorabo omnipotentiam dominum servire defendo."

The ground shuddered and the convent creaked. Loud, ominous echoes reverberated off the grey walls and the shelves shook, spilling books across the floor like broken butterflies. Dust sprayed from the cracks between the bricks as if the walls were bleeding dried mortar.

Sister Anne repeated the words, and this time Agatha felt the stone floor shift and crack. The blood of the symbol flared up, forcing Sister Anne to take a step back and leave the circle. The light was so bright it looked as if the blood were made of liquid sunshine. At that moment, the last of the actual sunlight faded from the windows. A stench of sulphur wafted through the air, turning Agatha's stomach, and the sound of glass shattering echoed through the library. The cracks in the floor grew longer and deeper, and thick, black smoke oozed up from underneath and crept across the floor, avoiding the blood circle. Agatha raised her head. There was movement within the smoke, as if something was alive inside it. The blackness moved towards the chanting nun, slithered up her pale limbs and under her long white chemise. The young nun screamed and dropped the book, which slid inside the circle of blood with a whoosh. Agatha saw the white of Anne's nightgown turn crimson, and a shadow poured out of her collar, turning into the shape of a broad claw tipped with sharp ethereal talons. It forced its way into the young nun's screaming mouth and gripped her jaw, pulling. Agatha heard a sickening snap and crunch as the lower half of Sister Anne's face was torn loose.

"Anne..." Agatha crawled to the edge of the blood circle, but noticed just in time that the shadows stayed clear of the circle's light. She could see them clearer now, translucent black creatures with long arms and big heads. Their skulls were oblong, with beady white eyes, and black teeth protruding from their hideous maws. Short torsos ended in smoky trails rather than legs, and the creatures used their sharp claws to pull themselves forward with incredible speed. Their movements made the convent tremble again. Stones fell from the ceiling and shattered on the hard floor.

This is what the spell looks like. We've conjured monsters.

Tentatively, Agatha stretched out her hand and touched the light with trembling fingers. It felt warm. A pleasurable heat spread between her thighs, and Agatha moaned. Outside of the circle, Anne fell to the ground as more shadows rushed towards her, ripping the skin from her carcass. The creatures swarmed over her body, feasting, tearing the flesh to ribbons with their needle-sharp teeth and claws until nothing but bones covered in shreds of bloody tissue remained. Then they moved away from Sister Anne and scurried towards the chapel in search of more fresh meat.

Agatha sat in the centre of the illuminated circle, one hand covering her open mouth, and she fought the tears as she looked at the bloody remains of her friend. The screams in the convent intensified as the voices of the Sisters of the order of Angels joined those of the children.

"What have we done?" Agatha sobbed, and wrapped her arms around her knees.

"Sister Agatha..." The voice was soft and otherworldly, but loud enough to cause the young nun to look up. A ghostly figure rose from the dead body, transparent but shaped like a human being.

"Sister Anne?" Agatha's voice shook. "Is that you?" Her sanity was on the verge of shattering like glass, and the young nun stifled a sob.

"I became the sacrifice, Agatha. I am part of this place now, bonded to the very ground the convent is built on. It is your task to finish the spell. The others will fall too, as I did. You must dispel the magic, not let its monsters reach beyond this sacred ground. Our souls will feed the master who sleeps for eternity, and the seal should be safe. You will be the Watcher of the Seal."

"It was I who should have died."

"No, you were meant to live."

"I don't know if I can finish the spell..."

"You can, and you must. If you don't, the monsters will be free."

On her hands and knees, Agatha crawled to the book. She pulled the leather-bound volume towards her. The pages were folded and cracked, but they appeared to be otherwise unharmed.

"What am I looking for?"

Anne's spirit closed her eyes, and the pages started to flutter by themselves. Agatha watched, holding her breath, until the pages settled. A salty taste flooded her mouth as her teeth clamped down on her tongue. The book stopped moving, and the text on the page glowed.

Agatha read the first words aloud, but the ghostly image of Sister Anne put a finger to her lips.

"Not yet... they aren't done yet. The sacrifice needs to be complete, otherwise this will have been all for nothing." The spirit cocked her head, listening to the distant wailing. The minutes passed with agonizing slowness while Agatha sat frozen to the spot, the muscles in her limbs burning with fatigue, but she didn't dare move. Finally the screams died down, and Sister Anne nodded.

"Now."

"My Latin, it's not..."

Something overtook her senses, and the words flowed from her lips. She called upon an ancient primal force and commanded it to pull the shadow creatures back through the cracks from which they'd escaped. The monsters screamed with bloodlust and rage. Their smoky talons tore deep scratches into the grey stone. The unseen fury compelled the monsters through the cracks, and then, suddenly, the convent was silent. Agatha clutched her chest and panted, her body drenched in sweat and blood; she shivered with cold. Warm liquid poured down her lip. Her fingertips touched her nose and found blood.

"You are now bonded to this place by blood. It is your duty to keep the spirits within." The voice of Sister Anne surrounded her. Behind her, dozens of white figures stepped into the library. Anne recognised most of the figures: some were the naked sisters of her order, others the children who had died in the convent that night. But she saw different spirits too; spirits of old nuns who had died years ago and of children Agatha had never seen before. There were men amongst them, and Agatha wondered who they might have been. Their translucent essence hummed slightly, and the young nun could feel their anger, fear and frustration pulsate through the air.

"What's happening?" Agatha looked around at the many souls. "Why do I feel this?"

"These souls are tormented, Sister Agatha. Theirs is an eternal suffering. The spell demands it. You are their Guardian."

"Can these spirits harm the living?"

Sister Anne looked at her with soulful eyes, and Agatha knew that her task would be greater than she'd ever imagined.

May God help us all.

Chapter 1

August 2014

The mansion bore the name 'Angel Manor', and was responsible for Freya's fierce childhood dislike of anything even vaguely resembling one of those creatures. Whenever her mother spoke about the old house, it was with fear and loathing, and now that she stood facing the building, Freya could understand why. She shuddered and clung onto the handle of the car, as if letting go would hurl her into a vortex from which she wouldn't be able to escape. Weak knees supported her weight as she looked at the large Victorian house standing on top of the remote hill on the Scottish Isle of Skye. The tips of the red pointed roofs reached up to the bright blue sky, and the windows in their white painted frames resembled dozens of tired eyes.

The last time she had visited the house, Freya had been only nine-years-old, and the visit had not been a pleasant one. Being back here made her feel like a child again. The grand building with its three wings and soft yellow bricks loomed down on her, the summer sunshine colouring the house in a golden aura. The courtyard looked a little barren but, beyond the gates, the garden was filled with high grass and wild flowers.

It's not as scary as I remember, she thought, and yet Freya couldn't fight the terror that licked at her insides. She knew there was nothing to be afraid of now, her grandparents having passed away a long time ago. Even her mother, who was terrified of this place, had calmed down a little since their deaths. Mum was still convinced that the solitude of the house drove people insane, but even the distance between the old manor and the nearby towns had changed since her mother's childhood. The nearest shops were only a twenty-minute drive away, and Freya had no intention of living up here in solitude. Nor did she have any intention of following in her mother's emotionally damaged footsteps. Her father had encouraged her to at least go and take a look at the house after she'd inherited it from her aunt.

She remembered that last conversation with her father. He'd had the slightly sad expression he often wore when discussing her mother, along with a tinge of frustration in his voice. "Freya, you've only seen the house once, and you were with your mother at the time. Your grandparents left her pretty traumatised, remember that. Your aunt wasn't the most stable of people either. But there's nothing wrong with that house. Go build your dreams there. Chase away your grandparents' shadows."

She had to admit to herself that she felt nerves she couldn't quite apply any sense of logic to. Her childhood memories, though extremely vague, played a part in that fear. She knew her mother and aunt were the victims of overbearing and abusive parents, and that was the only darkness the house truly carried, no matter how melodramatic her mother had always been about Angel Manor. Being here felt almost as if she were betraying her mother, dismissing her fears, yet at the same time, she was happy she had travelled to Skye. *Mum's past is not my own. I don't have to feel this way.*

"Is this it?" Oliver's voice rang over the sound of the passenger door slamming shut. He stepped up next to her, resting his hands on her shoulders. She could feel the heat of his skin through her thin blouse. A soft breeze tugged at her hair, making the grass and leaves rustle in soft harmony. The wind carried the scent of wild flowers, and Freya inhaled deeply.

"This is it." Her voice sounded small and feeble, so Freya cleared her throat. "Angel Manor."

His breath tickled the back of her ear when he responded, and she could hear the slow awe in his voice. "It's not at all what I expected."

The fingers on her shoulder squeezed a little, and she exhaled. A second car pulled up, a red Mini Cooper with a white roof and black stripes. Freya waved as Bam Green's pink and blonde head peeped out. Her American accented voice was high with excitement.

"This place is fantastic!"

"Glad you like it." Freya smiled as the girl got out of her car and ran over to them.

"It's much bigger than I thought it would be."

"Yes, that caught me by surprise too. I don't remember it being this big. Which is funny, because I always thought kids remember things bigger. I think I just remember this one being scarier."

Oliver let go of her shoulders to embrace Bam, and Freya finally took her hand from the handle of the car door. She rubbed her arms, despite the warmth of the sun.

"The way your mom described the place, I was at least expecting a few gargoyles, and maybe a hunchback servant or two." Bam laughed at her own joke, and Freya chuckled along. Oliver took a few steps forward, his thumb rubbing against his smooth chin.

"I was afraid that the building would need a lot of work on the outside, but it looks fine at first glance."

Bam ran past them both, her short frame appearing almost elfin against the backdrop of the Victorian House.

Oliver rubbed his nose, his eyes still fixed on the house. "I'm with Bam... this is nothing like what I expected. I was afraid it would be all dark grey stones and rotten windows. This is gorgeous though. I love the yellow brick. It makes the house look... friendly."

"Just wait until you see the inside..." Freya raked at the back of his head with her fingertips. "My aunt had the decorating skills of Morticia Addams from what I remember."

25

"The inside is what you have *me* for, darling." Bam's voice affected a false, aloof tone. "I'm the designated decorating queen. No inside can scare me, but this—" she waved her hands at the house and the area surrounding it, "—this can't be bought or changed. And it's perfect. This is the perfect place to start a new hotel. Look at the scenery."

"It is beautiful, I know. But this house—"

"Hotel," Bam corrected. She was halfway up the steps already.

"It's not a hotel yet. We still need to fix it. Anyway... whatever it is, this place is the only link to my scary relatives. My mother emigrated just to be away from them, and the house always played a big part in the stories she used to tell me. Apparently her side of the family were quite insane."

Oliver made a scathing noise, rolled his eyes and folded his arms. Bam just laughed and yelled: "Are you sure your mother didn't just move to marry that dishy Viking of hers? I mean, I would have totally followed him to the ends of the earth for a chance to spread my legs for him."

"It's not at all awkward when you talk about my father like that..." Freya wrinkled her nose at Bam, who didn't seem to notice, and instead ran further up the steps. "You might want to tone down that sort of thing, Bam," she called after her.

"What kind of thing?"

"That loud, blunt American thing you do. It was fine in Holland, at an international school with a bunch of other weirdoes... but here in the UK, you might seriously offend people if you talk about screwing their fathers. Ollie... you're English. You tell her." Freya turned to Oliver, but he was looking past her at the valley that lay far below. He took a few steps towards the edge of the hill. "Oh, look at that. Nothing can beat that view. I'm sure that guests will come here to be one with nature. We'll be fully booked as soon as we open, you mark my words."

The grass in the valley was a stark emerald colour, and in its centre was a deep inclination that looked like a large black hole against the bright green. Thousands of poppies surrounded the chasm, imitating a large blooming bloodstain.

"Do you know what the locals call that valley?" Freya moved up behind Oliver and whispered darkly in his ear.

"The bonniest valley in all of Skye? A must visit for any tourist?"

"Lucifer Falls."

"How... quaint."

"And you know why they call it that?"

"I'm sure you're about to enlighten me." A strong gust of wind pushed at their backs, edging them down the steep hill.

"Legend has it that when Lucifer fell from Heaven, he landed right there." She pointed at the dark circle. "That very hole is supposed to be the place where he entered Hell."

"What a... charming legend." Oliver turned away, and for a moment his face was cast with a shadow of doubt, but then he cheered up and gave her a mischievous grin. "We could work this to our advantage. People love local legends."

"Angel Manor has a nickname," she continued. "It's not exactly popular with the locals. They call it Lucifer's Lot."

"How very Stephen King." Oliver took a tentative step towards the deep drop. "Is it because of all the vampires that live there?"

Freya shrugged and let out a soft giggle. She hugged her arms around her shoulders and wrinkled her nose.

"Probably."

"Don't let silly stories scare you. The locals may not be fond of this place, but no hotel has ever been built for locals. Creepy myths are actually a great tourist attraction. It might not be as magical as the Faerie Glen, but it'll have its own appeal." Oliver turned to her and pressed his forehead against hers, his brown curls tickling her eyelids and cheeks, a faint hint of this morning's coffee on his breath. "This is going to be good, Frey. It's what we've been dreaming of for so long, a chance to get away from things and start something new. You told me yourself you needed to get away from your old life... what's more 'getting away' than moving to this island? This inheritance is going to be the best thing that ever happened to you, I promise." His hand forced its way under her arm and he pulled her along. "Let's go inspect that manor of yours. It's a lot bigger than I thought it would be. Imagine the potential."

Freya threw up her arms and sighed.

"I don't know... what if there's truth in the horror stories? What if this place *is* bad? My mum seems to think so, though I don't think she actually believes it to be bad in the supernatural sense of the word. Just... I don't know. She has a lot of demons here."

"Oh, come on, you don't even believe in... well, in anything, and suddenly you let a few scary stories get to you? Your mom is just really upset with her family, and the house is a symbol of that. It's not like she believes in real demons or anything, right? God, Freya..." He ran his hands through his hair. "You know how much I hate talking about supernatural mumbo jumbo. It's all bullshit." He bristled, then turned to her with an inquisitive look. There was a sharpness in his expression, and Freya felt naked under his gaze. "Is it the scary stories, or are you just getting cold feet? If you're changing your mind, then tell me now, Freya. I can't deal with this shit once we start. We're either doing this or we're not. It's up to you; it's your house."

"I'm not having second thoughts... I just..."

"For fuck's sake, Freya, we moved all the way from the Netherlands for this. I know I was moving to the UK anyway, but I turned down a perfectly good job in London to come live on an island, and Bam gave up moving back to the US and becoming a porn-star or something."

Freya slapped him on the arm, and Oliver chuckled. Then his facial expression changed to one of earnest. "If we're doing this we'd better be serious about it, and we need you on board, okay?"

"I told you coming here was hard for me. This isn't a new fear, Ollie. You're not being fair. I can't even tell you what I'm afraid of. Not the legends, honest; I know those are bullshit. It's more... I'm afraid of the family stuff, if that makes sense?"

"Well, sister... get over yourself. Look at the wonderful opportunity you have here. What else were you going to do with your dead auntie's house?"

"Sell it, like my mum begged me to do?"

Oliver's eyes twinkled and he winked at her. "That would be boring. Besides, if we can't make it work, you can always sell it."

Freya rubbed her face with both hands and inhaled deeply in an attempt to dispel the heaviness she felt.

She forced a smile. "You're right. You're absolutely right. This place will be amazing, no matter how bad the inside might be." She poked him in the ribs and ran after Bam, who was inspecting the courtyard. Freya knew she wanted this dream to work out as much as Oliver and Bam did. She longed for a new start. Her mother had been strangely silent about her decision, but mum seemed to contain her thoughts on her past better than she used to.

"Look, angels." Bam's sing-song voice rang across the garden, and Oliver and Freya ran up the stone steps to join her.

"This place is amazing, Frey. Look at the statues."

Two rows of stone angels stood on either side of the entrance. The sight of them made Freya's stomach drop, as they had when she was little. There were six on each side and they loomed like silent guardians against the backdrop of the Manor. She still didn't like the angels. There was something ominous about them.

"I guess that's why they call it 'Angel Manor'. Have you seen these yet? The stones around the house?" Bam's voice was high with excitement. She pulled up her hair and tied it in a bun at the nape of her neck. "Come and look." Like a child who had just found a new candy shop, Bam pulled Oliver and Freya by the arms and led them to the front of the manor. Opaque white stones, possibly milk quartz, were set in the base of the building at regular intervals, and in the centre of each stone were symbols inlaid with gold leaf. Freya looked at Bam, who was squatting down at the side of the house, and Oliver, who was bent over right next to her, and realised how happy she was her friends were here. *I hope they never get bored of this place and leave.* The thought was so powerful she felt a slight tremor go through her body.

"These look old." Bam ran her childlike fingers, decorated with bright pink nail varnish, across the stones. She yelped, pulling her hand back, and placed the afflicted digits in her mouth and licked the fingertips. "And static." Oliver followed her lead and placed his hand on the stone. The shock was so intense when his skin slid across the opaque material that Freya felt it from where she was standing.

"Holy shit..." She took a step back. Oliver pulled his hand away and placed it to his chest. "What was that? Oh my God, Ollie... your nose is bleeding." Freya squinted with a look of disgust.

"So is yours," Oliver shot back, then he pointed at Bam,

"and hers." They each touched their noses. Freya pulled her hand away and found it spattered with blood. A chill ran up her spine as she glanced at Angel Manor.

Why am I so afraid of something made from bricks and mortar?

"That's pretty creepy." Freya looked from one friend to the other. Bam scrambled to her feet and blinked, her childlike smile faltering for a moment.

Oliver handed them each a tissue to wipe the blood away with. There wasn't much; nevertheless, the three friends looked at each other in mute silence for a moment. Bam's eyes were round and the smile was frozen on her face. Freya wrapped her arms around her chest again, squeezing her bosom tight.

"I guess we just paid for the house in blood," Oliver said in a Transylvanian accent, dragging out the last word. He forced a laugh and put his arm around Bam, but his words made the hairs on the back of Freya's neck stand on end. She stared at the bright red stain on her tissue, and quickly put the whole thing in her pocket, out of sight.

"I'm a little freaked out," Bam admitted.

"Don't worry about it. We're pretty high up here, so I expect that we'll get nosebleeds more often. Seriously, don't blow this out of proportion, Bam. We all know what you can be like."

"Yeah... no." Bam forced a smile again, her eyes dull. "I won't make a big deal." Bam visibly collected herself and turned away from the stones. Then, as if a switch had been pushed, her round face lit up. At that moment, Freya felt grateful that her friend had the attention span of a squirrel, a blessing which often steered Bam clear of a potential freak out.

"I can't wait to see the inside... you know, see what I have to deal with, being the interior decorator. I'm thinking we should stay with the Victorian style. Keep it looking authentic." Bam's words rang across the courtyard as she skipped ahead, dragging Oliver along with her to the front door. Freya barely paid attention to Bam's prattling, her eyes focussed on the house as she walked forward. A slight movement from behind one of the third floor windows caught her attention and she slowed her pace.

There's nothing there. It's just your imagination.

Bam and Oliver's chatter hummed in her subconscious, and she followed them to the large wooden doors. Freya glanced up at the third floor window again, but she didn't catch any motion this time, and she scolded herself inwardly for letting her imagination get the better of her. Her friends' excitement was almost tangible, and Bam jumped from one foot to the other as she stood by the front door.

"Let's look inside. Get out your key."

The key was old and made of brass, as old as the house itself, Freya suspected. With shaking fingers, Freya pushed the key into the lock and turned it. There was a faint click, and she could have sworn the door shuddered.

All three friends held their breaths as the door creaked open to reveal the stale darkness lying on the other side. Light streamed in from behind them, reflecting off the tiny dust motes floating through the air like melancholy fairies, and the mouldy scent of old age invaded their nostrils.

"This is not what I expected." Oliver stood in the doorway, looking as if he'd been hit by a truck. "How long has your aunt been dead? Five hundred years?"

Her eyes followed his, and through the beams of light, she could see what remained of the entrance hall. The furniture lay in shattered ruins, and everything was covered in cobwebs. The faded yellow wallpaper, splattered in pungent, black mould spots, curled back, showing the brickwork underneath, and a gelatinous brown liquid oozed through large cracks in the wall. The remains of two large staircases curled up each side of a large oak door. Most of the steps were missing, and those that remained hung limp like wooden teeth in a rotting mouth.

"I... I don't understand. My aunt died less than two months ago. This place looks like it's been abandoned for years."

"I'm not surprised she died if she was living like this. That stuff looks toxic." Bam pointed at a nearby crack and the glistening brown substance, her mouth pulled in a grimace.

"I'm utterly gobsmacked." Oliver leaned against the doorframe, his hand covering his mouth. Bam nuzzled her face against his arm, looking even shorter than usual.

Bam licked her lips. "You know I said no interior could scare me? I was wrong."

"My aunt was a bit, erm... batty. I expected the place would need some work, but this..." The words trailed away, replaced with a wave of nausea.

"I've never seen anything like it." Bam looked as though she was about burst into tears.

"Who could have done this? Why did they break all the furniture?" Tears welled up in Freya's eyes.

"Look at the cobwebs. This wasn't done recently. Maybe your aunt was burgled, or suffered from vandals or something." Bam shrugged her shoulders in defeat and looked at Freya with a sad expression on her face.

"Suffered from vandals? You make it sound like a rodent problem." Oliver rolled his eyes. "Whatever happened, your aunt didn't bother to clean it up."

"I knew she was depressed. She'd lost all her kids in her lifetime. Who wouldn't be a little depressed? But to be honest, this is worse than I could have imagined. How could anyone live like this?"

"Did she live here all that time? I mean, she didn't go live with relatives, or check into a motel or something?" Bam's voice sounded muffled through Oliver's shirt.

"Yes, she lived here, right up to the very end. In fact, they found her dead in this house. No one told me it was in this state though. She died of a heart attack as far as I know."

"This place feels bad, Freya." Bam looked at her, and Freya could see that all the eagerness had drained from her face. "Oh hush." Oliver nudged her.

"I come from a long line of crazy people, Bam. That's all. Don't worry too much about it."

Oliver looked around and pointed at the debris on the floor. "Is there another way in? The dust looks undisturbed. I can't imagine anyone having passed through here for at least a few years."

"There are lots of entrances, so that could be possible. She was nuts, but I find it hard to imagine her living like this. Don't think she could abide cobwebs. The place was always a bit cluttered, but very clean, though I don't see how this could be undisturbed. The paramedics must have used the front entrance."

"Maybe they got in through a back door too?" Bam bit her lip.

Oliver shrugged. "Big house might have gotten the better of the old lass? If she was mentally unstable to begin with? You said she was depressed. Big house, all her kids dead... maybe she went loopy and embraced the filth?"

He gently pushed Bam aside and stepped into the entrance hall. With care, the three friends picked a path between broken chairs, vases, lamps, and even a rotted settee, while broken porcelain crunched under the soles of their feet. When Oliver opened the door to the main hall area, a stale smell assaulted their nostrils.

The main hall area was as disorganised as the entrance, with a large chandelier, made from hundreds of crystals, lying forlorn in the centre of the room. More broken furniture was scattered across the floor, and there was barely any wallpaper left on the walls.

"This place is depressing." The spark seemed to have left Oliver's eyes, and his shoulders slumped. "'Batty' doesn't even begin to cover this. I dread seeing what the rest of the house looks like."

The young man shrugged and shook his head. He walked to the white doors to the East Wing and opened them.

"What the fuck?" Oliver's voice sounded hollow. "Why is that walled up?" He stepped aside to reveal red brick and friable grey mortar.

"My aunt... she was pretty paranoid about this place. Not sure what about, but she was always acting crazy about it." Freya shot them a look between a grimace and a smile. "I'm not surprised she had parts of the house boarded up."

Freya spotted another worn set of doors on an adjacent wall. With a few strides, she reached them and pulled them open, but again, she found nothing but a flat expanse of brick and concrete. "This one is blocked too."

"This one isn't." Bam stuck her head past the doors she'd opened. "In fact... this wing doesn't look too bad. Maybe she lived in here." Freya and Oliver made their way over to Bam.

Something grabbed Freya's ankle and she screamed. When she looked down, she saw that part of a broken lamp had caught her leg, and she laughed in relief.

"Jesus, woman, you scared the shit out of me." Bam clutched her heart. "This place is creepy enough without you adding to it."

A deep red flush settled over Freya's cheeks. "I'm sorry, I'm just a little on edge. This house..." Her voice faded away, but Oliver offered her a sympathetic look. Freya shook her head and pulled her leg free from the lamp.

The wing that Bam found was untouched, and though every room was filled with big clunky furniture, the place looked relatively clean. There was some dust, but nothing a quick wipe wouldn't fix. And the smell was a lot better here too. There was a lingering odour of old people, but not of rot. The wallpaper was a soft yellow colour, spattered with a dainty white fleur-de-lis pattern, and the floor was polished cherry parquet.

"This is how I remember my aunt. A lot of... stuff... but clean and tidy. Terrible taste in decor, though." Freya picked up a porcelain figure of a little Dutch girl from a display cabinet.

"Well, at least we can work with this part. I think we could turn this floor into our own living accommodation. Then we work from there to turn the East and South Wings into hotel rooms. They're bigger, right?"

"I think so. *You* have the floor plans." Freya glared at Oliver. "I just have vague memories from fifteen years ago." She rolled her eyes, but Oliver wasn't watching. He wandered around the living room, opening drawers to cabinets and dressers while his fingers lightly caressed the furniture.

"There's a lot of stuff here. We need to figure out what we want to keep." Oliver held a crystal figurine of a dolphin between his fingers. "Maybe we can even sell some of this stuff online, or to an antique shop or something, to help finance the remodelling. The house is in a worse state than we could have imagined, so we'll need every pound we can get our grubby little fingers on."

"I'd like to keep this though." Freya pointed at a tall grandfather clock. It was a handsome antique, and instead of numbers, the clock had angels carved in the brass dial.

The figures were rendered with incredible detail, and on the top of the wood stood a last angel holding a tiny trumpet.

"I remember it from when I was little, and I've always liked it. You should hear it chime on the quarter hour. It's very pretty."

"These decorative plates look pretty old." Bam stood on her tippy-toes and pointed at one of the round metal plates that lined the wall. "They look like they're made of gold, but it's probably something fake. I mean... if they were real gold, or even just gold plated, it would mean there was a fortune here, right?" There was a soft hesitation in the short girl's laugh, a tuft of pink-tipped blonde hair escaping the bun at the back of her neck as she bobbed up and down. All three looked up at the wall. There were seven plates in total, hanging at regular intervals, and each of them gold. Oliver and Freya exchanged an excited glance.

"I remember these," Freya said, while Oliver climbed up onto a cherry-wood dresser. "My aunt was very proud of them. There was something about them, but I can't remember what."

The dresser groaned under Oliver's weight, and for a moment, he froze. Then he shifted slowly, and the dresser showed no further signs of protest. He lifted one of the plates from the wall. It was about the size of a serving tray, but much thicker. Seven symbols were carved around the rim with an angel moulded in the centre. He climbed down and flipped the plate over, his brow furrowed with concentration.

"This thing is heavy." He inspected the back, his fingers gliding over the surface. "I wish I had a magnifying glass."

"As if you know anything about carat marks." Bam snorted and leaned over the plate, her fingers sliding over the gold in search of a mark. "This could be something." The tip of her finger pointed at four little symbols incised into the metal. "Lemme see." Oliver held the plate out for her inspection, and Bam manoeuvred both him and the plate towards the light from the large Victorian windows.

"Yup, these are definitely gold markings." She squinted, bringing her face closer to the object. "It's not solid gold, because I see an H.G.E. mark, but the plating is 18-carat, which is pretty good." She looked from Oliver to Freya, shock and excitement mingling in her face.

"What would that mean? How much would they be worth?"

"I don't know, but each should be at least a grand judging by the size of them, depending on how much gold is on the plating. I'm thinking probably more."

"A thousand pounds? That's amazing." Freya felt her heart flutter, and she blessed her strange old aunt for her expensive taste.

"So, are we doing this?" Oliver turned to Freya as he held up the gold plate. "Are we selling these and getting our hotel?"

"I thought that was the plan?" Freya looked from Oliver to Bam, and she saw a look of worry in their eyes.

"We weren't sure if you still wanted to." Bam bit her lip and looked at Freya. "You've been a bit weird ever since you set foot on the island. We thought you might be chickening out."

"I do feel a bit weird. And to be honest, it doesn't help that half of what we've seen of the house looks like it's come straight from the abyss. But we said we would do this, and if we can find an affordable builder who can work wonders with houses that leak brown gloop, then I'm in."

Oliver laughed, and he carefully set the plate down so that he could hug Freya. "I say we go find the nearest pub and celebrate. Maybe find a bed and breakfast too, because I don't know if I'm so keen on sleeping here tonight. At least not until we've had that strange stuff investigated."

Chapter 2

Bam woke at five AM after a short, uncomfortable sleep. Her night shirt was drenched in sweat, and her head throbbed with a dull but incessant ache while her stomach churned with stinging acid. She couldn't remember her dreams, but she knew that they must have been disturbing. The small bedroom in the Redwood House B&B was still cast in darkness, and next to her in the bed, Freya groaned a little.

"Stop thrashing around."

Bam felt a hint of irritation. "I'm not thrashing, I just can't get comfortable. This bed is too damn small for the two of us."

"Well, get used to it. We'll be spending more time together until we find out if the hotel is safe to live in. We can't afford three separate rooms."

"I don't see why Oliver gets his own room and we have to share."

"Because he's the guy." Freya's voice sounded muffled through the soft, white pillow.

"As if we haven't slept in the same bed as him before. It shouldn't make a difference."

"Fine, we'll rotate. Whatever. Just please stop moving around. I feel sick enough as it is. I think I had too much cider. It went straight to a hangover. Didn't even get a nice buzz."

"I feel sick too."

"Well then, maybe you had too much cider as well."

"I drank diet Coke."

"Then you had too much diet Coke. I don't know. Just stop fucking moving and we can still be friends." Freya turned around and pulled one of the extra pillows over her head.

"Maybe it was something we ate." Bam bit her lip and tried to remember if there was something they'd had in common from the menu, but she couldn't think what it might have been. Oliver had ordered a burger, Freya's was fish, and she'd had a vegetarian dinner of stuffed peppers and goat's cheese. There was no link between their meals.

"Or we inhaled something nasty in that house." Her voice was a whisper now, and the thought sent tiny sparks of fear flashing through her brain. She sat up straight in the bed, a soft snore escaping from the pillow next to her.

"Freya." She pushed her friend's shoulder.

"What?" The voice sounded angry.

"What if the house poisoned us?"

"If it did, let me die in peace." Freya turned around and pulled the covers over her shoulder.

"I'm serious."

"The house didn't poison us."

"How do you know?"

"I just do."

"I've heard stories of people dying because they visited a tomb. Something about deadly spores or something."

Freya sat up, her face looking tired and pale under the long strands of black hair.

"When my aunt died, they did an autopsy."

"So, there was nothing suspicious about her death. What's your point?"

"I'm sure when they found her body a lot of people entered the house. Doctors, probably police officers. That brown stuff can't have just grown overnight, so they probably saw it too. Don't you think they would have investigated it to rule it out as a source of her death?"

"Maybe." Bam shrugged, unconvinced.

"We'll make some calls tomorrow okay? If we're not dead by then." Freya rubbed the top of her nose. "Though Lord knows, death sounds like a pretty sweet option right now. Just go to sleep."

"Yeah." Bam felt silly, so she slid back under the covers. Freya glanced at her, expecting her to say something else, but then she followed Bam's lead.

"Don't worry. Let's just try and get a few more hours of sleep. You picked a fine fucking time to freak out about the house, that's for sure. Just leave the stressing to me, and you go to sleep, okay?"

Bam closed her eyes and tried to relax her breathing. Something felt wrong, and she wondered if Freya was just being laconic or if she herself was overreacting.

***

Oliver woke from a dream. Sweat dripped from his forehead and his stomach tightened with cramps as if he'd swallowed glass. With shaking fingers, he peeled off his t-shirt and lay back down on the cold, moist sheets. A deep breath escaped from his lungs. He felt sick, and when he closed his eyes, he could smell the stale odour of Angel Manor. His mind reeled as he thought back to the nightmare which had plagued his sleep.

Angel Manor had been restored to its former glory. In his dream, he had walked through the rows of angels in the middle of the night towards a red-haired woman standing in the open front doors, a diaphanous nightgown revealing all her curves in the light of the moon. Her breasts pressed against the fine material, and he'd felt something stir in his loins.

"I'm yours now." The woman's voice was a low whisper, and for a moment, Oliver wondered if the words had come from her lips or if the house itself had spoken. "Come and claim me." She turned and ran into the house. Despite his misgivings, Oliver had run after her.

The hotel looked different in his dreams, not broken and old, but beautiful and whole. The floor shone under his feet, and the furniture looked in mint condition. A crystal chandelier sparkled with bright luminescence, casting thousands of stars around the entrance hall. The main hall was now a reception area, just as Oliver had envisioned it, and a fresh-faced receptionist in a Victorian black dress with a high collar and a blonde bun on the top of her head nodded at him as he walked by. There were people milling around, each regarding him with a reverence that made him feel like a king.

The woman in the nightgown beckoned him to walk further, and she led him to a large over-lit dining area, where hundreds of guests, dressed in beautiful gowns and three-piece suits, dined on delicacies served by at least a dozen waiters.

I want this, Oliver thought, *I have dreamt of this for so long, and seeing it makes me long for it even more.*

"This can all be yours. And there is so little you need to do in return, Oliver." The woman played with the strings of her nightgown. "I can be everything you want me to be... everything. I ask so little from you. But you can't leave me again, you bad boy. I miss you when you're gone."

"What do you want from me?"

"I want you to make me beautiful again. Can you do that?"

"Are you... are you the house?" He rubbed the bridge of his nose and looked at her through squinting eyes. Her face was so delicate, her symmetrical features making her look

42

like a porcelain doll.

"I gave my essence to this house a long time ago. I bonded with it, as you have."

"What is it that you want from me?"

"Fill the house with life. That's what I want. That's what we all want. A house needs the living. And this house is special, Oliver. This house guards secrets."

"What kind of secrets?"

She just smiled at him again and licked her lips.

"Bring us people. Let them walk on our floors and under our roof. That is all we want from you, and then you can have this..." she spread out her arms, showing him the people who sat eating and laughing in the dining room - eating *his* food, "...all for yourself."

"I want that."

"I know you do..." The pale hand pulled at another string of her nightgown, and milk-white breasts spilled from the fabric. They were modest, but enough for Oliver to feel his masculinity stir against his black cotton boxer shorts.

He couldn't quite recall what happened after that. All he remembered was the woman wrapping naked legs around him, the cold of her pelvis against his, and the welcoming wetness of what lay beyond her thighs. And how at some point she whispered in his ear: "Stay inside me."

As he lay on his side, eyes wide open, his thoughts wild, he realised that the house needed him. Being in this hotel felt like cheating, and Oliver was sure this was why he felt so sick. He wasn't meant to be here, and would have to return as quickly as possible. If he was going to turn the manor into the hotel of his dreams, he needed to be committed. The dream woman was right. A house, or in this case a hotel, needed life, and the only thing that could bring life to a building was people. He needed to get the hotel up and running as quickly as possible. Nothing would stand in his way. Not Bam with her bullshit and not even Freya. His thoughts were barely lucid, his eyes glazed over, and he turned to his other side as fitful sleep overtook him once again.

***

It had been Oliver's idea to return to Angel Manor the next day. Freya and Bam had struggled to get out of bed, and Freya had pleaded with him to let them sleep until they felt better. He admitted that he felt as sick as the girls, but he was eager to get started and somehow convinced Freya that the fresh air would do them good. Freya thought that he was probably right, because as soon as she stepped out of the car and onto the courtyard she felt the nausea retreat, and both Oliver and Bam looked decidedly less peaky.

The house looked different. She wasn't sure how, but for some reason the building looked more... *awake*. Her limbs felt heavy as she slid the old key in the lock. Sunlight streamed into the entrance hall, and to Freya's surprise, the place smelled different... fresher, as if someone had cleaned overnight, though there was still a hint of decay hanging around.

Freya pushed past Oliver and inspected the nearest wall. It was clean, and although the wallpaper was still torn and faded, the crack underneath it appeared as nothing more than a scratch. "I must be losing my mind."

"This was a huge crack yesterday, bleeding brown snot, right?" Bam said, her eyes wide as she looked from Freya to Oliver.

"Perhaps it wasn't that bad." Oliver made his way towards the wall and let his fingers glide over the crack. "I mean, it was pretty dark in here yesterday. The light must have been different or something. I think we saw it wrong."

Bam hugged her own arms "We saw it wrong? All three

44

of us?"

"It was pretty dark in here." Freya shrugged. She wasn't even sure if she had seen the brown substance or if it had just been an optical illusion. "The light must have played a trick on our eyes."

Bam shook her head and took a step back. Freya moved towards her and wrapped her arms around the smaller girl.

"Come on, Bam. We were all pretty shocked by the state of this place yesterday. Can you honestly say you remember seeing anything clearly?"

Pink hair tickled Freya's nose as Bam shook her head. Freya exhaled with some relief, knowing full well that they had just avoided a healthy dose of drama with their friend. Bam was easily rattled.

"I'm rather glad that our assessment of the place yesterday seemed a bit over-exaggerated. I think the appearance of the house just took us by surprise and we made it worse than it really was in our heads. It's still a mess, but it's not as bad as we thought."

Oliver cheered up, and put his hands on his hips and puffed out his chest. "True, we can clean most of this up, but I will still want my contractor to look at it."

"When's he coming?"

"Next Monday. He's Rudy's cousin, and he'll give us a good deal." Oliver pouted and placed his finger on his chin just below his bottom lip. "According to Rudy, the guy will do anything for him, and apparently Rudy will do anything for me, so yay us."

"Oh yeah?" Bam bumped her hip into Oliver's, and to Freya's relief she saw that the tension had been broken. "I remember Rudy. He was a hottie." Bam licked her finger and touched her bottom, making a sizzling sound between her teeth.

"Yes, thank you. Swell." Oliver ran his hand across the

back of his neck and smiled shyly. "Laugh at me all you like, but I think it works to our advantage that this guy has the hots for me, and I don't mind using my good looks to further our goal."

The girls laughed and hugged Oliver from either side.

"How refreshingly open-minded of you, Oliver. I took you for more of a lad than that."

His hands brushed his sleeves with demonstrative strokes. "I'm confident about my sexuality and therefore not threatened by gay men."

The girls laughed again and shook their heads. Then they looked at the debris scattered over the entrance hall, and the laughter died on their lips.

Freya eyed the broken furniture. "We should try to get as much stuff cleared out of here as we can before he comes."

Oliver nodded. "I'll order a skip this afternoon. I think we need to try and save up our money and make a space to live in the house. Hotel costs will eat at our budget." He looked at her, an anxious expression on his face. "Is that okay with you guys? Otherwise, I'll just stay here on my own for now and you can share a room." His eyes pleaded with them, and Freya felt a small pang of concern. There was something in Oliver's brown eyes that unnerved her.

"Stay here? Now? We don't have proper bedrooms yet. Nothing is clean. I think we should wait." She looked at Bam, who seemed just as doubtful, but her friend kept her mouth shut.

"Your aunt had to sleep somewhere. And what about her kids? I'm sure there are bedrooms somewhere."

"They could be in the same state as everywhere else. I really think we should sort out the mess before we think about living here. What about that brown shit we saw yesterday? What if it's some sort of toxic crap? Bam could be right."

"We saw it wrong. Do you see any sign of it now?"

"All three of us saw it wrong? What do you think it was, mass hysteria?" Freya folded her arms and straightened her shoulders.

"We probably saw something else. For all I know, it was just a big slug or something. I never investigated it... did you?"

"No, but—"

"Freya, the house is fine. Honest. You need to stop finding excuses. I know you don't like this place, but we're going to have to live here eventually. Might as well be sooner rather than later." He took a step towards her and gently grabbed her chin between his forefinger and thumb. "Face your demons, and all that lark." His smouldering eyes looked in hers and, for a moment, Freya remembered the brief time they'd dated as teenagers. She didn't want to stay in the house, especially not in this state. She didn't trust it somehow, and she knew it was insane not to trust a building... but there was just something about this place. And yet... Oliver had always held a strange power over her. When she told Ollie and Bam she had inherited the house, it had been him who had convinced her not to sell. Freya struggled to deny him anything, and she knew Bam was the same.

"I just don't know, Ollie. This is not what we planned."

"Well, I'm going to stay here." There was conviction in his voice. "I'd rather have you two stay with me, but if you won't... well, that's your choice. Bam? What say you?"

"I guess we can stay here." Bam looked miserable, but Oliver clapped his hands together.

"Splendid."

"Splendid? You sound like a villain from the old Batman series." Freya shook her head and muttered "kapow" under her breath.

"Ladies... let's go find the bedrooms and see if they're habitable. Then we can get our stuff from the B&B tonight."

He led the way and the two girls followed. Freya felt Bam's cold, clammy hand slip in to hers.

"You okay?"

"Yeah, I actually feel better." Bam smiled brightly, but Freya wondered how genuine it was.

Chapter 3

Clearing the house was less arduous than Freya had feared, and by the time the contractor came, most of the debris in the entrance hall and the central room had been thrown into skips. There was no way in hell they could get Bam to touch anything with cobwebs on it, so they sent her to collect anything that looked valuable instead.

"I wonder if we can get an internet connection all the way up here." Oliver grunted as he pulled a heavy bin-liner over his shoulder and made his way to the door. "That would be awesome."

"I wouldn't hold my breath for that." Freya wiped her arm across her moist forehead. "I can't get mobile reception up here, or anywhere around here, really. Lucifer Falls seems to be a bit of a dead zone. I know my aunt did have a phone line, though I think it only worked half the time. Mostly, she just used the landlines in the nearby towns. Hooking up Internet seems like wishful thinking to me."

Oliver smirked. "We could go retro, maybe get a modem?"

"Do they even make those anymore?"

"We'll do some research. I'm sure there's something that will work." Oliver patted her cheek in a condescending manner. "There are plenty of rural homes that have Internet; I don't see why this one would be any different. We just have to check it out."

"Yeah, I guess." Freya bit her lip and wrinkled her nose. "Though it would be easier to check it out if we had Internet. I need to get a UK mobile phone anyway. Mine is still Dutch, and it's costing me a fortune to use 3G."

Oliver didn't seem to hear her. Freya thought about how isolated they were all the way here in Lucifer Falls.

"I wonder what it was like for your mom to grow up in this place. Was it as crazy as it is now?" Oliver sat down on the floor, his hands shovelling bits of debris into a bin-liner.

"It was nuts, but not *this* nuts. Not like living in cobweb paradise. The house wasn't like this the last time I was here. I never met my grandparents. My mom made sure of that."

"She didn't like your grandparents?" He leaned his elbows on his knees and gazed at her.

"Mom hated them." Freya waved her hands to emphasize her point. "She didn't even go to their funerals. She told me stories from when she was a kid, and I don't blame her. Her parents were pretty sadistic."

Oliver stopped shovelling and looked at her with renewed interest. "What did they do?"

"When Mom was little, she and her sister were homeschooled by my grandmother. Mom told me that Gran would expect them to learn a part of the scripture each week, and if they got a single word wrong, Gran would whip them across the palm with a birch twig." She held up her hands and ran her fingers across her palms. "My mom still has scars on her hands. There were weird rules too, like they had to get up in the middle of the night to see if all the locks were still in place."

"Locks?"

"Yeah, Mom used to tell me the basement scared the crap out her and Aunt Miriam, and her parents would make them go and check if it was still locked. There was supposed to be a secret down there, but my mom never found out what it was. I guess Aunt Miriam did, because she walled the place up. Must have been pretty bad. I suspect my grandparents were into freaky stuff."

"Like a sex dungeon?" Oliver stared at her with raised eyebrows.

"God only knows. They were pretty fanatic religious people so I doubt it was a sex thing."

"Repression can do weird things to people."

Freya cringed at the idea of her grandparents having sex. "Anyway, the basement was forbidden to the girls, but at the same time they were in charge of the lock. They weren't allowed to go together either. Their mother would always make them check alone, and they weren't allowed to turn on the light." Freya shook her head and remembered the look in her mother's eyes when she recounted her journeys down to the basement. "Scared the hell out of my mother who, to this day, is still afraid of the dark." Her nails scratched at an itch on the side of her nose. "The darkness was another thing. My grandmother would blindfold them and tell them to go to a certain part of the house. They needed to be able to find their way at night without any lights, she used to say. They needed to know the whole house like the backs of their hands so that they could get away, no matter what."

"Why?" Oliver did a bad job of concealing his grin. Freya shook her head and laughed without mirth.

"God only knows. Maybe to get out if there was ever a fire, with the smoke and all? Whatever it was, I can tell you that this was a weird place to grow up in. My Grandmother could have been over-cautious, or maybe she was just a loony. I don't think it was healthy for two young girls to live in a place like this, so isolated from everybody. It's bound to make you a little crazy. Look what happened to my aunt." She waved her hand around and let the debris speak for itself.

"Mom ran away from home when she was fourteen. That's when she met my dad. She married him when she was seventeen and he was nineteen. I think if she hadn't run away, she'd probably be dead by now. Mom doesn't talk about this place much anymore, but I know she still has nightmares about it."

Oliver ran his hands through his hair. The muscles in his jaws were tight when he spoke. "That's pretty intense."

"Yeah, this place is. That's why I was a bit nervous about coming here. Not because I believe in ghosts or anything, but because I believe in human misery. This place, Lucifer Falls... a lot of people come here as an 'end of the road' kind of thing."

Oliver's eyes widened and he wrinkled his nose. "You mean...?"

"A lot of people have jumped off the cliff. It's a beautiful but tragic place, and it attracts people with a death wish." She tore off a new liner and shook it so that the plastic billowed, creating a parachute shape.

"That's a cheerful thought." Oliver inspected a piece of blackened wood between his fingers.

"It is, isn't it? I've always associated this house with misery. When I first inherited it, I wanted to get rid of it as soon as possible. But you guys made me see that there is a way to change the past, and maybe bring light onto a very dark family history. I would like to be the one who changes the reputation of Angel Manor, the one who makes it a place of beauty and life."

"Yeah, that's what this place needs," Oliver said with a dreamy look in his eyes. "Life."

***

The bedrooms were in almost pristine condition, and with the exception of the creepy art which lined the walls, were not as cluttered as the family room, dining room and kitchen. There were four bedrooms in all downstairs, with Bam claiming the biggest one for herself. She didn't get much resistance. The biggest bedroom had belonged to the aunt so Freya didn't want it, and Oliver was content to take a room with doors leading outside. To her surprise, Bam found that she liked the decoration in the bedroom, aside from the sinister paintings of angels covering their faces with pale hands, but she took those down the first night and put them with the rest of the antiques to sell. The walls were lined with blue velvet wallpaper, and the floor was beautiful polished parquet. In the middle stood a four-poster bed with curtains in the same midnight blue as the walls. The big windows let in enough light to counter the gloomy dark colours. When she closed the curtains, the room was cast in utter darkness, and Bam found she slept well in her new bedroom without any further worry about ghosts. The past three days had been wonderful. That morning, she had spoken to an interested antique dealer who promised he would come and take a look at the possessions left behind by the previous owner, and Bam had a suspicion they would have a nice little nest egg to put towards building the hotel after she was done.

With a sigh, she lay back on her bed and wondered how she could have ever felt fear towards the place. True, the first day she had entered the house, it had looked menacing, and she hadn't forgotten their bloody noses after they'd touched the stones, but it felt so friendly now. Welcoming... as if she had returned home after a long time away. Home was a new concept for Bam, who'd spent her life in boarding schools far away from her birth parents. That's how she'd met Freya and Oliver, at age twelve. She and her brother Chuck had lived in the same boarding school, and the four had been inseparable for many years. Oliver was Bam's secret crush, and she knew she would follow him anywhere. When Angel Manor had become an opportunity to stay rather than move back to California with her parents, Bam had grabbed it with both hands. The idea of starting a new life with Oliver excited her, and she hoped that when things settled down, she could lure him into her bedroom. They were meant to be together, Bam was sure of that.

For the first time since Chuck had died two years ago, Bam felt life could be sane again. She missed her brother, but a small part of her had to admit that she felt a little relieved she was free of his overbearing, and on occasion, abusive personality. She believed that it had been Chuck who had stood between her and Oliver, and because of him, she'd never dared tell anyone about her feelings. Not even her best friend. When Freya had dated Oliver for a brief summer, Bam had been emotionally crushed. Luckily, the two had about as much chemistry as two wet paper towels, and the relationship fizzled out before it had even begun. But Bam always thought it was her lips that belonged on him, not Freya's. She had dated many guys, none of whom were good enough for her brother, and he'd sabotaged every single one of her relationships. If she'd dated Oliver, their friendship would have been ruined forever. But now Chuck was dead, and Oliver only slept one room away from hers in the middle of nowhere. Her parents were in California, and she was here on this glorious island. Bam wrapped her arms around her chest and felt the firm silicone of her breasts push against her soft skin. She imagined it was Oliver holding her. Behind closed eyelashes, she saw, could almost feel, his lips touch the nape of her neck and her shoulder. Gooseflesh prickled her back and arms, and she hugged herself tighter, only to break away from the thought seconds later and get to her feet. This was no time for fantasies. She'd leave those to the darkness of the night and the privacy of a heavily-curtained four poster bed. If she wanted to impress Oliver now, she would have to show she was worth her salt.

She flung her legs over the side of the mattress, adjusted her NIN t-shirt, and pulled her jeans over her hips.

"Let's go sort out some antiques." With swift fingers, she pulled her hair into a ponytail and walked out to the living room area. There were quite a few items that could be worth some money in here. The aunt had kitsch taste, especially when it came to her knick-knacks, but there were a few things that could be worth something. The big gold plates were the most valuable, of course, and Bam didn't want to excite the others too much, but she had a suspicion they would fetch a lot more than a thousand pounds. She looked at the grandfather clock and wished she could sell that too. It would have made a pretty penny. The big hand landed on the angel representing the three, and soft, chiming music rang through the living area. It was pleasant, Bam decided, but she hated the clock when it struck the full hour; there was nothing dainty about those loud chimes.

The three friends had some money saved up. Bam, who was the child of rich parents, had the most to contribute. With the three years of her unfinished bachelor degree in design, and a natural flair for taste, she felt she had more than just cash to offer. Freya had a little saved up, and Oliver had the connections and the cooking skills. When the hotel was open, he would run the kitchens while Freya and Bam would manage the hotel. Every penny Bam could make from selling this stuff would be a blessing, and she intended to squeeze every last drop out of it all.

Bam climbed on a ladder and started to take down the plates one by one. She covered them carefully in bubble wrap, then slid them into cardboard boxes, after which she brought them to the conservatory.

Like the living room, the conservatory was in pretty good condition. A wicker table stood in the centre of the glass construction, surrounded by four matching chairs topped with white cushions. The glass trapped a lot of the late summer warmth so the room was stifling. Bam opened the doors to allow some fresh air in. The breeze brought the smell of wildflowers, intoxicating and almost noxiously sweet.

With care, Bam stacked the boxes in one of the corners of the conservatory, returning to the living room when she'd finished. The spaces where the plates had been were now large black spots. Bam blinked, sure that they hadn't been there before. She climbed the ladder again to inspect one of the patches. When she ran her hand across, a charcoal residue appeared on her palm, and Bam realised the wallpaper had been cut out in a perfect circle with exposed brickwork lying underneath.

"What the hell?" She rubbed the black spot again, and this time when she looked at her hand, it was covered in a thick red liquid. The black spot was crying blood. Bam yelped. Her foot slipped, and she clung on to the rung with her hands. The ladder wobbled dangerously, but eventually steadied. She clamoured down, fighting the urge to jump. Standing on solid ground again, she looked at the spot, but this time she only saw soot. Her hand shook as she held it up to her face, and to her relief she saw there was just black on her palm and no blood. The experience left her shaken, and Bam decided she needed a break and a coffee. She wouldn't tell the others what she'd seen; she didn't want to anger Oliver again. This was just her imagination. It wouldn't be the first time it had happened. If she gave into her moods again, it might ruin this opportunity, and she decided it wasn't worth it.

Chapter 4

Every bone in Freya's body protested when she got out of bed. They had worked throughout most of the night, clearing away the rubbish from the entrance hall and the central room until the skips were completely filled with broken furniture. The fear she'd felt had ebbed away over the past six days, and Freya believed that cleaning up the house had been very much like taming it. The work was arduous, and by the time she fell on her mattress at night, she'd be so tired that she would fall asleep instantly. Clearing out the house wasn't the horrendous task she'd expected it to be, and the hours passed quickly.

"What time is your guy coming?" Freya wiped the sleep from her eyes and ran her fingers through her obstinate black locks. The dark blue t-shirt with a picture of Kermit saying 'kiss the frog' hung to her thighs, and she caught Oliver casting an appreciative glance at her long tanned legs. She pulled the fabric of her shirt down a little in a self-conscious motion, and Oliver turned back to his coffee.

"Between nine and five." He glanced at the floor plans he'd spread out over the wooden kitchen table. Bam had done a great job cleaning the work area, and though the wallpaper and furniture were horribly outdated, the place was liveable.

"That's nice and specific." Freya pulled a face and poured herself a cup of the hot black liquid. The aroma filled her nostrils, and she realised she liked the smell of coffee more than she liked the taste. She poured in a generous helping of sugar and milk to mask the bitterness, sighed, and sat down at the table next to Oliver. "Why do they always need so much time? I mean, I can imagine that they don't know exactly what time they'll be here, but needing eight hours is a bit much."

"Hmmm?" Oliver looked up from his floor plans, but from the expression on his face, Freya knew he hadn't really been listening to a word she'd said.

"I'm going to have a baby."

Oliver sat up straight and stared at her with eyes wider than she'd ever seen them.

"You're what? How? Why?"

"You need me to tell you how babies are made?" She couldn't hold back her laughter. "It's Bigfoot's baby."

"You're taking the piss." His shoulders sagged a bit and he took a deep breath. She laughed louder and punched him in the arm.

"That'll teach you for not listening." Freya raised an eyebrow in mock disapproval, but then her face turned serious again. "I might go into town today. Get some cleaning supplies and some more milk."

"Pick me up some aspirin, and I think we're almost out of bin-liners too."

Freya got up to grab a notepad. "Sure. What would you like for tea?"

"Hamburgers." Bam's sleepy voice came from the doorway. "And fries."

"Chips. No fries here, darling." Oliver looked up at the short girl, and when she stuck out her tongue to him, Freya just snorted.

"And it's burgers. Hamburgers are American."

"*Burgers* it is." She scribbled some groceries on the list and handed Bam her cup. "I used the last of the milk, so if you want you can have my coffee."

Bam muttered a quiet 'thank you' and took the cup between two hands, blue painted nails intertwining around the porcelain. She inhaled the scent of coffee and, with slow deliberation, took a sip from the cup, then grimaced as she pulled her face away.

"Jesus, Frey... did you put enough sugar in there?"

Freya shrugged, rose to her feet, and tore the top piece of paper from the notepad. "I'll try to be back by ten. Hope the guy doesn't come before that."

"What guy?" Bam looked from Freya to Oliver.

"The contractor. He's coming today to make an estimate."

"Right, I'd forgotten about that. Wednesday the guy from the antique thing is coming." Bam sipped the coffee again, followed by another wince.

"I can't wait until we can really get started on the renovation." Freya folded the grocery list into a solid little square. "I'll be back. Bam, don't forget to eat. There's bread on the counter." She ran off to have a shower, leaving Bam and Oliver in silence at the kitchen table.

***

Freya enjoyed the trip to the grocery store. The ride had been pretty. She couldn't get enough of the bright green rolling hills, which were so different from the flat Dutch countryside, and the sky was a deep blue that offset the colours of the wildflowers and the grass.

She'd had a bit of a headache when she'd left, but that seemed to have cleared up now. The fresh air was doing her a lot of good. Bam greeted her at the steps of Angel Manor, and from the excited look on her face and the way the girl hopped from one foot to the next, Freya surmised she had good news.

"Did you get a good estimate for the antiques?" Freya's words came out in pants, her lungs not yet used to the hills on the Scottish island compared to the flatness of the Dutch countryside where she'd grown up.

"No. I told you earlier, that guy won't be here until Wednesday." Bam sounded absolutely giddy. "This is better." She seemed to contemplate her own words for a moment. "Well, no... not better, but still pretty damn good." She giggled, her thin fingers wiggling in front of her mouth like the legs of a spider. "The contractor is here." Bam giggled again and shot Freya an impish look.

"Eh... okay?"

Bam turned around and ran up the steps.

"Hey, feel free to give me a hand with the shopping," Freya cried, and she held up the heavy plastic supermarket bags as far as her arms would allow. Bam stopped in her tracks and muttered an apology, then turned and skipped back down the stone steps to help.

"Not sure what the reason behind walling the place up was. We tried to look through the windows to see what's on the other side, but it's too dark and the windows are very dirty. It's probably just more rubbish, as this place was pretty smashed up when we first found it. We didn't dare to knock down any walls though. I thought it best to leave that to the professionals." Oliver's voice echoed through the hallway as Freya and Bam made their way to the main hall, where he and two contractors were in the midst of their conversation. One of the men, tall with dirty blond hair, stood with his back towards them. The other was a man in his mid-forties with a friendly face and short brown hair.

"Oh, here's the owner now." Oliver moved his hand towards Freya, and the tall man turned around. A pair of sharp green eyes held hers for a moment, and a casual smile played across handsome lips. He was the most beautiful man that Freya had ever seen. He looked like a movie star, and she suddenly understood Bam's excitement. Her knees felt weak, and blood rushed to her cheeks with hot tingles.

"Freya, meet Mr Masters and Mr Philips."

The beautiful man, who Freya had now elevated to the position of Greek God in her mind, took a few steps forward and extended his hand.

"Call me Logan."

"Yes." Her words were meek, and she simply stared at the extended hand, the grocery bags dangling by her side. There was an awkward silence between them as their eyes locked.

"I'm sorry." The stranger shook his head. "How rude; you're carrying shopping. Let me take those from you." He nodded at the other man. "John?" Freya couldn't find the words to respond, and she let Logan take the bags. The man he'd called John stepped forward and took Bam's bags. Oliver moved towards them, his eyes boring into Freya.

"I'll show these gentlemen the kitchen," he said, and as Logan walked away he hissed at the two girls: "Meanwhile, maybe Freya can find her brain?"

Freya and Bam stared after the men as they went through the double doors leading into the West Wing. Then Bam turned to Freya and punched her in the arm, the little fist with pointed knuckles making quite an impact.

"What's wrong with you?"

"That, ladies and gentlemen, is how Freya flirts." She brought her arm and head down on Bam's shoulder and pretended to sob.

"That was awful."

"Wasn't it just?"

"I'm amazed you ever get laid with techniques like that."

"It's not easy, let me tell you."

"Seriously, that was so bad it was almost impressive. You should write a book."

"Please let me suffer in silence."

When the men's voices became louder once more, Freya bolted upright and pretended to be studying one of the doorframes.

"Smooth," Bam whispered with a chuckle, and Freya waved a hand at her in irritation. Her stomach flipped when she saw the contractor making his way towards her again.

"Take two," Logan said. He shot her a winning smile, and Freya felt her stomach drop into her pelvis. Her smile was weak, and she gave him an awkward handshake, cursing herself inwardly.

"Freya Formynder."

"Logan Masters. That's quite an exotic name you have there." The skin of his hand was hot against hers, and to her horror, Freya noticed that her palms were sweating.

"My dad gave it to me," she said lamely. "I mean... he's Norwegian... it's his last name. My first name... um... it..."

"It's very pretty." The tall man winked at her, and acid bubbled in her throat.

"Thank you. You're pretty too." She grimaced. "Your name, I mean your name is pretty. No... not pretty... handsome. No, not handsome either... it's a good name." Her eyes betrayed her discomfort, and she looked at Bam and Oliver, who were standing at a distance, trying their best not to laugh out loud.

"My name is John Philips." The other man cut in with a sympathetic smile, his hand extended. Freya gripped it, somehow regaining control of her motor skills.

"Nice to meet you, excuse me, I have... um, a thing to do." Freya pushed past Logan and John, walking as quickly as she could without breaking into a run to her bedroom. Less than a minute later she slammed the door behind her and fell onto the bed. She buried her face in the pillow and moaned.

A few minutes passed when a knock on her door forced her to leave the comfort of her bed. Oliver leaned against the doorframe.

"What the fuck happened to you?" His eyes twinkled and he had a cruel smile on his face. Freya threw her head back and covered her eyes with the backs of her hands.

"That was horrible. I can't believe I turned into Cletus the Slack-Jawed Yokel."

"So, you think our new contractor is attractive, do you?" He rubbed his chin and gave her another crooked smile.

"I was hoping to be less obvious about it."

"Yeah, I was hoping you would be too. But unfortunately, you were about as obvious as a baboon flashing its big red arse."

"That's a nice image, thank you. This helps my crushed ego quite a bit."

"Well, stitch it up, kiddo." Oliver attempted an American mafia voice. "You better get used to this fella being around, ya hear?"

"Stop it. You're not funny." She sank onto her bed, and Oliver sat down next to her.

"I'm not kidding, Frey. I talked to Logan, and he can do us a real sweet deal. He works with problem kids that are trying to get their lives together. They take on big projects like this for little more than room and board."

Freya sat up, leaned on her hands, and gave Oliver a scrutinising look.

"Do they deliver professional work? We can't have the hotel looking shoddy."

"From what I've heard and seen, they do an amazing job. Logan only works with really talented kids that want to make something of their lives. He showed me a portfolio of some of his projects. Rudy vouches for him, and you know what Rudy is like."

She nodded slowly, doubt gripping her stomach.

"Don't pull that face. Let's be honest; even with the sales from the antiques, we would have never had the money to do up the whole hotel and get it running. We probably would have had to rent out rooms when only one of the wings was ready and fix up the rest along the way. This way, we can do the whole project at once. We have to pay for the materials, the room and board. I figure we let the kids stay here, and at the end they all get a little 'internship money', which is really no more than a bonus. Do you know how much cash that will save us?"

"But these kids..." Her fingers twirled around the purple sheets of her bed. "You said they were problem kids?"

"Minor stuff. Nothing too serious. Vandalism, petty theft, stuff like that. Come on, everyone deserves a second chance, Freya. I expected you to understand that." He pushed her shoulders with a jovial smile, but Freya saw an intensity in his eyes. "They'll be supervised."

"By Logan and that other guy, erm... Philips?"

"Yes, and another guy. There are a few professional builders who help out. And Logan has some connections for electricians and other tradesmen. He said he'd get us discounts from them too."

"It sounds almost too good to be true." Freya forced a smile and leaned against Oliver. The sweet musk of his Calvin Klein aftershave hung around him like a protective blanket, and she inhaled the familiar scent.

"Who said that we can't ever get lucky?"

"Who indeed."

"Plus... Captain Awesome will get to live with us for the better part of a year." He turned his head to look at her.

"Do you think you can handle that?"

She punched him on the leg. He retaliated by pulling her onto the bed and tickling her. Freya screamed with laughter and fought to defend herself. After several minutes, they both fell onto their backs and looked at the ceiling.

"When can they start?"

"Next week sometime."

She exhaled, blowing a wayward lock of hair from her face. There were several minutes of silence between them, and Freya listened to the birds chirp outside her window. She thought about Angel Manor, and how the house had already transformed in her mind. It wasn't frightening at all. The only thing that had made the house frightening was her weird aunt and her creepy cousins, but they'd all died, and they'd left her the house. Angel Manor was *hers* now.

"This is really happening isn't it?"

"It is. We're making it happen."

"Yes," she said with a deep sigh. "Yes we are."

***

Logan turned to look at the house one last time. He had to admit that it was a gorgeous building, and it would be the biggest job the 'Second Chance project' would have had to date. Yet there was something about the house that bothered him, and he couldn't quite put his finger on it.

John stood next to him and followed his gaze. "This'll be a perfect project to do with some of the more difficult lads, like Terrence Jones and Roger Mace."

Logan rubbed his nose between his thumb and forefinger. "It would be, wouldn't it?" He inhaled deeply. It was away from bars, or any other goddamned place, so he wouldn't have to be afraid of them running amok. And yet, when he looked at Angel Manor and the row of creepy angels leading to it, something nagged at him. "It's going to be a long project, this one."

John frowned. "Yeah, but it looks like a good one though. This house is amazing. The only thing I worry about with the lads are those two young ladies in there."

"We'll have to keep an eye out for that, yes. It's a good thing they're in a completely different wing of the house from where we'll be working. That little blonde looks like she might be some trouble." Logan raised his eyebrows and mussed his hair with his hands.

"That girl with the dark hair, Freya, seemed to take quite a fancy to you." John shoved his shoulder against Logan, a dirty grin on his face.

"She was cute."

"I hope you're not going to be a problem on this project." John winked at him and pulled a packet of rolling tobacco from his pocket.

"I'm nothing if not a professional."

"These projects take a long time. I can imagine a man might weaken his resolve, having a pair of grey eyes give him that dreamy look and fluttering eyelashes at him all the time."

"A man might." Logan looked at the rollup and pulled a face. "You're not smoking that in my car, mate. Let's go. It's a long trip back to Edinburgh."

The two men climbed into the vehicle and drove off down the narrow road, away from Angel Manor and Lucifer Falls. Logan couldn't quite shake the feeling that the house was watching them as they left.

Chapter 5

The last of the antiques were hoisted into the dealer's van by two large men who smelled like they hadn't showered in a week. The dealer himself, Mr MacDougal, was an elderly man with bad teeth and thin white hair brushed messily over a glossy scalp.

"That'll be the last of it, Miss. It was a pleasure doing business with you." A hint of the man's halitosis hit her, and Bam fought against a grimace. He shoved a gloved hand towards her and she grabbed it, feeling the soft leather creak between her fingers.

"You made a good deal here."

"So did you, Miss. There are a lot of pieces that will need restoration, and we came all the way out here to pick everything up." When he spoke he inhaled sharply, which made his words sound like a chuckle.

Bam nodded in response, feeling out of breath just listening to him. She had hoped to get a little more money, but in the end she'd caved because MacDougal had offered to take everything off her hands in one go. If she could have spent more time, she knew she could have secured a better price, but everyone had agreed they just wanted the furniture cleared out before the kids arrived.

"There you go, as promised." He handed her a crisp envelope, and Bam took it between her thumb and forefinger. She didn't want to touch the man again. His bulging eyes were lined with puffy skin, and he blinked at her in a way that reminded her of a frog.

"Good luck with your, uh, hotel." MacDougal looked around. "Beautiful spot, Lucifer Falls. Not the best loved though. But you know how tourists are. They don't mind the occasional ghost story."

"Ghost story?"

The halitosis and annoying breathing were instantly forgotten. Bam suddenly found herself very interested in what the man had to say.

"Don't you know the stories?"

She shook her head. "I only know the one about Lucifer Falls being the place where the devil supposedly fell from the sky and fell straight through the earth and into Hell, if you mean that one?"

"No, though that is a part of it." He leaned in conspiratorially. "You see, Lucifer wasn't the only angel that fell from Heaven. He took several with him. Some believe that not all demons made it into Hell, but that some remained in the land. Almost two hundred years ago, a convent stood on the very spot where this house stands. The nuns of the convent were the guardians of unadoptable orphans. The whole thing went up in flames. There were only two survivors, one of them a nun and the other a little girl. It's said the girl later built this house."

"I didn't know that." Bam bit her lip.

"I'm sure there'll be archives about it somewhere. It's become a bit of a local legend. Every island has its dark side; this happens to be Skye's." The man grabbed his hat from the table and placed it on his glistening scalp, little wisps of white hair escaping from under it. "They say the nuns still haunt this place. Called themselves 'Angels', they did." He gave her a knowing look and adjusted his headwear.

"Spooky." She wrapped her hands across her shoulder and shivered. The man gave her a smug nod.

"Well, I'll leave you to it. Thank you again." He put on his brown raincoat. Bam held the door open for him and watched him walk towards his van, where the two movers stood having a cigarette. She stayed in the doorway until the van drove out of sight, her skin an exposition of tiny goose bumps.

"What are you staring at?"

Bam yelped and turned around to face Oliver. His brown curls hung flat around his head like withering flowers, and sweat stained his old work-shirt.

"Nothing." She felt a pang of guilt because she had been thinking of ghosts again and Oliver hated talking about ghosts. "I got the cheque." She held it up with false cheerfulness.

"Good job, Bam. I'm proud of you, girl." He leaned over and kissed her forehead, his lips burning hot on her skin, and Bam felt a tingle in her crotch.

"Thanks, I wanted more, but—"

"You did fine. This will provide us with a nice little buffer. It'll give me the opportunity to build a proper kitchen in this place." He took the cheque from her hand and held it up. "This is absolutely brilliant."

"Plus, now all the stuff is gone, we can redecorate the living room."

"Yeah, that's the plan. While the builders do the hotel, we can focus on our little part of the house."

Bam plucked a piece of plaster from his shoulder. "I'm not very good with the technical stuff, but I'm one hell of a decorator."

He chuckled, and the sight of his crooked smile made the butterflies in her stomach twirl. Oliver wasn't the most handsome man she had ever met – his nose was a little too broad for that and his chin was weak – but there was something in the way he spoke and smiled that turned Bam to pudding.

"Let's go have some lunch." Oliver put his arm around

her shoulders, but Bam pushed him away, her nose wrinkled.

"Get off. You stink!"

Oliver bent forward and wafted the scent from his armpits in her direction with his hand, and Bam screeched and ran away laughing. Oliver chased her into the kitchen, his fingers pulling at her shirt. Bam came to an abrupt stop when she saw the expression on Freya's face. She was sitting at the kitchen table, a letter in her hand and her brow a knot above her nose.

"What's up?" Bam slid onto the seat next to her and gave her a worried look.

"This came today from the inheritance lawyer. They missed it somehow, but my aunt wanted me to have it."

"What does it say?" Oliver took a seat on the other side of Freya and looked over her shoulder at the letter. Bam felt her stomach tighten, and she fiddled nervously with the plastic floral tablecloth that she'd used to bring a bit of colour to the dreary wooden kitchen.

"It's just insane." Freya sounded exasperated, and she sat back in the wooden chair, never taking her eyes off the letter. "I knew the woman had issues... but for God's sake..."

"I'm curious now." Oliver raised his eyebrows and leaned further forward.

"Okay, I'll read you bits. It's very long so I'll spare you all of it. Here it goes.

"*Dear Freya,*

"*If you're reading this, I'm probably dead, and I never had a chance to instruct you with regards to Angel Manor. I will try to leave the instructions as clearly as I can in the journal since you are on your own now.*" Freya turned the letter around to see if there was any mention of a journal.

"I haven't quite figured out what the journal is, or where it is. It didn't come with the letter. I'll have to ask if it got left behind."

"Go on," Oliver urged.

"'*Your mother was the natural heir to this house, but she passed over her rights many years ago, and I don't think she'll serve as a Guardian. You are humanity's last hope, Freya. I know you come from a Godless family, but the good Lord has a plan for you, and it is very important that you follow through with that plan. Not just for you, but for all of us. Without the Guardians, the world will be doomed. I don't know how much your mother has told you about Angel Manor, but it's different from any other house you will have encountered. It has secrets, which I've explained more about in the journal. What you need to know is that this house is not just bricks and mortar. It's as near alive as any building can be. It was built that way almost two hundred years ago. The house protects the secret, but at the same time that very secret taints the house. It can be cruel and needy, much like an old family member, but it will love you and those who you choose to love too. But be careful, because it can get jealous, and like a scorned lover, the house will lash out, and it may try to hurt you if you don't treat it properly.'*"

Bam's teeth gnawed on the soft flesh of her bottom lip, and she looked from Freya to Oliver with big round eyes. "That's the scariest thing I've ever heard. This house is alive?" The walls seemed bigger and darker to her, and she couldn't shake the feeling she was being watched. Oliver hissed between his teeth and rolled his eyes, but kept quiet.

Freya looked up and pursed her lips. "She goes into quoting the Bible here a lot, so I'll skip that part. But this is where it gets interesting, and really crazy.

"'*In order for you to live your life in relative safety, I have built a safe haven in the West Wing. There, you can live away from the spirits that dwell in the house. We walled up the other wings and used salt in the mortar. The spells in the house are strong, but they are fragile, and I fear for the shadows that you will bring from your previous life. This place gives them strength. Learn the spells to protect yourself. It's important. Should you ever accidentally release any of the souls, I've placed seven golden seals in the main room of this wing. It will be your sanctuary.*

"'During the seasonal equinox, you need to leave the house. Make sure there's not a single living creature in the house at that time, this is very important. The spirits will feed off their life-force and become stronger.

"'You will bond with the house the way I have, and once it has you, it will never let you go. The house will destroy itself if it doesn't have a human bond, and all the secrets will spill from its core. You are blessed as well as cursed.'"

Freya rolled her eyes.

"Yada yada, a whole bit about Jesus saving me, and how he will protect the spirits of the house, and that I must forgive them because they weren't meant to be evil, but the magic made them that way or something. Here's another good bit..."

She cleared her throat.

"'Never enter the basements under the house. They are old and dangerous, and what lurks there is an unspeakable evil. The house is built as a fortress atop the basement. The knowledge of what lies in the dark has been lost for several generations. It's our duty to protect it.'"

Freya looked up from the letter and pulled her lips into a thin line. "And then there is a bit that says it's my duty to make sure there are heirs to the house. And she pleads with me to take her message seriously."

"Holy smokes, Batman." Bam put her hand over her open mouth and looked from Freya to Oliver.

"More like Holy smokes, Batshit, if you ask me." Oliver

whistled between his teeth, and Bam laughed nervously.

"I know, right?" Freya put the letter down, but she still stared at the blue handwriting, and Bam followed her gaze. The writing was scratchy, with straight thin loops that pushed through the lines on either side, and most of it was illegible to Bam. Her eyes met Freya's, and she saw her friend's face change a little.

"You know this is crazy, right, Bam?" Freya looked worried. "No such things as ghosts or spirits. There's nothing in this house. I think my auntie might have been schizophrenic or something."

"Oh, right." Bam's voice was barely audible. She pulled her knees up to her chest, resting her heels on the edge of the wooden chair. "There are a lot of rumours around this place."

"That's no surprise." Freya leaned over and kissed her on the head. "There are a lot of stories about this area, so add a house to the mix, inhabited by crazy people, and voila... instant myth. Look at it this way: We've been here ten days now and we haven't seen a single weird thing, so the place really isn't haunted."

Bam rested her chin on her knees and bit her lip. Her eyes wandered around the kitchen, then settled on Oliver.

"Except that we all got mysterious nosebleeds when we first arrived."

"Probably just the air up here. We're quite high up you know." Oliver waved her words away with a flick of his hand, but Bam wasn't ready to give up so easily.

"After we all touched the stones? Bit of a coincidence, don't you think?" She saw a darkness in his eyes then, one she'd never seen before, and part of her wanted to give up, but her innate tenacity wouldn't let it go. "What about that brown stuff we saw? Or how the house suddenly looked a lot better the next day?"

"Come on, we talked about this." Oliver slammed his palms on the table and got to his feet. "Why do you keep bringing up this bullshit? Bam, there are no ghosts. And until you bring me evidence that they exist, I don't ever want to talk about this again." His eyes shifted with an agitated passion that surprised Bam.

"Maybe we should just get those golden plates back... you know, just in case?" Her eyes watered, but she fought the tears. Freya shifted on her seat, clearly uncomfortable. She was the peacemaker, Bam knew, but Bam also knew that Freya was on Oliver's side in this. Her friend was uncomfortable with the house, but for different reasons than Bam was.

"We can't. We need the money. I'm not missing out on all that cash just because you're superstitious, or because of some crazy letter from an even crazier woman."

She sighed and suddenly felt utterly ridiculous. Her legs slid off the chair and she leaned forward.

"I'm sorry. I don't know what came over me. For the record, I do believe in ghosts, but you're right, this house doesn't have any or we would have noticed by now." A silence fell over the kitchen, and Oliver looked at Bam with suspicion. She returned his glare with a wet smile. "Promise, I'm not going to bring it up again. Let's just eat lunch, okay?"

Freya slid her arms around Bam's shoulders again and squeezed tightly. "Good idea. We should eat."

They ate their sandwiches in silence, and all Bam could think of was visiting the Portree Community Library later in the week to do some research on the house, and on spirits.

Chapter 6

The minibus buzzed with voices and laughter. The young men referred to themselves as 'Chancers'. They were a rough bunch, and Logan wouldn't normally have picked the combination of these six young males in particular, but John had insisted it was time to teach them the ropes on a bigger project. Up until two days ago, seven guys had been picked for the project, but Tyrell Jones, Terrence's brother, hadn't shown up. The two brothers were his biggest concern, and Logan had decided not to wait for Tyrell to show his face. He would get another chance down the line as soon as Logan found a way to make the young man feel the consequences of his absence. It was one less troublemaker to worry about, and Logan knew that if he could keep Terrence Jones and Roger Mace in check, the other four would be a cakewalk.

He shifted in his seat and looked at his crew. They ranged from eighteen to twenty, all kids who had felt too little love in their hard young lives and now stood on the brink of adulthood. Logan himself remembered what it was like, and if he hadn't been saved by a project much like this one, he would probably have ended up in jail, or worse. He loved these boys and he understood them, but he was a strict mentor and took no shit from any of them. They loved him for it, he knew, and he was always happy to see another youngster fly the nest. Logan was only twenty-eight himself, but he sometimes felt like he'd lived a hundred years already.

"Put that cigarette away, Terrence." He glared at the black guy who smiled at him with an unlit filter cigarette between his straight teeth. "You light that and there will be hell to pay."

Terrence seemed to contemplate his words for a

moment, but then he took the cigarette from his mouth with a dramatic gesture and crammed it back in the almost empty packet.

"So, no love for a fellow London boy then, Logan? Is that how it's going to be?"

"Rules are rules, Terrence. Doesn't matter where you're from."

Terrence wasn't a bad kid. Logan liked him more than his brother, but he came from a terrible home and all he knew was how to fight. The only way he knew how to get attention was by acting out. His mother was a junkie who'd tried to clean up her life when she'd left London and moved to Edinburgh. There, she met the boys' new stepfather, who was a good for nothing son of a bitch who liked to beat both of them bloody. Terrence and Tyrell lived more on the streets than they did in their own home, and Logan often found them a place to stay during the internships. It would be good for Terrence to be away from his stepfather, and Logan decided it might be a blessing in disguise that he would also be away from his brother for a bit. He was intelligent, and Logan hoped he could convince Terrence to do a bit of side-study at some point. First, however, he needed to learn some discipline. All these guys did.

The boys leaned against the seats, bored and sluggish after several hours' driving. The play fights had died down a bit, and now they were just talking. Two had even fallen asleep. The weather made the minibus hot, and even Jim McLeod, the third mentor, snored softly in his seat. His bald head sagged forwards, and his thick, red beard rested on his ample chest.

"You need a break from driving soon?" Logan peered at John, who shifted in his seat for the fifth time in less than a minute.

"Naw, I'm okay. Me back is just acting up. Can't wait to get there."

"Yeah, I wonder what the boys will make of it."

"They'll be gutted that there's no pub nearby."

"The first few weeks they'll be too tired to want to go to a pub. We'll wear them out. And we'll provide some entertainment at the weekends. Plus, they get to go home for a weekend every fortnight."

John shook his head and gave Logan a sad glance.

"Naw, lad, most of them won't want to go home. You know that."

"Still, got to give them the option." Logan leaned back and looked out of the window. Nothing but green hills and blue sky. He loved being away from the city. One day, he wanted to build a house of his own and get away from it all, maybe fall in love and get married... a wife and a kid... a few animals. It would be living the dream. He closed his eyes, and the picture of the girl with the black hair appeared in his mind. *What was her name again? Freya?* He thought of her flushed face, those big grey eyes and the curves on her body, and for a moment, he imagined what it would be like to unbutton her cotton shirt to reveal the flesh beneath. Then Angus Reid and Lyndon Farrow tore him from his daydream with loud laughter. They stood, Lyndon half-leaned over the seat, punching each other in the arms.

"Settle down you two," Logan snapped, and when they didn't respond, he raised his voice. "Oi! Settle the fuck down."

The guys sank back into their seats, each still chuckling. Logan turned around again, but the fantasy of the pretty girl with the black hair was ruined, and he felt a little agitated.

***

The countryside looked dull to nineteen-year-old Terrence Jones. He was still angry with his older brother for skipping out on the project. It wasn't like Tyrell to not even let him know that he was going to cop out, and though he would never admit it to himself, Terrence was actually a little worried. The prospect of being away from his stepfather was the only good thing about this whole trip, but he had never been away from Tyrell for long and he hoped that Logan would allow his brother to join them later on. Sure Tyrell was a stupid fuck for not being there, and he knew that Logan was angry, but he also knew that Logan was an all right kind of bloke.

Another thing that Terrence didn't like was that the house they were supposed to be fixing up was in the middle of nowhere. On a fucking island, no less. How much worse could it get? There would be little chance of finding nice looking birds on an island, Terrence had decided, and he'd probably only have old fogey pubs to hang out in. Logan had told them that they would be camping too, until the place was cleared up enough for them to sleep in. Terrence didn't mind camping. He'd spent enough nights on the streets of Edinburgh, sleeping on cardboard, to be able to rough it out anywhere. Most of the guys in their crew had been homeless at one point or another.

He looked out his window as they drove up a steep hill, and in the distance he saw the large looming shape of Angel Manor.

"That's a fucking big house." Mason Applebaum pointed at the window, and all the guys got up from their seats and moved to get a first glance.

"Is that it, Mr Norris?" Gary Feltman asked.

"That's it. Angel Manor."

"Whoever lives there has to be well rich," Angus muttered. "That looks like a castle." There were more mutterings in agreement, but Terrence felt a pang of annoyance.

"Don't be stupid. That's a mansion, not a castle." He

flicked Angus across his mousy brown locks and made a hissing noise between his teeth.

"Fuck you."

"That's enough." Logan's voice cut across the bus, and Terrence felt his temper settle down.

"That's the house that we're turning into a hotel. Yes it's big, so it'll be hard work. I need you guys to be on your best behaviour."

"Och, we know the speech," Roger muttered from the back of the minibus, loud enough for everyone to hear.

"Well then, I'll save giving it to you again." Logan looked at each of the young men and let his gaze linger on Terrence a little longer than on the others. "Three strikes and you're out: I ship you back home. This will be a wonderful opportunity for you to learn some skills..."

"Oh aye. I got me some mad skills," quipped Lyndon Farrow, while he half got to his feet and grabbed his crotch. All the boys laughed in response.

"I'm sure you know how to work your tool, Lyndon; just keep it in your pants please. No one wants to see it." More laughter and a few jeers, and Lyndon sat down again, shaking his head. "Like I said, this will be a good project for all of you. From here, you could go on to work for actual construction companies. This will look great on your CV."

Terrence had thought about his future a lot. It wasn't something he'd even considered before he'd joined the Chancers, but he found he liked the idea of having one. The thought of a good job with a steady pay check was appealing, maybe a little flat all to himself... or he could share it with his brother. It was all good, and he could get away from that white gob-shite, Paul. He might even leave Edinburgh, go back to London... or move somewhere else altogether. He liked having possibilities.

He looked at the house. It was big like Mason had said,

and it was beautiful. Terrence imagined what it would be like living in a place like that, and he pictured himself in a swanky suit with an FHM girl on each arm. The closer they got to the house, however, the images of busty females faded and he began to feel uncomfortable. Something was off about the mansion. Sure, it was all yellow stones and sunshine on the outside, but somehow it didn't feel very welcoming, as if the building itself were judging him. The window of the bus felt cold against his skin, and Terrence wrapped his arms around himself, his eyes never leaving Angel Manor.

**

"I think I saw a van pull up on the driveway." Bam peered around the door into the kitchen, her hair falling over her face. "We should go greet them."

Freya nodded and got to her feet. "Have you called Oliver?"

"He's seen them. Told me to come and get you."

"Okay." Freya put her cup in the sink and rinsed it so the tea wouldn't stain.

"Frey?" Bam looked at her with big eyes and a guilty expression.

"What?" Freya raised her eyebrows and put the cup upside down on the counter to dry. "What's bugging you?"

"Remember when I went out yesterday?"

"Yeah?"

"Well, I did a bit of research... on... on psychics." Bam's voice was barely above a whisper and Freya opened her mouth to object, but her friend held up her hands in defence. "Hear me out. This woman and her team are very respectable, and they could just check out the house to find out if there is anything here. I called her and she said she was interested in this house."

"No, Bam... just no." Freya shook her head. "Psychics are charlatans. We're not going to be paying con-men."

"She doesn't want money."

"I don't care what she wants. For fuck's sake, you're taking this ghost thing too far. Oliver is right..." She stopped her words when she saw the hurt expression on Bam's face.

"Just think about it, okay?" Bam handed her a piece of paper with scribbles on it in blue ink. "This is her number, in case you change your mind."

Freya took the paper and considered throwing it away, but instead she put it in the top drawer, closing it with a firm movement. "Okay."

Bam nodded and left the room with Freya following her, feeling a little anxious about meeting the work crew.

They don't look so bad. Freya eyed the six young men who stood shoulder to shoulder in the entrance hall. *They're just kids.* Some of them looked close to being her own twenty-five years of age, but a few of the boys hardly looked old enough to shave. Their clothes were old and a little dirty. The way they stood, eyes wide and mouths a little slack, staring at the grandeur of Angel Manor, she could almost relate to them. When she was younger she had known those feelings well.

She'd hoped she would be a little more resistant to their mentor's good looks, but when Logan Masters shook her hand, her knees turned to jelly again. The thought of having him around was both exciting and terrifying, and Freya fought hard to hide the blush she felt creeping into her cheeks whenever he looked her way.

Don't be such a silly little girl. It's not like you've never seen handsome men before, she chided herself. But this guy was different in some way, and butterflies swarmed in her stomach like locusts.

Freya stepped forward and offered each of them her hand. Two of them, a pale kid with reddish hair and a guy with dark skin, shot her leery, appreciative looks that made her skin crawl.

One of the mentors, a stout Scot with muscular shoulders and a big red beard, cleared his throat. "We'll set up camp outside the house."

"Camp?" Freya looked at him with surprise. "This is a big house. We can make space for nine people..."

"Thank you, Miss. When we finish some of the rooms in the other wings, we'll gladly make use of them, but for now we'll stay outside. We don't want to get in your way."

"You won't be in our way. The West Wing is large enough to share. It's not in the same state as the rest of the house, and there are rooms upstairs."

"With all due respect, I don't think it would be a good idea to have boys in the same wing as you, Miss."

Freya's eyes flicked to the red-haired guy who'd leered at her, and she saw a look in his pale blue eyes that she didn't like.

"Oh." Her skin ran cold and she hugged herself, pulling her gaze away from him. *This was such a bad idea.*

The big man obviously saw something in her face, and he waved his hands in an apologetic gesture. "No need to worry, Miss. Honest, these are good boys. But they might be rowdy, especially at night. We like to have them where we can keep an eye on them. That's all. They won't harm you in any way. They wouldn't dare."

"I understand," she responded. A sense of relief washed over her when she saw the shadows of Oliver and Bam stand in the doorway. "Here are my partners in crime now." She winced at the word *crime*; it had slipped from her mouth before she'd realised it. She laughed sheepishly to cover up for her mistake, but nobody seemed to have noticed.

"This is Oliver Jardin, and this is Bambi Green." One of the boys, Freya couldn't see which, whistled through his teeth. There were more leery looks, and Freya felt her stomach drop. Bam just giggled and shook their hands. She wore a tight, white Breeders T-shirt that stretched across her silicone breasts and a pair of cut-off jean-shorts that revealed just a hint of the rounded cheeks of her buttocks. Her hair was done up in a playful ponytail, and Freya saw the appreciation in the young men's eyes. It took all of Freya's self-restraint not to slap her hand over her eyes and sigh.

"So many boys to keep us company," Bam crooned, and Freya saw from the way she wiggled her hips when she walked that she was savouring the attention.

"Down, girl." Oliver grabbed Bam by the wrist and pulled her away. "Let's give our crew time to settle in. We can make them some tea or something."

"Is there anything we can do for you?" Freya tried to ignore the stares that followed Bam's gyrating backside.

"I'd bam that," the red-headed one said under his breath, and the black guy laughed with appreciation.

"Naw, we're good, Miss. Logan and John are finding somewhere to set up the tents, so we'll go help them. Tea would be nice though."

"Then tea it is." She turned and left, grateful that she could stalk towards the kitchen while self-consciously wondering if the guys were staring at her backside too.

This is going to be a long year, she sighed.

Chapter 7

Freya and Bam's slender fingers intertwined as they watched the young crew and their sledgehammers from the doorway of the West Wing.

An unexpected silence had settled over the main hall. The boys, who had been wild and giddy only moments ago at breakfast, stood around with serious faces as they listened to John Philips' speech about site safety. Freya glanced at Bam, who looked as nervous as she felt. Her heart drummed slowly and heavily against her chest, and her palms were moist with sweat.

What are you afraid of, Bam? Ghosts? she thought, but didn't dare to say the words out loud. *What am I afraid of? Am I afraid that the monsters my mother feared lie waiting behind that wall?*

The silence was broken when the first hammer hit the brickwork, the blow ringing through the rooms with such clarity and intensity that Freya felt Bam's body shake. For a moment, she thought that the house had shuddered, and a sickly feeling crept up her throat. She bent forward to look at Oliver, who stood leaning against the wall. One of the corners of his mouth was curled into a slight smile and his eyes blazed as he watched the hammer strike the bricks. It was no surprise he was pleased the wall was coming down. Freya knew that he'd been waiting for this moment. Oliver had talked about how this was the symbol of a new beginning, the first step to creating his future. His excitement was almost palpable. Oliver hadn't been himself the past few days. He'd been distant and less jovial. She thought that the pressure of the project might have got to him. Last night, she'd heard him talking to himself, and that could never be a good sign. She hoped she was wrong, because the work had only just started and she needed

Oliver to keep a clear head, especially now that Bam seemed so twitchy. If he was having some sort of a nervous breakdown, it would be extremely bad timing.

Once again, she wondered if she'd made the right choice by keeping the house. Perhaps its curse wasn't ghosts after all, but stress. The house was large and hard to maintain. Maybe that's what drove people over the edge. She slid her arm around Bam's shoulders and rubbed her friend's skin with her thumb. Her mind wandered to her aunt, a thin woman with wild red hair and bulging eyes that always had an expression of accusation in them. A thought occurred to her that they'd found no pictures during the clean-up. Not of her aunt, nor of her children. Freya could hardly remember her cousins at all. She remembered playing with them, but the memory didn't go much further than the fact that they were ginger and a bit odd.

The hammer struck again, and the wall spewed pieces of brick and crushed mortar like a boxer spitting out broken teeth. The dust particles in the room danced in the languid sunlight filtering in through windows in golden streams. The young men cheered as the hole in the wall became bigger. Freya felt a change. She couldn't say what it was, but it tingled down her spine. She told herself it was just cold feet over starting a hotel so far away from home.

***

Ethereal eyes fluttered open from a deep sleep. *Equinox?* the tormented mind of Sister Agatha thought. The idea came with difficulty, slow and distorted. She had fought hard to keep her mind intact after her death. Without a body and a brain to make connections, the spirit was no more than a shadow of its former self. And the house... this house, it wanted to taint her as it had the others. It was alive. She could feel its essence in the bricks and mortar, tempting her over to darkness.

Why am I awake? she mused, as instinct kicked in and she materialised from her resting place.

The spells... something is breaking the spells. Panic surged through Agatha and she forced herself to concentrate on the house. *Strangers, there are strangers in Angel Manor. They're destroying the spells.* She could feel the heat of their bodies, even at this distance, and Agatha fought her longing to be near them. Life was so painful to the dead, and the warmth of the pulsing blood stirred a hunger, even in the docile nun.

Where are the living Guardians? Where are those who are supposed to protect the house? Agatha reached out with her essence and touched upon the descendant of the bloodline. The heir was here. And she had brought others. And the house had bonded with them. Two so far, but there would be a third. She focused on the heir again, a pang of worry shooting through her soul. *There is something different about this heir... something bad.*

For several decades, Sister Agatha's soul had known peace. The spells had protected her resting place, had kept her away from the living, letting her sleep in blissful ignorance through the year except on the equinoxes and the solstices. However, this was neither the equinox nor the solstice, and if the barriers to her domain were broken, the other boundaries would soon follow. Their absence would awaken the lost souls trapped inside Angel Manor.

But there were worse things...

The living might release the Angels themselves.

***

The last of the bricks fell with a crack, and the crew stood back, coughing as the lime dust tickled their throats. Mutters of appreciation hummed across the lips of the builders as they craned their necks to peer inside the East Wing. The darkness stretched away into unseen depths, and Freya's heart pounded against her ribcage.

"What happened to the windows? Where's the light?" Terrence pulled the dust mask from his powder-covered face and wiped the residue from his hair with a gloved hand. He dropped the sledgehammer, and the loud thud made Freya cringe.

"We're wearing PPE in there. The structure looks good, but we don't know how long this place has been boarded up or what we might find." John Norris handed out hardhats.

Freya gazed into the darkness beyond the rubble. She waited for everyone to make their way through, then watched Oliver step into the void.

"Don't forget your hardhat." Logan handed her a yellow monstrosity. Freya ran her hands over the deep black scratches and scuffmarks, hesitating to put it on for a moment.

"I wouldn't go in there without one." He winked at her and she responded with a watery smile.

"I think I'm a little intimidated by the thought of what's in there. The two rooms we cleared out were pretty bad. I can only imagine what this place is going to look like."

"Well, I wouldn't worry about it too much. You've got us to help you now." He touched her arm, and she felt a little jolt as he did so.

"You know what's weird?" She looked into his deep green eyes. "I've only just realised something."

"What?"

"There were so many cobwebs... but I haven't seen a single spider yet..."

"I'm sure we'll come across a few. And other creatures I expect. They tend to nest in old houses like these."

"I've not seen a living creature anywhere near here. Not even a fly."

"Well, I would say that we're pretty alive." Logan pointed at himself and made a gesture towards the guys.

Freya's cheeks flushed a soft pink, and she put her hat on to mask the embarrassment she felt.

"Of course... I meant... no animals."

Logan pushed the hardhat further onto her head, the plastic pinching her temples. "I know." Another wink accompanied by a smile. He held his hand up towards her, and she placed her palm in his. Logan led her through the door and into the East Wing.

There was a smell, sickly sweet with a hint of rotting meat underneath, so overpowering and sense-dulling that Freya was forced to take a step back. She lingered in the doorway, her face set in a grimace.

"What's that smell?" Her voice was muffled by the cupped hand around her mouth and nose.

"What smell?" Logan looked at her with sincere confusion. "I don't smell anything. Well... maybe it's a bit stale, but not nearly as bad as I thought it would be."

Freya looked at the others, who were investigating the dark wing. The only light came from the portable builder's lamps that they carried. No one else seemed to have noticed the stench, so she carefully inhaled again. It was still there, but not as strong this time, only a vague scent. A nervous laugh bubbled in the back of her throat and she bit her lip to keep it from escaping.

"Are you okay?" Logan adjusted his hardhat and cocked his head at her.

"I'm fine. It's just... darker than I would have liked. I don't do so well in the dark."

"Ah. Don't worry. We're here with you." He grabbed her hand and squeezed it, and Freya felt a hot tingle throughout her body.

She turned her eyes to the long corridor of the East Wing and gave a soft sigh. Yellowish-green wallpaper hung in tattered curls; it looked as if someone had deliberately shredded it in the centre. A residue of lime crunched under the soles of her shoes, giving the illusion the floor was made of gravel rather than marble.

"It's like another world in here. I feel like I've just landed on the moon or something." Freya's voice was no more than a whisper, and Logan nodded.

"It does a bit, doesn't it? This is one of the oldest buildings that we've had the privilege to work on. It's fascinating what kind of state these places can be in." He smiled at her, and her legs went weak again.

If only I could just lean forward and kiss him, she thought. *If only he could be mine.* The words echoed through her mind, and she felt a familiar tremble in her body. Logan was still talking about the house, his eyes sparkling as he spoke.

"Though I have to admit, so far I've been pleasantly surprised. This house looks like a sturdy old girl." He tapped the side of a wall with his free hand, the other still wrapped around hers. A sudden jolt of static electricity ran from Logan straight into Freya as his palm connected to the plaster, and Freya pulled her hand back in reflex. The house shuddered on its foundations, a tremor that Freya had felt before.

"Holy shit!" Logan cupped his nose. "Terrence, shine a light here. I don't know what the fuck that was, but I think it gave me a bloody nose." A light beam illuminated his face, and Logan looked at his hand. A generous splash of blood covered his fingers, and Freya's hand automatically went to her own nose. Her hand came back red. She looked around to see if anyone else was bleeding and, to her horror, saw both Oliver and Bam dab blood from their nostrils. *Not again.* Her blood ran cold, but Freya didn't want to come across as hysterical, so she fought to keep her face even.

"You're bleeding too." Logan stepped closer, grabbed her chin and pushed it up to inspect her face. "Did you feel that?"

"Yes."

"Mental."

"It's happened to us before." Bam's voice was high with panic. "When we first arrived, we touched the building outside, and we all got simultaneous nose bleeds. It's happening again." She held her hand up into the light, streaks of blood still visible on her upper lip, and there were tears in her eyes.

Her words seemed to freeze time for a second; no one moved or spoke, and all eyes were on Bam. It was Lyndon Farrow who spoke first.

"That's just fucking spooky. Like the kind of shit you see in horror movies." Some of the guys exchanged glances.

"If this place is haunted, I'm out of here," Lyndon said, his hands moving with agitated gestures as he talked.

"Don't be ridiculous, Lyndon." John's voice had the stern, no-nonsense tone of a drill sergeant.

"Awww, is wittle Wyndon scawed of ghosts?" Roger pouted his lips and fluttered his eyelashes at Lyndon, who responded by punching him in the shoulder.

"Shut up!"

"Come on, guys, don't fool around." Logan glanced around the group. His stare was met with silence, and Freya wasn't sure how to react herself. She wanted to be dismissive again, but wasn't sure if she could a second time.

"Let's see what work needs to be done, okay?" He wiped his nose with a paper tissue and handed Freya one too. Bam had her own pack and she shared them with Oliver. Freya was amazed that Bam appeared to be taking the bloody nose so well, acting very calm as far as she could tell, but she didn't trust it one bit. She'd heard the panic in her voice only minutes before, which left her wondering if Bam was just afraid of Oliver's wrath.

Oliver, who seemed rather unperturbed by the whole thing, grabbed one of the builder's lights and beckoned to Freya. "Let's go check out how many rooms there are."

Freya nodded, deciding this was neither the time nor the place to push the nosebleed matter, and followed Oliver. She looked back at Logan and smiled at him. He returned it with a small salute with his index and middle finger. The young crew seemed to be ill at ease after the nosebleed incident, but the strict voice of John Norris cut through the stillness of the East Wing, forcing the boys to focus on their tasks.

There were fourteen rooms on the bottom floor in total, all various sizes and in various states of disrepair. Someone had painted the windows black, and the light from outside struggled to get through the parts where the paint had peeled, casting eerie shadow patterns across the floor. The most unnerving of all was an old dining room. The floor was covered with broken crockery lying in shards across the decaying carpet. A broad antique table, which looked to be in rather decent shape, was surrounded by eight high-backed Victorian chairs. The velvet on the seat cushions had worn thin and frayed, but otherwise there was little damage. A large centrepiece sat on the table. Freya guessed it used to have flowers, but only an elaborate vase remained, covered in cobwebs that spread out from the centre to the rim like a fragile tent. Through the delicate webbing, Freya saw plates, cups, and cutlery made of silver. Oliver plucked at the cobwebs to reveal more of the perfectly-set table. He pulled out a sizeable silver serving dish, the ladle clinging to a black sticky substance lining the inside.

"That's a little creepy. I wonder why this table is still set, and how long it's been here."

"I find this whole place unsettling." Freya rubbed her arms. "I think it would be best if I don't come back in here until it's all been stripped bare. It's just freaking me out too much."

"It's just a house, Frey," Oliver warned, his tone sounding like an automatic response, his eyes firmly focused on the table.

"This is exactly the kind of darkness my mother is afraid of. I don't need to feel this kind of crazy. Set tables in dark rooms... cobwebs, it's more than I can handle."

Oliver blew a stray curl from his cheek. "You're being stupid."

"Maybe, but I like to think I'm more problem eschewing. I'm going to stay in the part of the house that doesn't look like it's Pinhead's vacation home, and I'm taking Bam with me. She's been acting crazy enough lately. I don't need her in hysterics either."

"Fine, stay in the West Wing. You'll only be in the way here, anyway."

She touched his shoulder but he pulled away. "You're so tetchy lately. I feel that every time I say anything negative about this house, I'm insulting you somehow. What's up with that?" The muscles in his neck stood out, and she saw how tense his shoulders were.

"I need this to work, Frey. I don't want to go back home to my old life. It was bad, and this is a new chance for me. There's something about this house... it just speaks to me. Whispers sweet nothings in my ear about having my own kitchen, cooking the food I want to cook. It will be awesome. Imagine if this takes off? Imagine if guests come to this hotel just to taste my food?" Freya pushed her hands in her pockets and rocked back and forth on the balls of her feet. It had been a while since she'd seen that spark in Oliver's eyes. For a moment, she'd forgotten that this meant more to him than it did to her, that this was living his dream. Or at least part of it. He had always wanted to cook, and the hotel would provide the perfect opportunity for him to do so. While she was worried about hiring hotel staff and working the front desk, Oliver was dreaming of kitchens and menus.

Freya let out a deep sigh and slapped the side of her leg with some determination. "I'm sorry. I need to stop being such a big baby about this place."

"No, that's okay. I think it might be better if you stay in the West Wing. When the rest is done, when this place doesn't look so filthy anymore, you won't feel so freaked out."

"I think I let Bam get to me. The bloody noses were pretty freaky."

"Yeah, I don't know what keeps causing that, but I have to admit, that weirded me out a little too." He nudged her with his elbow. "Disadvantage of staying on the west side of the house is that you'll see less of Mr Fantastic."

Freya flicked Oliver's ears with her thumb and forefinger.

"I think that might be a good thing." Freya shook her head. "I'm going to grab Bam and take her with me to the supermarket."

"Don't forget to get loo paper." They smiled at each other and Freya turned to leave. For a moment, she froze as she looked into a pale female face with gaunt cheeks and sunken eyes.

"Oliver..." she gasped.

"What?"

She wanted to tell him about what she'd seen, but it was gone as fast as it had appeared, and Freya wondered if she'd seen it at all.

"Er... do we need more bread?" She didn't dare say anything else.

"No, we're okay for bread. When we get the new kitchen installed, I might start making my own."

"That sounds great." Her voice cracked slightly, but she doubted Oliver had noticed the uncertainty. Freya stumbled out the door, the blood drawn from her face, the lime debris unstable beneath her feet. Déjà vu tugged at her mind, nudging her to remember something from years ago. She had been here before... no, not here... it had been in the South Hall. The one time she'd come with her mother. The memory was so vague. Aunt Miriam and mom were fighting in the living room, and the wings hadn't been closed off then. She closed her eyes and suddenly she remembered the incident as clear as day.

Paul, the eldest of her cousins, took her hand and told her: "This house has secrets. There's a monster here, and if you listen carefully, you can hear him cry."

The hallway had appeared so long to her infant eyes. The roof was high, and the large windows let in bright rays of light that reflected off the shining marble floor. Their steps still echoed through Freya's memory, and if she concentrated, she could hear their voices.

"I'm afraid."

"You should be. Our monster is really scary. It lives in the basement."

Freya's heart raced, and her little palm was sweaty and slick against Paul's skin.

"Do you want to see it?"

She nodded, her throat too thick and dry to answer. Her knees wobbled, but she steadied herself. They walked further down the hallway to the middle, where the sunbeams diminished and the shadows deepened. Behind a stout metal door lay the basement. A large chain hung to one side, wrapped around a crank. Paul pushed down on it, and the door creaked open.

"Why do you have to do that?"

"Because, if the monster escapes, we need to be able to close the door quickly." Paul gave her a pinched smile. He was a rather unattractive boy, Freya noted. His hair was flame-red, and his face was long and milky white, splattered with honey-coloured freckles. Pale grey eyes, as grey as her own, peered from beneath barely visible golden eyebrows.

"Are you too afraid to go down there?"

"No." It was a lie. She was terrified, but she didn't want him to see her fear. With a raised chin, and a knotted stomach, she placed her foot on the first step. Once more, she glanced back at Paul, who towered over her, his face set in a curious grimace. Then she turned and walked down the stairs, her steps slow but deliberate. When she reached the bottom, a loud bang, followed immediately by darkness, told her that the door had been shut. Something grabbed her around the neck and pulled her back. Freya screamed, and a warm stream of urine bloomed in her tights, leaving a hot damp trail against the grey wool. Somewhere through a haze of panic, she heard laughter, but she couldn't focus enough on it to stop wailing. She kicked out, and the hands let her go with a curse.

"Shut up you stupid brat!" The voice was young and familiar… a boy. Freya fell to the ground and sobbed until her throat was a dry, raw mess.

"You're such a baby."

The door above opened and the light poured in, streaming down the stairs like a waterfall of safety. Paul's figure cast a looming shadow against the light. Lucas and Constance hovered over her, but Freya kept her eye on the door, determined to escape.

"Did it work?"

"Didn't you hear her scream?"

"No, dummy, you can't hear a thing once the door is closed."

"Get up." Constance pulled at her arm, but Freya shrugged her off. *"Don't be so stupid. Get up. Or we'll leave you down here with the real monster."* Constance pointed at a second door just visible on the other side of the basement.

Much like her brothers, Constance had a long, horsey face, pale and freckled. Her mouth was more gums than teeth, which made her look a little slow. With the back of her hand, Freya wiped the cooling tears from her cheeks. She sniffed and looked at her cousins, then got up.

"What you did was really mean." Her voice was still strangled from crying. She took a few steps back until her heel hit the stairs.

"Watch out for the salt, you daft cow." Lucas grabbed her arm and pulled her forward.

A hint of genuine fear crossed Constance's bland features. *"Fix it,"* she hissed. *"Put the salt back."*

Paul hurried down the stairs, and suddenly all three children were brushing the scattered salt into a neat line, their eyes round with terror. Freya blinked, and her eyes scanned the floor and the stairways. Words she could not read were daubed on the walls with black paint, accompanied by symbols that made her skin crawl.

"What is this place?"

Paul got to his feet and stood right in front of her, his pale grey eyes hard. *"A prison."* As if to confirm his words, a loud noise, as if someone was beating a rod against a metal door, clanged through the basement.

"What was that?" Her voice quivered. Constance just shook her fiery red head, her braids swaying across her shoulders. *"I don't think this is funny."*

"You need to check the lock, Paul." Lucas turned to his brother, whose eyes were transfixed on the door at the end of the basement. *"You need to see if it's still safe."* Paul froze for a moment, and then he raised his hand. Freya saw his fingers tremble.

"Paul, go." Constance's voice seemed to snap the older boy out of his trance, and he ran towards the door. Freya wanted to take a step forward to see what he was doing, but Lucas pulled her arm again.

"No you don't. Upstairs with you. You don't need to be here." His mouth was a thin line. *"Now go."*

He didn't have to tell her twice.

Freya turned and ran.

***

She hadn't thought about the incident in years, and Freya was surprised at how deeply she'd suppressed the memory. But now it seemed as if it had happened yesterday, and even the faces of her cousins, who had been no more than pale blurs in her mind, were now sharp and clear. The thought of the basement made her skin crawl. She knew it had been just her cousins playing a trick on her, but she had been so young and impressionable at the time, and that childhood fear still lingered. A shiver ran up her spine and an acid taste rose up her throat.

Pull yourself together, girl. Now you've got yourself seeing actual ghosts. They don't exist; you're just letting your imagination get the better of you, Freya told herself, but her whole being screamed, *I don't want to be here.*

Chapter 8

The curtains billowed in the gentle breeze, the folds of fabric flapping with a continuous rhythm while shadows danced across the floor. The night was muggy, and the air hung thick in the bedroom, creating pearls of sweat on Bam's near-naked skin. She wore a sheer chemise nightdress, a baby pink colour, with a matching pair of knickers. The set wasn't exactly comfortable, though it felt cool enough, but Bam had a suspicion that Oliver would knock on her door that night. He had told her that he wanted to discuss something with her, and that he would come find her later. Of course when he came, she would pretend that she'd merely forgotten and had dressed for bed. She didn't even care if he believed her or not. However, the idea of opening the door to him like this was enough to make her jittery.

If only it wasn't so stiflingly hot. Bam had opened all the windows, and still the room felt oppressive. She'd pushed all the curtains of her four-poster bed open to let in as much fresh air as possible, and the blankets lay discarded on the floor. The room was lighter than normal, the moon and stars peering through the open window like welcome guests. Bam fell back onto her bed and exhaled. Things had been crazy in the house ever since the builders had arrived, and she thought it might be a good idea to take a break soon, maybe get away for a few days. Freya was so uptight about the house, and Oliver was just busy the whole time. Bam hadn't felt comfortable since the day she'd seen blood on the walls, and the opening of the East and South Wings hadn't increased her love for the house. She closed her eyes and tried to think cool thoughts.

A soft breeze tickled her right leg, as if fingers were tracing their way from her knee to her thigh. When she felt it again, Bam bolted upright. But there was nothing there, and she pulled a face at her own paranoia. When she'd first seen the cobwebs, she'd been afraid that the whole house would be riddled with spiders, and she still hadn't been able let go of that idea. She laughed at herself and lay back down on the bed, but as soon as she closed her eyes, she felt another tickle in the same place. This time she merely raised her head, and to her surprise, she saw a dark shadow move near the foot of the bed. Quick as a snake, Bam pulled her legs up and crawled to the headboard. She hugged her knees, looking into the darkness with wide eyes and a pounding heart.

"Who's there?" she whispered. "Oliver?"

The darkness remained silent, but a chill had enveloped the room. The heat wasn't nearly as oppressive as it had been only seconds ago. She crawled back to the foot of the bed and pulled on the blankets lying on the floor. Her eyes scanned the dark, and she did consider running to the living room where Freya and Oliver were probably still watching TV.

Something moved again in the black, and she yelped, pulling the covers up to her chin with a jerk and sliding back towards the headboard.

"F... Freya?" her voice trembled as she covered herself with the blankets, hoping they would somehow magically protect her. "This isn't funny, guys, I'm really scared." There was a whine to her tone, and she could feel the tears sting behind her eyes. The blankets were twisted in a knot, and no matter how hard she kicked and squirmed, she couldn't get the fabric to cover her.

From the corner of her eye, she saw movement to the right, and she heard strange hollow footsteps around the room. A tear escaped the corner of her eye while a taste of bile climbed her throat into her mouth. Floorboards creaked.

"Why are you doing this to me?" More tears spilled from her eyes, and she sat curled up tight against the headboard, still fighting to get the covers in place.

"Shhhhht."

Bam wasn't sure if she'd heard a voice or if it was the wind playing tricks on her, but the tiny hairs on the back of her neck stood on end.

"Bambi."

She was sure it was a voice now, and to her horror, she realised who it belonged to.

"No." The word came out of her mouth as a moan, and she pulled her knees tighter to her chest, the blankets now forgotten. She pressed the palms of her hands against her eyes with such force that her eyeballs stung. "No, I'm dreaming and you're not real."

"Have... you... missed... me?" The voice was slow, sounding as if each intake of air was a struggle, each word a battle.

"You're not real. You died. You can't be here."

But she knew her words were empty, because her brother's place was at her side. Wasn't that something he had always stressed? How connected they were?

A figure stepped from the shadows. Not a person... he was too frayed at the edges to be real. Instead, he looked like a reflection peering up from dark, muddy waters, rippling in the current.

A sob, the kind that made her throat feel like she'd swallowed nails, escaped from somewhere deep in her soul, and the tears flowed freely now. "Chuck." The word came out in a wet heart-breaking lament. Grief pulled her shoulders and head down as if gravity had increased, and her mind was drowning in a flood of memories and emotions. "Oh, Chuck." She rested her temple on her knees and gazed at the shape of her dead brother through her tears.

The figure floated closer, the temperature in the room dropping a few degrees. Goosebumps rippled up Bam's skin in a flash. Her whimper was barely audible, but her body was immobilised in a combination of terror and fascination. Seeing her brother again tugged at her heartstrings. Her relationship with Chuck had not been a healthy one in his lifetime, but it had been a familiar one. Seeing him brought forth a longing she'd forgotten she had, the feeling of being part of something. Of being important.

"Bambi." The whispering voice was gentle. Invisible fingers stroked her cheek with a touch as light as breath. "You brought me here, Sis. I can exist here. I can be with you again, if you let me."

She shook her head, her fists clenched into balls. "No, you're dead, and you don't have any power over me anymore. I'm free from you now, and I can live my life the way I want." There was no real strength behind her words, though.

A shimmer shook through the figure, and its features became more defined, enough to resemble a living person, albeit a translucent one. The image of Chuck ran his hands through his hair in the same way her brother had when he was aggravated, and he paced the floor by the foot of her bed.

"I don't understand, Bambi. You brought me here, you pulled me to this house, and now you reject me?" He stopped moving and looked at her, his eyes dark and deep in his head as if he hadn't slept for months. "Do you know how cold and lonely it is here? How much I miss you, how much I long for your warmth?"

"I'm sorry, Chuck." Her strength and resolve cracked like a thin sheet of glass at his display of grief. "I'm so sorry." She moved to the middle of the bed, her heart beating so heavily that it made her feel queasy. She had never been able to disappoint her brother or deny him anything he wanted. His presence stirred those same feelings, along with a terrible guilt, because she hated herself for wanting him dead. She had felt relief when he'd died, and that had stung. He hung his head, and it looked as if he was weeping. He seemed so real, not like a ghost at all, but like a projection of her brother. There was something about his presence and his sadness that was almost palpable. The temptation to reach out to this broken creature who once had been her brother led her to crawl further along the bed. His head rose and he looked at her, his eyes pleading with her the way they had in life when he'd wanted something she hadn't wanted to give him.

"I love you, Bambi."

She gave in... as she always had. Old habits die hard.

"I love you too, Chuck." Her knees peeked over the rim of the bed, and she clutched her elbows with her hands. Her breasts pushed against the sheer fabric of the nightgown.

"Have you missed me?" he asked again, and he leaned forward so that his face was close to hers. Cold flowed from his very being. She closed her eyes and tears stung her corneas.

"Have you missed me touching you?"

"No." She opened her eyes, and she felt her resolve harden. "That was wrong, Chuck. You took advantage of my love for you." Her mind raced back to all the times her brother had visited her bedroom at night, the times when he had manipulated her into touching him, and into letting him touch her. She could still feel his eager fingers on her skin, and the duplicity of the abusive relationship weighed heavily on her mind. The price she'd paid for his love had been too steep.

"Damn it, Bambi. Don't you talk to me like that. You know I'm the only one who loves you." Chuck's eyes widened and his mouth twisted in a cruel sneer, one that Bam also remembered too well.

"You don't get to do this to me again. You're dead." She

102

hissed the words through clenched teeth. "You're dead, and I'm alive. I'm going to live my life without you... and you know what? I'm *glad* you're dead." Her hand shot out, grabbing one of the pillows on her bed, and with all her might, she threw it at the figure. The pillow went straight through him, and Chuck's spirit exploded in a burst of tiny luminescent particles just as if she'd thrown a stone into a pond filled with duckweed.

"You can't hurt me anymore, Chuck. I'm not going to let you. I'm going to let you go. Be at peace brother, and let me be at peace too." She yelled the words, a song ringing in her heart.

I'm free, she thought, *for the first time I'm really letting Chuck go. I needed to cast him out of my life, I needed to let go of both my hatred and my love for him.* She felt elated, and so very strong.

Something touched her hair and, before Bam had a chance to look round, she felt a tug followed by a rough pull. Her body flew back against the bed and an unseen force dragged her further upward. Bam screamed.

Her scalp burned and a cold fear clutched at her heart. She struggled to get up, but invisible hands pinned her down. Above her, Chuck's face materialised, only he appeared different now. He looked dead. His body was no longer transparent, and the weight of it crushed her. His skin was greyish, possessing a waxy quality. His eyes lay deep within his thin face, skin pulled tight across the skull to reveal long, broken teeth. Rot had set in on his left cheek, and a cluster of maggots wriggled from the dead flesh.

"You think I can't hurt you, little sister?" Maggots and dirt fell from his mouth when he spoke, and he waggled a black, shrunken tongue at her. "You are oh so very wrong. I have power here, little sister. And you are still mine, as you always have been."

"You're scaring me, Chuck." Her words were a high-pitched whine, similar to the one she'd used when she was younger. "Please, stop."

The face above her changed, becoming once again the handsome face of her brother, and he looked at her with curious eyes. There was nothing ethereal about him now; he was a normal human being, the way he'd been in life. His hand touched her cheek, and he furrowed his eyebrows.

"I scare you?"

"Yes."

He blinked at her, his head cocked and his fingers stroking her cheeks and lips. The weight of his body made it hard for her to breathe. Then he forced the fingers of his left hand into her mouth. Bam tasted the rot, and she gagged. The dead man's skin was as cold as ice. His other hand pushed up against her thighs, against the thin fabric of her underwear. She felt his fingers press against her pubic mound, the pressure bruising her soft skin. A sharp breath whistled against her teeth as the fabric of her underpants cut into her flesh.

"I'll do a lot more than scare you, Sister. I will claim you." Two fingers slipped past the fabric of her underwear and pressed between the warm lips of her vagina. The cold digits burned against her hot, slick insides. Bam screamed again, past the dirty fingers in her mouth, in the hope that someone would hear her. Chuck's left hand forced its way across her face, stifling her yells, as his right hand pushed deeper inside her. Bam fought against her dead brother, but ghostly hands grabbed her wrists and legs. They pulled at her limbs until she lay sprawled, weak and defenceless. Her brother sat up, his legs between hers. He looked normal, but she couldn't chase away the image of his rotting skin and maggots. His eyes glanced over her, the way they'd done that first night he'd visited her room, when she was thirteen-years old. The night she'd got her first bra.

Chuck had entered her room in the boarding school that night wanting to see the bra. There had been a look in his eyes which had frightened her even then. Her brother was two years older than she was, and to Bam, he was the world. With cold fingers, he had touched her nipples. Soft at first, he marvelled at the reaction they had from his touch, but then his fingers were cruel and hard. He pinched her until she cried, and even then he wouldn't let up. That night, she'd got off lucky, but after that his visits became more frequent, and he hadn't stopped at just touching her breasts.

"I like what you're wearing." Back in the present, the tips of his fingers touched the material of her nightgown. "Did you put this on just for me? Or were you trying to be a little whore? Did you mean to seduce someone else?"

"No." She sobbed, terrified of angering him even further. "I did this for you."

Chuck nodded in approval, and he lifted the material of her nightgown between his thumb and forefinger, a lascivious smile on his face.

"I'll fuck you, sister. Because I know you want me to." He pushed aside her underpants, exposing her pink vagina to the moonlight. Every muscle in Bam's body tensed, and she shivered with panic. Her brother's image changed again to the rotting cadaver, and he pulled at his pants to reveal his erect, maggot-coated penis.

"Please, no." The soft plea built up to a scream, and suddenly the lights went on. The image of her brother disappeared with such abruptness, it was as if he had never been there in the first place.

"Are you okay?" Freya's voice sounded like an anchor of sanity in a sea of madness. The room instantly returned to stifling summer heat, and the smell of rot was replaced by Freya's gentle perfume. Bam screamed again. She thought she would never stop. Freya rushed to her side and wrapped her in her warm arms, and Bam clung to her while she wailed and cried salty tears.

"Bam... stop screaming." Freya pushed her face into her neck. "Please, just stop." Eventually Bam calmed down and the two girls sat on the bed, rocking back and forth.

"Jesus, what happened?" Oliver stood in the door opening, his face drawn with fatigue. "Why is she like that?"

"I don't know."

"Do you need my help?"

"No, best you just go. I'll talk to her alone. She probably had a bad dream."

Oliver retreated, and Bam heard him walk away. She felt grateful; she didn't want him seeing her like this, but she couldn't stop crying. After what felt like an eternity, she finally calmed down enough to speak.

"He was here." Her voice was strangled and raw.

"Who?"

"Chuck."

"Oh, sweetheart, you had a nightmare."

Bam pulled away from her friend and furrowed her brow, her eyes flaming with anger.

"This was *not* a nightmare. Chuck was here, and he tried to rape me."

"Bam..."

"Don't you *Bam* me. I know what happened. I felt his fingers inside me, Freya. This was no dream."

"I didn't see anything." Freya insisted, but Bam's throbbing groin didn't lie.

"There's something wrong with this house. I knew it as soon as the fucking brown slime disappeared. I don't know

106

how it happened, but it brought Chuck here."

"That's impossible."

"Fuck you. Don't you say that to me. There's something weird going on in this house, Freya. And you can feel it too. I can see it in your eyes. Even Oliver knows it, but he's too busy putting his head in the sand to acknowledge it. We made it worse. We took away your crazy aunt's protection shit, and we let some bad things out."

Freya got to her feet and spread her arms in despair. "Bam, listen to yourself. This is nuts. What do you want me to say? I've invested my life savings in this house. This was going to be my salvation, and now you want me to what? Walk away? Because you had a nightmare. You realise how unhinged that sounds, right?"

A gentle breeze brushed across her skin, and a pang shot through Bam's heart when she looked at Freya's sad expression. She buried her face in the palms of her hands, the tips of her fingers digging into her hairline.

"I don't know what I'm asking you, Freya. I just know that I can't do this anymore. Your mother was right." Her words had an instant impact on her friend, she saw the hurt in Freya's eyes.

"That's not fair. My mother is afraid of this place because her parents used to torment her here. But my mother never told me that the dead came to visit, Bam." Freya wagged her finger as she talked, her eyebrows knotted at the top of her nose. "She might be a bit nuts, but you're the one who's talking crazy here."

Bam pinched the bridge of her nose and gave Freya a mute stare. Something softened in her friend's face, but the sadness was still apparent.

"We've got builders here now, Bam. Money is being invested, and we've ordered the materials. I can't back away from this now. It's too late." She ran fingers through her hair. "It was you and Oliver who wanted this in the first place."

"I know." She couldn't bear to look at Freya. "I know, and I'm sorry. But... I can't do this anymore." She pulled open her wardrobe and wrestled a suitcase from the bottom. The smell of cedar wood and fabric softener flowed from inside. The plastic handle dug into her palms, and Bam struggled to get the case free. With a rough jerk, she pulled the suitcase away, dragging a red silk dress behind it, but she didn't care anymore.

"Bam, come on. What are you doing? It's one AM; where are you going to go at a time like this?

"I was almost raped by a ghost, Freya. I can't stay here." Her fingers trembled as she unzipped the lid of the case and flipped it open. With a soft huffing sound, the lid bounced on the mattress, and Bam walked back to the wardrobe, where she plucked clothes from the hangers.

"How about we stay in Oliver's room? The three of us, like old times. If we're there, nothing can hurt you, right? Please don't leave in the middle of the night. Just go in the morning, when it's light."

"You promise you won't leave me?" she pouted, blinking the tears away that threatened to well up again.

"I promise. We'll eat biscuits and natter all night if you don't want to sleep, okay?" Freya leaned towards the door. "Ollie?" There was no response, and she held out her hand to Bam. "Let's get out of here first, go to Ollie's room."

Bam took her hand, a surge of gratitude washing over her, but the fear still clung to her like a dark cloak.

Tomorrow, I'll leave.

Chapter 9

Lyndon Farrow and Roger Mace moved through Angel Manor, their footsteps crunching through the debris of the South Wing. Both boys tried their best to be quiet, but it seemed as if the house had other plans. The meagre light of their torch illuminated a stream of white across the dark floor. In the distance, they could hear the old clock chime, but the noise was soft enough not to startle them.

"Watch where you put your feet, you elephant!" Roger pushed Lyndon, and he almost lost his balance. He felt a surge of annoyance, but he kept quiet. No one messed with Roger, except maybe Terrence, and Lyndon wasn't about to try.

"You're not exactly twinkle toes yourself, pal," was the only retort he dared to give. He listened to the hiss of raindrops beating against the windows.

Roger clicked the piercing in the side of his lower lip against his teeth and punched Lyndon in the arm. He pointed at a heavy door. "Let's go to the basement, in case Norris or Masters come looking. I don't want them to catch me smoking dope again." He pulled a joint from his jeans pocket, placed it carefully between his lips, and lit it, taking a long drag and holding it. After a few seconds, he exhaled a cloud of pungent smoke. "I don't know why you wanted to go in the house, anyway. It's fucking creepy here at night."

He held the spliff between his thumb and forefinger and passed it to Lyndon, who in turn inhaled deeply.

"You're such a numpty. This place is fucking awesome." Roger pulled at the metal basement door, the weight forcing him to use both hands. His red hair, cut into spikes with a slanting uneven fringe at the front, made him look like the singer of an indie band. The door opened with a loud metallic creek, and Roger grunted with effort. Lyndon quickly moved forward to help his friend.

"Why is this door so heavy?"

"Don't fucking know."

"Looks like it's knackered." Lyndon pointed at a broken pulley.

"That probably helped keep it open or something. Stop your fucking whinging, bawheid."

They propped the door open with some rubble, and Lyndon prayed the stones would hold. He piled on a few more just in case. Roger grabbed the joint back and took another hit. He shone his torch down the stairs, and to Lyndon's dismay, there was very little to see. Just a set of concrete steps covered in a thick layer of dust.

"Has anyone even been down there?" Lyndon tried to sound nonchalant, but his voice shook when he spoke and a clump of nerves knotted together in his stomach.

"Naw, pal. We'll be the first. Should be fucking epic though, two-hundred-year-old basement. Maybe we'll find some rats or shit. Who knows, there might even be something down there that's worth selling. I'm hoping they left some antiques lying around that everyone forgot about or something." Roger handed him the spliff and nodded his head towards the entrance, indicating for Lyndon to walk through.

"You got the torch." His eyes glanced at the light in Roger's hand.

"And I'm lighting your way." Roger's thin, pale lips pulled into a tight smile, and his watery blue eyes were harsh. Lyndon considered arguing, but he decided against it and descended the old stairs. The faint light of the torch swayed in front of him, colouring the steps with a bluish white hue, but it did little to illuminate anything, or to take away the fear blossoming in his stomach like a poisonous flower. The darkness from below seemed to engulf the light completely, and then Roger moved the torch to the wall, leaving Lyndon standing in darkness.

"What the fuck, Roger?" His voice went a few octaves higher with panic. "Bring the light back!"

"Look at this, man. There's writing on the wall." The big, circular beam of light wavered over grey bricks, revealing painted black letters. Whoever had scrawled them had done a sloppy job, and the pigment had run down in thin streaks, giving the words the appearance of bleeding.

"This place is messed up." Lyndon almost forgot his fear of the dark, the ominous letters somehow appearing so much worse. "That's not normal graffiti, Rog." He shook his head, his mouth twisted in a grimace.

"Pussy." The light beam moved from the wall and aimed straight into Lyndon's face.

"Cut it out." He followed the light down the stairs. Something caught his eye, and he stopped walking. "Shine the light over here..." He pointed to the ground, and Roger followed his finger with the torch. There was a thick line of white stuff at the edge of the stairs. Lyndon jumped over it, and Roger followed his lead.

"Coke?" Roger quipped, but Lyndon couldn't force himself to laugh. The basement was cold and dark, and he decided he hated this place more than anywhere else in the world. If anything happened, he was out of here. He didn't give a shit if Roger thought he was a pussy. Roger's torch caught the string of a light switch, and Lyndon pulled it. Soft yellow illuminated the basement. It wasn't a lot of light, but it was enough for them to see by.

"This place could certainly use a higher watt light bulb. Can't see shit." Roger shrugged and tapped the bulb with his index finger.

"There's something weird about this place, but I can't quite figure out what it is." Lyndon took a tentative step into the empty basement. Roger inhaled deeply, the tip of the joint flaring, throwing weird shapes and shadows across his pale face. His eyes rolled up and he let the smoke flow across his top lip like a reverse waterfall, inhaling it back up his nose. He clicked the torch off.

"No dust." Roger's voice was strained, and he exhaled between his teeth. "It looks like someone has cleaned in here. But that doesn't make sense. The stairs are plenty dusty and there are no footsteps."

"That's just creepy." Lyndon bent over and touched the floor with his fingertips. The cement was cold as ice, but no residue of any kind clung to his fingers... the basement was spotless. "Can we go now? I really don't want to stay here."

"We'll go in a bit. I want to see what's in here." His face scrunched into a stoner's smile, his eyes nothing more than little slits.

"There's nothing in here, man... let's just go."

Without warning, a loud metallic sound reverberated through the basement; Lyndon nearly jumped out of his skin.

"That's not nothing." Roger took another toke from the joint and passed it back to Lyndon.

"Fuck this noise..."

"Come on, what can it be? Ghosts?"

Lyndon didn't answer. Instead, he looked at the joint in his hand and took a hesitant drag. Roger stepped deeper into the basement, Lyndon hanging back while taking a few more puffs on the joint. Roger stopped a few feet away from the door in the back and smiled.

"I wonder what's behind this door. Could be a wine store." He ran his hand across the surface. "If it is, I'm pinching a few bottles."

"Wine bottles don't make noises, mate." Lyndon rubbed

his face with his hand while wrapping his lips around the roach and inhaling the last few sour tokes. The leaves burned against his lips, and he flicked the butt to the ground. His mind was sluggish. This was not a nice buzz. He felt stressed out about everything, and more than a little paranoid.

"Probably rats or something. Maybe something fell over." Roger clicked his torch on again and pointed to the darker areas, then squatted to his knees and picked something up from the floor. "More of that white stuff here." He smelled his fingers and turned to face Lyndon, the torch on his face. "I think it's salt or something." He got back to his feet and grabbed the door handle. "Ready?"

"Naw."

The door creaked as Roger pulled it open. Lyndon took a few steps closer, but remained at a safe distance. Beyond the opening was pitch darkness. The beam from the torch crossed the door and landed on a figure of a large, nude woman. Bulbous folds of skin spilled over each other, while large vein-splattered breasts topped with liver-coloured oval nipples rested on her stomach. Her round face was a mask of death, deep-set eyes only showing the whites. Thick meaty chins covered any evidence of a neck, and her skin was an unnatural pale tone. Lyndon cried out and Roger took a step back, his shoe crunching on the salt line, smearing it over the ground.

"What the fuck, what the fuck?!" Roger screamed.

"Roger, close the fucking door, ya bawbag!"

"I'm trying. Come and help me." Roger threw his full weight against the door, but it wouldn't budge. His voice was high with panic, and Lyndon took a step forward to help his friend out, but the fat woman flickered for a moment and suddenly appeared on the other side of the door.

"Nah, fuck that shite, man. This isn't happening. I'm not

seeing this. I'm not seeing shit." He stumbled back, waving his arms over his face. The figure of the woman was so terribly silent. A fat hand, tinted a greyish hue, rose towards Roger, who just sagged to his knees and flopped towards the ground.

The woman moved with uncanny speed, grabbing the falling young man by the hair, her pudgy fingers tangling in his flaming locks. Roger half hung in her grip, his eyes wide with fright, and he stared straight at Lyndon, who in turn thought he was going to throw up from fear. The naked woman lifted Roger's head a bit higher, then slammed his face down onto the concrete. A sickening dull crack rang through the basement as Roger's nose exploded like a ripe melon, spraying blood, teeth and torn flesh across the floor. The sight of the blood stirred Lyndon into action. He turned and ran towards the door just as something flickered in his peripheral vision.

Before he had time to react, a second naked woman appeared, this one so close that Lyndon struggled with a rising panic. She was tall and thin, her lanky body the same pale grey as her fat companion. Her face was too hard and angular to be pretty; she had a strong, masculine chin, and big white eyes with long lashes made her look like an unpainted porcelain doll. Long blonde hair fell across her small pointy breasts, and the liver-coloured nipples peeked through the greasy strands. Stunned, Lyndon stared at her, from the small breasts to the narrow belly button and down to the waxy blonde pubes that lay between her thighs like a promise of golden treasure. His eyes trailed back up to her face, and she cast him a black-toothed grin. Her image flickered and disappeared for a fraction of a second, but then reappeared right in front of him, her hands shooting out before cold fingers dug into the skin of his temples and cheeks. He felt hot blood run from the wounds. Her white eyes narrowed with malice, and her jagged teeth snapped at him from behind blistered blue lips. A smell of rotting flesh emanated from her, filling his nostrils and mouth. Lyndon gagged.

She made no sound, and her body was strong despite being light. He could barely feel her weight as she jumped on top of him. For a brief second, she disappeared, and moments later, dark teeth bit into his chin. Serrated incisors cut through skin and fat until they scraped across his jawbone, and Lyndon screamed as a flap of his skin came away. When the spirit flickered out of existence again, he saw his chance and sprinted towards the stairs.

He made it up five steps when his foot landed wrong and he fell awkwardly. His legs flailed as cold, sharp fingers grabbed his ankle, dragging him down. Teeth sank viciously into his calf, tearing through the fabric of his jeans, through the muscle, spilling hot blood across his leg. Summoning all the strength he could muster, Lyndon kicked back and scrambled up the stairs. The spirit released him as abruptly as it had grabbed him, and he almost fell again, his fingers clinging to the stone steps just enough to hold on. His body shook as he looked over his shoulder to see the woman standing at the bottom of the steps, just behind the white border of salt. She touched the air experimentally, as if an invisible wall stood between her and Lyndon.

Behind her, he saw the fat woman squatting down over Roger's limp form, her meaty thighs spread wide and her fleshy folds engulfing a large portion of his lower back. She pulled his head back again. Roger's eyes were bruised and swollen, his nose was a shattered mess of blood and cartilage, and his mouth was a gaping, toothless hole. Fat fingers held his hair and pushed into his mouth, his moans echoing through the basement. Lyndon grimaced, his eyes glancing at the door from which the fat woman had stepped. To his horror, he saw several other naked figures, all female. One, a woman in her late forties, perhaps a little older, used an old-fashioned saw to slice into the flesh of her own leg, a thick black liquid oozing from the wound. Her greying hair framed her oval face in electric wisps, while bulging white eyes peered from sunken, cadaverous sockets.

She smiled at him, the way the thin woman had done, and Lyndon decided there was nothing more he could do for Roger.

Fuck him! He opened that fucking door. I told him not to.

He turned away and limped up the stairs, his chin and leg throbbing with pain. He couldn't put weight on the leg so he pulled himself along as much as walked. The dust from the stairs got into his mouth and lay thickly on his tongue, tasting of lime and filth. Once more, he looked back. Roger was being dragged into the back room, his hands clawing on the concrete in an attempt to get away from the eager hands pulling at his legs. For a moment, it looked as if he might get away, but then he was dragged into the pitch black with a heartbreaking wail and the door slammed shut behind him, muffling his screams.

The woman who stood at the bottom of the stairs looked at Lyndon one last time, and then she too disappeared. Lyndon snapped out of his trance and crawled out of the basement. He pulled himself up by the doorframe and limped out of the South Hall.

"Fuck, fuck, fuck..." His frantic voice was no more than a sigh in the emptiness of the abandoned wing. "What am I going to do now?" He thought about waking John Norris or Logan Masters. Heck, he would even settle for Jim McLeod right now, though the beardy Scot would probably make fun of him.

"I don't know what to say..." Tears streamed down his eyes as he stumbled through the hall. "What if they think it was me who killed him? Who's going to believe that there's a bunch of psychotic, naked women in the basement?"

He didn't know what to do; all he wanted was to get out of the house. Fatigue gnawed at his senses while the slow buzz of marijuana and blood loss made him sluggish. The hallway felt as if it would never end, and he cried softly. Lyndon didn't come from a loving home, yet for the first time since he'd been a child, he longed for his mother. The house was so dark without a torch, and fear consumed him. He saw ghosts in every shadow, his paranoia flared up, and more tears came.

As he entered the main entrance hall, he heard soft, wet footsteps on the marble floor behind him. Lyndon whimpered. He couldn't look back; the fear was too great. He tried to increase his pace but his right leg still hurt too much.

"Please, please..." his voice cracked. The footsteps followed him as he shuffled through the rooms, trailing blood behind him in long, slick tracks.

Relief washed over him when his hand closed over the doorknob of the entrance. The metal was cool under his hot, sweaty palm. He flicked his wrist and pulled the door open, a rush of fresh air caressing his skin as he stepped outside. For the first time, Lyndon dared to look back, and he saw the shape of a woman in a thin, white nightdress. She was different from the other spirits, less malevolent somehow, but there was something in her blank eyes that terrified him, and he stumbled away from the house. Soft humming voices filled his mind, and he scratched at his blood-soaked temples, his nails sinking into the deep wounds.

"Naw... I got out, please, I got out! Leave me alone!" Something landed under his eye and he slapped at it, the impact of his own hand making his ears ring and his jaw tremble. The skin flap on his chin tore a bit further, and Lyndon cried out with pain. His path was obscured by shadows that flitted around him with increasing speed, and though his leg hurt, Lyndon quickened his pace, desperate to put some distance between himself and that terrible house. "Get out of my head," he screamed at the whispers, and he broke into a run, his bad leg barely holding him up. "Get out."

He failed to see the cliff, not until he was right beside it. The toes of his Doc Martins peered over the edge, and he had to flail his arms to stay balanced. The shadows disappeared instantly, clearing his vision.

"I can't let you go, I'm sorry." The voice was soft and feminine, and Lyndon slowly turned to face the speaker. It was the woman in the white nightgown.

"Who are you?" his words were no more than sobs. "What do you want from me?"

"The Angels have claimed you, and it's time for you to join us, Lyndon."

"How do you know my name?" he whined, his shoulders slumped. His heart was heavy and he felt so tired. The idea of having to live with what he had seen, to know what was out there, was a burden he wasn't sure he could carry. He couldn't picture himself going back home to his parents, to sleep alone in a bed again. To close his eyes would mean seeing that woman again, her black teeth snapping at him. It would be seeing Roger's nose explode with blood and gore... it would be reliving those terrible minutes back in that basement.

"You know what to do," the woman urged him. Lyndon nodded. He looked down at the cliff and back to the spirit who floated a little above the ground. Then he stepped off. His body plummeted down, and for a moment, Lyndon soared like a bird. It was a magnificent feeling. His body released endorphins, and his trousers tightened against his erection. The world was the most beautiful place from here, and he had never been happier in his whole miserable life. Then he hit the first rocks. The impact shattered his collarbone and shoulder. The next hit broke both his legs, and the third collision smashed his skull, the bone splinters penetrating his brain, killing him instantly.

By the time his body reached the bottom of the cliff, there was very little left that was recognisable as Lyndon Farrow. His battered corpse landed in a patch of poppies, which gently kissed his dead flesh in the summer breeze.

Chapter 10

The heat made sharing a bed a special form of torture, Freya decided, but the way Bam lay shivering against her clammy body, she couldn't bear to tell her she needed more space. Her friend was hot, yet she had the covers pulled up to her shoulders and goose bumps were visible on her skin.

That must have been some dream, Freya thought, so she let the tips of her fingers slide across Bam's arm.

"You're awake too?" Bam's voice quavered.

"Yeah."

"How can anyone sleep in this heat?" Oliver sounded muffled through the pillows. "Three in a fucking bed too. We must be insane."

"Sorry, Ollie." There were tears in Bam's voice. "I'll go if you want."

Oliver turned around, his eyes shining mildly in the dim light of the bedside lamp.

"I'm sorry, Bam. I didn't mean that. I'm just tired. It's been a weird day."

"That it has." Freya sat up in the bed. She couldn't sleep anymore, and she just wanted the sun to come up. "Do you remember when we used to sleep like this all the time? Back in school?"

Oliver moaned, turned around, and threw his head demonstratively into the pillow.

"Yeah, good times..." Bam's voice trailed away. Freya's mind conjured the image of the four young people lying in two singles pushed together to make one bed.

"Chuck was still alive then." Bam looked at her with sad

119

eyes.

"I'm sorry, I didn't mean to..."

"Don't be sorry. Those were different days. Chuck... well, things were different then."

"Why do you think you started dreaming about Chuck, Bam?"

"It wasn't a dream." There was no venom in Bam's voice, and she pushed herself up against the headboard until she sat next to Freya. "I don't think it was." Her eyes fluttered and she leaned back, a sigh escaping from her lips. "Maybe it was a dream. I'm not sure now. Everything is so messed up."

The regular sound of Oliver's heavy breathing indicated that he had fallen asleep. Freya envied him for his ability to sleep under any circumstance. Sleep didn't come easy to her at the best of times, and being in a bed with her freaked out friend on a hot summer's eve wasn't helping. Something was bothering Bam, and Freya wanted to know what it was. She didn't believe her friend had been attacked by a ghost, but something had definitely rattled her pretty badly.

"This ghost or dream, or whatever it was, must have come from somewhere." Freya ran the back of her index finger down Bam's arm. "I think you might know why. Care to tell me?"

Bam crossed her arms over her chest and hugged her shoulders. Her head hung down and tears glistened in her eyes. Freya's brow furrowed in worry.

"You know you can tell me anything, right?"

"I think it's because I have the potential to be happy here. It's bringing out all my demons."

"What do you mean?"

"When Chuck was still alive, our... our relationship was

complicated." Bam didn't meet her eyes, her chin resting in the cross where her wrists came together.

"Chuck was a little overbearing, I remember. He was overprotective."

Bam gave a snort filled with bitter resentment, and she turned her head sharply to Freya.

"It was worse than overbearing, Frey. He wasn't overprotective, he was possessive. Chuck considered me to be his, and he didn't like sharing his toy. He only tolerated you two because he liked you." Bam's pretty face was screwed up and ugly with the malice from her words.

"I don't understand."

"You have this effect on men, Freya. Look at the builder guy; he's totally into you."

"What does this have to do with Chuck?"

"The only reason that Chuck hung out with you is because he found you attractive, which was fine with me, because that meant he let me hang out with you too."

"You've lost me. You really have. What are you trying to say here?"

"That Chuck treated me as his possession. That he ruined any chance I had of happiness with other guys. Not because of love, but because he was a horrible person." The tears came so sudden and with such ferocity that Freya was taken aback by Bam's outburst. "And I let him, Frey. I let him rule me, and I did everything that he wanted."

"What did you let him do?"

"I let him decide who I could date, what I could wear... I let him touch me, Freya..."

The words hit like a mallet to the head, and every muscle in Freya's body tensed. Her back pressed into the headboard as she tried to comprehend what her friend was telling her.

"You... let him... touch you?" She tried to keep her voice steady, void of emotion, but the image of Chuck touching his sister made her stomach cramp up. "He forced himself on you?"

"It's more like he guilt-tripped me into sex. Chuck always had this power over me, and I would do anything for him. He knew that."

"He raped you."

"I wouldn't call it rape. I never said no."

"This is disgusting."

"You're making me feel dirty." Tear-stained eyes turned to her, and guilt knotted Freya's thoughts.

"No, not you... him. You were a victim in this, Bambi..."

"Don't call me Bambi, please. You know I hate my real name."

"Sorry. This... this is so much to digest." Freya threw her arms around her friend. "I had no idea, Bam... if only you'd told me. I could have helped you."

"I couldn't tell you. I was a part of this, Freya. I didn't say no. I agreed to everything. It was just how it was."

"He used you. Don't put this on yourself. That's not right." She leaned back and looked at the ceiling. "Jesus, no wonder you dreamed what you did."

"I... I don't know. I just want to be happy, and I thought this place would do it for me. I'd be with you and with Ollie, and everything would be okay. But it's not. I think I may be losing my mind, and I have to admit, I'm frightened of this house now. Maybe you're right, maybe it was just a dream, but I can't stand having another dream like that again. I just can't." She shook her head with such force that Freya feared she would bump her head against the wood, and so she pulled her friend towards her, wrapping her arms around her.

"You need to find some help, and work your way through your past."

"I know." Bam's tears flowed freely again, Freya could feel them stain her t-shirt. "Oh God, Frey, what am I going to do?"

Freya rocked her back and forth for several minutes in silence, her heart heavy and her mind spinning. She didn't know what she would do without Bam, but she knew that her friend couldn't stay here. There was too much going on with the house and Freya couldn't play babysitter. She wished she could, but this was the worst possible time for Bam to have a breakdown.

"How about you take a break? Go see your parents in Los Angeles for a while? Take in some sun, go see Disneyland. Maybe get some therapy while you're there?" She pushed her gently away and lifted her tear-streaked chin, forcing Bam to face her. "How does that sound?"

Bam nodded, but there was doubt in her eyes, and Freya knew that sending her friend to parents who had neglected her all her life wasn't ideal, but she had no better ideas.

"We'll drive to Glasgow in the morning. Find ourselves a hotel and get a ticket for you to go to LA."

A loud snore from Oliver made both girls jump. They exchanged another glance and laughed softly.

"I don't want to go to my parents."

"Anywhere else?"

"No, LA will be fine. I have some other relatives there. But I'll be back as soon as I can. I want to do this; I want to run this hotel with you guys." The corners of her mouth curled. "Pursuit of happiness and all that shit." She sniffed, but with a brave smile.

"Good girl. Nothing can keep you down for long."

"Unless you find out that this house really is haunted. Then I'm not coming back."

"If that's the case, I'm burning this place to the ground and moving to LA with you." They hugged, laughing softly into each other's necks. Freya hoped that she was doing the right thing in sending Bam away.

Chapter 11

"You haven't slept a wink. Are you sure you can drive?" Oliver examined her with a critical look on his face. He looked funny with his mussed hair and tired eyes, Freya thought. She wasn't feeling too chipper either; her body complained at the lack of sleep, and even her coffee sat in her stomach like a lead brick.

"I'll manage."

"It's over five hours to Glasgow."

"Bam and I can take turns."

"She can't drive at the best of times, let alone without sleep." Oliver frowned at her, and Freya fought a surge of annoyance.

"Ollie, we'll be fine."

"I could drive her."

"No, I need you to oversee the builders. Besides, I think Bam could use a little girl time right now. I owe her that much. I feel bad enough for sending her away."

"Are you actually sending her off?"

"Sort of. It's... it's just complicated."

Her words froze him for a second, then he tilted his head and slid to the chair next to her around the breakfast table. "You're not telling me something, Frey. We've never had secrets before."

"Yes we have, you ninny." She tried to laugh it off, but she wasn't that good an actress.

"Not like this. What's going on?" He leaned in, and she could smell the bitter mixture of coffee on morning breath.

"Bam had a nightmare and suddenly she's shipping off to LA?"

"It goes deeper than that, Ollie. I'm sure when Bam's ready to tell you she will. But it's not my place to talk about this with you."

"But it's bad though?"

"Yeah, I'd say it's bad. And I think if Bam stays here, she's going to keep having these panic attacks."

"Do you believe she saw a ghost?"

"In a way, maybe. Not a real live ghost, but I think she's being confronted by her own ghosts from the past. Add a house in the middle of nowhere, a lot of stress, and a dollop of creepy stories, and you have the recipe for a nervous breakdown."

"Please don't you go have one on me too, okay? I need you here."

She looked at him over her coffee cup, one eyebrow raised and a sneer curled around her lips.

"I think I'll be fine, thank you."

"What's Bam going to do with her car if you're driving her?"

"She's leaving it here. No sense in paying the parking costs, and she can't take it with her. You can drive it if you like."

Oliver couldn't manage to keep the mild disgust off his face and Freya giggled into her coffee. A sound caught their attention and they turned to see Bam pulling her pink suitcase across the threshold into the kitchen.

"I didn't get everything, but I have enough to keep me in clothes for a few weeks. I can buy stuff in LA too. I'm sure Mom will take me shopping if I ask her nicely." She gave them a smile that didn't reach her dark-encircled eyes.

Freya jumped to her feet and grabbed a cup from the counter. "Coffee?"

"Yes, please." Bam abandoned the case on the floor and squeezed in around the table. "I need caffeine. We might have to pick up a couple of cans of Red Bull on the way."

"They make my heart explode," Freya said with a hint of drama in her voice. Bam snorted into her coffee and rolled her eyes.

"You look better than you did last night." Oliver grabbed Bam's shoulder, and Freya noted a strange expression on her friend's face when he touched her.

"I think I'm just relieved that I'm going away for a bit. I guess it's just all too much for me right now."

"You'll be back though?" Oliver arched his eyebrows and gave Bam his best impression of puppy eyes, which made her giggle.

"As if I could stay away from you." She punched him playfully in the shoulder.

Freya's coffee cup made a hollow sound when she put it on the table. "We should get going soon. It's a long drive and we still need to find a hotel."

Bam held up her own half-filled cup. "Let me finish this and I'm ready to go."

***

Logan woke to the sun shining through the thin, grey canvas of his tent. The night had been hot, despite being low to the ground. He had zipped open his sleeping bag hours ago, and was now lying on top of it wearing nothing but a pair of black boxers covered in printed pink lips – a present from an ex-girlfriend. The tent was stifling, his back and face sweat-soaked, and he decided he couldn't wait until they moved into the house. Luckily, the East Wing had several showers the Chancers could use, and Logan intended to make good use of them that morning. He pulled a t-shirt and a pair of joggers from his rucksack and wrestled them across his limbs. His muscles were stiff from working, and he groaned when he crawled out of the tent and into the morning. He was pleasantly surprised to see most of the guys already up and about. John was handing out plastic cups of coffee that Oliver filled from a large thermos. He stretched his back and scratched his hair with a satisfied groan.

"Morning, Logan. Sleep well?" John handed him a cup, and Logan inhaled the aroma.

"It was a bit hot."

"Aye, that it was."

"Where's Jim?"

"He's looking for Mace and Farrow."

"What do you mean looking for them?"

"They weren't in their tents this morning." There was a look of worry on the older man's face. "I don't mind Farrow not being there. The worst he would do is smoke a joint. It's Mace I'm worried about. That kid is bad news."

"Roger needs tough love." Logan ran his hand through his hair and cursed inwardly. Roger had been a bit of a risk to bring along, and it hadn't taken long for him to act up. Logan had hoped that by taking him away from his normal surroundings, he would behave a little better. "Is Terrence accounted for?" He scanned the young men and saw Terrence's face sticking out from one of the tents.

"Aye, I'm glad to say that Jones and Mace aren't up to their usual mischief. To be honest, I really think Terrence is trying to make something of himself here. I'm proud of the lad."

Logan nodded in agreement. He too felt a certain glowing pride at the way Terrence had behaved during this project. So far, he had worked harder than all the other boys, and even his usual rowdy attitude seemed subdued.

The only thing Logan worried about was the eyes he cast at the little blonde girl, but he could hardly blame the guy. Logan himself was having less than appropriate thoughts about the other female.

From a distance, he saw Jim approach, holding an unlit torch as if it were a weapon, his face expressing his dark mood.

"Find anything?"

"No sign of the buggers." Jim's forehead wrinkled, the wild hairs of his eyebrows making him look owlish. "I'm writing them up for this."

"Yeah. They'll be back though. I mean, where can they go?"

"I don't know. But I wouldn't put it past them that they made it all the way to Portree or something, the daft little sods." Jim shrugged. He looked tired.

"How long have you been looking?"

"An hour at least. I was up early and noticed they'd gone."

Logan slapped the other man on the shoulder. "They're bound to show up somewhere."

"Aye, but meanwhile, we're two men short."

"We'll manage." He looked past the larger man and his eyes spotted Freya making her way out of the house with a pink suitcase, her blonde friend in tow. In a few strides, he reached her and took the case from her hands.

"Going somewhere?" To his pleasure, he saw a soft pink blush touch her cheeks, and she cast her eyes down.

"I'm taking Bam to Glasgow."

"Day trip?"

"No, she's going to catch a plane to Los Angeles." Her

eyes looked directly into his, and then she quickly looked away again. He saw something in them... a sadness.

"You're not going with her, I hope?" He knew he was showing more of his feelings than he should, but he was curious to see her reaction. Her cheeks flushed a deeper pink, almost a red colour, and the corners of her mouth twitched.

"No, I'll be back tomorrow."

"Good." He lifted the pink suitcase onto his shoulder; the wheels would only slow him down on this uneven terrain. "I won't have to hold your suitcase hostage then." The other girl stepped up behind Freya, and Logan noticed the nudge she gave her. He walked ahead of them to Freya's car and put the suitcase down.

"Thanks Logan, I appreciate it." She smiled at him, and he imagined taking her cheeks in his hands and kissing those heart-shaped lips with all the passion he could muster.

"Drive safely," was all he managed to say, and he saluted the girls with his fingertips. Then he turned and walked back towards Jim, who was writing notes on a clipboard, his face folded in a grumpy expression. When Mace and Farrow showed up, Jim would have some unpleasant chores for them. He looked over his partner's shoulder at the retreating car, and he felt a pang of longing.

She's only going for a day... why do you care? he wondered. *She shouldn't be leaving the house. She belongs here.* The voice in his head sounded unfamiliar, and the sound of it caused a chill to crawl down his spine.

Chapter 12

By the time they saw Glasgow's church spires in the distance, Freya felt as if her stomach was trying to flip itself inside out. She'd been mildly nauseous when they'd left Angel Manor that morning, but as the day progressed, the feeling had only intensified, and she'd been tempted to stop the car several times. The idea of lying down in a hotel room and resting was the only thing that kept her going. Whatever she was suffering from, Bam wasn't feeling well either, and Freya suspected that the lack of sleep wasn't sitting well with either of them.

When she finally hauled the pink suitcase up the stairs of the cheap B&B, she was about ready to fall over.

"Maybe we need to eat something healthy." Bam said, looking dubiously at the plastic bag that they'd used to dispose of the pastie and chocolate wrappers. They'd picked up food from petrol stations along the way, but the dry, sugary treats did nothing to improve their stomachs.

"Yeah, maybe. So, not going out for a curry then?" Freya quipped with a weak smile. She felt as if the saliva in her mouth had dried up, leaving her tongue rough and sandy. Something scratched the back of her throat, and her head throbbed. The thought of food was off-putting at best, but she agreed with Bam that maybe a healthy meal would make them feel better.

The room in the B&B felt oppressive and dark. There were two narrow beds on each side of the cramped space, a wine-red carpet with more than a few dark stains, and walls that were coated in snot-yellow flowers and dark green hummingbirds. A small window looking out onto a busy street let in a hint of light, but did nothing to dispel the sombre atmosphere. The two beds were covered with matching off-white counterpanes, their ruffles hanging to the floor. The room smelled of fabric softener.

"Well this is... um, quaint." Freya tried to make her voice sound cheery, but in fact she just wanted to lie down and go to sleep.

"This place is horrible."

"It's just for tonight. Tomorrow, we're going to get you your ticket, and then we'll have you off to LA in no time."

"I need to lie down. I feel like shit." Bam flopped onto the left bed, her arms spread out. "That car ride was the worst."

Freya inhaled deeply and fell down on the other bed. "It really was. Maybe just one nap, and then we can get some tea."

"Yeah, just a nap."

***

"You need to go back to the house."

Freya blinked. She was sure she had only been asleep for a second, but when she opened her eyes, the sunlight from the little window had been replaced by darkness.

"Bam?" Her voice was hoarse and she sat up on the bed, trying to determine exactly where she was again. Bed and Breakfast. She knew that much, but why? Then the memories returned, a wave of nausea hit her, and her mind spun. Something pushed at her subconscious. There was something important that she was forgetting. Scraps of her dream returned to her, but not enough to remember clearly. Freya rested her head between her hands. *What am I supposed to remember?* Frustration pounded at her temples and she fought back the tears. An overwhelming sense of homesickness overtook her, and for the first time, she realised she had begun to think of Angel Manor as her home. She never thought she would, but the house had grown on her. She had made it her own. Once it was renovated, it would be free of the stigma that her crazy family had put on it, and it would be all hers. And here she was... in a strange hotel, while she could be home now. It wasn't even a hotel, just a crappy bed and breakfast, miles away from the beautiful views of Lucifer Falls. Freya wanted more than anything to be home. The emotion was so strong she was having a physical reaction to it, and she had to jump up to make it to the tiny en-suite bathroom. Seconds later, she emptied a sour-tasting mixture of pasties, scotch eggs and chocolate into the murky white toilet bowl. She wretched with such power that her stomach stung with cramps.

"Are you okay?" Bam's voice sounded drowsy.

"No, I'm not. This place is making me sick."

"You just need some more sleep, and you'll be fine."

"I'm not kidding, Bam. I need to get out of here. I want to go back home. This place is making me sick."

"Don't be ridiculous. I'm feeling ill too. We probably just have a virus or something. But we can sleep it off, feel better in the morning."

"No." Freya struggled to get to her feet and staggered towards the small sink. She twisted the silver tap and let the water flow. Cool, clear water streamed between her fingers, and she brought her face to the current, rinsing the rancid substance from her mouth. "No, I can't stay here. I need to go. You should come with me. You can't fly if you're sick, so you might as well stay home with me."

"That place is not my home, Frey." Bam put her hands on her hips, and her eyes flashed with anger. "If I can't fly, I'll stay here until I feel better. I'm not going back to Angel Manor. And neither should you. Especially not in the state you're in." She pointed at Freya. "Look at you. You were just throwing up, and now you want to drive five and a half hours in the dark to get back to that hell house?"

Freya turned to inspect herself in the mirror. Her face was as white as a ghost's, thick dark circles framed her eyes, and her mouth looked like nothing more than a dark gash in her flesh. Her chin was wet with the water she'd gargled with, and her eyes looked wild and filled with pain. Something pulled at her, some unseen, unknown force. She couldn't explain it, but she felt she had to go back to the house. It was as if her life depended on it.

"I'm going. I'm sorry, but I can't stay here." She pleaded with her eyes, but her friend crossed her arms. "Please come with me."

"No, I'm staying, and I'm getting a ticket to Los Angeles."

"Your mobile should work here. I'll call you tomorrow from Portree or something, okay?" Freya moved her head so she could rub her hand across the back of her neck. She opened her mouth again, planning to say something else... anything... to convince her friend to join her, but then she changed her mind. Bam looked at her with round eyes, sucking in her bottom lip.

"You're really doing this?"

"Yes."

"You're going?"

"I'll try and call you later today, okay? I want to know what time your flight goes." Freya opened her arms to hug her friend, but Bam shied away. She fought the tears that were threatening to spill, got up, and walked to the door. "Do you have enough money?"

"Got my credit card. I'll be fine." Bam didn't look her in the eyes when she spoke. "I'm going to phone my mom in the morning, let her know I'm coming."

"Give your mum my love." She opened her arms to hug Bam, but her friend took a step back. "Don't be like that, Bam. Let's not leave like this. I love you, you know that?"

Bam raised an eyebrow and seemed to mull the words over in her head, then she nodded and stepped forward, arms wide. They embraced in a tight hug that was a little painful, but heartfelt nonetheless.

"Drive safely." Bam's voice trembled.

"I will. You be safe too, okay? Don't do anything crazy."

"I won't."

Freya opened the door to the room and took one last glance at Bam before stepping through and pulling it closed behind her.

Chapter 13

A gust of wind pulled at the tent with such violence that Logan woke instantly. Rain hammered down on the canvas, drumming with a deafening rhythm. The tent jerked again, and Logan imagined an invisible giant trying to lift the whole thing with him inside it. Outside, the storm howled. Another tug. The pole leaned at an unnatural angle, and Logan realised that the tent wouldn't be able to withstand this storm for much longer. As he struggled to get dressed, the pole snapped and the canvas landed heavily on him. His hands beat against the material, and it took some effort to find the exit. Logan tried to protect his face from the driving rain with his arm, but it was futile. The wind blew the rain in all directions, and there was no protection. Around him voices echoed through the wind.

"Logan." The voice was hollow and far away. Logan screwed his eyes up, desperately trying to see through the howling maelstrom.

"John," he shouted into the storm.

"Logan, we need to get the boys inside the house."

"Let them grab their sleeping bags."

The world around them was chaos. Tents were ripped from their moorings, flapping in the wind like angry crows. The grass was treacherous and slick underfoot, and Logan fought to keep his balance. He grabbed his own sleeping bag and stuffed it under his shirt in an attempt to keep it dry. He made his way to the next tent over and struggled with the thrashing flap. The edge caught him across the cheek with a sharp snap, stunning him slightly. Logan bent down to look inside and found Terrence and Angus staring back at him, their eyes wide with fright.

"Get dressed, grab your sleeping bags and come on. We're going to the house." He had to scream so hard to be heard that his throat felt raw, but they understood. The young men pulled on their clothes and stuffed their sleeping bags under their shirts, following Logan's example. He bent over, his back catching all the rain, and he wondered how dry any of his clothes were going to be in the next ten seconds. His shirt was already heavy, cold and wet, and it clung to his back like a sickly second skin.

Logan indicated for the guys to follow John and Jim. They ran to the house whooping and screaming, a mixture of excitement and terror. John opened the door for everyone to run through, and the large empty hall of the house was an oasis of calm and quiet compared to the violence outside. The smell of wet fabric mingled with the subtle limey aroma lingering in the air.

"*Welcome home.*" The words were little more than a whisper and Logan turned around to see where they came from, but there was nothing behind him. His heart was going like an express train, and he felt a cold lump in his stomach. He looked at the boys, but none of them were paying attention to him. He shook his head and tried to calm his nerves.

It must be the wind… and my imagination playing tricks on me. This place is as quiet as a tomb.

A whistle cut through the stillness, and Logan glanced around to see Jim look out of one of the large windows. "That's some storm, boys. They can get pretty bad up here."

"Luckily, we were close to the house." Logan pulled the sleeping bag from his shirt and inspected it. It had some dry patches, but not enough for a comfortable night's sleep. "Damn it," he mouthed under his breath.

A light beam shone from the doorway and Logan saw Oliver dressed in a pair of striped blue pyjamas.

"Are you guys okay?" He took some tentative steps closer. "That's quite a storm out there."

"Do you mind if we stay here tonight?" Logan ran a hand through his wet hair.

"Of course not. If you look in some of the old rooms, there are a few mattresses you can use. I might have some blankets still, though I don't know if I have enough for everyone. The girls won't mind if we use theirs." His torch created a trembling oval on the swept floor.

"That would be very kind."

The light moved to each man, illuminating them one at the time.

"Is that everyone?" Oliver's eyes met Logan's, and the blond man rubbed his neck.

"No, we're missing two guys. But they've been gone since last night."

"Oh." There was worry on Oliver's face, and Logan cursed himself that he had to tell him. "You didn't mention it."

"We figured they'd be back by now."

"I hope they're okay."

"Yeah, me too."

An awkward silence hung between them, neither man making eye contact. It was Oliver who spoke first.

"I'll go get those blankets. The storm has cooled the night down and I don't want you and your boys to get cold."

"Thanks." Logan said gratefully.

Oliver nodded and hurried off.

"John, can you take the guys upstairs to the South Wing, second floor, and grab some things to sleep on?" John acknowledged the request and urged the four young men to follow him. Logan stepped up next to Jim and looked out the window. The rainstorm was so intense it was hard to make out anything outside.

"Worried about Mace and Farrow?"

"Aye, I hope those wee pricks are okay." Jim sighed heavily, his meaty hand rubbing his bald scalp.

"I'm going to the town tomorrow and calling their parents. I was hoping I wouldn't have to do that, but they've stayed away too long." Outside, a flash of lightning lit up the falling water and the grass below, and seconds later a deep rumbling sound chased it.

"Like their parents give a shit. Neither of them lives at home anymore."

"Still, I feel I should notify someone."

"They could really fuck up this project, you know that?" Jim grunted and turned to Logan. "I can't believe they just left. I mean, they've done crazy shit before, but they've never just left without saying a word, you know? And I feel responsible."

"Well, we *are* responsible."

"I don't mean like that. I mean because I convinced you to bring Mace along. I know you were hesitant about him and Jones, but I insisted, and if we hadn't taken them..."

"That's bullshit, Jim, and you know it. Could have been any of these guys. Technically they're all adults, and it's not like they're forced to stay here."

"Yeah but if they're going to piss off, they should at least say something."

"You're not wrong there. But these are some messed up lads. I'll have a stern word with them when we find them."

"*If* we find them." Jim grimaced. Logan shook his head

and slapped the older man's shoulder.

"We will." Logan grinned, but he wondered if Jim believed him. In fact, he wasn't at all sure that they would find the boys.

***

Pearls of sweat trailed from her forehead, down past her temples, and onto her neck, tickling her skin as they dropped. Freya wondered if she had a fever. She felt so tired, and yet a strange urge motivated her to drive on. The traffic whizzed past, loud and fast, like roaring metal animals. The drive had been quiet for the first two hours of her journey, but as the world around her woke up to start its working day, the roads became gradually more crowded. All she wanted was to be at home, to be in the calm cool space of Angel Manor.

You're almost there... almost. The bridge to Skye was only a twenty minute drive from where she was now, but she felt so tired. *Maybe I should stop and rest.*

"Don't stop." The voice came from behind her and Freya looked in the rear view mirror. To her horror, she saw a pale elderly woman sitting in the back seat. Freya jerked the steering wheel. The car next to her swerved, honking its horn loud enough for Freya's heart to beat so fast she believed it was about to jump out of her throat. Her hands tingled with the surge of adrenaline, and she needed to take several deep breaths to regain her focus. She glanced at the mirror again, but the figure was gone. The car felt a lot colder than it had moments ago, so she turned off the air conditioning.

I'm going insane.

From the corner of her eye, she saw a presence beside her. Her mind reacted, but her body was ready for it this time, and she turned her head a little to see the old woman sitting next to her.

"Aunt Miriam?" The figure turned to look at her with

140

soulful eyes set in folds of translucent skin. "Am I hallucinating?" There was no answer, and for a moment, Freya thought about pulling the car over to the side of the road.

"Don't stop." The voice didn't exactly come from Aunt Miriam, more from all around Freya, but she knew it was the old woman who spoke.

"Why are you here?"

"The house. You belong to it now. You mustn't ever leave again."

"Oh God, I think I do have a fever. This isn't happening." Her hands gripped the steering wheel even tighter until the stitching bit into her palms.

"You mustn't leave the house again."

"Well, I can't just stay inside. Surely you went outside once in a while. To go shopping or go on a holiday?" She glanced at the pale figure again. Aunt Miriam looked so old, much older than her mother.

"You must care for the house, and you mustn't do so alone."

"You said that in your letter."

"Find the journal."

"What journal?"

"Find the journal." The image flickered a few times, then faded.

"Aunt Miriam?" But she was gone, and the temperature in the car returned to normal. "This is nuts." Freya needed time to make sense of what just happened, but she didn't dare stop. *Another hour and a half tops, then I'll be back home,* she thought, *back in my haunted house. Oh, fuck... I think Bam might have been right.*

Chapter 14

The rain refused to let up, so Logan had decided to let the guys sleep in. There had only been six mattresses clean enough to sleep on so the young men shared three between the four of them, while each of the mentors had their own bed. Being in the house seemed to keep the four boys docile all night, and Logan felt grateful for small miracles.

Movement on the communal mattresses indicated the guys were waking up, and Logan took this as a sign to get out of bed himself. He'd slept like a baby, oddly enough, better than he had in the tent. The house spooked him a little, and yet at the same time it felt comforting. Logan couldn't figure out why, but he felt a connection to the old place.

"Morning." John stretched his pudgy arms and scratched his naked chest, his face rumpled from sleep. "Och, this wasn't so bad, was it?"

"Not at all."

"It's still raining." Jim, already standing by his spot at the window again, said with a heavy voice. "Still as bad as last night. The wind seems to have died down a bit, though."

"Well, as soon as it stops, we'll collect the rest of our stuff." Logan got to his feet and pulled his mattress to the side of the hall, where he stacked it against a wall. "Might be better if we sleep in here from now on. Should make it harder for boys to run away too." He regretted the words as soon as he said them, seeing the grimace cross Jim's face.

Terrence was the first of the guys to get up. He folded his blanket in a neat square and put it on Jim's bed. His dark eyes met Logan's, and he could see he wanted to say something.

"What's on your mind?"

"I don't get why Roger and Lyndon aren't back yet."

"Do you know where they went?"

"Nah, man. But knowing Roger, they probably had some wacky baccy, and they went to light one up. I didn't hear of no plans otherwise. Roger would have told me."

"Should we be worried?"

The young man shrugged, the corners of his full mouth curling down. "I don't know, man. I really don't. This could just be one of Roger's little games. It's just different from the shit he usually pulls, you know?"

"Yeah. I hear you."

"Wouldn't surprise me one bit if the fucker is just hiding in the house somewhere, you know what I'm saying?" He wiggled his thick eyebrows at Logan, who raised his own in return.

"I never even thought of that."

"Wouldn't put it past him." Terrence shrugged.

"We'll go check the house today. Look at the places we haven't searched for them yet." Jim rubbed his neck, obviously agitated.

Terrence swung his wiry arm to loosen the muscles, and he looked around. "So what are we doing today, Boss? Are we searching for our missing brothers or are we clearing up more shit? I personally can't wait until we get to do some of the bigger projects."

"Jim and I will search the house for our two runaways. I don't want you boys roaming through the house, so you focus on clearing up. Mr Jardin should have the plans his architect drew up for us by next week. That's when this party is really going to get started." He winked at Terrence, who replied with an impish grin.

"This is a pretty cool job. I hope Roger and Lyndon show up though. We'll need all the help we can get on a job this size."

Logan's eyes inspected the high ceilings of the entrance hall, his hand fiddling with the collar of his t-shirt. "That it is, Terrence. That it is." He turned to the boy. "Don't you worry. If they don't come back I'll call the centre, see if we can drum up some more volunteers. I'm going into town today to see if anyone has heard anything from our two escapees."

"I hope you'll find them. And maybe you could give calling Tyrell another shot?" He seemed genuinely concerned, and it touched Logan's heart. Terrence had come a long way from the loudmouth he'd met over a year ago, and he felt a surge of pride.

"I'll think about it." Logan winked and ruffled the boy's scalp.

***

Dark clouds hung heavily above the Isle of Skye, but as Freya's car approached, she felt as if she were chasing them away. Ahead of her, rain fell in torrents, but her vehicle never made it to the rainclouds. Her head swam, and beads of sweat dripped down her brow, their salty liquid landing in her eyes, stinging them. Twice, she felt the grass under her tires as she slipped a little off the road, causing her heart to pound.

"Stay on the fucking road, Freya; you're high up, so don't drive off a fucking cliff," she hissed at herself through clenched teeth. It took all her might to keep the steering wheel steady. Freya felt as if she were driving through a dreamscape, her surroundings almost surreal in her feverish vision. She leaned forward, the heat of her face so intense she could feel it on the backs of her hands. The falling water mesmerised her, but she kept focusing on her destination, praying that she would make it without crashing the car.

As she drove up the steep hill towards Lucifer Falls, the sun peered through the grey mass, and when she entered the Angel Manor lot, the rain stopped abruptly. Freya gasped and halted the car. It wasn't that the rain had ceased without warning, but her headache and nausea had disappeared as if by magic as well. She sat still, eyes wide, both wrists on the steering wheel, gaping at the clear blue skies, dumbfounded.

There was not even a trace of the fever she'd had only minutes earlier. In fact, she felt the epitome of health. *What the actual fuck is going on here? Am I just going insane?*

Her muscles complained as she flung her legs outside the car, but other than that, she felt fantastic. With her recovered health came a pang of guilt for leaving Bam behind in Glasgow. She had to remind herself how terrible she had felt only moments ago, and that it had been a good decision to go. Perhaps she could convince her friend to come and join her. As soon as she'd had something to eat and a bit of a rest, Freya would drive down to Portree and give Bam a call to see if she was okay. And she'd ring the guy from the phone company too, because not being able to call from the comfort of her own home was a pain in the backside.

The door to Angel Manor opened and the guys spilled outside, each looking up at the sky in wonder. Logan was the last to leave the house, and Freya's eyes caught his. The intensity of his gaze made her legs tingle and almost buckle. With a few steps, he reached her and offered her his hand, which she took gratefully.

"You're back early. What time did you leave?"

"I set off a little before half four." She blushed and bit her lip. "The B&B was just... too stifling." No other explanation came to mind, and she was aware of how lame her reason for leaving was. Now that she was back at Angel Manor, she felt a hint of shame at how she'd acted.

"Did your friend get on her plane?"

"No, she still has to buy a ticket. I have no idea when her flight will be." Her cheeks burned a little and she cast her eyes down at her feet. "I may not have won any friendship of the year awards today."

"You drove her to Glasgow, not to the nearest train station. I think that deserves some kudos." His fingers wrapped around her wrist, and sparks ignited in the depths of her soul.

"You do know how to make a girl feel better."

"I try."

She noticed that the young men all looked as if they'd just got out of bed, their hair ruffled, and they were dressed in t-shirts and shorts rather than the tatty jeans and long-sleeved shirts they normally wore while working on the house.

"Did you guys sleep in the house last night?"

"Yeah, there was a bad storm. It ripped our stuff to shreds." He pointed at the campsite and the remains of four tents scattered across the soaking grass. Several of the airbeds had made a break for it. One of them was clinging to an overgrown topiary near the house.

"Oh my..." Freya's hand rested on her lips.

"It was still raining until about two minutes ago. Then it stopped... just like that." He snapped his fingers with a loud click.

"It stopped right before I arrived."

"Maybe you brought the sun with you from Glasgow."

"I didn't know the sun lived there." She tilted her head and curled one side of her mouth.

"No, I guess it doesn't." He chuckled softly, his hand never leaving hers, their eyes meeting for a moment.

"Freya?" Oliver's voice broke the spell between them. She wasn't sure why she did it, but she pulled her hand out of Logan's grip.

"Hey, Ollie."

"I didn't think you'd be back until tonight. Or tomorrow even." His hair was wet from what she suspected was a shower, and his face looked bright and fresh. "You missed one crazy storm last night."

"I heard." She nodded her head towards Logan. "It sounded intense. Maybe it's a good idea to create a space for the guys to live in, seeing as their tents are pretty much ruined." She pointed at the campsite, and Oliver's eyes followed the direction of her finger.

"Oh my God, it's worse than I thought." He tangled his fingers in his wet brown curls. Freya could smell a hint of aftershave. "We can absolutely make space in the house. I know you didn't want the boys to be in the same wing as us, but things seem to have been going very well, and with Bam gone..." Oliver glanced from Logan to Freya, "... there's only Freya now."

Freya rolled her eyes, but then she nodded. "I really don't see the issue either. The guys have been very well behaved so far."

In the distance, the four young men were picking their scattered belongings from the ground, all a little quiet and solemn. One of them, she thought his name was Mason, cupped his hands so that Terrence could have a leg up against one of the trees to rescue a dangling backpack. It was a sad sight.

"I guess we can try."

"Good."

Chapter 15

"Today I will get up," Bam whispered, her voice no more than a raspy croak that garbled most of the pronunciation. She had spent the past forty-two hours in the cramped room with no food or drink, hallucinating from an intense fever. In her dreams, a dark figure sat on her chest, preventing her from moving, sucking the energy out of her.

For the first time in hours, she had a lucid moment, and she was shocked at the state of her body. Flaky dry tatters hung from her lips, and every breath hurt. Her skin hung like a loose sack around her bones.

"Can't get away, Sis. You're dying."

"You can't be here, Chuck... you can't be." Her tongue was thick and dry, and it stuck to the roof of her mouth.

"Don't worry, Bambi... I'm not here. This is only a projection. My soul is stuck in Angel Manor."

"You can't hurt me."

"I can't... not now. But you're hurting yourself plenty." Bam detected a hint of smug cruelty in her brother's words. "You see, my dearest, I can't leave Angel Manor... but neither can you. You are as stuck to that house as I am."

"You're wrong." She turned on her side, all her organs groaning in protest. *If only this room wasn't so hot.* "You're stuck in that house, and I got away. I got away from you." She cried but no tears came; she simply didn't have any fluid left in her. Bam wanted to drink, but she couldn't bring herself to do so. Something was holding her back, but she knew that if she didn't break out of it, she would die.

"No, you didn't get away. Only part of you left, Bambi. You bonded with the house, and it owns your soul now. It still has you, sis. That's why you're so sick."

"How can it have my soul when I'm here?" Her eyes rolled to the back of her head, and her tongue lolled from the corner of her mouth. If anyone had been present in the room, they wouldn't have been able to understand her, but to Bam it felt as if she were having a lucid conversation. The muscles in her body cramped up with acidic pain flashes, her hands knotted into claws. Her once beautifully manicured nails were now broken and bitten down to the quick.

"You should have told Freya how you were really doing, sis. She could have saved you. She would have come to get you and brought you back. But you didn't. And now the battery to your phone is dead, and you're going to die in the next few hours."

"I got away from that house." The words were slow but determined.

"You didn't get away from the house, sis. Something got away all right... but it wasn't you."

"Fuck you, Chuck. What do you mean, something got away?" Bambi coughed, her throat was so scratchy it felt as if she'd swallowed needles.

"When your body left the house, it took a part of the spell with you. It seems to have grown, Bambi dearest... and it wants you dead." Chuck squatted next to the bed and cocked his head at her. She wanted to claw his eyes out.

"You're full of shit. All I need to do is drink some water, and then I'll be fine. The water is right over there."

"It won't matter. Can't exist separated from your soul for too long. It knows it too."

His taunting tone powered her with a sudden determination, and Bam gathered all her strength to push herself up from the bed. She made two failed attempts, where her arms simply refused to carry her weight, but the third time she managed to sit up straight.

"Third time's a charm," she muttered with an air of victory. Her hands sought support on the mattress, and she felt a cold clammy substance, filled with hard dry clumps, squelch under her fingers. *I fucking shat myself, this has to be the most disgusting thing I've ever done.*

Her knees buckled as she got to her feet, and she fell to the floor with a meaty thud. Every inch of her body hurt, as if her skin was just one big bruise that throbbed and ached. She crawled on all fours, the weight of her body bearing down heavily on the bones in her hands and knees, but she ignored the sharp pain. Slowly, she inched forward, the ghostly presence of her brother hovering just outside of her peripheral vision.

"I'm going to drink that water, and then I'm going to be fine... you'll see." Her elbows wobbled and she pushed herself forwards with her legs. *Why didn't I drink before? The water was right there... why did I wait so long? Could there really be something in here with me? Is this part of the spell Chuck spoke about?* She tried to remember the past two days, but they were a blur. All she remembered were the dreams that had kept her in bed. She didn't want to leave the comfort of the mattress because she was feeling so very ill. She drifted in and out of strange, vivid dreams about the house. The memories came flooding back to her. Angel Manor had been calling for her, demanding her return, but she had ignored it. Instead of answering the call, she had given in to the sickness and the fatigue. Bam hadn't been lucid in days, and now realised it may be too late. From the corner of her eye, she thought she saw a dark shadow, but she wasn't sure.

She staggered on, putting one hand in front of the other, gripping onto the red carpet. The house had poisoned her spirit, had destroyed her body, and she had just accepted it. The sight of Chuck had broken her, and she hadn't fought back. *But I will now. I will fight you, you evil bastard, and I will get better. Just you wait and see. Fuck you, fuck the house, and fuck whatever else is in here with me. I'm going to survive this. I'm stronger than you.*

Her elbows finally gave out when she reached the bathroom. The sink loomed high above her, seemingly unreachable from the tiled floor. Her eyes, hazy with delirium, glanced around the bathroom and spotted the tub. The tiles were so cold, they made her shiver as she hoisted herself up the three small white steps that led to the narrow half-bath. Once she reached the cool smooth rim, she tried to lower herself gently, but her hand slipped and she fell hard into the tub, landing on her elbow and hip with a sickening crunch.

The pain was excruciating, and her hip pushed against the metal plug of the bath. With her last strength she opened the cold tap and let the water flow down. Her muscles screamed as she brought her face to the stream, the water pushed against her cheek and teeth with such force that she coughed and spat. Thick bilious liquid rose from her stomach and leaked from her mouth as she coughed, and she tried to roll on her side, but didn't have the energy. The water poured over her face and throat and Bam struggled to look away. She felt a pool of cold water form around her body, sticking her clothes to her. The level rose slowly but steadily, pulling gently at her hair. Bam stared at the tap, and she understood that the tub was filling up, that she needed to turn the tap off, but when she attempted to do so an unseen force yanked it to the other side so that the water came out faster. Then the handle broke. The water poured down, hitting her in the face and chest. Bam pulled herself up to crawl away. She grabbed the side of the tub, her fingers sore with the strength of her grip. She inhaled deeply and concentrated.

Come on, you can do this. It's just a fucking tub. Get it together, Bam. She pushed herself up. Carefully, she moved her limbs, positioning herself so she could stand. Her body was weak, but she managed to get to her feet. Relief washed through her, and Bam began to step over the edge of the bathtub when something pulled at her hair, knocking her head against the silver spout. Her skull banged against the metal with a dull thud, and bright red and white stars exploded before her eyes. Her head swam, the blow blurring her vision. Something heavy pushed down on her chest, and through her eyelashes she saw a shadowy figure squatting on her. Bam slapped at it, but her hands only hit air. The weight pushed against her head and hit it against the porcelain of the tub, dealing her already pained skull another blow. A moment of emptiness overwhelmed her and Bam understood that her brother had been right. She didn't have a soul after all.

She should have returned to the house while she still could. The house owned her very essence, and she belonged to Angel Manor as much as Chuck did; as much as all the others did. She could almost see them now, the multitude of souls bound to the bricks and mortar, some brought by the living, others because they died there. With a trembling hand, she reached for the shadowy image again, and then the lights went out for good. Her frail body floated in the pool of water, which continued to rise, covering her face and body. She drowned without ever waking up, and it was two hours later, when the water started to rain down in the room below, that the owner found her battered body.

***

Freya woke from a bad dream, but the images faded as soon as her eyes opened. All she was left with was an uncomfortable feeling that lingered like a forgotten memory. A hint of familiar perfume hit her nostrils and, for a moment, she was convinced Bam was lying next to her in the bed, but when her hand explored the spot, she found a cold, flat mattress. She sighed and remembered that Bam wasn't here, but somewhere in Glasgow, or perhaps LA by now. The only time Freya'd managed to reach her friend, she'd sounded very sick. She didn't want to come back to the house even though Freya had offered to pick her up, and eventually she'd given up. She hadn't been able to contact her after that, and it frustrated Freya that she had no clue what was going on.

With a sigh, she turned on the little nightlight on the

bedside table. The alarm clock told her it was one AM. She'd only been asleep for two hours. Her mouth was so dry that her throat felt sore. A thin layer of slime coated her tongue, and she sighed with resignation when she realised that she needed to get out of bed to get a drink.

She grabbed her pyjama bottoms from the chair at the foot of the bed, then slipped her feet into a pair of fuzzy, giraffe-head shaped slippers. Bam had given them to her for Christmas, and though they were completely silly, Freya loved them. She took a few steps towards the bathroom, and then changed her mind. She would rather have a hot cup of tea than cold water. For some reason, the idea of drinking from a tap made her shudder with revulsion.

Freya couldn't be bothered to lift her feet as she walked, and the bottoms of her slippers swished as she dragged them over the marble floor. Yawning, she scratched the exposed skin beneath her short t-shirt as she made her way across the kitchen to the fridge. Opening the door, Freya remembered that she was going to make tea, so she closed the door again and turned around.

A scream escaped her mouth as the lights went on, every muscle in her body tensed and her heart pounded fiercely in her chest. She stared at Logan, who looked as shocked as she was.

"I'm sorry. I didn't mean to frighten you..." He held up his hands in defence. There was a book clutched in his right hand. "I forgot my notebook here earlier, and I couldn't sleep... I wanted to look at something, but I couldn't find it. Then I remembered it was here. I didn't mean to intrude on your privacy. Just assumed everyone was asleep." He looked truly miserable, and Freya couldn't help laughing.

"Don't worry about it. You can come to the kitchen any time you want. I just wasn't expecting you."

"Well, that makes two of us. You weren't exactly what I was expecting either." His hand rubbed the back of his neck, his head tilted forward, and his eyes met hers with a shy smile. "I like your shirt." He pointed at her top, which showed a picture of Yoda looking up at the incredible Hulk, the subtext read: "Hulk, your father I am."

"It matches my slippers." She held up a foot and wiggled it about. Logan's eyebrows shot up and his head moved back in surprise.

"Wow... those are some, um, slippers." He chuckled, placing his thumb on his bottom lip.

"I'm making a cup of tea, would you like some?"

"Sure. If you don't mind. I know it's late."

"I could use the company." Butterflies fluttered through her stomach, and Freya tried to keep her face neutral. The idea of spending time alone with him in the middle of the night made her nervous and giddy at the same time.

"What kind of tea do you like? I have flavours." She pulled down a wooden box filled with teabags from the top shelf and showed him the assortment. Logan laughed.

"I thought you meant real tea, not the posh stuff, but I'll have whatever you're having. We can share a bag."

Freya liked that idea, though she wasn't sure why. "Sure." She picked a brightly coloured paper from the lot and inspected it. "Apple and cinnamon okay?"

"Sounds great."

The kettle weighed heavy in her hand as she turned on the tap, and the stream of water brought with it a feeling of irrational panic. She stared at the water, her brow in a tight knot. The sound of the rushing current was offensive to her ears, and she stood frozen.

"Are you okay?" Logan shot forward to close the tap, and took the kettle from her hand. "What happened? You don't look so good."

"I..." Freya peeled her eyes away from the tap. "I don't

know what just happened. I just... just freaked out, but I don't even know why."

"You must be under a lot of stress, with the house and all." Logan wrapped an arm around her shoulders, pulled her away from the tap, and set the kettle down on the kitchen counter. "Your friend left. That's probably affected you a little too."

"You don't know the half of it." She let him guide her to the table, the tea-making abandoned. "I don't know. I feel like I've been going a little insane lately. Starting to see things that aren't there." An oppressive feeling filled her stomach, and she wondered if she had said too much. She didn't want Logan to think she was nuts, or unhinged, or anything like that. What she wanted was for him to be impressed with her, but tonight she needed to be honest.

"Stress can do that to you. I've had some weird moments in my life too."

"See any ghosts?"

"No, did you?"

She shrugged, her skin going cold. "I don't know. I think I might have been hallucinating at the time. When we went to Glasgow I had a bit of a fever. It's just that weird things keep happening, and I don't know if it's just stress, like you say, or if it's my imagination getting the better of me... or if there's something more to it."

"Tricky. I wish I had some answers for you. I can imagine that a house like this can get to you though. Not hard to see ghosts in old buildings." His long, slender hands rubbed through his tousled hair and his eyes seemed far away. "I've seen my share of old places over the years, and some houses are creepier than others. Some almost feel alive."

"Angel Manor feels alive. My mom used to say that as well."

"Is it an old family home?"

"Yes, I inherited it from my aunt." The inside of her mouth did a great imitation of cotton wool and Freya wanted a drink. The idea of opening the tap again didn't appeal to her, so instead she got up and opened the fridge. "The house is too big for just me to live in. Also, I'm not a fan of being the hermit of Lucifer Falls. So when I told Bam and Oliver that I inherited the house and wanted to sell it, they convinced me to turn it into a hotel instead. It's big enough." She pulled a carton from the fridge and held it up.

"It sure is. Good location too. Great for nature lovers."

"Exactly. Would you settle for iced tea?"

"Of course." He got up and grabbed two cups from the counter. "Quite a big adventure to undertake with friends. You must be very close to want to start a hotel together."

"We're like family." She poured the tea and handed him a cup while they both sat down around the table again.

Freya's hands squeezed the cup. She felt so silly. She didn't want to talk about her weird connection to Angel Manor, but she didn't want the conversation to be over yet either. It was nice to have Logan to herself for a little while, to talk to him and listen to his deep and even voice, to look into those bright green eyes of his. She imagined what it would be like to kiss him, but pushed the thought from her mind when she felt a hot blush creep up on her cheeks.

"How about you, what got you into this job?"

"That's a long story."

Freya looked around the kitchen before shrugging her shoulders. "I have the time."

A smile spread across Logan's lips and he exhaled a mock sigh. "Very well."

His eyes rolled up to the ceiling for a moment as he gathered his thoughts, and Freya leaned in a little. She could smell his aftershave mixed with a hint of body odour, and the butterflies in her stomach danced in response.

"I started with the Chancers ten years ago, only then I wasn't a coach, I was one of the kids." His eyes pierced into hers, his face a mask of expectation.

"Wow, it's great to see that the project can be such a success for people," Freya said, giving him an awkward smile while inwardly cursing herself for being so lame.

"It is. That's why I wanted to stick with it and pay it forward. I was eighteen when John Norris approached me in Edinburgh. I didn't have an education and I had no real place to go. I'd run away from London years before, lived everywhere and nowhere. Like you, I had a mother who was unbalanced, only mine tried to balance herself out by doing drugs. Never knew my father. Needless to say, I dropped out of secondary school when I was fifteen, and I ran away from home. I did a bit of thieving here and there, nothing too terrible, but enough to give me a record. The Chancers saved my life. I would have gone downhill from where I was. Having a proper job can give a misguided lad a new sense of self respect, it did that for me."

"And here you are, helping others out."

"Yeah, and it's a great feeling. Though it's always tough when you find out that some people just don't take it seriously."

"You mean the two boys who ran away?" Freya pulled her foot onto the chair, resting her chin on her knee.

"Yeah."

"Did you ever find out what happened to them?"

"I went to the police station in Portree yesterday. You know, just in case. Their mums don't know anything, but that doesn't surprise me much. They didn't spend a lot of time at home, if you know what I mean."

"What did the police say?"

"Well, it's two guys with a track record for running away. Both of them are legally adults, so I don't think the police will be looking too thoroughly."

"Do you think something's happened to them?"

"I hope not, but as long as I don't know where they are, it'll eat at me, you know? I'd go look myself, but I wouldn't know where to start. You know, I expected this from Roger Mace, but Lyndon disappearing bothers me. He's just... not as much of a troublemaker. I'd have thought if any two were to run off, it would have been Terrence and Roger, not Lyndon and Roger." He tapped his index finger on his lips, his eyes narrow. "In fact, something that Terrence said keeps nagging at me."

"What did he say?"

"He said he wouldn't be surprised if they were still in the house."

Freya sat up straight, her raised leg slid off the chair and landed on the ground.

"In the house? Why would they do that?"

"Don't worry, I think he's wrong. If they were hiding in the house, we would have found them by now. They've been missing for three days. I don't think they would go that far with a joke. They'd need to eat, after all, so unless one of the other guys is in on it, they're not here. I don't see the point of such an elaborate prank anyway."

The thought of two young men roaming around Angel Manor without supervision unnerved Freya. She bit the edge of her thumbnail.

"I hope you'll find them soon."

***

It was cold where Bam was, but she could feel the warmth of the two nearby. The house was so much larger now, and her mind was clouded with the confusion of the newly deceased. She was an echo of the person she had been, and she was trying her very best to cling on to what little remained of her sanity. Her body had died somewhere far away, but her soul had never left, not since the day she'd first set foot in Angel Manor. Her soul was strong, as all the recently dead's were, still very much tied to her previous existence, and her thoughts were still a clear reminder of who she had been. Part of her didn't truly understand that she was dead, though in time her essence would dilute and become increasingly part of the house, as the others had.

She could sense the presence of the other spirits in the house, tormented and trapped, just like she was. Her soul felt so tired, but Bam knew she would never rest, not as long as the house imprisoned her. She would only lose herself more and more to this building as it fed on her. Before she lost the last bit of her humanity, she had to warn Freya. There was something in here with them. Not the spirits. Something bigger. More dangerous. It was currently dormant, but not fully asleep either. Whatever it was, it demanded sacrifice. She felt its pull humming softly like white noise.

In her current state, she could see things she'd never seen in life, like the souls and the chains of pure energy binding them to the house. She had a chain of her very own, and through the bright white light she saw a red and black vein pumping with poison.

The house around her was very much alive. Partially because of the spells that kept it together, but also because of the unseen force spreading out through the bricks and mortar like thin black spidery veins, filling the building with darkness. Whatever this force was, it was buried deep, but not deep enough.

Bam lamented the loss of her life. She had been too young to die and her spirit was frightened and confused. She was a lost soul, so when she saw Freya sitting at the table in the kitchen, alive and well, talking to the man she liked, something in Bam broke. She saw the hot pulses of body heat, the rhythmic beating of both hearts and the signs of sexual excitement in them both. Bam was perfectly torn between a feeling of love and hate.

Chapter 16

Terrence couldn't sleep. The temperature in the house was stifling, not helped by the fact that he shared the same room with the three other guys and the counsellors. Plus, Mr McLeod snored like a drowning warthog. He'd preferred the tents. Surely if they were going to sleep in the house, there should be at least two rooms available to them. This place was big enough.

He pushed the thin sheet away from his wiry body and carefully crawled off the mattress. He didn't want to wake anyone, but he needed to stretch his legs for a while, so he cautiously placed his foot between the sleeping forms of Angus and Mason. A loud, unexpected snort from Mr McLeod almost caused him to step on Gary's outstretched hand, and the scare made him suppress a laugh as he snuck out of the room. Once he closed the door behind him, he felt like he could breathe easier. With a little lift in his step, he made his way through the dark corridors of Angel Manor.

The house appeared different at night, away from the other people who filled the solemn rooms with laughter and banter. The night made the building seem strange... unfamiliar. Ceilings appeared higher and corridors wider. Colours became muted monochromes. The moon peeked in through the long, glass windows, shining brightly enough inside for Terrence to walk comfortably without a torch. His eyes were already accustomed to the dark. The sound of his footsteps echoed dully off the walls, making him sound bigger than he really was, and for a moment, Terrence pictured himself as an important man taking a leisurely stroll through his own mansion. He opened one of the doors and walked through the room to a set of balcony doors. He fiddled with the lock, but it was stuck.

A movement caught the corner of his eye, and his heart lurched in his chest.

"Who's there?" Terrence wished he'd brought a torch with him now, or a knife. There was no answer. It was cold here, and his body shivered. "If this is someone fucking with me, I'm going to punch your face in."

"Don't do that, bro," a familiar voice whispered in his ear. Terrence jolted and turned.

"Tyrell?" His eyes widened and his mouth hung slack. "What the fuck are you doing here in the middle of the night?"

"You called me, bro."

"Like hell, I did. How the fuck did you even get in here, man?" Terrence's brain fought to catch up with this new development, and it took him a few seconds to feel the happiness of seeing his brother again.

"Now, that would be tellin' wouldn't it?" Tyrell threw his head back and laughed, and then he snapped forward again and gave Terrence an unsettling look. Terrence wanted to run up and hug his brother, but there was something about the way Tyrell was standing, the way he looked, that stopped him in his tracks.

"Where did you go, T? Why didn't you come on the project with us?"

"I ran into a little bit of trouble, bro." His brother didn't move, just stood there, waving on his feet as if he were a flag in the wind. "Actually... I ran into a *lot* of trouble." There was pain in his voice, but no real expression crossed his features, just like one of those Botox bitches on TV looked: a flat, expressionless mask.

"Well you're here now. Logan will be proud."

"I came because you called me here."

"You keep saying that. I didn't call you. My phone don't

162

work up here."

"They hurt me, Terrence. They hurt me real bad."

Terrence took a step forward, squinting his eyes to get a better look at his brother, but Tyrell was shrouded by the shadows in the empty room.

"Who hurt you, T?"

"They found me with Billy Sanders."

"Billy the Queer? What the fuck were you doing with Billy the Queer?"

"I loved him, bro." The voice sounded sad and haunted, and Terrence's muscles tensed.

"Nah, man. Don't sell me that bullshit. You ain't gay." But his heart sank because he knew he was wrong. His brother had always been a little different, and though they never talked about it, Terrence had known. His stepfather had suspected it too, and he was even rougher on Tyrell than he'd been on him.

"I loved him, bro," Tyrell repeated.

"I don't think this is the time to talk about this, T. Let's wait until morning, you know... just... I haven't seen you in weeks. It's a bit sudden and shit."

"I don't know how much time I have."

"What the fuck are you talking about?"

"My mind... I don't know how much longer I can hold on. I'm fading fast. This house... it's stronger than I am."

"Have you done fucking drugs again?"

"Listen to me, Terrence. Don't go down to the basement. There are things in there... they're awake but trapped, and they're hungry. So very hungry."

"You're creeping me out, T. I don't like this. It's not

fucking funny."

"Don't go into the basement, Bro. Get out of this house while you still can. Though I'm not sure it will let you go."

"Cut it out, Tyrell. This isn't funny. I'm going to smash your face in if you don't stop with the bullshit."

"You called me here, and now I'm trapped in this house."

Terrence felt his frustration turn into fury, and he stepped forward to lash out at his brother, but his fist found empty air. Terrence shrieked.

"What the fuck! What the fuck?!" He couldn't get his voice below anything more than a loud, high-pitched shriek.

"They hurt me, bro. They hurt me so bad." The soft voice of his brother was audible even over his own screaming, and Terrence noticed his sibling's bruised face. He had looked normal only seconds ago, but now his jaw and nose were clearly broken and his eyes were swollen. "You brought me here."

"No, man. No. What the fuck is going on?" Tears welled up in his eyes and fell down his cheeks in long glistening trails. "Am I dreaming this?"

"This house, there's something with this house. It gives us a form, but it takes something from us too."

"Who is 'us', T?" Terrence's face twisted with grief, his mouth pulled back in a grimace, tears and snot gathering on the groove above his upper lip. Everything in his mind told him to run, but Terrence stood rooted to the spot. "Who is 'us'?"

"You know, Terrence. I can see it in your heart."

"I don't know. I don't know anything right now. I don't even know if I'm seeing you or if I'm dreaming this."

The figure stepped forward, flickering out of existence

for a second, and then reappeared right in front of Terrence's face. "You think this is a dream, little brother? You think you're having a nightmare?" Tyrel's hand grasped Terrence's wrist, and he screamed in fear. The touch was painful and strange, as if he were held by hot air rather than a fist, yet he couldn't pull loose.

"I don't know, T. Let me go, man."

"This is not a dream, brother. This place will swallow you whole if you don't get out." The apparition rested its head against Terrence's, and unlike the phantom hand, the head felt cold and clammy. Terrence whimpered, but he didn't dare pull away. He just shivered and cried. "It got me, and it wants me to get you too, so that you stay here with the rest of us. But I can't do that to you, bro. I love you too much. I don't know for how much longer I'll love you, but I do now."

"What should I do?" His voice was barely audible over his sobs, but the spirit knew what he'd said.

"Leave."

***

The new souls hadn't gone unnoticed by those already connected to the house. Their presence fed the very essence of Angel Manor, and Sister Agatha, who was linked to the house in a way only one other was, felt a surge of energy through her core. She felt the hunger grumbling in the depths of the building like a famished predator waiting to leap on its prey.

The autumn equinox was nearing, and that would bring the house to life. There were too many living within the walls of Angel Manor, and their energy would feed the dead. Sister Agatha would have to find a way to communicate with the child of the bloodline, but she hadn't communicated with the living for so long, she wasn't sure she could pull herself together enough to warn the girl. The presence of the living was making her stronger, she felt that much, so perhaps there was a way.

The lost souls roamed through the halls, and more would come. The living always brought their dead, and the house would always adopt them. The girl who had bonded with the house stood on a threshold. She would have to choose between who she was and who the house wanted her to become. A choice that Agatha herself had made when she'd died. There were few like Agatha who had been able to resist the pull of Angel Manor's darkness, but the nun hoped the girl would fight the urge to give in.

Sister Agatha froze as another presence entered her domain.

"Who dares?" The words were mere thoughts, but the other spirit understood them, and the image of Sister Anne materialised, a spirit who she hadn't encountered since she had been alive.

"How did you get free?"

The spirit smiled at her, and though her face was pretty and sweet, there was a wolf behind that smile and a darkness in her eyes that frightened Sister Agatha.

"The one I've been waiting for has finally arrived. She will set us all free, Agatha. Even you. You can't protect them anymore."

"You wanted to protect everyone at one time, remember?"

A flicker of emotion crossed the spirit's features, and for a moment Agatha saw the soft-hearted Anne who had given her life to save the children. Then the face hardened and the wolf grin returned, filled with hunger and bloodlust.

"That's not what the house wants, Agatha. We must appease it, for it serves the sleeping master." The nightgown flowed around Anne's form as if she were surrounded by water, the white fabric billowing in the still air, and her red locks writhing like live tentacles.

"The master is appeased by the sacrifice we made. No more blood needs to flow, Anne. That's why we cast the spells, remember?"

"Can you not feel the hunger?"

She could. She felt it in every part of her being. The others could feel it too: the sisters in the basement, the members of the bloodline who were buried outside the house and no longer able to pass the threshold of Angel Manor.

"Are you keeping the living here?"

"I can't, and you know it. I can only tempt them to stay. Only the child of the bloodline can bind them to the house... to the spell. Only she can force them to stay, not I."

"What about the boy you killed?"

"I didn't kill him, he killed himself. I just made him see it was the right thing to do."

"I'm surprised you didn't let him go."

"Why would I let any of them go?"

"Because he would have told others. And there is one thing that will draw human beings... telling them not to go somewhere."

Sister Anne seemed to contemplate her words, and then her face broke into a smile again. "I don't need to tempt them. The Guardians will do so themselves. They will bring us new life in abundance."

Sister Agatha reached out with her mind and found Anne's. She saw the face of one of the guardians as he spoke to Anne, promising her many visitors to Angel Manor.

"They plan to make this place a hotel?" Her voice was high with panic.

"They will succeed. A new age dawns for us, the special

one has arrived. She woke us all outside of the equinox."

"No one knows what the prophecy means."

Anne gave a sly smile. "We shall see what fate has in store for us." And with that, her spirit disappeared, leaving Agatha with a growing sense of foreboding.

Chapter 17

"Are you headed into town?" Oliver didn't even look up from his newspaper when he spoke.

"Yeah, I'm going to call Bam at her parent's house. She didn't call me when she landed so I'm starting to get a bit worried. I hate that it's so hard to reach anyone here. I'm going to call BT as well."

He took a sip from his coffee, still not making eye contact. "Don't bother, I've already phoned them. They're sending an engineer out on Monday."

"That's a relief. It means I won't have to drive into Portree every bloody time we need to make a phone call. I can live another two days without a phone."

"Oh, don't go all the way to Portree. There's a small town just south of Lucifer Falls. I think it's called Aingeal or something. That place has a shop, a library and everything, even a phone booth if you can believe it, and it's only half the drive."

"It's just off Lucifer Falls?" Freya raised her eyebrows.

Oliver nodded. "Yeah, instead of going right, go left at the junction down below."

"Thanks for the tip." She raised her thumb, and quickly felt awkward, so she rubbed her hands across her stomach as if she were straightening the fabric of her shirt.

"Bring me some aspirin okay? We're out."

"Again? I bought a whole box a few days ago... what happened to them? Have you been pretending they're Pez?"

"No, I just get a lot of headaches. Must be the stress."

169

The paper rustled and Oliver's brown eyes peered over the rim. "It's not like I'm the only one who's been taking them. Those damn guys keep asking me for aspirins too."

"Sheesh, no need to get so defensive, Oscar the Grouch." Freya wrinkled her nose at him and tried to cheer him up with a funny face, but to her disappointment, she didn't see a smile. "Why are you so grumpy?"

"My nights have been a bit restless," he admitted. He flicked the page of his paper with a noisy gesture and broke eye contact. "Lack of sleep makes me grumpy."

"Want to talk about it."

"No."

"Fair enough. I'm going to head out and get this over with." Freya inhaled deeply, her whole body resisting the idea of having to leave the grounds. She knew that as soon as she stepped off the property, the headaches and nausea would start. The thought alone made her quicken her step, but as she strode through the entrance hall, a voice stopped her in her tracks.

"Are you going out?"

Logan was standing against the doorframe of the South Wing, dressed in a pair of dusty blue jeans and a white sleeveless t-shirt. The sight of him made her squirm.

"Yes, just into town for an errand."

"Can I hitch a ride with you? I want to pick up a few things too."

"I can get them for you if you'd like. It's no bother."

"No, I'd rather go with you. It gives me a moment to myself, and I like the company. Unless you mind, of course." The corner of his mouth curled in a twisted smile, and she laughed.

"Not at all, I'll be glad of the company too."

He strode casually towards her, both hands in his pockets. "I enjoyed talking to you last night." He winked and she fought the rush of hot blood to her cheeks, failing miserably in the attempt.

"Me too." She didn't quite know how to act, so she picked up her pace again and opened the door. With a hop and a skip in her step, she darted down the stairs, Logan in tow.

"Are we going to Portree?"

"No, apparently there is a place that's closer. Might give that a try. Portree is pretty far, and I don't like staying away for too long."

They stepped into the car, and Freya mentally prepared for the journey. Then she pushed the key into the ignition, turned it, and the car hummed to life. Logan fixed his seatbelt, and they pulled away from the manor. As soon as they left the grounds, Freya felt the familiar headache resurface, and she was unconvinced this was a coincidence. From the corner of her eye, she saw Logan pinch the bridge of his nose.

"Are you okay?" There was something hopeful in her voice. She wanted him to confirm how she felt, just so that she would feel less crazy.

"I don't know. The worst headache just hit me. I hope I'm not getting a migraine."

"I have that headache every time I leave the grounds. Then as soon as I get back, it disappears."

"You said something like that before."

Freya frowned and swallowed a lump in her throat.

"I think Bam had it too. That's why I'm so worried about her. I just hope that it goes away when we've been gone long enough from the house. I would hate to think that she's in the US with a stinker of a headache for the next few months." She imagined Bam walking around with an icepack on her head and snarling at her parents. Her friend was not the most gregarious of people when she was unwell. The thought almost made her laugh, and Freya chewed on her lips. She tried to focus on the road, the urge to return to Angel Manor already nagging at her subconscious.

***

"Mrs Green?" Her hand clutched the black plastic handset of the old payphone. "This is Freya Formynder. I was wondering if Bambi had arrived home yet. I can't seem to reach her on her cell phone. I dropped her off in Glasgow a few days ago and she said she was going to catch a flight to LA."

"Freya?" The voice sounded broken. "You... you haven't heard?"

"Heard what?" A cold fear clutched Freya's throat.

"Oh, my poor baby..." Heartfelt sobs came through the phone and Mrs Green wailed words that Freya couldn't understand.

"Mrs Green, what happened to Bam? ... Mrs Green?" The woman wouldn't respond, and Freya wanted to reach down the phone line and shake her. She pictured the overly-tanned woman, with her leathery skin and bleached blonde hair, screeching. A deeper voice sounded through the cries, and seconds later Mr Green's baritone came through the phone.

"Who is this?"

"Freya Formynder, sir. I was calling to see if you'd heard anything from Bambi?"

"You mean, you don't know?"

"Know what, sir?" Freya felt tears well up in her eyes and her throat was dry and raw. "Has something happened?"

"Bambi is dead, Freya. She died in Glasgow."

"What... no..." Freya took an involuntary step back, her hand covering her mouth. "No... that can't be. I only saw her a few days ago."

"She slipped and fell in the bathtub. Hit her head. Drowned." The man struggled with his words.

A high pitched wheeze escaped from her open mouth, but no other sound came. The grief was too deep, too painful to verbalise. Freya felt her knees buckle, and she sank to the floor of the phone booth, her forehead hitting the glass with a thud. The receiver didn't reach that far down and it dangled near the top of her head. Freya was only dimly aware of the door opening, and Logan's strong hands pulling her to her feet and out of the booth, where he allowed her to sit down again. She made herself small, sobbing, and he picked up the phone.

"Hello?" He listened for a moment. "This is Logan Masters, who am I speaking to?" There was a pause, and Freya buried her head in her pulled up knees. "Mr Green, I'm a friend of Freya's. I don't know what you told her, but..."

A voice crackled from the other side of the phone and Logan was silent again.

"Oh God... I... I'm so sorry. We weren't expecting that. I..."

More crackling from the other side, Freya turned around and looked at him through her tears. He offered her a look of sympathy. "Mr Green..." The other man must have not let him speak because Logan was quiet again, and a hint of impatience flashed across his features. "I understand, sir. I'll tell her.... yes... thank you. Goodbye." He placed the receiver back on its cradle and stared at it for a moment, then he turned back to Freya.

"I... I'm so sorry."

"It's my fault." The words burned at her throat as she spoke, but she needed to let them out. "If I hadn't left... If I hadn't left her there all alone..." Her chest ached, every muscle in her body cramped and a foul taste coated her tongue. Logan knelt down beside her and gathered her in a tight hug. He hurt her a little, but Freya welcomed the pain, there was a certain reality to it in a world that suddenly felt unreal.

"Shhh," he soothed, rocking her back and forth. "This is not your fault. You aren't to blame."

"She was sick, like me... and I left her. I left her, Logan. I left her." Her tears bled into his shirt, and she balled her fist around some of the fabric. "Oh God... I left her there to die."

"Stop it, you did no such thing."

"I should have known... but all I could think of was getting back to Angel Manor, so that I would feel good again. I was so selfish."

"No, you weren't. Don't be crazy."

"I asked her to come, but she didn't want to." Her words were deep, sore hiccups. "I begged her to come back with me, but when she didn't want to I gave up. I gave up on her. And now she's dead, and I'll never see her again. Ever... because she's dead. Dead!" The word sounded alien to her ears, as if she had never heard it before.

This can't be happening, Freya thought. *Not to Bam. Not to a girl who was so alive, who was so full of energy. She can't be dead.* The idea of Bam lying in some coffin somewhere, it was just too absurd for words. Her smiling face, the mischievous sparkle in her eye... Freya could think of nothing else. Snippets of memory that made up the puzzle of who Bam had been in life flooded her mind. The way she hiccupped when she laughed, or snorted drink through her nose when Freya made a face at her. The way she would crawl into Freya's bed when she was scared, her body always the warmer of the two. The way she held Freya when she was sad, or stroked her hair with those brightly painted nails to ease a broken heart. All of that was gone. Bam would never be there for her again. Bam would never demand her attention again. All that was left was a void. For the last fourteen years, she had spent most of her days with Bam... that was more than half her life, and she would never see her again. Freya would have given anything to relive those last moments over again.

The shopping lay forgotten, as did Logan's errands. The tall man half-supported, half-carried the crying Freya to the car, where he put her into the passenger seat with as much care as he could. She pulled her legs up to her chest, not even bothering with the seatbelt.

"Give me the keys, I'll drive."

She pushed her hand in the pocket of her jeans. The rough denim pressed into her thigh and scraped at the tops of her fingers, but she found the sharp metal key and freed it from its fabric prison. The car roared to life and the wheels crunched over the dirt road.

"The man on the phone... Mr Green?"

Freya nodded in response, her head resting heavily on the back of the seat and her eyes fixed on the window. Outside, the green of the countryside rushed past, trees flickered like the slats of a picket fence, creating a stroboscopic effect.

"He told me they had Bam's body flown over to the US. The funeral will be held there. I think he told me what day... I... I can't remember."

Freya closed her eyes to fight the strong wave of nausea.

"Stop," she moaned, and Logan brought the car to a halt. She opened the door and leant out. A spray of white foam gushed from her mouth, leaving a burning coat of acid on her tongue in its wake. A second wave followed, cramping her stomach with stabbing pains, and then a third and final flood of vomit landed in a loud splash on the ground. She hung out of the car for a moment longer, and finally, when she was confident she wouldn't be sick a fourth time, Freya wiped her mouth and sat back down.

"Got it out of your system?" Logan handed her a crumpled tissue, and she took it gratefully.

"Let's hope so. Don't want to gross you out with puking in here."

"Hey, it's your car. I deal with kids who have to overcome drug problems. If you think a little vomit is going to scare me..."

"Thanks." She scrunched the tissue in her hand and stuffed it in her jeans pocket. Her eyes refused to meet his; she just couldn't look at him.

"Do you want to go home, or do you need a little longer?"

"I feel an urge to go back to the house." She glanced over to him this time, and noticed his knuckles were white from gripping the steering wheel. Her eyes went up to his face, which was pale and drawn, and to his tousled hair.

"I feel the same urge." His voice was low, and he gave her a solemn nod. Seconds later, they were driving back up to Angel Manor.

***

Bam watched the car approach the manor. She wrapped her arms around her shoulders, something she used to do as a child. The house was whispering incoherent sentences at her, tugging at her, demanding her servitude. Most of her soul wanted to comply, but there was a stubborn little part of her which rebelled. She wasn't like the others, and though she couldn't completely ignore the demands of the house, she could move more freely than the other spirits. This gave her the opportunity to stay away from her brother's clutches. She could feel his presence, his desire for her. The house wanted him to get her - the house demanded her pain - but Bam wasn't willing to give in just yet.

Outside, she saw her friend get out of the car. Her heart sang out to Freya, and she hoped that her best friend could mean the end of her damnation. She knew the house wanted to protect the bonded humans, and Bam hoped that she could use that knowledge to her own advantage. It was too late for Oliver. Bam felt how deeply his soul had embedded itself into the house, even more so than her own. Freya was a different story. She was tied to the house, but the house didn't own her. Her friend still made her own decisions, and she was Bam's only hope. She wanted nothing more than to be free from Chuck.

Chapter 18

"What's the matter with you, Terrence?" John Norris sat next to him on the stairs they were repairing in the entrance hall. "You look like shit."

"I've been having these nightmares." Terrence rubbed the dust from his eyes and rested his elbows on his knees. The hammering of the tools thumped through his skull and his lungs burned with exertion.

"Nightmares?"

"About my brother. I keep dreaming he's dead."

"Jesus." John's meaty hand slapped on his shoulder, and his elbow slipped from the impact, causing him to almost tip over.

"The scary thing is that the dreams are so realistic, I almost believe that it's really happening to me."

"I had a dream like that once. I dreamt I was going to die. It was the scariest thing ever because I was just waiting for it, you know." John rubbed his temples, his eyes far away with the memory. Terrence just nodded; the coach's words did nothing to ease his mind.

"Yeah, it's just a dream, right?" Long legs clad in dirty overalls stepped around him, pushing him aside to get up the stairs.

"Maybe the dream is trying to tell you something? Maybe you need to go spend some time with your brother? You could go and see him this weekend."

"Yeah... maybe." Terrence stared at his hands, but he knew that if he went back to Edinburgh for the weekend, he might never return. "Could be that these dreams are just me trying to sabotage myself again."

"How do you mean, son?" John squeezed his shoulder, and Terrence felt a weight lift from his stomach.

"I don't finish shit, that's my problem. I find all these fucking excuses to leave before I can get the job done. Now there's this, dreaming about fucking ghosts. And all I want to do is get out of here, but I wonder... is it because of the dreams, or am I just looking for another excuse?"

"Those are some wise words. You are a smart lad. What do you think?"

"I don't know. The dream I had last night, it was just so fucking real. I was actually in this house speaking to my brother's ghost. Then he disappeared and I went for a walk. I even remember crawling back in bed and everything."

"Do you think you saw a real ghost?" The hand squeezed again.

"Nah, man. I don't believe in ghosts."

"And even if you did, why would your brother be all the way out here if he'd died in Edinburgh?"

"He said something about me calling him here."

"Did you?"

"Hell, no. Why the fuck would I do that?"

"Because you miss him? Because you love him?"

"Truth is, Mr Philips, I think it might be a blessing for me to be away from Tyrell for a bit. It lessens the drama, if you know what I mean? Just... Tyrell is home for me, you know? He brings the troubles that come from home. I'm glad to be away from that."

The coach rubbed his hand over Terrence's short hair, and he smiled. "Good lad. I think you'll be all right. We've all seen a change in you on this project. You seem serious now."

"I am, Mr Philips, I really am."

John got to his feet and wiped the dust from his overalls. "Logan is going to Edinburgh this weekend to get some more recruits and see if he can find out what happened to Mace and Farrow. If you change your mind about going to see your brother, let me know, okay?"

"Will do, sir... will do." He scratched an itch behind his ear and smiled. Somewhere in the depths of his mind he heard his brother's voice again. "*Leave.*" Terrence was determined not to let his fear get the better of him. *Not this time.*

***

"You are so beautiful." Oliver ran his fingertips over the icy skin, pale and blue veined like marble. Black eyes looked at him with longing, their hunger almost palpable. She smelled of poppies and the faintest hint of decay. "You become more alive every day. I can feel your skin." He lowered his head and kissed her stomach. The past few days, she had cast off the diaphanous night gown and appeared to him with the promise of more than just a glimpse. All he had to do in return was bring more life to the house. She fed off their energy, and that made her more complete. Oliver could touch her now, and soon he would do more than touch. Soon she would be his. He had dreamt of her since the first day he'd arrived in Angel Manor, but the dreams had gradually become more of a reality. Oliver knew he was obsessed with this creature and he didn't care.

"When are you going to tell me more about yourself?" He kissed her flesh again, and the woman on his bed flickered in and out of existence for a brief second. "You're fading..." His eyes filled with panic, but she sat up and put a cold finger on his lips.

"Only for now. I get stronger every day, and soon you will be able to have me." Her soft breasts pressed against his chest, but to his disappointment they felt only slightly denser than air.

"Let me become whole again."

"I'm trying."

"You know what I am, right?"

"Yes, you are Angel Manor."

"I am. I was alive once, like you. But I became part of this house... as you have. Remember what I told you?"

"My soul... it... it's bound to this house?"

"Yes. You are a guardian, and you are forever tied to here... to me."

Oliver leaned his head back and inhaled, a smile set firmly on his face. "I like that."

She shifted her shape and curled her body around him, light as air and a little warm. His penis twitched in his pants, anticipating a touch that never really came. "You are special, Oliver. You see what the others can't. You know some of the secrets of Angel Manor, and yet you love it. Like a true guardian should. You will protect us, and you will provide us with what we need. Convince the others to help us." Her voice tickled his cheek like a soft breeze.

"Yes, I'll make them see."

"They can't leave here. The house has claimed them. If they leave, they will die."

Oliver nodded, his eyes thick-lidded and the irises turned up, revealing the whites underneath his fluttering lids. His thoughts were no longer lucid in the spirit woman's presence, clouded by intense emotions and longing.

"We must appease the sleeping Master. If he wakes up, we will all be doomed."

"Yes."

"Do you remember how to appease him?"

"Through blood and sacrifice."

"And pain," she added with a deep sultry voice. "Don't forget the pain. It is pain that cleanses a soul. The blood is merely the vessel for the pain."

"Yes, I remember."

"Bring us life, Guardian. We crave it. The souls in Angel Manor grow restless."

"I shall."

"The autumnal equinox draws near. You know what to do?"

"Protect the guardians and bring more life to Angel Manor."

"Good, you will serve us well."

She disappeared like snow before the sun, leaving Oliver with an empty feeling, his own thoughts slowly returning to him.

"There's not much time," he said, still in a daze. "I must hurry."

***

Strong hands guided Freya to the front door of the yellow-bricked building. The presence of the house soothed her, while at the same time making her uneasy.

"I'll be damned," she heard Logan mutter.

"Your headache is gone, right? No more nausea?" Their eyes met, hers still filled with tears.

"I think it went as soon as we came up the drive. Not sure, but I've only just realised it."

"I told you."

"That's just odd. Do the others have it too?"

"I... I don't know. I think Oliver and Bam..." her voice trailed off as she said the name.

"They had it?"

"Yes. And the further away we went, the worse it got. Or maybe it was the longer we went away... I'm not sure. I don't know how this works. To be honest, I thought it was just a coincidence at first."

"I went into town before but it never bothered me. Only this time... and the last, now that I think of it. I remember having a whopper of a headache when I spoke to the police about Mace and Farrow. Just thought it was stress at the time."

"After you had the bloody nose."

Logan cocked his head, silent with his own thoughts for a moment, his index finger tapping his lips. "Yeah, I think so." His brow furrowed and his hold on her tightened. He had said the words quietly, but it still made the hairs on the back of her neck stand on end.

"There's something really weird going in this house, and it frightens me. Bam knew it... and now she's..." Tears spilled from her eyes again, the invisible hand of grief gripping her throat. Logan pulled her towards him, holding her firmly against his chest, where she could feel the steady beat of his heart. His hand gripped her hair tightly, and Freya unleashed another wave of tears. After a few minutes, she managed to compose herself and wiped the tears from her slick cheeks.

"I need to tell Ollie."

Logan held the door open for her, and she stumbled through. Two of the young men were having a coffee break in the entrance hall, and they looked up from their paper cups with raised eyebrows.

"You okay, Miss?" the fellow with dark skin asked.

"I'm okay," she croaked. "Have you seen Oliver? I need to speak to him."

"Did something happen?" He looked alarmed, but Freya couldn't find the energy to put him at ease. She shrugged and bit her lower lip, the muscles in her face cramping with grief.

"Not now, Terrence, okay? I'll talk to you guys later about this." Logan put his arm around Freya again and gently pushed her towards the West Wing. "Get back to work."

The young lads stared for a moment longer, then put their coffee cups on the plastic table and picked up their tools.

"Freya?" Oliver stood in the door opening, his body language stiff and his face filled with concern. "What happened? Why are you crying?"

She pulled away from Logan and flung herself full force at her friend. Oliver was her strongest link to Bam, and she held on to him as if he could somehow undo Bam's death.

"It's Bam..." she managed to say between loud sobs.

"Oh no..."

"Bam..."

"No... don't say it. No."

"Ollie..."

"She's okay, right? She just had an accident or something, but she's fine. Is she in the hospital?" He pushed her away from him, still gripping her arms. "Freya, tell me she's okay."

She couldn't look him in the eyes; instead, she hung her head and cried hot salty tears. Her shoulders shuddered uncontrollably.

"Freya." He shook her firmly, her teeth rattling in her

skull. "Freya, what happened?" The words were slow and deliberate, his tone a mixture of anger and frustration.

"Bam's dead."

Oliver let go of her arms and gave her the most heartbreaking of looks. A second later, his knees buckled and he sagged to the ground. He placed his hands in front of his eyes and a low wail escaped from his mouth, slow and dark, like the howl of a wolf. Freya bent over and wrapped her arms around him, soothing him, his grief giving her the strength she lacked before. His wail grew louder, mingling with sobs and tears.

"Hush, Ollie, hush. It's going to be okay." It wasn't going to be okay, and she knew it, but Freya couldn't think of anything else to say. "It's okay, it's okay," she repeated over and over, her hands raking through his dark brown curls, her own tears joining his. Bam appeared behind Oliver, a wavering vision, distorted by salt water. Freya blinked. She had to be mistaken... she just had to be. As she wiped the tears from her eyes, the figure disappeared and Freya felt an emptiness in her heart.

Chapter 19

The smell of meat and tomato sauce spread through the kitchen, a hint of paint lingering underneath. The paint buckets were still stacked next to the counter, waiting for Freya to finish turning the kitchen into a sunny yellow and bright white modern dining experience. The dark wood, hospital green wallpaper, and loud blue and green tiles that greeted them every morning were too unpleasant. She didn't feel much like fixing or changing anything at the moment, and Freya knew that if she had the luxury of leaving, she would have packed her bags there and then. But the thought of getting one of those terrible headaches was even less appealing than staying. Especially when she considered what had happened to Bam.

Oliver set the Mr Men placemats, one of the many treasures they'd inherited from Bam, on the table. As he was about to set the third one down, he froze.

"I keep forgetting... we only need two now."

"No, not tonight. Put down three. I invited Logan to come and eat with us."

He blinked at her. His movements had been slow the past three days, and Freya was worried about him. Oliver's reaction to Bam's death had been weird: one moment he was grieving, and the next he seemed to be obsessing about the house. She didn't know how to respond to him anymore, and he'd begun to make her feel uncomfortable.

"Something smells nice." Logan stood in the door opening, and Freya felt a surge of gratitude for his presence.

"Thanks for coming, Logan. We're having pasta." Freya put plates of her homemade spaghetti in front of Logan and

Oliver. "I thought it would be a good time to talk." She had just taken one of the pans to the others in the East Wing dining hall. It had surprised her how nicely the room had cleaned up, and with a bit of wallpaper and some new furniture, it could be a very comfortable lounge area for the guests. Only Freya wasn't so sure she wanted to turn the house into a hotel anymore. In fact... she wasn't sure what she wanted to do with it at all.

"I feel we need to talk about the house. About what's happening, but also about our futures."

"What do you mean, about our futures? We have to finish this house. Bam's death shouldn't stop us from doing that. She wouldn't have wanted that." Oliver dropped his fork in the bowl of food and glared at her. His body language was tense, his voice high-pitched with nerves, and something about the way he moved reminded her of a junkie in need of his next fix.

"Everything has changed since Bam died. Not just emotionally, but practically. We're down one person, and that will make running the hotel more difficult. And we don't have Bam's share of the money anymore, which means the first few months of start-up that we planned are almost impossible."

Oliver raised his hand and opened his mouth to reply, but Freya lifted her finger and shot him a stern look. "No Ollie, let me finish. This is about more than money. We need to face it... there is something wrong with this house. I... I don't believe in ghosts, or at least I didn't, but I'm worried. There are things going on that I can't explain. And we need to take them seriously."

Oliver slammed his hand on the table and got up from his seat. "Don't you start with this haunted house shit. Bam..." He swallowed his sentence and sank back down again.

"Yes, Bam felt it too, and she left... and now she's dead."

"Bam slipped in the bath and drowned. In *Glasgow*. Don't blame the house for her death. There was nothing supernatural about it."

"Well, I do." Her hand shot in front of her mouth. It was the first time Freya had said or even thought the words and suddenly, all her feelings came in to focus. "I do blame this house. It makes us sick when we leave, Oliver. I didn't want to believe it, but it does. I've tested it out too many times. Everyone who has had a nosebleed here is stuck in this house. And I'm sure Bam slipped because the house made her so sick. When I le... when I... left her she was very ill. I shouldn't have left her there, but I wasn't thinking straight myself. She didn't get better, but I did... as soon as I set foot back in Angel Manor."

"This is ridiculous. You're full of shit."

"Logan?" Freya's eyes pleaded with the tall man.

"It's not. She's right. I've tested it out the last few days since we got back. I get sick every time I so much as set foot off the grounds. And the further I go, the worse it gets." He scratched his chin. "Duration works too, but less drastic. If you stay near Angel Manor, you're fine except for a small headache. Go further away, the pain grows more rapidly. Though it doesn't lessen when you come back to the area, it only goes away when you step back on Angel Manor property."

"You've been testing it out?"

"Yeah, I wanted to see if it was real."

"You're both nuts." Oliver threw his fork onto the table. It skidded with a loud noise across the surface before jangling against the tiled floor.

"Go and try it yourself. You had a nosebleed, didn't you?"

A silent stalemate played out, the two men staring at each other with daggers in their eyes. Freya sighed. Anger gripped her stomach, but she fought to stay level-headed.

"If the house has that effect on us, we need to get the other people out of here. They don't seem to be bound yet. Let's not wait until they are."

"No." It sounded more like a whine than a word and Oliver slammed both palms on the table this time. "We can't build the hotel on our own. We need their help."

"We're not going to build the hotel. I can't risk having more people tied to this place."

"Do you realise how insane this is?" Ugly red blotches appeared on Oliver's face, and his curls bounced wildly as he spoke. "You want to call off the building project... No, you want to call off our *future* because you think this house is haunted?" He shook his head and stared at her as if she were crazy. Freya began to lose the battle with anger.

"Explain to me why we can't leave the house then? Huh? Give me a good scientific reason? Because Lord knows, I would love to hear one. I don't believe in ghosts either, Ollie, but since I've been here I have seen some weird shit. And I can't deny it anymore. We ignored it before, and now Bam's dead. Dead! And it's our fucking fault." Her hands slammed on the table, palms down, mimicking Oliver's earlier behaviour.

"Fucking hell, Freya..." He threw up his arms in exasperation. "Have you even called a doctor about this? I mean, what you're claiming is outrageous. You could just have some sort of flu."

"That magically stops when we get back to Angel Manor?"

"I don't know. Have you seen a doctor? Wouldn't that be the first logical step?"

She glared at him, his words making her feel sheepish. Freya wasn't a fan of going to the doctor's office, and Oliver knew it. Here, in this strange place where she didn't have her own doctor, she was even less likely to go. There was a good point to what he was saying, if only her instinct wasn't screaming that she was right. Flu wouldn't explain the spirits she'd seen, and it wouldn't explain why Bam had been so frightened, yet she knew she couldn't win this argument with Ollie if she didn't at least get herself checked out.

"I'll go see a doctor, but I still want to stop the work. We can't take any chances."

"We can't stop building. This is our dream." He begged her now, his voice soft and nasal.

"*Your* dream. This was never my dream. I never wanted to come to this fucking house. You and Bam... you wanted this."

Ollie half rose to his feet again, one hand resting on the table while he thrust the other towards her in sharp jagged motions. "You said you were on board. You promised me you were okay with this. Remember? Back before we spent all this time and money? Before Bam died..."

"You're being unreasonable. Don't you think that things have changed?" Their angry voices filled the kitchen and Freya wondered if the young men could hear them.

"Unreasonable? Freya, you're asking me to abandon a project and go home just because you think you might have seen ghosts."

"I'm not asking you to leave, you asshole. That's exactly what I'm saying... we can't fucking leave. This house makes us sick when we do, and I don't know what's going to happen if we stay too far away from it. We might end up like Bam."

"You're really blowing this up out of all proportion, Freya. This isn't like you."

"I just don't know what we're dealing with here. It's starting to freak me out a little. I kept telling myself I was imagining things, but I'm just not so sure anymore. What if there is something going on?"

"See? You're not even sure. You just changed your tone completely. You aren't sure this place is haunted."

"I'm sure enough. How can you deny that weird things are happening?"

"I haven't seen anything weird yet. No furniture has mysteriously moved, and I haven't seen any ghosts. All I have are you and your stories of nosebleeds."

"How about the first day we got here? Remember the brown snot? It disappeared the day after. That's pretty weird, right?"

"We saw it wrong."

"No we didn't, we all saw it."

"Freya... I don't know what to say to you anymore. I think Bam's death is affecting you. You need to stop feeling guilty about it. You didn't leave her to die."

His words were like a punch in her stomach, and for a second, Freya fought for air.

"That's not fair. What you're saying... it's not fair. I..."

"Listen, let's make a deal, okay? Get a doctor to come out here, let him check everyone out, just in case. Please, do that much for me?"

"But what if the house claims more people?"

"Really? Come on. How is it going to claim more people? There haven't been any accidents. Logan, have your boys mentioned anything weird?"

"No. I only know that one of my guys has been having nightmares about his brother's ghost."

Freya pointed at Logan but her eyes remained on Oliver. "See? What if it wasn't a nightmare and he actually saw a ghost?"

"No." Logan shook his head. "I don't think so."

"What do you mean?"

"Tyrell is still alive as far as I know. Unless he died recently, but then we would have heard something. I call in to the centre once a week, and no one has reported anything."

"And without a dead guy, we can't have a ghost." Oliver folded his arms and shot her a smug smile, but Freya wasn't convinced. "So, no one has actually seen a ghost, aside from you and Bam? The two people who have suffered from a fever twice, I believe? And you're sure you're not just sick?"

Freya frowned, the words stuck in her throat, and she fiddled with the nails of her left hand. Part of her wanted to believe Oliver. The world would make a lot more sense if there was no haunting, if Bam had just slipped and fallen in the bath, if her aunt in the car had just been a hallucination. But what of the woman she'd seen the first time they'd broken down the wall to the East Wing? How could she explain her? And the nosebleeds? Could it really be some sort of virus? Suddenly she wasn't sure.

"If we are sick, then the people exposed to us need to be checked out." Oliver took another bite of his food and looked at her over his bowl. There was something in his eyes that she didn't like. *Do I see victory? Does he know he has me?* She turned to Logan, but she saw doubt in his face too. Oliver's truth sounded more plausible than anything supernatural. Why wouldn't he doubt?

"We can't just stop building, not even because of Bam's death. We'll mourn her, and we'll have to make do without her share of the money, I know. But come on, think about what you're saying, think about what you want to throw this all away for? For a hunch? A superstition? You're suggesting we stay behind in a house that's unfinished... a builder's project. It's dangerous, and we can't finish it ourselves."

"He has a point." Logan pulled on Freya's arm, urging her to sit down, and she obeyed.

"We can't risk the guys being here."

"The boys have been here for several weeks now and they're fine. Like Oliver said, there's no real proof that anything is happening in this house. Could be that we really did get some weird virus, or maybe it's the stress. Who knows?" He rubbed his chin and then placed two hands on her cheeks. "I'm not saying you're not right, I'm saying... we just don't know yet. And we need to do a bit more research before we make any decisions. It's not fair on the guys either. This is a big chance for them. These guys come from abusive homes, have been involved with petty crime, and some have nowhere to go back to. Being here is good for them."

"What about your two missing boys?"

"They didn't have nosebleeds as far as I know, and they were runaways. Let's not make more of this than what we've experienced."

"It just feels so wrong."

"Think of it this way: If nothing's happened so far, why would something happen now? Let's get some more information first. How does that sound?"

"Yes." Oliver's voice was eager and there was a hunger in his eyes. "Let's at least try to make it through September."

Logan looked from Freya to Oliver, his face nonplussed "Eh... yeah."

"If they're going to stay, maybe they can put up those walls again?"

"No, let the house be as it is now," Oliver snapped. "I

don't want to put the walls back up."

A sigh escaped Freya's lips, and she felt like she was losing any ground she'd had at the beginning of the conversation.

"What about you, Logan? You're as trapped as we are?"

"I say get that doctor in here before we do anything drastic. Maybe there are other things we can do, like research the history of this house, perhaps talk to some of the locals. I'm sure there are plenty of stories."

"Well, maybe, if you all believe that this house is haunted, we could get some experts in?" Oliver sounded nonchalant, but Freya had a sneaky suspicion there was more to his words than he was saying.

"Only a minute ago you were telling me that I was insane for even suggesting ghosts... and now you're telling me we should get ghost experts in? Make up your mind, Ollie. You're acting weird."

"I'm acting weird? Look at yourself. I'm only accommodating your crazy."

"My crazy?"

"At least then we'll have answers." The smile on his face was smug, and Freya narrowed her eyes, but she had to admit there was some sanity in his words. If there *was* something wrong with this place, she wanted to know about it.

"Fine, Bam did some research on psychics." She walked towards the drawer and pulled it open. Her fingers ran through the clutter of band-aids, matches and other little knick-knacks until she found the piece of paper she was looking for. She fished it out between her thumb and forefinger. With a triumphant smile, she held the piece of paper up and waved it about. "I'll call this lady. It's what Bam wanted all along."

"Let's get on that as soon as possible."

"Whatever. I'll call her in the morning, shall I? To get you your confirmation. And if I do... we're having this conversation again." Freya pushed her bowl of food away from her and got up from the table, her voice tight and her stomach swirling with hot acid. "I don't know what's going on in that mind of yours, Ollie, but you've been acting weird lately. I don't know how to deal with it." She wanted to lash out more, to fight against the defeat she felt, but part of her knew that she couldn't outwit Oliver, not with the arguments he had. She was defending ghost stories for fuck's sake. How could she ever sound sane?

Oliver knew it too, but his slight smile changed to a frown when he looked at her.

"Where are you going?"

"I'm going to search the house and see if I can find that diary Aunt Miriam was talking about in her letter. Maybe that can clear some stuff up."

Logan pushed his chair away from the table with a loud screech, his food also forgotten. "I'll come with you. Best not to wander around the house alone. Everything seems pretty solid, but you never know."

"Thanks." She turned to Oliver again, who was staring into his food with a distant smile on his face.

I don't like how he's acting. I don't like it one bit.

***

"Why did you agree with Oliver to leave the guys here longer?" Freya flicked on her torch as they entered the south corridor. "You could have shipped them out tomorrow."

"I can't just tell them that this project is over... especially not because of a ghost story. I need some time to sort this out."

"I get that."

"Besides, I wasn't kidding when I said most of these boys don't have a good place to get back to. I need to give them time to make arrangements. They were expecting to be here the better part of a year, not the lesser part of two months."

"Yeah."

"I don't fully disagree with Oliver either. Nothing has really happened as far as we know. There are too many variables. Quitting a project is very expensive."

Freya shrugged. She wanted to say something clever, but she was too busy feeling stupid.

"My story sounds pretty crazy, huh? Maybe Ollie is right. Maybe the stress of losing Bam, and the guilt I feel... it... well, I suppose it could be getting to me. Maybe I'm just losing the plot."

His warm hand landed on her lower back, sending jolts of energy through her body.

"Don't be so hard on yourself. I'm a little suspicious too. The 'feeling sick' thing, I've never encountered anything like it before."

"Is it strange that I feel relieved that you at least partially believe me?"

He smiled and his hand rubbed softly against her lower back, and a spark of longing exploded between her thighs. Freya jumped away from his touch.

"What?" Logan took a step back, his eyebrows arched, and he held up both hands in the air. Freya could feel from the heat in her cheeks that her face was most likely beet-red.

"I... it's just..." She struggled to find the words to explain. "That part of my back... when you touch it... I mean... I feel... um... you know..."

"Ticklish?"

"Yes..." she mulled the word over in her mind. "Ticklish will do." The beam from her torch painted his face with light and shadows. His presence had become so familiar to her over the past few days, as if she had known him all her life, and she wondered if the attraction she felt for him was mutual or if he just thought she was nice. She could still feel the warmth of his hand on her skin even though he was no longer touching her, and the arousal she'd felt lingered softly. Logan cocked his head and narrowed his eyes at her, a curious smile playing around his lips, but he didn't say anything.

Freya cleared her throat, the blood still pulsating in her cheeks.

"We should go about this logically. I don't think the diary would be in any random place. My aunt mentioned it in her letter, so she must have assumed I already had it. So what place could I have got it from?"

"Her inheritance lawyers?" Logan moved towards her, the light from her torch spreading across his chest like a blooming night flower.

"Well, yes, that would be logical. But seeing as I didn't get any diary from the lawyers, we should stick to searching the inside of the house."

"You lead the way, I'll follow."

Chapter 20

"Weekend's coming up, guys. Anyone want to go home?" John pushed his Stanley knife into a spotted yellow apple. The skin curled against the side of the blade and fell into his hand, its sweet fragrance escaping into the air.

"Can we go do something else instead?" Angus Reid grabbed one of the apples and sank his crooked teeth into it. "I don't fancy going home much, but I'd like to get out of this house for a bit."

"Yeah. Maybe get a few pints somewhere, you know?" Gary piped in. His skin was greasy and pocked with acne, and he was missing one of his front teeth. Mousy brown hair hung in dirty strands across his shoulders and forehead.

"You can get a few pints in Edinburgh." John watched the young men's body language. They didn't want to leave, he could tell. There was a peace and harmony to the group since they'd come to Angel Manor. It was as if something had clicked with them, that the thought of a new future somehow seemed more promising. Perhaps it was the fresh air that had done them good, or perhaps it was just being away from it all. They had behaved so well over the past few weeks. Even without television, computers and phones they'd been all right. No shenanigans at all. They played card games, read books or listened to their I-pods, or whatever the damned things were called.

It's like the air is filled with tranquilizers or something, John mused, and chuckled at his own joke. It helped that the biggest troublemaker had run away, and that the second biggest seemed keen to turn over a new leaf, though he felt a little worried by how peaky the Jones boy had been looking.

This was the first time the guys had said anything about entertainment. They hadn't complained at all so far. Come to think of it, he hadn't really felt as homesick as he thought he would either. There was no way of calling the missus every night like he usually did, and he didn't really mind. The house had a homey atmosphere, and John felt a pang of guilt for not missing his own home more than he did.

"We'll see what we can do. You've behaved very well so far, so I don't see why we can't go out sometime."

Mason, a geeky-looking boy with glasses, pulled out a deck of cards and held it up. "Who's up for a game?" Two of the three hands shot up; only Terrence looked uninterested. He put the ear buds in and fiddled with the dial on his mp3 player. John was always amazed at technology. He remembered having a Walkman when he was a kid, and that was at least twenty times the size of the little white device. The melancholy look on Terrence's face bothered him, so he got up from his seat and sat down next to the kid.

"How about you go with Jim this weekend? Go home, check out your brother. I know you're worried about him."

Terrence pulled one of the ear buds out and turned to John. "I don't want to."

"Why not?"

"Because if I'm right and my brother *is* dead, I'd rather just not know for a bit longer."

John slapped the young man's shoulder. "I get that. But he's not dead. Those were just dreams. Nothing more, I promise."

"You know, in my dreams he tells me to get out of this house?" His deep brown eyes were round with worry. "He tells me to get out while I still can. But I can't go. I don't know why, but I just can't bring myself to leave here. There's something very comfortable about this place, like I belong here or something. Does that make sense?"

"Yeah." The word popped out of John's mouth before he had time to think. He felt it too. As if the house was asking him to stay. Of course this was a ridiculous thought, and yet... somehow... it wasn't.

***

The attic was cast in the soft glow of moonlight and stars shining through the large bay windows. During the day it was filled with light, but now it looked desolate, and frankly, a little creepy. Freya contemplated turning around and heading back down the thin wooden stairs, only coming back when the sun had chased away the dark shadows. Logan stood right behind her, leaning over her shoulder. His body was warm against hers, and she felt the butterflies flutter in her stomach once again. He reached past her to something dangling in the darkness, and with a firm yank, he brought an array of light-bulbs alive. The light chased away some of the shadows whilst deepening others in the corners. Dust particles danced elegantly in the light beams.

"At least the lights work up here." Logan grinned.

The attic was gigantic, spreading out over the entire house and splitting off over the different wings. Most of it was empty, but in the centre they found a cluster of old furniture, covered by large white sheets giving it the appearance of fat ghosts.

"Maybe we should come back here in the morning." Her voice faltered a little.

"Aren't you curious?" His breath was hot on her cheek, and she was awkwardly aware that she just had to turn her head and her lips would be on his. Her need to get away from the attic was suddenly overpowered by her longing to spend time with Logan.

"I am, but I'm also creeped out."

"Where's your sense of adventure?" He pushed his way past her, his body pressed against hers, and she wondered if he'd done so on purpose. "Besides, I'm here with you. What could happen?"

"Well, I'd rather not tempt fate, thank you." She wrinkled her nose at him, but the scent of his body made her head spin.

"Even if this place is haunted, I've never heard about a ghost harming a person, have you?"

"I've heard of possessions."

A look of worry crossed Logan's face. "Oh right, yeah, there are those. Did anyone ever die from those?"

"I don't know. I think some exorcisms might have gone wrong."

"Well, if we see a ghost, we'll run. Besides, if there are ghosts up here, what's stopping them from getting into the rest of the house? As far as I know, ghosts won't be stopped by walls."

"You're really not helping."

"I'm really not, am I?"

They both laughed, though their laughter was laced with a nervous shrillness. One of the light bulbs flickered slightly, making the shadows dance, and Freya took an involuntary step towards Logan.

"Is it me, or did we just land in a horror movie?"

"If you're real quiet, you can hear the ominous background music." Logan hummed a tune from a slasher film that sounded very familiar, a wicked sparkle in his green eyes.

"Oh, stop it. I would have to at least be in my bra and knickers, running around and calling out 'Billy? Is that you?' Maybe fall down a couple of times."

Logan pinched his chin between thumb and forefinger and gave her a scrutinizing look before nodding in approval. "I'm liking this bra and knickers thing. We should try that out."

She gasped and laughed at the same time, and punched him in the arm. Suddenly the attic didn't seem so frightening, not with him here. *He's flirting with me,* she thought, *or, at least I think he is.* Doubt whispered in her ear.

"You, sir, are no gentleman." She winked at him, secretly afraid he would back off.

"Well, you're making it difficult to be a gentleman if you're talking about running around in your delicates."

She giggled. She hated herself for it, but she giggled. Her legs felt lighter, as did her heart, as she walked further into the attic.

"I wonder what's stored up here." She pulled one of the sheets off the furniture with a loud swishing noise. A snowfall of dust whirled down on her, tickling her nostrils and filling her mouth with the taste of old cotton. A cherry-wood secretary desk gleamed darkly in the sickly yellow light, the wood smooth and polished. Logan grabbed another sheet and pulled.

"Okay, that's more than a little sinister." His voice was quiet, and her skin broke out in goose bumps.

"Sinister?" The lump in her throat made her voice sound high, and she took a few steps in Logan's direction. Her gaze fell onto a faded white lace bassinet, decorated with a large, faded pink bow.

"What's creepy about it? It's just an old cradle."

The corners of Logan's mouth turned down, creating thick creases in his skin, and his eyebrows knotted above his nose. He took a step back from the bassinet and pointed a finger at something inside. Her heart pounded as she stepped closer. In the shadow of the brittle lace curtains, withered with age, lay a porcelain doll. One of the eyes was missing, leaving a dark hole. The remaining eye lay deep within the socket, its pale blue iris and pinprick pupil staring back at Freya. A cobweb of tiny cracks ruined any sweetness on the childlike face, and the side of its mouth was completely blackened. The doll had black hair, perhaps once dressed in curls or another pretty coiffure, but now the hair was thin and stringy, like that of an old woman, and it started too high on the forehead. It was dressed in a white high-collared dress, which was in remarkably good shape compared to the rest of the doll.

"That's the scariest thing I've ever seen." Freya was about to say more when she saw the doll move. Two large, black, hairy legs poked out from the eye socket, and Freya fell backwards against Logan. More legs followed as a fat spider crawled out from the doll's empty eye.

"Nope, I was wrong... *that* was the scariest thing I have ever seen."

"Not a fan." Logan grabbed the white sheet from the floor and chucked it over the bassinet. "Let's never look at that again."

"First spider though."

"What do you mean?" he asked.

"First spider I've actually seen in the house, which is strange, because when we first came here the whole entrance hall was covered in cobwebs."

"Now that you mention it, I've not seen anything either. No spiders... no rats, or anything else. That is a little odd." He plucked at the sheet, making sure it covered the whole crib. "Let's see what's under the rest of them."

"Hopefully, no more spiders."

**

A soft summer breeze played with the curtains of his

bedroom. Oliver sat on the large four-poster bed, eyes fixed on the world outside his window. The temperature in the room lowered and the lucidity of his thoughts became muddled, like ink droplets in a glass of clear water. A smile spread on his lips, his eyes dreamy and distant. Cold fingers ran across his trousers, fingertips tracing his swelling penis.

"Freya wants to send the boys home. To protect them."

"We can't let her do that. We need those young men. We're hungry for company." Her face was close to his, and though he felt a tickle of cold air, he knew it wasn't her breath... not exactly. She was dead, after all, and somewhere in the back of his mind, Oliver was surprised that this didn't bother him. He wasn't afraid of death anymore, not since he met Anne. He believed that death in this house was not that different from life. Angel Manor filled a hole in his soul that he could never define. Oliver, a child of boarding schools and neglect, felt a part of something for the first time in his life. The house wanted him, thought he was special, and he had fallen in love with it. Part of him was jealous of Freya. He knew she was something even more special to the house. She was one of the bloodline. What that meant he wasn't sure, but he felt it. He also knew that when she died she wouldn't live in the house, and he was glad of that. Because when he died, he would stay here, and he would be with Anne.

"You need to give us more living creatures to feast on. We're getting stronger with the equinox approaching."

"The equinox will be this Wednesday. I convinced Freya to get a group of psychics to come and check out the house. That will be more people for you."

"Good."

"It's not easy to invite people here. I can't do too much, or Freya will get suspicious. She has the power to kick me out. It's her house."

"You can't leave here, Oliver. You're mine now." The entity moved closer to him, her face different from before. Less a shadow, more physical. Her pale skin was lined with black veins, and her eyes were set in dark circles, the irises white, with deep, dark pupils that stared into the world the way only the dead could. "You're so warm." The woman's mouth leaked black fluid that dripped in languid trails down her greyish skin. "I crave your warmth." She crawled on top of Oliver, straddling him. He could feel her through his clothing; she had the temperature of meat fresh out of the fridge. There was weight to her shape now, delicious weight that pushed against his pelvis. She moved slowly back and forth, pressing the fabric of his underwear tightly against him. "I was a virgin in life. You will be the first to enter me. Would you like that?"

Oliver nodded, lust exploding like fireworks in his mind and his loins. He didn't see the lecherous corpse that crawled on top of him; instead, he saw something that he desired more than anything else. In the dead white eyes, he saw the power of Angel Manor.

Greyish fingers, topped by broken black nails, peeled away at the fly of his trousers and pushed away the fabric of his boxer shorts. His erection burst forth, and Oliver shuddered when the cold hand wrapped around his warm flesh. She smiled at him, the black liquid dripping further, running over her exposed breasts. Long, glistening trails ran past her dark blue nipples, where they fell like inky raindrops. She lowered her head and pressed her mouth against the tip of his manhood. Oliver closed his eyes and his body shuddered with pleasure.

"I will give you anything you want."

***

To Freya's relief, the rest of the furniture was not nearly as macabre as the bassinet: just an old single bed, a wardrobe, and a table with three chairs. The wardrobe held a plethora of old dresses which looked to be at least a hundred years old. Freya pulled out a green dress and held it in front of her body.

"I think this might fit me."

"Would look nice on you."

"I'd have to wash it first, though, maybe even perform an exorcism before I put it on." She ran a hand over the stiff taffeta. Logan responded with a loud snort.

"Well we could always opt for the bra and knickers thing. I'm still a fan of that idea."

"You're not letting that go, are you?"

"Not anytime soon, no."

Her hand hid her smile as she put the dress back in the wardrobe.

"I think that writer's desk will be our best bet, if we can get it open." She stepped closer to the cherry-wood piece and inspected the brass lock holding the rolling shutter closed. Underneath there were four drawers, each with their own identical lock. "We didn't happen to come across a key anywhere, right?"

"Let me give it a go." Logan fished a Swiss army knife from his pocket and pulled a thin blade out. "How attached are you to the desk? I can't guarantee that I won't scratch it."

"Hack away. I have no need for it."

Logan placed the tip of the knife in a small crevice at the bottom of the rolling shutter. He pried at the metal, and seconds later, a small click signalled his success. With nimble fingers, he pulled the rolling shutter up, revealing a solid desktop underneath. There were a few writing utensils, placed in such an orderly way that it took Freya by surprise. A dark blue leather-bound notebook, the cover cracked with age, sat in the middle of the desktop. Around it lay three old-looking fountain pens and a dried up inkwell.

"Could this be the journal?"

Freya shrugged and carefully picked up the leather bound volume. The leather crackled under her fingers as she opened the cover. The pages were yellowed and brittle under her touch. The words were written in a cursive handwriting, impossible to read in the dim attic light.

"I don't think this is it. Too old. My aunt said she wrote me instructions, but this looks like something before her time. I'm curious to read what it says, though."

Logan looked over her shoulder, his chest pressed against her back and his cheek against her ear. "That's interesting handwriting. Very legible."

"Might have to go over that tomorrow." She closed the book. "Maybe there's something in the drawers. Do you think you can get them open too?"

"Shouldn't be too much of a problem." Logan leaned over and took something from the desk. With a bright smile, he held up a brass key, the same colour as the locks. "This might just make it a lot easier."

Freya made a huffing sound and snatched the keys from his fingers. She squatted in front of the dresser and opened the locks to all the drawers one by one. Carefully, she pulled the bottom drawer open, but found nothing but tiny scraps of dried-out paper and a thick layer of dust. The second drawer was equally empty, and with a surge of impatience, she skipped the third drawer and went straight for the top one. A large scrapbook filled the space, and Freya wrapped her fingers around it and lifted it from the drawer. Its pages were fragile, though not as brittle as the notebook's had been, and from the cover, she guessed it wasn't as old. A plethora of cut-out newspaper articles filled the pages, as well as black and white photographs which had turned a beige colour over the decades. All the articles had something in common: Angel Manor.

"There has to be answers in here. We should take it

downstairs and read it in better light."

"Sure." Logan touched the lower part of her back again, his fingers running teasingly along the rim of her jeans.

"Stop that," she gasped.

"I'm sorry." He smiled and didn't look sorry at all. "I forgot you were... ticklish." Then his arm reached out again and she felt his fingers press against her lower back once more. Another surge of energy tingled through her body, more intense than she'd ever felt before.

"Stop it." She panted the words, taking another step back.

"Say Uncle." He grabbed her wrist and pulled her towards him.

"Uncle, Uncle!" she yelped, "Please, don't tickle me there. I'm serious... it's not just ticklish... I..." She looked up at him and the smile melted off his face, replaced by a look of incomprehension.

"Oh, sorry... uh..." Realisation dawned on him and his eyebrows shot up. "Oh. Do you mean..."

"This is so embarrassing." She hid her face in her sleeve. Logan removed her arm and tugged her towards him. Then he placed his hand on her lower back and stroked it gently. She looked into his eyes, and he held her gaze with an intense stare. Her whole body responded to his touch, and when he lowered his mouth onto hers, she eagerly accepted his kiss. Their mouths worked together in a harmonious rhythm, and Freya's knees weakened.

The floor shuddered under their feet, and the temperature around them became a few degrees warmer.

"Did you feel that?" Freya broke away from the kiss. "I think the earth just moved."

Logan didn't answer her; his eyes were glazed over with hunger. His lips met hers again with even more passion, and his fingers pulled at the buttons of her white cotton shirt, exploring the naked skin underneath. She answered his kisses, but more tentative this time. She felt uneasy... watched. Logan pushed her towards the single bed and she resisted a little, putting her weight against him, but he was too strong. He laid her down on the mattress, which smelled stale, like unwashed laundry.

"Not here," she muttered through his kisses. "Let's go downstairs." But if he heard her, he didn't respond, his hands pulling her blouse away from her breasts. Freya tried to fight the lust she felt, but it was too overwhelming, and she couldn't pull away from his touch. His lips pressed to hers, his fingers slid underneath the white lace of her bra, and the tips of his first two fingers clenched her nipple, creating a burst of pleasurable pain. She pushed her body against his, a haze settling over her thoughts, her hands pulling at the zipper of his jeans. Somewhere in the back of her mind, she heard the buzz of voices, too far away to make out, yet she knew what they were saying. They talked of life and love and sex, of guilty pleasures and of hedonism. Something was controlling her actions and she couldn't resist it, so instead, she gave in to the delicious feeling.

In the wrestle of passion, clothes were discarded, naked bodies entwined. Freya spread her legs and welcomed Logan inside her.

***

The house shuddered as it felt the energy flow from the living souls in the attic. The heir of the bloodline connected to the essence of the house in an unconscious way, her lust merging with its hunger. Never were humans as alive as they were during copulation, and the house trembled with ecstasy. This new heir was everything it had been promised, and it had waited for her for more than a century. Change was palatable. Even the spirits felt it, and they roamed restlessly around their enclosed spaces.

Angel Manor had been fed only a few scraps over the

years, keeping the souls from previous deaths in its walls but rarely finding the opportunity to pick fresh meat from living bones. The Guardians had seen to that. As soon as a soul was bound to the building by the heir, they were protected from the house's ravenous appetite. However, the spirits could be creative, and fear, lust and anger still filled its needs.

The autumn equinox was near, and it longed to deliver sweet pain and suffering. More spirits would mean a more developed consciousness for Angel Manor; it fed on their essence and turned it into its own being. The house wanted to fill its halls with more souls to punish. The master who slept demanded it. It was the bargain that had been struck.

***

Bam watched the two bodies merge, and she felt a mixture of desire and fear. She wanted to warn Freya, to tell her that her lust was feeding the house, making it stronger, but she couldn't. Her freedom was so limited. Somewhere below her, she could sense Chuck searching for her. It took all the energy she had left to keep him at bay, but Bam knew that soon she would lose the struggle, and he would find her. When he did, Bam feared she might lose her last bit of freedom.

***

Freya didn't notice the first spider until it was on his cheek, fat and hairy, tapping its long legs with slow impatience. Freya groaned with pleasure as Logan thrust himself inside her, her hips moving in perfect harmony, until she saw it. At that moment, her moan of pleasure turned into a scream. Logan stopped, his glassy eyes suddenly cleared, and he shook his head. Freya couldn't stop screaming, especially when she saw the other spiders, and there were many. Dozens or more, crawling all over his naked body... and to her horror, she saw they were crawling on her too. For a second, the world seemed to stand still, then the two lovers broke loose, each scrambling to their feet and smacking the swarming creatures from their bodies.

Freya screeched and jumped around from side to side, slapping herself with such ferocity that red marks imprinted on her skin. Logan's movements were calmer, but from the look in his eyes, Freya could tell he was freaked out too.

"What the fuck, what the fuck, what the fuck!" Freya chanted, still slapping at the eight legged intruders. "Where did they come from?"

"The mattress." Logan swatted a large spider from his shoulder and flicked at another on his leg. He shuddered. "They must have come out of the mattress."

"I told you we should have gone downstairs. What were you thinking? This place is the scariest part of the house, and we have sex here?" With a yelp, she brushed a row of spiders from her breast. "Oh God, are there any on my back? Get them off, get them off!" She continued hopping about, smacking and flicking. Logan, who must have seen her need was greater than his own, moved forward and helped her.

Even when he assured her all spiders were gone, and she could see he didn't have any on him, she could still feel their legs all over her. Her heart pounded.

"Where did they go? I can't see a single spider now." Logan scanned the floor, the position of his shoulders betraying the tension he felt.

"I don't know, and I don't care. This place gives me the creeps." Freya stepped into her pants, then fumbled with her bra, hooking up the back as fast as she could. Logan inspected his jeans then pulled them on over his boxers. He leaned over to grab his shirt and froze.

"Logan?" Her voice sounded childlike with fear. "What's wrong?"

"You were right." He stood, the shirt forgotten at his

feet, his long muscled torso straightened to his full height.

"About what?" Freya's lip trembled slightly and lump formed in her throat.

"Ghosts." His hand rose with an aggravating slowness, and his finger pointed towards a dark corner of the attic.

She knew she had to turn around, even though she didn't want to. Her head rose slowly, as slow as Logan's finger had, and when she looked, terror gripped her.

In the dark depths of the corner, away from the window, stood at least a dozen children of different ages, all huddled together. They were near naked, dressed in old camisoles and tattered underwear, stains covering the greyish white fabric. Their hair sprung in knotted, greasy tangles from their scalps. Some were tall and some short, but they were all malnourished and gaunt.

"Oh my God." Freya's hand moved to her mouth. She felt frozen to the spot. "Logan, you see them too?"

He didn't answer her, but she felt his hand wrap around her arm. She followed him slowly, her eyes still on the children. Her thoughts flashed towards her aunt, who had sat next to her in the car, to her mother who had always feared this house, and to her time as a child in the cellar. All she wanted was to get away from the dead children with their melancholy stares. The children stepped forward, moving as if someone was pulling their strings, their thin arms outstretched. They opened their mouths in unison, and the sight of the dark, wide openings was more than Freya could bear. She turned and ran, Logan right behind her. The children's cries echoed through the attic, long wails, wordlessly pleading for rescue. Her heart pounded in her throat as she reached the stairs, and she clung on to the railing to avoid falling. Even on the floor below, she could still hear the children crying. Something inside her knew that the children didn't want to harm her, but that didn't lessen her fear.

"Are you okay?" Logan wrapped his arms around her and held her tight. The house went silent again, and Freya burst into tears.

"I don't know, Logan. I really don't know."

Chapter 21

The boys were lively as they piled into the narrow pub. The interior was bright with its fresh, white paint and wooden tables and chairs. Terracotta tiles lined the floor, smelling faintly of spilled ale and floral cleaning products. The crowd inside was varied in age and appearance, and Terrence guessed that there were quite a few tourists mingling with the locals. He had been afraid that they would walk into a pub filled with old geezers who would stare at them and give them a right bollocking for being young and foreign... but there were plenty of other English people sitting around the tables. He even spotted a few ladies that were a bit of all right. Terrence smiled. This could be an interesting night after all.

They made their way between the scattered square tables, Mr Norris leading them with Mr McLeod bringing up the rear, until they found a nice, quiet spot near the back. It was early still, and Terrence wondered if the pub would get livelier. There were certainly a few people here, but the younger ones might move on somewhere else later. It was anyone's guess how the evening would pan out, but Terrence felt a small pang of gratitude for being out of the house. As long as he was in the house, he felt fine, but now that he put some distance between himself and Angel Manor, he wondered if it wasn't a good idea to go back to Edinburgh after all. There would be other projects, and he was a bit worried about his brother. He decided he'd try his brother's mobile phone to see if he could get in touch with him.

Everyone took a seat, either on the wooden chairs or the stone bench sticking out of the wall on the other side of the table. Mr Norris got up to get everyone a pint. Terrence slipped his hands in his pockets and fished out two pounds and three fifty pence coins, scanning the room for a phone.

"Don't worry, Terrence, drinks are on John and myself tonight. You boys deserve it."

"Oh, thanks, Mr McLeod, but that's not what I got the money out for. I was going to call Tyrell."

"Oh, sure. I think I saw a phone over there." Mr McLeod pointed in the direction of the toilets.

"Thanks." Terrence got to his feet and slid past Gary, whose fingers fiddled with one of the cardboard coasters. "Move aside, you fat fuck." His knee connected with Gary's leg, and Gary made himself as small as he could, his eyes shooting daggers at Terrence. To make up for his rudeness, Terrence ruffled his friend's hair as he walked past.

He spotted the phone from a distance, but was distracted by the lovely ladies at one of the tables he passed. There were three of them, a natural redhead, a dye-job blonde, and a girl with milk chocolate skin and bleached extensions. They wore tops that showed off their breasts, and Terrence was a man who admired female chests of all sizes, especially when they were on such lovely display. He gave the girls a smile, and to his satisfaction, they smiled back in a flirtatious way. After his phone call, he would have to see about buying these ladies a drink with the few bob he had in his pocket. His mind automatically went to Tyrell, who had always been his wing man, and he thought of what his brother had said in his nightmares. *No way are you gay, T,* Terrence thought. *You're better at pulling birds than I am.*

He picked up the black receiver and pushed the coin into the slot, waited until there was a dial tone, and pressed Tyrell's mobile phone number. After several rings, the phone went to voicemail.

"A pleasant evening to you, ladies and gentleman," Tyrell sounded from the other side, a hint of laughter in his voice, imitating a posh accent. "I am presently unavailable to converse with you over the telephone..." he actually snorted when he said the word 'telephone', "... but if you would be so kind as to leave your name and number, I shall return your call at my earliest convenience. Otherwise, I would kindly ask you to go fuck yourself, you impatient cunt." A sharp beep interrupted his laughter, and Terrence shook his head with a smile of his own.

"Yo, T-Dog. It's your baby brother. My mobile doesn't work in the house and I forgot to charge it before I came out, so I'm calling you from a payphone, but if you could drop me a line, send me a text or something... I'm a bit worried about you." His ears felt hot when he said the words, and he pictured his brother laughing at him for saying them, but it was how he felt, and he would rather Tyrell call him back to mock him than not call him back at all.

With a sigh, he hung up the receiver and placed his head against the cold plastic of the phone. He knew that the ghostly image of Tyrell was just a dream, but he'd feel so much better if he could hear his brother's voice for real, not just through voicemail. He took a deep breath to collect himself, then managed to conjure a smile.

On his way back, he stopped by the table with the three girls. He guessed them to be his age, maybe a year or so younger, and he slid onto the stone bench next to the dye-job.

"Evening, ladies. I thought I'd come and say hello." He offered a toothy smile and a wink, and the girls giggled.

"Just a hello?" The blonde had a thick Scottish accent. Her eyes were dark blue and stared at him from under heavily made-up lids. Thick black lines made her eyes almond shaped, and the purple eye shadow brought out the blue of her irises nicely.

"Well, I'd ask you how you like your eggs, but I reckon we need to save that question for the morning." He winked again, and she rewarded him with a crooked smile.

"Bless ye," she giggled. "What's yer name then?"

"Terrence."

"Well, Terrence, ah'm Emma, this is Lindsey," she tapped the black girl on the arm then pointed at the redhead, "and that wee lass over there is Bonnie."

"Are you local girls?"

"Aye, that we are. And where are you from?"

"London."

The girls made 'whoooo' noise and turned to each other with meaningful glances.

"Eh, and what's a Londoner doing on our little isle, then?" It was Lindsey who spoke, and her dark eyes gleamed at him. He liked how the red of her lipstick stood out against her beautiful skin, and he imagined running his hands through her extensions and pulling them slightly.

"Well, I've been living in Edinburgh for the last eight years."

She cocked her head and gave him a wry smile. "Why come to Skye then?"

"I'm here on a job."

"A job, eh?" Her eyebrow raised slightly, the corner of her mouth curled in an attractive manner.

"Yeah, I'm one of the construction workers in this house called Angel Manor."

The girls stared at him.

"You mean Lucifer's Lot?" The dark girl's mouth twisted in an amused sneer.

"What?"

"That creepy old house on Lucifer Falls. We call that Lucifer's Lot."

"Have ye seen any ghosts yet?" It was Bonnie who spoke

up now, her accent so thick he could hardly understand her. She had a very soft lisp, which was most apparent when she said the word 'ghosts'. Terrence didn't like where this conversation was going. It had taken a lot of energy to convince himself that he hadn't seen anything supernatural, and now these three girls were telling him that maybe he had. He lost control of his thoughts for a few seconds, but then the sight of Angus snapped him back. Angus had spotted him too, and he sat down on one of the empty chairs.

"Hello then. What's this, Terrence? Been keeping these lovely ladies all to yourself, have you?" Angus grinned at the women, who looked a little startled at first, but then broke out into smiles and giggles.

"Angus, meet Emma, Bonnie and Lindsey. Ladies, meet Angus." They shook hands and exchanged smiles.

"What were you talking about then?"

"Ghosts." Emma cocked her head at Angus and fluttered her eyelashes.

"Eh?"

"Angel Manor... apparently the house has another name." Terrence raised one eyebrow and touched the side of his nose with an index finger. "And it's a real fucking charming one too."

"Do tell?"

"Lucifer's Lot. You know because of Lucifer Falls." Lindsey smiled.

"Well, ye know that tha place used ta be a convent about two hundred years ago, right? They took care of little orphan children. Until one o' tha nuns burned it doon." Emma looked around the table and smiled at her captive audience. Terrence liked the way she smiled, and he was tempted to put his hand on her knee under the table.

"Only two people survived: a nun and a wee girl. They

218

thought tha nun might'a torched tha place, but no one knows tha real story. Ye know how things go; people talk an truth turns in'te urban myths."

"Emma loves her myths," Lindsey giggled, and took a sip from her pint of cider.

"It's an interesting place." Emma focused her gaze on her glass, her finger moving around its rim in a circular motion. Terrence could see the excitement in her face. "Years after tha convent burned doon, tha wee girl came back. She'd been an orphan, but this rich family adopted her, so she had a lot o' coin. Her adoptive parents died or something. There's stories that say she killed them, and tha t'was tha little girl who set fire ta tha convent." She put her lips to her glass and took a sip, allowing her audience to mull the words over. "Whatever happened, tha nun and tha child built tha house and called it Angel Manor, in honour of tha burned down convent, because tha t'was called tha Holy Angels Convent, see? They used to call tha nuns tha Angels."

"Aye, only they weren't angels at all, were they, Emma?" Lindsey raised her eyebrows.

Emma leaned forward, lowering her voice. "No, ah hear that tha Sisters were really Satan worshippers. There was an article about tha convent. The kids went in, but never came out. No one ever knew what happened ta them. And that convent was centuries old, but there was no record of any o' tha kids after they got to tha orphanage. They just disappeared." She leaned back with a smug smile. "There'll be some stuff on it in tha library."

"I don't know. I think in this case, 'ignorance is bliss' works fine for me," Angus muttered. "I've got to sleep in that house, you know? I'm already happy no one died in the house itself, just in that convent."

"Are ye kidding? Lots of people died in that house." It was Bonnie who spoke now, her soft voice cutting through the background noises of the other customers. "Some of them even died in our lifetime."

"Aye, like the previous owner and her three children. Everyone who's ever lived in that house has been a complete recluse, but apparently two o' tha old lady's children tried ta run away from tha house a few years ago, both adults mind ye. One o' them fell in love and wanted ta get married and have kids, tha other just followed. Both died within four days of leaving."

"What does that have to do with the house though? They didn't even die there." Angus lifted his hands in front of him as if he were defending himself against blows, and Terrence snorted.

Emma ran her fingers through her hair, her eyes dark. "They say that once tha house has ye in its grasp, it won't let ye go."

"That's comforting." Terrence felt the blood drain from his cheeks, and he thought of the dreams he'd had about his brother again. They'd been so realistic.

"Anyway, tha old lady and tha last son died in tha house itself. He went first. Killed himself he did."

"Nice." Angus pulled a face.

"That whole house is built on blood," Emma said. "It started with tha construction. At least four men died during tha building o' tha house, an' another two disappeared without a trace."

Terrence and Angus exchanged a look, and Terrence saw his own worry reflected in his friend's eyes.

"Disappeared? Two guys disappeared?" Terrence stared hard at Emma. "Two?"

"Aye, two... why?"

"Fuck, mate... we had two guys disappear from our group. The coaches think they ran away, but I'm not so sure now."

"Ye're having me on." She leaned back a little, an incredulous smile on her face.

"Nope. Go ask if you don't believe me. We called the police and everything."

"What did tha police say?"

"Well, the guys who ran away are notorious for sodding off. They contacted the boys' parents and stuff, so I guess if they don't show up sooner or later, they'll make a case out of it."

"Could just be them then, not tha house."

"Yeah, could be. But it just struck me as odd, them leaving like that."

"Maybe the house ate them." Lindsey said and laughed. Bonnie giggled along, but there was an eager gaze in Emma's eyes.

"Ah've always wanted to see that house from tha inside." She looked directly at Terrence now. "Do ye think ye could sneak us in?"

"Eh..."

"It sounds like a right scary place. And ah always get really horny when ah'm scared." Her bottom lip pouted a little and she fluttered her eyelashes.

"Yeah, we can sneak you in," Angus said. He clapped his hands together with anticipation. "How about tonight? Unless Sunday night isn't convenient for you. Don't know if you have school in the morning or something."

"We'll be fine, right girls?" Emma looked at the other two, and Terrence saw that Bonnie looked a little frightened. He didn't like the idea of the girls going to Angel Manor, but at the same time, the thought of having horny girls to play with in the dark cancelled out any fears he might have had.

"You can't ride with us. The coaches won't have it. Do you have a ride?"

"Aye, I got a car." Lindsey lifted her hand, the action almost childlike, and they all laughed a little.

"Well, if you go to the house after one o'clock, that's when everyone's usually asleep. We can sneak out and let you in through the back door. Make sure you park your car out of sight."

The girls nodded.

"This is gonna be so cool," Emma said, and something about her keenness made Terrence's heart sink.

***

Freya squinted at the letters on the page, but they were difficult to read and she felt like flinging the notebook across the room. Instead, she let out a stifled scream and punched the armrest of the chair.

"Why did this person write in chicken scratches?"

"Found nothing, eh?" Logan looked up from his own study with a weak smile. He cleared his throat and scratched the back of his neck. "I can't really concentrate on mine."

"Can you at least read it?"

"Yes, but..." His green eyes sought hers, but Freya looked away. "Damn it, Freya, should we talk about what happened in the attic?"

She raised her eyebrows. "The ghosts? We talked about that, and now we're trying to find out who they are."

"No, not the ghosts..." He put the book down, got up from his seat and crouched down next to her, his hands on either side of her, gripping her arm rests. She couldn't look away from him; he was too close. "Freya, we had sex. Very weird sex... we should talk about this."

"What's there to talk about?" Her cheeks burned.

"I don't know... maybe just what you think about all this. I mean, I know I wanted to have sex with you, but I'm not even sure if you had voluntary sex with me or if... if..." He looked from side to side, desperately trying to find the words.

"Or if it was the house?" She finished the sentence for him, her confidence blossoming from his insecurity. His face lifted, the expression he wore either hopeful or tormented, Freya couldn't tell. "It wasn't the house. Though perhaps the house sped up the process a little." She put a hand in front of her mouth to hide her smile, but it soon turned into a laugh. Logan's face cleared up with obvious relief, and he joined her laughter.

"It was certainly intense." He shook his head, still laughing.

"Oh God, and the spiders. That was just... horrifying."

"Yeah, that's a night I won't soon forget. I wish it could have been different though. I would have liked it to have been a bit more... special." He leaned forward and pulled her hand away from her mouth.

"Protection would have been a good idea too."

Logan recoiled a little. "I didn't even think of that. Holy shit, are we in trouble here?"

"No, I'm on the pill, and I'm pretty sure I have no icky diseases. I hope you don't."

"Clean." His face was stern. "I've been tested recently. I... I... like to be safe."

She nodded, her eyes averted. "That's good then. I think we should be okay. Just... if we're ever going to do this again... maybe better safe than sorry?"

"So..." He tilted his head and raised an eyebrow, offering her a crooked smile. "There's a chance we might do this again?"

Chapter 22

"Ah can't believe we're doing this." Bonnie shuddered and pulled her coat close around her. The end of summer was still warm, but the nights were getting chillier. "Noo, ah don't mind going inside that spooky house, but do we have to do it at one in the bloody morning?"

"Ach, where's yer sense o' adventure?" Emma pushed her hip against Bonnie, who had to take a step to the side in order to keep her balance. "What if we see a real ghost?"

"What if the house eats us?"

"Dinnae be daft." Emma made a 'pshhh' sound and waved her hand at her friend. Her mind was wrapped in a happy fuzz from the alcohol, and Lindsey, the only sober one, clung on to her arm as they made their way up the hill towards the old Manor.

"Are ye sure we needed to park the car all the way down there in the bushes? Ah don't think anyone is expecting us, ye know?" Bonnie glared down the steep hill to where the vehicle was parked, but it was impossible to see it in the moonlight. "Ah think we might be being a bit too James Bond about this."

"Better safe than sorry." Lindsey winked at Emma, who nodded in agreement.

"Always wanted ta see tha inside of that house." Emma slurred. She added as an afterthought, "Jesus, this hill is a wee bit steep, isn't it? Ah wish ah wasn't wearing heels. Ah'm too pissed for this bollocks."

"Oh please, ah've seen ye a lot worse than this." Bonnie giggled, and Lindsey laughed along. Emma just shrugged and rolled her eyes. The three girls climbed the steep hill and carefully made their way towards the building.

"Look at those angels," Bonnie said with a deep sigh.

"Those survived tha fire," Emma said. "They cleaned them up apparently. T'was a miracle they didn't burn with tha rest o' tha stuff."

"Does stone even burn?"

Emma shrugged. "Ah don't know, ah guess it does, considering tha convent burned ta tha ground."

"Don't be stupid." Lindsey shook her head. "Stone doesn't burn. The convent burned to the ground because buildings often have wooden structures inside. They burn, and then the stone collapses, usually breaking when it does."

"Oh." Emma felt a bit sheepish. "Well, there ye have it then. Tha angels miraculously survived tha falling stones."

"Can we go look at them up close?" Bonnie inched forward.

"They're right in front o' tha front entrance. Ah'm not sure if that's such a good idea. We're supposed ta meet tha guys round back or something."

"Psst." The harsh whisper cut through the darkness, and the three girls froze in their tracks. Emma felt Lindsey's fingers dig into her skin and she hissed with pain.

"Ladies?"

The voice came from the shadows, and it was Emma who first moved towards the sound. Lindsey trailed one step behind, her hand still around Emma's arm. Two guys were standing near some bushes, and one waved at them.

"There ye are," Emma whispered loud enough for everyone to hear. "We were wondering how we were going ta find ye. This house is pretty big. Ah had no idea where we were supposed ta meet." The two young men stood side by side, their faces cast in shadows. "Lead tha way."

"We'll go in through the back. The others are waiting for you inside."

"You're going ta give us a tour of tha house, right? Show us some of tha really scary places?"

"Of course. Come on." The black guy made a motion with his hand and walked towards the back of the large mansion. He was shorter than Emma remembered. The other guy trailed behind. He was handsome, his tousled hair a mousy brown colour, though his face looked a little gaunt in the moonlight. He was dressed in a thick black jumper and had his hands pushed deep into his jeans pockets.

They snuck around the building. The girls followed the lead of the dark-skinned guy, who crouched as he walked, and they all tried to be as quiet as possible. They stopped at a pair of white painted terrace doors, and the guy held open the door for them. Emma smiled gratefully.

"Thank ye, Terrence."

The boy paused for a moment, then he smiled. "I'm Tyrell."

"Ah thought ye said yer name was Terrence?" She squinted at him.

"Terrence is my brother."

"Och, well ye two look a lot alike." Emma shrugged.

"We've been told that before." He smiled at her, and a shiver ran down Emma's back. His eyes didn't smile along with his mouth, she noticed. "Go on in."

***

Bam watched the three girls from the window. Her eyes were fixed on Chuck, who leered at the living flesh the way he used to focus his attention on her. She still feared him and the sight of him turned her cold.

227

A wave of emotion passed over her, amplified by the Manor. The young women were suddenly the focus of her attention, as an inner predator took over her senses. Thoughts of pushing sharp blades into their skin and watching the blood well up made the space between her legs tingle with the heat of desire. She pictured peeling their skin and plucking the gleaming muscles underneath like a harp.

Something in her shifted, and the murderous thoughts were replaced by a deep inner shame.

These are not my thoughts. I don't want to hurt anyone. Yet she knew part of her did, now that the inhibitions of life were gone. The house egged her on, toyed with her thoughts and feelings, made demands... but she couldn't just blame the house. That primal hatred had been inside her when she was alive, but she'd kept it at bay with kindness and logical thoughts. Now that she was dead, all of those deeply hidden emotions were beginning to surface. They were confusing and a little exciting too. In this new existence she had choices to make. Bam narrowed her eyes as the girls disappeared into the manor. She pictured them dying... screaming.

***

"I don't think your girlfriends are coming." Gary Feltman patted his arms. The night was nippier than before, and he was only wearing a t-shirt. "I've been standing here freezing my nuts off for over an hour, and still no sign of them. When did it get so cold anyway? It was positively balmy last night, and it was fine when we came out here."

"Women are always late," Angus retorted with false wisdom. "They could still come."

"Were they hot?"

"What?"

"The girls, were they hot?"

"Two of them were. One was a bit pasty." Angus wrinkled his nose to show his distaste for girls with red hair.

"I... I don't mind pasty." Mason Applebaum muttered, grinning in his shy way. The young men laughed in return, and Angus hooked his arm around Mason's neck. Mason struggled, but Angus was stronger and he pulled him down, his knuckles rapping against the top of Mason's head.

"Fuck this. I'm going back in the house," said Terrence, who had been sitting on the lowest branch of a tree in the hope he could see further down the hill. "They're not coming. I'm sick of this."

"Fucking prick teases." Angus let go of Mason, his voice dripping with disappointment. "Scary makes them horny, my arse."

"Welcome to blue ball city." Gary laughed at his own joke, but the other guys were too glum. They walked back to the house, none of them having spotted the red car in the bushes a little further down the hill.

***

The high ceilings, in combination with the empty walls and floors, made the South Wing intimidating, and the smell of the place was less than pleasant, like an animal had died somewhere long ago and no one had quite managed to get the scent out. Lindsey felt a slight pang of regret for coming along to this house in the dark. She wasn't sure where she stood on the idea of ghosts, but being here alone with several young men while no one knew where they were suddenly seemed like a bad idea. They knew nothing of these guys, and the house was miles away from civilisation. If the boys were up to no good, no one would ever find them. The thought worried Lindsey, but she didn't want to voice her concerns out loud. She had been fine with the idea when it was first suggested. In the pub, the two boys looked charming and attractive, but when these two had come to collect them, she'd lost her confidence. There was something in the way the white guy looked at her. His eyes were intense and so dark, Lindsey wondered if he was high on something. She knew there were four of them here - that's what that cutie Terrence had said - but now four guys sounded like more than three girls could handle.

"Are ye going ta give us tha tour then?" Emma's whisper sounded like a hiss.

"We're going to take you to the others first. Then you can roam the house as much as you like." Tyrell's voice was cold and distant, and it made Lindsey's skin crawl.

"Where are the others?" Lindsey forced her tone to be airy.

"In the basement."

"That's a little sinister... the basement. You're not serial killers are you?" She laughed at the joke, but there was no mirth in her laughter. Tyrell stopped walking and turned around, his face clear in the bright moonlight shining through the windows.

"We're in the basement so we don't wake the owners."

The white guy took a step behind her, standing too close for comfort. His accent was American. "You're not afraid of going to the basement, are you?"

The basement scares the shit out of me, Lindsay thought. She caught Emma's eye, and pleaded silently with her. She knew how badly Emma wanted to see the house, and she knew she was being silly. Of course these guys weren't going to harm them, they were nice guys, or so they had appeared to be in the pub. And there was supervision somewhere in this house, so they wouldn't really try anything. She was sure of it.

"I'm not scared." She put her hand on her hip and looked at the black guy with arrogant confidence that she really didn't feel. "Lead the way."

Tyrell began down the hall. There was something almost robotic in the way he moved, but Lindsey convinced herself that she was being melodramatic. They had gone to stranger places with stranger guys, she decided, and they'd been fine then too.

"This is the place, ladies." Tyrell stopped at a heavy-looking door, different from any other doors they'd passed. It looked like metal. Any doubt that Lindsey had pushed aside came rushing back when Tyrell opened the door, revealing stairs leading down into darkness.

"I'm not going down there. That place looks crazy." She folded her arms around her chest and planted her feet firmly on the ground. "Show us someplace else."

"Aye, it's too dark for my liking as well," Emma said, staring down into the darkness. "Ah don't want ta go down there."

"We need you to be one of us, then you can roam the house."

"And what the fuck does that mean? Be one of..." The words died on Lindsey's lips. Thick dark blood oozed from Tyrell's left temple, his eyes were sunken more than they'd been before, and the brown of his irises were covered with a film of white. "What the fuck have ye done to yer head?" Lyndsay's words were cut short by Bonnie's scream. The white guy's face had started to rot, and thick, yellow maggots wriggled around the corner of his mouth.

"The house wants you ladies, and the house shall have you," the American guy said. "The Angels are waiting." Lindsey took another step back, her eyes fixed on Emma and Bonnie. She realised what Tyrell was about to do a second too late, and before she could warn her friends to move away, the black guy slammed the heavy door against them. Emma fell backward immediately, but Bonnie fought back, trying to push the door away. Tyrell didn't allow her to move. He wasn't exactly holding the door, his hand merely stretched out towards it, his fingers barely touching the metal, but Lindsey saw Bonnie struggle. The ginger girl's eyes were round with terror; she cried and pushed with all her strength. Lindsey wanted to step forward, but a cold hand gripped her around the throat. For a moment, it looked as if Bonnie was winning the fight, then something pulled her into the darkness. The door shut with a loud clunking sound, making Lindsey's bones and teeth shudder, and cutting off the sound of Bonnie's screams.

Tyrell turned towards her, his hollow eyes impassive, blood drizzling from his temple, but now Lindsey noticed it wasn't just blood, but a lumpy grey mass. She moaned, her legs giving way, but the cold hand around her throat held her up.

"I'm sorry, girl," Tyrell said, "I have no hatred for you, but I am part of Angel Manor now, and I must do as she bids. She wants you. I'm incapable of doing you real harm, but my friend Chuck here has more strength and more drive than I do. I shall leave you in his expert hands." Tyrell nodded at her then disappeared, leaving Lindsey with her captor. Fear pushed at her senses, yet it gave her strength and Lindsey fought with all her might. The hand let her go. Her feet hit the floor hard, and her heart threatened to burst through her chest, but she ran.

***

The stone steps collided hard with Emma's flesh, and time appeared to slow down as she fell further into darkness. At the bottom of the stairs, she landed on concrete with a sickening crunch, hot pain surging through her arm. The wind was knocked from her lungs, and a wheezing sound escaped weakly from her lips. Blue and red stars exploded before her eyes. The distant slam of the door, followed by the sound of something heavy falling and bouncing off the stairs, brought her to an abrupt state of alertness. A heavy body landed on top of her, and pain shot up her arm again.

"Bonnie?" Her voice trembled. The body on top her moved a little and moaned. "Bonnie, get off. Ye're hurting me." The weight shifted.

"What just happened?" Bonnie's voice sounded weak and afraid, and Emma wished she could see her friend better.

"Emma... did ye see that guy's face?"

"Aye." She had seen it; she couldn't banish the sight of it from her mind. Bonnie's words made it even more real because, for a moment, Emma had prayed it was just her imagination.

"Do ye think he was a ghost?"

"Aye." Emma bit her lip and pushed herself to a sitting position. Her back, arm and head hurt, but to her relief, she found she could still move. "We need ta get out of here as fast as we can."

"What about Lindsey?"

"We'll get help for her."

"What are we goin' ta say? Ghosts got Lindsey?"

"Ah don't care what we say, we need ta get out of here, and we need ta get help, ye daft cow." She regretted the words as soon as they came from her mouth. "Sorry, Ah didnae mean ta be such a bitch."

"It's okay."

Something to their right made a sound, as if someone was pulling a chair over the concrete.

"What tha fuck is that?" Emma could barely say the words. To her left something scuffled, and she fought a wave of nausea bubbling in her stomach.

"Emma?" Bonnie sounded near tears. "There's something in here with us."

Emma crawled to her feet, her head throbbing. She stumbled forward, disoriented, and looked for the stairs, but she couldn't find them. Something slid across her eye and cheek, and she screamed, swatting it with her hand. It caught in her fingers, and realising that it was a light chord, she pulled it. A sickly yellow light filled the basement, and Emma had to close her eyes. The contrast between utter darkness and the light was too sharp, and her head was still sore. She opened her eyes slowly, her vision clearing, but before she could register what was going on around her, Bonnie screamed.

More than a dozen women, all of them naked, surrounded them in a semi-circle. The females were all different shapes and sizes, but they all wore the same expression on their faces: hunger. A sob echoed through the basement, and at first Emma thought it was Bonnie... but when the hot tears burned her cheeks, she realized it was she who was crying.

***

He was behind her. Lindsey knew he was, even if she couldn't hear his footsteps. And that smell... it was strong here. Lindsey ran down the moonlit wing and cursed the moment that she'd set foot in Angel Manor. She had never even considered that the ghosts from the stories could be real; she'd been worried about lustful men, not rotting ones. And yet, here she was, running for her life. The house wanted her? Well the house could fuck the hell off, she decided. The wing looked bigger than it had when she'd walked through it the first time, but she was pretty sure that most of it was one straight corridor. Twice she lost her balance and fell, but she was determined. On her left, she saw a door open and she recognised the room. Her heart was singing with hope and relief when she made the sharp turn and slowed her pace. It was the room that they had entered through, and the doors were still open. As she stepped over the threshold, the doors to the outside swung shut, stopping Lindsey dead in her tracks. Then the door behind her slammed and Lindsey was trapped. In the corners, she saw movement.

"Don't worry, baby... I'm only going to hurt you a little." The voice behind her spoke in the familiar American drawl. "I'm just going to fuck you to death." She turned, blood draining from her face, to see Chuck standing behind her, the fly to his jeans already open. The maggots were gone now, and he looked almost alive from where she was standing. In the corners of the room, Lindsey saw more people.

"Please help me?" She looked at an old woman who had her hands wrapped around the shoulder of a young girl. "Please?" Tears flowed down Lindsey's cheeks, and her mouth filled with saliva.

"Don't look at them. They're only here to watch. No one can help you now."

"This can't be happening."

He disappeared for a moment, and then reappeared, looking more solid than before. "Oh but it is." His hand yanked at her extensions. Lindsey screamed, but Chuck was stronger than she was, and he pulled her down onto the floor. She pushed against him, her hands connecting with his chest before slipping through into nothing as if he was in between states of being.

Rough hands pulled at her skirt, pushing it up towards her thighs. She clawed at him, his face momentarily made of flesh, and managed to tear some skin off, revealing a dark glistening substance underneath.

"I thought you would appreciate me looking more human?" He smiled at her, revealing teeth blackened with the same oozing substance. "But if you would rather fuck me in my ghost form, I can oblige." He bent forward and licked her cheek, leaving a wet trail of dark mucus.

"No, please... please." She didn't know what else to say, and when he pressed his lips to hers, the maggots poured into her mouth. They squirmed against her tongue and the inside of her cheeks, and Lindsey vomited against the cold wet lips. Her hands pushed against him, digging her nails into the rotting flesh, and she wriggled her knees under him, nudging against his legs. The figure pushed himself up and looked at her, his cheek still dripping with black, the skin peeled back.

"Lie still, girlie."

She turned on her side, heaving up the maggots, and tried to slip away from his grip, but he grabbed her right arm and brought it back with so much force that Lindsey could feel her bone snap and her muscle tear. The pain screamed through her body, and in her agony, she vomited again on the floor. Her mouth was filled with the hot sour taste, and now that her arm hung loosely at her side, Chuck rolled her over with ease. He grabbed her other arm and pulled on that with the same force. With a pop, her arm dislocated itself from her shoulder, and a new wave of pain washed through her.

"No more running now, or I will get your legs." The intense eyes held hers, though Lindsey found it hard to focus through her tears. Her underwear cut into the skin between her cheeks as rough hands pulled at it. Three tugs and the fabric tore, leaving her exposed. The fight was punched out of her with the breaking of her arms. Chuck parted the lips between her thighs and pushed his cold, dry fingers inside her. She moaned with pain again, her face slick with tears and her mouth a tormented sneer, cables of spittle running from her top lip to the bottom one.

"You're so warm. Life is so sweet and warm. I just want to consume you." He leaned forward and sank his teeth into her shoulder. She groaned as hot blood poured down her naked skin, past her broken arm. Then he pulled his fingers free and pushed her legs wider apart so that he could force his erection between her legs. His penis was even colder than his fingers, and it scraped against her insides as if she were being raped by a wooden stick. He grunted, his bony hips boring into her soft thighs as he thrust with the ferocity of a bull, back and forth, back and forth. His body

236

decomposed further as he drove deeper into her; flesh wrinkled and tightened across bones, darkening with each movement, and his hair grew long and white. Skeletal hands tore at her shirt. Her chocolate breasts spilled out from the fabric of the cream coloured bra, and his rotting, bony fingers pinched at her dark nipples. His rhythm picked up speed. There was a look of ecstasy on the decaying face, and when the jaw crumpled and loosened from the skull, another hail of maggots fell out. A pool of them landed on her stomach, crawling around, and she felt them moving between her legs as his rotting penis pushed them deep inside her. Then the figure started to come apart, and black dirt splattered down onto her body. She was covered in the stuff, from her face to her pelvis, but Lindsey found the courage to move for the first time since he'd broken her arms. She flopped from her back to her stomach, battling to get away from the dirt. She couldn't use her arms, so she rolled towards a wall and pressed her back against it, then she pushed with her legs until she was in an upright position. She stood, a little wobbly on her feet, her arms hanging limp and useless to her sides, and she stepped with determined strides towards the double glass doors.

Her arm screamed in pain when she raised it to grab the brass handle, but she bit through it. She pushed down with every ounce of strength she had left, but the door wouldn't budge.

"No, please, no." Tears poured from her eyes again. The familiar scent of rot tickled her nostrils, and before panic could make master of her, something grabbed the back of her head and slammed her face against the glass. A deep star appeared in it, intricate as a spider's web. Lindsay's eyes rolled into the back of her head and she fought to stay conscious.

"You don't get to leave yet. I told you I would fuck you to death." The dry cold penis pushed into her exposed anus with such force that she almost fainted. He pressed her against the window, the cool glass a painful hard barrier for her soft warm breasts. The blood on her face left a smear on the cracked glass. Then the fingers pulled at her hair again, and he smashed her face into the glass several more times until it gave way, leaving only large jagged shards. Chuck pulled her head back one final time and drove her eye into one of the long spikes. The pain was brief. The glass cut through the soft tissue of her eye and embedded itself in her brain. Her body twitched a few times before it became still and Lindsey felt the house embrace her in the cold and the darkness.

***

Bonnie pressed herself against Emma, her body trembling with cold and fright. She wished that Emma hadn't turned on the light, because the sight of the women was more than her sanity could handle. And yet, the idea that she would die in the dark didn't appeal to her either. Her mind found it difficult to grasp what was going on around her. The scent of rotting flesh hung thick in the air, and though the women were obviously animate, they didn't quite seem alive. There was something wrong with the colour of their skin, with the way their eyes were glassed over, the way dark blue veins lined their skin. It reminded Bonnie of the time she and her sister found Nana after she died in her sleep, but seeing the same deathly stare in the hollow-set eyes of the women who surrounded them was so much worse. Bonnie couldn't conjure up a single moment in her life that was more terrifying than this one.

Her eyes darted to the right, where a homely looking woman with small, sagging breasts and a thick cluster of reddish brown pubic hair walked back and forth like a caged tiger in front of the other women. In her hands, she held a linked chain, which extended in three loose ends that dragged behind it like metal tails. Each end was tipped with a metal hook, and the links themselves were covered in steel spikes that pressed into the woman's pale flesh. When she walked, the chain cut into her skin, causing thick lines of black blood to run down her back.

"Emma?" Bonnie had difficulty finding her voice.

"We need to move backwards, get to the stairs." Emma spoke in low calm tones, the tears already drying on her cheeks, which gave Bonnie a surge of hope. Their hands found each other, and their fingers interlocked. Emma took a careful step back and Bonnie followed her lead exactly. Then another step, never looking away from the semicircle of women. The woman with the chain stopped and bared her teeth at the two girls. Bonnie stifled a scream. The thin woman pulled the chain from her shoulders, the skin ripping even further, and raised it above her head as if she were wielding a simple whip.

"Now," Emma cried, and they turned to make a run for the stairs. To her horror, Bonnie saw that they were further away than she'd thought. *How can they be that far? We just fell down them. How did we end up in the middle of the basement?*

She picked up her pace, Emma a few steps ahead of her, still holding her hand, and then a metallic sound filled the basement. Emma stopped in her tracks as the three ends of the metal chain coiled around her, the hooks digging into her skin through the little black dress she wore. Emma looked at Bonnie, just for a brief second, but the expression of fear on her friend's face broke Bonnie's heart. Then Emma was pulled from her grip with such force that she stumbled to keep her balance. Emma landed on the floor, blood pouring from her wounds, and the naked woman leered as she pulled the struggling girl towards her, the way a cowboy would haul in cattle. Bonnie made a decision then, and she turned and ran. She was going to make it, she knew, and when her foot hit the first step, she almost smiled with relief, but then cold hands wrapped around her ankle and pulled. Bonnie lost her balance and fell, her chin connecting with the concrete stairs. Her jaw shattered, blood and teeth spilling from her lips. Her face skidded across the steps until she landed on the floor, the hands still pulling at her without mercy. She blacked out, and when she woke up, she was on her back. Above her, in a cobweb of metal, hung Emma. She was naked, like the women around her, and blood poured down from several cuts on her body and face, tinting her white skin red.

Bonnie attempted to call out her friend's name through her shattered jaw, but all she was rewarded with was pain. She tried to move her arms and legs, but they were tied down, her limbs spread out. Emma's face turned in her direction. Instead of eyes, she had hollow sockets from which blood poured; her tongue and teeth were missing too. One of the naked women, a tall, fat one with a chest like grey udders, put a large machete under Emma's left breast. The round, firm flesh hung perkily over the metal. The ghoulish woman smiled at Bonnie, as if she were enjoying having an audience, then her smile turned into a wicked grimace and she brought the machete up, slicing neatly through the firm tissue. Emma screamed so loud, Bonnie's bones vibrated under her skin. Her voice screamed along in unison with the painful wail of her friend.

The machete, dark red with blood, found its way to Emma's belly, and the woman wielding the blade looked at Bonnie again. Bonnie wanted to look away, but somehow she couldn't. It was as if someone was holding her head and she couldn't close her eyes. Then the woman pushed the blade into Emma's abdomen and cut across. A coil of wet, slippery intestines slid from the folds of open skin like a grey garden hose. Emma made a strange sound, somewhere between a cry and a moan, and then she hung still while her intestines uncoiled and fell to the floor with a wet thud.

Tears rolled from Bonnie's eyes, past her ears, and round to the back of her neck. She was alone now, and she knew it would be her turn to die. The woman with the machete smiled at her again, revealing those horrible black teeth, then she pointed at something behind Bonnie. Two more women, one young and pretty with long blonde hair and soft features, the other old and haggard with grey hair and a long, bulbous nose, stood near a large metal device.

Bonnie wasn't sure what it was, or where it had come from, but it looked like a wheel from the Middle Ages. The two women each held a lever, and they started to turn. The wheel spun under the pressure, the sound of rattling chains filled the basement, and Bonnie's arms and legs were pulled further apart. She lifted her head and looked around the room. The women had all gathered around her, their faces eager and hungry. The chains cut into her skin, pulling at her bones and muscle, and only then did Bonnie realise what was happening.

"No, please..." she moaned, but her words turned into screams when her limbs were stretched beyond their limits and her body was lifted into the air. Her eyes darted to the women who were turning the wheel; their momentum seemed to be gaining. Her muscles tore under the pressure and her bones slid from their sockets. With an agonising slowness, her skin began to tear, and Bonnie screamed with a pain she'd never before experienced. Blood gushed from the tears, welling up against her pale flesh. The scream only lasted a few seconds as she came apart. The last vision she had was of her legs flying in different directions, blood and tissue trailing behind them. Then the world went dark, and the house welcomed her soul into its midst.

Chapter 23

Oliver wasn't at his usual spot at the breakfast table, and Freya thought about peeking around the corner of his bedroom to see if he was up. She decided against it, a little relieved that he wasn't awake. Oliver seemed out of sorts lately, and his presence bothered her. She didn't want anything to spoil the semi-good mood lingering from the night before. This was the first time since Bam had died that she felt anything other than deep rooted despair. True, the house was haunted, but she had spent a rather delightful evening with Logan, and it made her almost giddy... almost. She was ashamed by the knowledge that a man could have such an effect on her, and she promised herself that she wouldn't take the Angel Manor 'situation' lightly just because she was falling in love. *Oh God, I am... aren't I... falling in love? I must have the worst timing ever.* She poured herself some coffee and leafed through the picture book they'd found in the attic. She had given up on the notebook; someone else would have to decipher that one for her.

Yellowing tape held faded photographs to the pages. There were pictures of an older Angel Manor, of some of the owners, and of the interior. She didn't recognise any of the people in the pictures until she saw a tired looking nun and a young woman standing in front of the ruins of what looked like an old church. Freya peeled the photograph from the page and turned it around. Written in faded pencil were the words: 'Beth and Agatha, 1844. Convent of the Holy Angels.'

She'd seen the nun before... in the house, so Beth had to be her ancestor. She stared at the young woman. She appeared to be in her twenties. A piece of parchment paper was taped on the opposite page, a newspaper article from 1822.

'Fire at Lucifer Falls – the Convent of the Holy Angels at the top of Lucifer Falls burned down last night during the summer solstice celebration. It is estimated that twenty-eight Brides of Christ and around fifty children between ages four and fourteen died in the fire. The only survivors are Sister Agatha and one of the orphans. The cause of the fire is as yet unknown, as is the fate of the convent. The church will decide whether or not to restore the holy order.'

Freya pictured the frightened faces of the ghostly children, and she suspected they hadn't perished in the fire, that a deeper darkness had taken them. Her jolly mood dissolved as she turned back to the picture.

With a sigh, she pulled the piece of paper from her pocket again and studied the curly handwriting of her now dead friend.

Oh Bam, if only I had listened to you. If only I'd believed you, maybe you'd still be alive. Freya thought about how the house held on to its souls, and she wondered if Bam was roaming the halls too. She also wondered if the angels would torment Bam if they found her, and she had to push the thought away in fear of crying. She had to find peace for all those who were bound to Angel Manor, and if a psychic woman could help her with it, then so be it.

***

Just outside the small village to the east of Lucifer Falls, Freya found a spot where her mobile phone could pick up reception. She cursed herself for not thinking of it earlier instead of relying on payphones. A little recess in the underbrush allowed her to park her car safely to the side of the road, and she opened the driver's door to let her legs dangle out of the side. Her fingers trembled as she dialled the number on the piece of paper. The phone rang a few times before a female voice, with the slightest hint of a French accent, answered.

"Hello?"

"Is this Miss, or Mrs, Florifera?"

"Speaking, dear. I'm a Miss, but you can call me Marie-Claire. How can I help you?"

"My friend Bambi called you a few weeks ago?"

"About the house on Lucifer Falls?" The voice sounded eager now. "Yes, I remember."

"I... would like you and your people to come and have a look at it. It's haunted, and... and... we need an expert."

"I see. What did you have in mind? An exorcism?"

"Um... if that's what's needed. I don't know what needs to be done. But there are spirits here and they're stuck. I just need help."

"Yes, Bambi told me that when we spoke. She wasn't sure about the ghosts, but you seem pretty convinced?"

Freya wanted to blurt out that Bam was dead, and that she was afraid the house might have something to do with it, but she worried that if she said this, the woman would change her mind and not come.

"Yes, I'm very sure Angel Manor is haunted. Not a doubt in my mind." Freya wondered if she sounded convinced or perhaps a little insecure because of the way her voice shook. "Can you help?"

"Of course. I can be there by tomorrow morning if you'd like. Would that be okay with you?"

"Yes, Miss. I appreciate it. Bam... Bam didn't tell me about payment. How much do you charge?"

The woman on the other end of the phone laughed, her voice pleasant and warm.

"Keep your money, but I would like to use the pictures I take and the story of Angel Manor for a book I'll be writing. If that's okay with you? I don't have to use your real name. I can change that much."

"I don't mind. But please, just come and help."

"We'll be there tomorrow around noon, dear. I'm looking forward to it. We hoped you would call, you know."

"Thank you." Freya said, brushing away a single tear. "I'll make sure we'll have some tea ready."

The woman on the other end of the line laughed again, her voice as clear as a glass bell, and Freya felt deeply stupid for her comment.

"Can... can I ask you something?" Freya squeezed the phone, the sharp edges digging into the palm of her hand.

"Of course."

Freya cleared her throat. "Have you ever heard about ghosts being dangerous? Have ghosts ever killed anyone?"

There was silence on the other end for a moment.

"That's a tricky question. But if you mean can spirits cause physical damage, then you don't have to worry. I've not come across any evidence that spirits are able to harm people. However, they can manipulate their surroundings. And they can influence the mood, and sometimes even the minds of the living, so they aren't completely harmless either."

She pinched the bridge of her nose and inhaled before she spoke. "But having them in the house... it's not dangerous? I don't have to evacuate everyone?"

"No, I think you should be fine. The spirits will most likely try to reach out to the living, though. So it will be good to help them pass on. But even malevolent spirits tend to just be mischievous at best, though I wouldn't recommend anyone being exposed for a long period of time. The dead aren't the same as they were when they were alive."

Freya thought of Bam. "Thank you, that's a bit of a relief."

"No problem, dear. Listen, I have to run off now, but I'll see you tomorrow. Bye!" The voice transformed into a dial tone and Freya's thumb found the black button to put the phone into sleep mode. She leaned back, a deep breath escaping from her lungs through her lips, and let the tears flow.

***

Oliver woke up around noon. His head throbbed as if he had been on a three-day drinking binge, his forehead was hot and clammy, and he was pretty sure his temperature was raised. The more solid Anne was becoming, the more his body seemed to suffer from her touches. In the mornings, he felt so drained, and every muscle in his body ached, but her caresses, though cold and painful, were filled with lust and promise. She filled a void that Oliver had never even known he had. She was the perfection he sought. No living girl could compare to his spirit woman, and Oliver loved giving himself to her, and to the house.

The doorbell rang, the deep sound vibrating through the whole house, and Oliver slipped on his bathrobe and slippers. He walked to the door with slow, sluggish movements and opened it. A man stood in the driveway, inspecting the row of angels. When he spotted Oliver, he waved and took the stone stairs two steps at a time.

"Mr Formynder?"

"Jardin, my name is Jardin. *Miss* Formynder isn't here right now."

"My name is Harry McDougal, I'm here to install yer phone lines." He was a middle-aged fellow with a thick beard which could have used a trim. Faded brown corduroy trousers clung to his thin legs, and his large belly was clad in a too-tight white t-shirt. A red plaid shirt hung open and loose, matching his red cap. In his right hand, he carried a square black case with a red sticker on the top.

"Come in, Mr McDougal. Would you like a cup of

coffee?" Oliver waved his hand to welcome the man in.

"Aye, black please, two sugars," the man replied with a toothy grin, and Oliver almost grimaced at the sight of the yellow teeth, but he managed to keep his face pleasant.

"Coming right up."

"As far as I know, this house has had a phone line before, right? We got a signal, but it just seemed rather outdated." McDougal put his thumbs through the loops of his trousers and hoisted them up as he spoke, then rocked back and forth on the soles of his feet like a cowboy.

"Yes, I believe so."

"I'll have to see about ye're master socket. It would be helpful if ye could show me ye're junction box, then I can have a look to see what we're dealing with here." The man nodded. "I should be done in a jiffy, I should think."

"But first... a cup of coffee." Oliver forced a sickly smile.

"Aye, first coffee. Are ye okay, lad? Ye're looking a little peaky."

"I'm fine, thank you. A bit of flu," Oliver lied. He led the man to the kitchen and offered him a chair.

"I was very excited when I got this job. This house is a bit of a legend ye know?" McDougal accepted the coffee cup and put his thin lips to the rim, his moustache spilling over the top.

"Oh?" Oliver tried to sound interested, but he wasn't feeling it. He didn't care what people said.

"Oh, aye. Most people think this place is haunted."

"Do you think it's haunted?"

"Nae, I'm not the sort who believes in ghosties. But might tell me mates down at the pub that I saw a monster or two. For a bit of a laugh, ye know?"

"Delightful." Oliver smiled weakly.

They sat in silence across from each other for several minutes, drinking their coffees, the other man becoming gradually more uncomfortable with the silence. He fiddled with his coffee cup, and his nostril twitched with some sort of a nervous tic. He glanced around the kitchen as if he was looking for something to talk about, and several times he opened his mouth, but nothing came out. Instead, he pushed his empty coffee cup away and looked at his hands.

Oliver sipped slowly, amused by the man's discomfort. Then, when his coffee was finished, he turned to the man and said: "If you'll follow me."

The chair made a loud scraping noise across the tiles when McDougal got to his feet, and Oliver winced, his head still throbbing. He waved impatiently at the man to come along and led him to the junction box just off the main hall.

"There you go. I hope you don't mind if I leave you to it?"

"That's nae problem at all, lad." McDougal gave Oliver a thumbs-up, put his black case down on the floor and opened it with two determined clicks. Oliver stalked off, desperate to find an aspirin for his headache.

***

Hungry. It wasn't a word she heard exactly, nor was it the feeling she had in her stomach when she was alive... the house whispered it to her somehow. Bam knew she was hungry for life; she craved pain and blood. Every fibre of her wanted to kill, wanted to torment. The presence of the new living soul in the house was too overwhelming for her to ignore. The house wanted her to have this, wanted her to taste the feeling of blood on her lips, to feel the sensation of heat again, to consume life. Bam closed her eyes and concentrated on the man... he was near the entrance.

***

As Harry suspected, the router was terribly out of date. He grabbed his newer model and applied it with professional skill, rubbing his hands together in admiration when he was done. "Do you think the phones will work now?" A female voice with an American accent asked.

He turned to see a young woman standing behind him. She was short, and a little weird looking according to Harry's taste. She had blonde hair with pink streaks in it, and Harry decided that if she were his daughter, he would make her wash that crap out. He did notice she had a very nice chest, and he felt like a dirty old man for admiring a girl so young.

"Phone should work fine. Let me test it first though." He took out his receiver and plugged it into the junction box. To his great satisfaction, he heard a dial tone. "See, there ye go. Connected to the rest of the world now. I'm not sure if ye can get Internet up here though. Ye'll have to talk to the company about that. I just do phones."

"Is that all?"

"Aye, it's that simple. Now it's up to the main office to give ye a phone number and get ye connected, but that should take only a few minutes, and they do that from a distance. I'm done here."

"Would you mind looking at the other junction box too?"

"What do ye mean?" Harry scratched under his red cap, his nails scraping across his balding scalp. "There's only one junction box."

"No, I'm sure there's another one in the South Wing." The girl put her hands in her pockets and brought her shoulders almost up to her ears.

"Are ye sure?"

"Yes, I live here. I think I would know these things. Didn't Oliver tell you?"

"Nae. But... it's highly unlikely that—"

"Can you at least just look at it?"

"Aye, lead the way." Harry shook his head, convinced that the girl was wrong, but he had a few minutes to kill and his curiosity was piqued.

The South Wing, as the girl had called it, was in worse shape than the main hall, and Harry hoped it would be safe to walk here without a hard hat. There were large lumps of concrete on the cracked marble floors, which must have come from somewhere. He eyed the walls, but they looked solid enough, and the ceiling, although very high up, didn't look too damaged. It was a nice house, though, and with a bit of love and care it would fix up great. But as it was, it suited the ghost stories that were told about it. All it lacked were large paintings with stern, old-fashioned characters looking down on him.

"Down here." The girl opened a large metal door, and she waved for him to go down first. "You'll find the light switch at the bottom of the stairs. It's a rope. You can't miss it."

"All right." He shrugged and walked down the stone stairs. Harry didn't mind the dark, given how often he had dealt with it in his career, but there was something about this basement that gave him the creeps. For one, the temperature was too low.

"I'm so sorry." Her voice sounded far away. "I belong to Angel Manor now, and I must obey. I never meant to hurt you." Before McDougal reached the end of the stairs, the girl closed the door with a heavy bang.

Harry swore.

***

Bam leaned against the door. Phantom tears ran down her cheeks; she was torn between who she was as a living person and who the house wanted her to be. It would be so easy to just give in, to merge with the others and feed. Bam knew she would be more fulfilled, but if she did, she would lose all sense of freedom and all sense of self.

She had no qualms about killing, not now... not when she knew what death truly was. The fear that the living had for the afterlife was unnecessary and a little ridiculous. Death was in many ways like life... it simply was, and no amount of thought would change it. And like life, death forced you to choose a path. Bam was ready to choose, and she knew her aim would be freedom. If the house wanted living souls, it could have them. But she would not feast along.

***

"Open the door, lass. It's very dark in here," Harry called to the closed door. There was no reply, and he considered heading back up the stairs, but the work had to be done and it was only a few more steps to the light switch. He stepped onto the solid ground and grabbed into the air to find the rope. After several failed attempts, his fingers finally clutched around something and he pulled. The weak yellow light turned on, and Harry found himself staring at a group of naked women.

"Is this some kind of joke?" He almost laughed, the situation was so absurd. "My wife won't appreciate this, ladies." Harry stared at an attractive blonde woman with small perky breasts. In her hand, she held what looked like a rusty sickle. Nerves surged through his body, there was something about the colour of the women's skin and the way their eyes looked that he found truly unnerving. He averted his eyes, hoping to make the situation less awkward.

"Look at me, Harry," a sultry voice said, and Harry stared into the pale eyes of the blonde.

"How did you know my name?"

She brought the tip of the sickle to the corner of her mouth and licked her lips. With slow determination she pushed the metal through her cheek. Harry groaned.

"We know you, Harry." Black blood ran past her chin, and she stepped forward. "You are one of us now."

She sliced the blade across his chest, cutting through his shirt and the skin underneath as if she were slicing through butter. Harry cried out in pain.

"What are ye doing, ye crazy bitch?" He took a step back, but another of the women moved behind him. The sickle came down across his skin again, and his shirt bloomed with crimson as two other women swept at him with knives, their sharp blades cutting into his back. He held up his arms protectively, but hands clutched onto him, forcing his arms down. The blonde stood before him again, her eyes filled with hunger. She brought the sickle back and pushed it into Harry's soft throat with force. Skin and cartilage ripped under the pressure, and for a moment it didn't even hurt. Then the pain hit him, searing and screaming, while hot blood poured from his wound. His face was a mask of surprise, and he saw the light slowly dim. *This wasn't the day I was supposed to die,* were his last thoughts as hundreds of voices called out to him, telling him to join them. Harry's body slumped to the ground, his spirit melting into the deep magic of Angel Manor.

Chapter 24

The van from the phone company was parked near the house, and Freya smiled as she drove past it. The thought of being able to phone from Angel Manor and not having to cross the invisible border to the land of headaches and nausea made her want to sing with glee. She parked her car and made her way to the front door, where she was greeted by some of the young men having a smoke break.

"Hey, guys. How's it going?"

"Fine, we finished the stairs today. The main entrance is starting to look pretty snazzy." Angus flicked his cigarette aside and stood up. He glanced over her breasts, and his expression reminded her of a cat stalking a mouse. She pulled her shirt over her cleavage and raised an eyebrow at him.

"Good to hear you're making so much progress. Have you seen Oliver?"

"No, he hasn't been about much lately."

"I'll find him." She pushed her way past and stepped into the house. Angus had been speaking the truth; the entrance hall really was cleaning up nicely. All it needed was a lick of paint, and if the psychic could indeed perform a successful exorcism, Freya might still consider a reception area. If Angel Manor could become ghost free, maybe it would be a good idea to proceed with their plans for a hotel. She hadn't decided yet – it would be so different without Bam around – and at the same time, Freya hated the idea that it would have all been for nothing. "Oliver?" She peered around the corner of the kitchen, but there was no sign of her friend. "Ollie?" She made her way to his bedroom and found him lying on the bed. He looked pale, and his eyes were glazed over.

"Are you okay?"

"I will be, as soon as the equinox is here." His voice was soft and dreamy, then he sat up abruptly. Freya yelped. "Frey? When did you get here?"

"Just now, I asked you if you were okay." Her hand clutched her chest in an attempt to calm her pounding heart. "Jesus, you scared me."

"What are you doing in here?"

"Looking for you, knob-end. Why are you still in bed? It's past one."

"I wasn't feeling well."

"You don't look well." Freya sat at the end of his bed and placed her hand against his forehead. "You're burning up."

"Yeah, just leave me be for a bit and I'll be fine." He turned to his side, his back towards her, and pulled a pillow over his eyes. After a moment, he pulled the pillow from his face and glared back at her. "Speaking of not feeling well... I thought you were going to phone a doctor to have everyone checked out?"

"No, something came up that made me wonder if getting a doctor was necessary."

"It couldn't hurt." Oliver narrowed his eyes at her, and Freya cringed.

"I guess... whatever, let's focus on one thing at a time here, okay? I came in to ask you something."

"What?" Oliver looked over his shoulder.

"The phone guy, did you let him in?"

"Yes, a while back. He came just after you left."

"Where is he now? I didn't see him when I came in."

"He probably left, Frey. Why are we talking about this?"

"He didn't leave. His car is still here."

"Is it? Maybe he's eating lunch or something."

"Because that makes sense." Freya threw her hands up in the air and shot Oliver an incredulous look. "Why would he be eating lunch here? Jesus, Ollie, tell me you didn't leave him to fend for himself?"

"What was I supposed to do?" Oliver lifted himself on his elbow, the bed creaking under his movement, and he looked at her through a mass of tousled curls. "Hold his freaking tools? Why are you whining at me?"

"You're useless, that's why."

"I'm fucking ill, Freya. Stop nagging."

"You could have asked Logan to see him in. Damn it, Ollie, we can't let strangers just roam around in here."

"No, we've been over this. The house isn't dangerous. It's just a house for fuck's sake." He fell back onto the bed and waved at her to go. "Piss off, you're making my headache worse."

She slid off the bed, her feet landing solidly on the ground, and she stared at her friend. Oliver was different somehow. She couldn't quite put her finger on it. Perhaps he was more irritable... or just a different kind of irritable. The close bond they'd once shared felt frayed lately, but life had been a little insane, so Freya didn't want to make too much of it. She left the dark bedroom in search of the missing man from the phone company.

***

"Still no sign of the phone guy?" Logan sat next to her at the kitchen table, his face covered in a thin layer of dust.

"No, but his van is still here."

"Where do you think he could be?"

"I don't know, but I'm worried, Logan. What if something's happened to him? People are going to come looking. I really don't want to deal with that. What if they arrest us? We can't leave the premises without getting sick."

"Calm down. Nothing has happened yet. Let's not panic until we know more."

"He's been here for eight hours, Logan... at least. And not one sign of him. It's hard not to panic. What if he ran into something? Like those angels the children talked about? Or something else?"

"I'll have my boys do a full sweep of the house, okay? Could be that the guy just injured himself and he's lying at the bottom of some stairs with a broken leg."

"Is it bad that I'm hoping that will be the case?"

"What else could it be? We met the ghosts, and we're still fine."

"True, but..."

Logan bent forward and took her hands in his. "Listen, let's not drive ourselves crazy okay? Let's not panic before we know more. Deal? If we haven't found him by the morning, we'll come up with something." He sat back and let go of her hands. "Worst case scenario, we push his car off Lucifer Falls, into that big hole in the middle. No one will find it there." He laughed at his own joke, but Freya didn't have the heart to laugh with him. She worried, if it was the house, the boys would have to leave here as soon as possible.

"Did you manage to reach that psychic?" Logan's words cut through her thoughts.

"What?"

"You were going to call the psychic today, weren't you?"

"Oh yes, she's coming up here tomorrow morning."

"That soon?"

"She seemed quite keen."

"Well that's good. That will give us some more clarity."

"If she isn't a charlatan."

"If she isn't a charlatan." Logan nodded.

***

Oliver woke as the sun was setting. He had spent most of the day in bed, feverish, but now he felt oddly refreshed. The equinox was drawing near. He wondered why the house chose him over Freya, but in the back of his mind, he knew it wasn't that the house had chosen him, it was that he had chosen the house. Freya never loved the place, not the way he did. Oliver loved the house before he'd ever set foot in it, and the promise of what this place could become was what bonded him to it. He needed the house more than Freya did, and that's why it wanted him.

His dream of being a chef had faded; he cared little about rebuilding the kitchen or feeding guests his carefully crafted food. Instead, he dreamed about his bond with Angel Manor and how he would bring it everything it needed. He was its Guardian, and the task suited him well. He would bring the place souls to feed on, like a bird would bring its offspring worms. With each passing day, he gave more and more of himself to the house, bonding with the ancient magic within. He understood how the spirits felt; he was one of them, the only difference being that his spirit was still housed in a shell made of flesh and bone.

Somewhere beneath the brick and the concrete, something else pulsated like a slow throbbing heart, its magic running through Angel Manor like tiny black veins. Being a part of something this big and this important, Oliver could scarcely remember what it was like to be someone ordinary. He would never be unloved or unwanted again, the house would see to that.

"Thank you for the gift." He hadn't seen her enter the room, but he felt her presence almost immediately. She looked as human as he did now, the dawning of the equinox having affected her greatly.

"What gift?" Oliver raised his eyebrows, then realisation dawned on him. "Oh... the phone guy. I'm glad he pleased you."

"The house is very pleased."

Pride filled his chest, but a moment later the smile faded from his lips.

"I'd better get rid of the van before Freya gets too suspicious."

"Yes, but first, it's time to show you something."

"What?"

"Why we are here. Why this house is what it is."

"I can sense it. It's underneath the house, right?"

"Yes, I will show you where the master sleeps, and the importance of the solstice and the equinox."

"Show me." He looked at her through half-lidded eyes. She beckoned him with a long, pale finger, inviting him to follow her, and he obeyed.

Chapter 25

Marie-Claire Florifera stared at the car window. Although her blind eyes could not see the world passing outside, she liked feeling the sunlight on her face. Something far below sang to her, something as old as the world itself. Though she sensed the magic, it was obscured from her second-sight. Her corporeal eyes saw nothing of the mortal world, yet they were very sensitive to the world beyond the veil, and she could see spirits as well as those with 20/20 sight could see people. Why she had this talent, she didn't know. All she knew was that she had always been able to see the dead, and she didn't fear them anymore.

She had seen many haunted places in this world; some were truly haunted while others only bore the ghosts of overactive imaginations. Marie-Claire had encountered some truly spectacular occurrences, and she had felt a little guilty when she lied to the girl on the phone about the dangers of spirits. She knew how dangerous they could really be, but it was in no one's best interest if the living feared the dead. That would only give the spirits more power.

It was rare for spirits to be corporeal enough to do actual physical damage to the living, though Marie-Claire had encountered a few places in the world where this was the case. Usually there was an outside factor involved, such as magic or even an artefact. Land could be magical too, and it would draw spirits towards it seeking strength and power. Often those were exactly the kind of spirits that shouldn't have either, and that's what made them dangerous. Marie-Claire suspected that Angel Manor might be the kind of place filled with such magic.

Angel Manor had been on the top of her list for many

decades. She had heard stories about the house, but the previous owners had been more than reluctant to even let her near it. When the girl, Bambi, contacted her, Marie-Claire had been over the moon, but now that the day had finally come for her to inspect the building, she didn't feel so confident anymore.

"I'm curious to see what this house has to offer." Pierre, the newest member of her team, spoke to her from the front seat. Marie-Claire moved her head in the direction of the words.

"Yes, Angel Manor is rather infamous. As is the place where it's situated."

"Lucifer Falls?"

"That's the place." She folded her hands together on her lap, the smooth, silk gloves brushing against her fingers.

"Is it true that Lucifer landed there when he fell?"

"I doubt it, but I'm sure there is something about that place. The living, even those who do not possess the second-sight, tend to be very sensitive to paranormal activities. They don't see spirits like I do, but they feel that something is out of the ordinary. Often they make up stories about highly spiritual places, and they get a reputation even though no one has actually seen anything. I must admit I'm picking up some vibrations from the area, so I would like to inspect the actual place at a later date... see what I'm sensing from here."

"It will be interesting to get some interviews done with the locals." It was Julie who spoke. Marie-Claire could hear the thick Australian lilt in the voice.

"Indeed, I feel that there will be a lot to write about this particular project."

Some people thought Marie-Claire was psychic, but other than her astounding second sight, she had no powers of prediction, only a strong understanding of logic and deduction. She had never contradicted those who called her psychic, they obviously needed to give her a label they felt more comfortable with, and she had been called worse by those who feared her gift. Witch was just one of the many names Marie-Claire had to suffer in her long life; devil worshipper was another common one. She didn't care about any of them. Her life was her own, and the judgements of others meant nothing to her.

"It's up there. We can see the house, Marie-Claire," Ruben, one of her oldest companions, reported as his hot, sweaty hand found hers. He was as eager about this house as she was.

"What does it look like? Describe it to me." Ruben was used to being her eyes, and he knew exactly which details she wanted to hear.

"It's different than the pictures, more alluring somehow. The bricks are yellow, and the windows are large. You can't really make out the cross shape from this angle, it looks more like one of those Victorian mansions. The gardens are a little wild, and I can see the angel statues from here."

The car pulled onto the long driveway to the house and Marie-Claire's blood ran cold. Her eyes suddenly picked up dark clouds, and a heavy pressure settled in her stomach. Her old heart pounded, loud and slow. Marie-Claire slumped in her seat, overwhelmed by the sheer magnitude of the paranormal activity around her, and she fought to stay conscious.

Around her, voices tittered, calling her name and touching her arm. It took her several minutes to fight against the feeling enough to sit up and acknowledge what was going on in the mortal realm.

"She's coming round."

"Marie-Claire... talk to me."

"I'm quite all right. Please stop fondling me." She waved at the hands that touched her, her voice conveying the irritability she felt.

"What happened?" It was Julie who spoke. "You looked as if you were having a stroke."

"I'm fine... I think. Though I must admit, of all the places I've ever been... I've never felt anything like this. This is truly incredible. We must tread with caution, my friends. This house has a lot of spirit." Marie-Claire's arthritic fingers touched the wrinkled skin of her face. Her lips felt rough, and she found a little bit of spittle in the corner of her mouth, which she wiped away hastily.

"Spirits?"

"Well, that too, I suspect. But it's more than that. I... I... feel something else, a deeper darkness, but I can't quite see what it is. There is magic here, not just spiritual magic. I have encountered similar locations before, but never this strong. I assume the spirits here can be dangerous, so we need to be on our guard."

"This should prove interesting." She heard the excitement in Ruben's voice, and she would have shared it had the oppressive feeling not scared her more than anything else had in her life.

***

Nerves raged through Freya's body. She had been jittery from the moment she'd got up. To her relief, she saw the installation guy's van was no longer parked outside, and though she couldn't come up with a reasonable explanation why it had gone that morning after it had been parked outside all last night, she decided it was one less worry for now. The psychics were her main concern.

She talked to Logan about giving the guys the day off, and Logan convinced Jim and John to take them on a day trip through Skye. He argued that there was enough for them to see, and because they had behaved so well up until now, they deserved a little treat. The two counsellors had not been pleased, and both had argued that planning would be required, but she had pleaded with them, and they gave in. She wondered if they felt something was off about the house too, or if they attributed her somewhat irrational decision-making to the recent loss of her friend. Either way, she would rather meet Florifera and her crew away from any prying eyes.

Logan and Freya watched the van pull away from the house, and he wrapped his arm around her as soon as it was out of sight. The warmth of his body felt reassuring, and her skin still tingled at his touch. With all that was occupying her mind, Freya was amazed she could have romantic feelings about anyone, but there they were... the feelings, and they were so strong they overcame all the stress. Being near Logan made everything more bearable, his presence casting a thin emotional quilt over her anxieties.

"I haven't seen Oliver yet. Is he still in bed?" She half turned to Logan, lifting her face up to him. He looked down at her, his nose close to hers, and for a moment she thought, she hoped, he would kiss her again, but he didn't.

"Is he still ill?"

"I don't know. I've been so busy, I haven't really checked up on him. I won't be winning any 'friend of the year awards' this year, I'm afraid."

"It's not that bad." He tightened his arm around her and laughed softly. "Most sick people want to be left alone."

"Well, I'd better go bring him some coffee and tell him that those people are coming."

"You do that. I'm going to pop into the shower quickly before they arrive."

She pictured the hot water of the shower running down his naked body, and bit back the lewd remark resting on the tip of her tongue. She didn't want to scare him off. *If I get this wrong, he might never touch me again,* she thought, and she wanted Logan to do that above all else, so she merely nodded and trotted off to the kitchen.

Her hand trembled as she poured the coffee, spilling hot drips onto the countertop. She wiped the side of the mug, picked it up, and made her way to Oliver's bedroom. Her knuckles rapped on the wooden door three times, and when she heard no response, she pushed down on the brass handle. The room was dark, the heavy curtains still closed, and Freya put the cup on Oliver's nightstand. With a hint of cruelty in her heart, she walked over to the window and pulled open the heavy curtains. Sunlight exploded into the room in fierce, yellow beams, bright enough for Freya to avert her eyes. The words 'rise and shine' died on her lips as she turned to wake Oliver. His bed was empty.

"Ollie?" She said. There was no response. His en-suite bathroom was empty also.

"Ollie?" Her voice filled the room. "Goddamnit." She bolted for the door, a sense of irritation mixed with dread clutching at her.

"Oliver? Ollie?" She spent several minutes wandering through the West Wing, opening doors and peering inside. *Maybe he went out and I didn't see him? Maybe he's just doing some shopping?* She stomped towards the entrance hall and looked out the window, but Bam's car was still there, as was her own. Freya swore again and punched the wood of the windowsill. "I don't need this shit, Oliver. Not today." She turned on her heel and headed for the new staircase. Now that it was finished, it looked even more impressive. Freya admired the beauty of it for a brief second, then she ran up, taking two steps at a time.

"Oliver?" She pushed open a few of the doors on the second floor, carefully avoiding the boys' sleeping quarters in fear of invading some sort of privacy. "Ollie?"

The door to the bathroom opened and Logan's head peered around the corner. His wet hair hung across his forehead, dripping water across his face. He blinked at her.

"What's up?"

"I can't find Oliver anywhere." Her voice cracked, and she fought back the tears. "I wish everyone would just stop disappearing in this fucking house. It's not funny anymore, and I'm starting to get seriously worried. How many disappearances can we discount as 'coincidences', and when do we start to blame the house for this?"

"Calm down. You're panicking." He stepped out of the bathroom, a green towel wrapped across his hips, drops of water clinging to his shapely figure. "Let me get dressed, I'll help you look."

"That's all we seem to do here lately, play fucking hide and seek with everyone."

"Give me a moment to get dressed," he repeated, but his words lost their effect when the doorbell echoed through the house. It was a low and ominous sound that reminded Freya of the bells of Notre Dame.

"Oh perfect." She rolled her eyes and made a dismissive gesture with her hands at Logan. "We'll deal with Oliver later. I need to get through this meeting first." She turned and ran towards the door.

Chapter 26

Marie-Claire Florifera looked like she'd just wandered out of a Hammer Horror film, Freya thought. The psychic was an elderly woman, her long, white hair a stark contrast to her coffee-coloured skin, but what stood out to Freya most were the white eyes. They had neither irises nor pupils, and their sightless stare frightened her more than the ghosts in the attic had. The woman wore a white dress which flowed to her bony ankles, topped by a long, light blue vest, making her look like an ethereal nymph from a fairy tale more than a human woman. Freya needed a moment to compose herself, and only when her eyes fell on the man who was holding the old woman's arm, did she regain her voice.

"Please... come... come in." Her voice sounded high and cracked to her own ears. The man, who was only an inch or so taller than the blind lady, nodded. He had light auburn hair that receded into a sharp crow's peak, and tanned, freckled skin lined with age, much like old leather. He wore light grey pantaloons that reached up to his waist, a white shirt with blue checks and an off-white coat. It seemed that time had stopped moving for him around the 1980's.

"Are you Miss Formynder?" The old woman's voice was clear, sounding more like a young girl's.

"Yes. Please, call me Freya." She held out her hand and then felt silly, but the man tapped the woman's right arm and she stretched her hand out to meet it.

"This is quite a house you have here." The woman gripped onto Freya's hand, her bones protesting under the pressure. "I have no doubt Angel Manor is haunted. There is a lot of paranormal activity here. It's up to us to determine what exactly seems to be going on."

"Of... of course." Freya navigated the woman past the doorframe and into the entrance hall. "I have some tea on."

"Please, child, do me a favour. Give my team a spot of tea, let them settle in, but I want you to take me on a tour of the house. Just the two of us. I want to get acquainted with it first, and I can sense you have a strong bond with this place, so I insist that you are my guide."

"If that's what you wish." Freya turned to Logan, who nodded his head in acknowledgement.

"You can go now," he said. "I can take the others to the kitchen."

"Would you? Thank you." Freya stalled for a moment, wondering if she needed to introduce herself to the rest of Florifera's team first, or if she should just get on with the tour.

"This is Ruben, and I will introduce you to the rest of my colleagues after our tour, dear." The old woman smiled as if she had read her mind, and Freya felt her skin break out in goose bumps. Ruben gave her a curt nod, then turned his back on her and walked back to the vehicles standing in the driveway.

"Come now, dear. Show me this extraordinary house."

***

"Be careful with that FLIR camera. It's fragile, you clumsy oaf!" Ruben sneered at Pierre who had just piled the large laptop case on top of the camera bag without much delicacy. "*Imbécile stupide*, don't you know this stuff is delicate?" He swore under his breath in French. The young man got on his nerves, and he had from the moment he'd joined Florifera's crew. In the years that he'd worked with Marie-Claire, Ruben had seen many people come and go, and he knew the type Pierre was. *A thrill seeker.* Guys like him never stuck around for too long, not when they realized that ninety-percent of the work was dull, and that most of the haunted spots they would visit were just made up by those looking for attention. He had to admit, though, things were less crazy since they'd moved to the UK. They'd still met some annoying, attention-craving homeowners, but they also had the luxury of seeking out their own locations, which tended to weed out a lot of the fakes.

There was a time when their crew had been bigger, but now they numbered just five. It would be enough for Angel Manor, Ruben knew, though he had to admit Marie-Claire's reaction on entering the grounds of the manor had worried him. He had never seen her so overwhelmed before. This would be one of those experiences they wouldn't soon forget, Ruben felt sure of it. He didn't have any paranormal abilities, but even he'd felt the oppressive atmosphere on entering the surprisingly friendly-looking edifice. His stomach had become heavy with a foreboding feeling, and his frustration focussed itself on his clumsy new companion.

"That's a lot of equipment." A tall man, who Ruben instantly dubbed 'Lover Boy' in his head, said, while he helped Julie with one of the tripods.

"Yes, we need all of it. Do you have a place where we can set up? We need somewhere to hook up the laptops."

"Maybe you can show us the places where you've experienced the most activity?" Julie said. She was looking at Lover Boy as if she wanted to lie down and spread her legs right then and there. Ruben thought she was a bit of a silly girl, but he preferred her to Pierre.

"No." Ruben shook his head, still irritable. "We wait till Marie-Claire comes back. She will have a much better sense of where the hotspots are."

Both Lover Boy and Julie gawked at him, and he realized his tone had been a little harsh. Something about this house was making him grumpier than usual, and Ruben wasn't the most gregarious person to begin with. He hated to admit it, but this house had him spooked.

"Of course. How about I show you the kitchen? I have some tea ready. After that, we can find a good spot for you to set up."

"That would be fine. Let's get the rest of the stuff out of the car first. Can we leave it here?" He pointed at the space at the foot of the large staircase where the equipment was stacked in neat piles.

"Yes, of course."

"Tea might be a good idea after our long drive." Ruben put his arm around Julie's shoulder, his mute way of apologizing for his crass behaviour. They walked together towards Pierre and Darren, who were getting the last pieces out of the van. Ruben's eyes fell on the row of Angels in front of the house, and his stomach flipped.

There is something wrong with this place, something very wrong.

***

Rather than giving Marie-Claire Florifera a tour, Freya felt as if she were the one being guided around the house. The medium walked a few steps ahead of her, waving a pendulum made from a milky-blue stone on a silver chain, and the way she manoeuvred around certain areas, Freya would have never guessed that the psychic was blind.

"You are the one who is bonded with this house by blood, are you not?" The woman's soft, musical voice pierced her cloud of thoughts.

"Yes. Angel Manor belonged to my aunt, and my grandparents before her." Freya cleared her throat, her voice sounding a little strangled.

"It was built by an ancestor, was it not?"

"I... I think so. To be honest, I don't know that much about it. What I do know is that the house has always been given to the next generation. My mother left home when she was fifteen. She rarely speaks of it anymore, or of her life with her family. And when she does say anything, it's seldom good. She used to mention it when I was little, but my dad would try and change the subject."

"Yes. I can see that." The woman's French accent was very slight, but it gave her voice a sing-song quality. "I feel a lot of grief in this house, both from the dead and the living."

Florifera stopped in her tracks and turned towards Freya, her white eyes looking straight into her soul.

"Now tell me what it is you are hiding from me."

"I..." Blood rushed to her cheeks, and Freya fought a wave of nausea. She wanted to say that she didn't know what the woman was talking about, that she wasn't hiding anything, but she couldn't lie. "The girl you spoke to... Bambi?"

"I remember her."

"She's dead."

The expression on the woman's face didn't change. Instead, she just stared at Freya with those stern white eyes.

"She didn't die here." It wasn't a question.

"No, she died in Glasgow, in a B&B room."

"I see. Yet you blame the house?"

Freya looked at her feet. She felt like a ridiculous child.

"I... I don't know."

"You do know. You blame the house?" Florifera flicked the pendulum up and caught it in her hand, her fingers making a protective fist around it.

"Yes."

"Don't keep up pretences. I'm here to help you. I've

already acknowledged that this house is haunted. You don't have to feel shame for acknowledging the same thing."

"Is it possible to blame the house for something that happened miles away?" Freya's fingers found the bottom of her shirt, and she wrapped the material around her fingers.

"I can't answer that. This house is certainly a strong influence, and spirits can travel from one place to the next. I know the human psyche can be very fragile when it comes to the world beyond, but I don't know with certainty if there is a direct causality between the house and her death."

"I don't think there is. Or there shouldn't be... I just... I feel like there is."

"I understand." The woman dropped the pendulum from between her fingers, the blue stone bouncing a few times before hanging still. Florifera closed her eyes, and a deep wrinkle creased the skin between her eyebrows. Freya stared at the pendulum. It hung completely still for several seconds and then, without provocation, began to swing in circles. Faster and faster, the milky blue stone spun. Freya watched closely, but she was unable to detect any movement from the hand that held it.

"I sense several different sources of paranormal activity. The strongest is beneath us. Perhaps in a basement... perhaps even deeper than that. There is strength in what lies beneath, and darkness." The blood drained from Florifera's face, tinting her skin an ashen grey, and she took a step to maintain her balance. Freya moved forward to support her, but Marie-Claire waved her away.

"I'm fine, child, just a little overwhelmed by the intensity of what's in this house." She wiped her hand across her brow and closed her eyes again. "The second strongest source is upstairs. That's where the other half live. The two are connected, one needs the other. I have a feeling that there is a bit of a cat and mouse game going on between that which resides below and that which exists above." She raised her head towards the ceiling, and Freya followed her gaze, but she saw nothing.

"Those above fear those below. And then there are the strays, the stragglers. Those who don't truly belong to the house but have become a part of it. Some died here, and some were brought here by loved ones."

Cold chills ran down Freya's spine. She felt the blood drain from her own face this time, and her heart pounded madly.

"How many spirits are here?"

"Many, dear, I sense many. I sense the house too. Its presence is rather loud."

"The house?"

"This world has places which are more connected to the spirit world. Where the veil, for lack of a better word, is at its thinnest. The influences of the afterlife weigh heavier in these places. Angel Manor is built on one of the strongest paranormal sites I've encountered in my life so far. It's overwhelming. And I can tell you, dear, I've seen a lot in my sixty-eight years."

"So what's going to happen now?"

"Well, in the following days, we'll be trying to make contact with the spirits and see what we're dealing with. Then we'll work on trying to find a way to get them to cross over."

"Like an exorcism?"

"Of a sort, yes." Florifera took a step towards her and reached out her arm. "I changed my mind, dear. I don't want a tour after all. This house is a little too strong for me, and I don't think it's a good idea to go wandering without a bit of back up. I can't see the spirits yet, but their presence is already tugging at me."

"Is that bad?"

"I don't know yet. But let us go and drink a cup of that tea you promised me, and then we'll get the equipment set up. That will give us a better idea of what we're dealing with."

"Okay." Freya took the frail arm.

"And over tea, perhaps you can fill in all the other things you forgot to tell me."

"What do you mean?"

"You haven't told me the whole story. The ghosts you encountered would be a good start."

Freya took a deep breath and grabbed the woman's arm. A sense of relief flooded over her, and she felt safe. This woman knew about the house, and she wouldn't think Freya was crazy. A weight lifted from her shoulders as they both made their way back to the kitchen.

***

It took Florifera's crew two hours to set up their equipment. The blind medium led the way, pointing out the rooms where they would have to place various infra-red cameras, heat and motion sensors, voice recorders, and other electronics that made little sense to Freya. It had been decided to make the kitchen the headquarters for the laptops. It had everything within arm's reach as well as plenty of electrical outlets. Plus, according to Ruben, it was conveniently located. The kitchen table and most of the counters were covered with computers and other machinery that Freya couldn't even put a name to. Two of the crew members, a young guy with white blond hair and a large nose, who introduced himself as Pierre, and a very short man with long brown hair, who had said his name was Darren, sat behind their respective laptops. They tested the visuals on the different cameras, concentration written across their faces, while the other two looked on over their shoulders, muttering technical things that bored Freya to tears.

Marie-Claire had made a half-hearted attempt to introduce Freya to the team, but the ghost hunters were too busy setting up shop and barely gave her a second glance. Freya didn't like the way the young, overweight Australian woman with the face full of freckles looked at Logan, and she felt a little threatened by her presence.

"Tell me when you began to experience strange feelings about this house? What's happened during your time here?" Florifera grabbed her hand and took a seat at the kitchen table.

"I think it started on the first day we got here. I mean... it's not like we're constantly overwhelmed by ghosts, and I haven't seen any furniture flying around like in the movies or anything."

The old woman laughed, her voice clear as crystal chimes, and she threw her head back.

"No, things are seldom like they are in movies."

Freya couldn't help but wonder if a blind woman was capable of watching movies, and if she did, would she get any satisfaction out of them.

"When we first got to the house, shortly after my aunt died, we had a bit of a shock. The entrance hall and the main hall were both in ruins, covered in cobwebs, and I mean *covered*, but there wasn't a single spider in sight. And there was this stuff coming out of the walls... like slime."

"Slime?" The old woman looked genuinely confused. "What do you mean?"

"Well, I'm not sure, because it was gone the next day, but there was this slimy stuff oozing from cracks in the walls. We all saw it, but when we returned the next day, it had disappeared. Maybe we were mistaken."

"No, this is very possible. There have been physical manifestations of paranormal occurrences, some mediums would argue that you encountered a substance we call ectoplasm."

"That sounds like something out of Ghostbusters." Freya scrunched up her face and tried to hold back her laughter; the whole idea seemed so silly. But the thought of the children in the attic brought her thoughts back into perspective.

"There is more though. I... we... some people are connected to this house. We can't leave without getting sick."

"You are bound to this house?"

"Yes, it seems that way. The longer we're away from the house, or the further, the worse it gets. Bam..." Freya felt a surge of emotion well up from within and had to take a moment to regain her composure. "Bam left and got sick. She... she died a few days later."

The older woman looked her straight in the eyes, and Freya found herself wondering once again if those white eyes could see after all.

"That's interesting," was all she said, her expression encouraging Freya to continue.

The words spilled from her lips like a waterfall. She rambled about the attic, about the children and the spiders they'd found. She talked about the house, and the spirit she'd seen when they'd first opened the East Wing, about Bam and how frightened her friend had been, about Oliver and how he was acting out of sorts. She told everything she could remember in chaotic sequence, and by the end of her story, she was sure none of it had made sense.

"And people keep disappearing too. At least, I think they do. The phone guy was gone for hours, though his van's gone now so he must have left. But there were two builders that never came back. They could have run away, but... Oh God, those guys will be back tonight." She placed her head in her hands, and without provocation, the tears started to pour from her eyes. "I didn't even think about that. And Oliver... he's missing now too. I can't find him anywhere."

"Hush, dear." A hand rested on her shoulder. "If they are gone, we will find them. Let's not panic just yet. You are no longer alone." The words blew through her mind like a warm wind.

"I'm not. I'm so happy you're here. I just want to be able to leave this all behind me. But I can't."

"I know, dear. And everything will be okay. I've seen some things in my life, and I've always been able to help. We will find out what your house wants and then we will force it to release you. We—"

Her words were interrupted by excited chatter and cheers.

"Unbelievable," Ruben said. "Marie-Claire, we already have evidence of activity. We've never had such an instant response before."

"What did you see?"

"We just saw a figure cross through the corridor in the South Wing."

"In daylight?" Marie-Claire's white eyebrows arched.

"In broad daylight."

"Now that is unusual."

"We're picking something up on the EVP as well." Julie held a set of headphones against her ear and fiddled with the dials. "There's a noise. I think that someone might be trying to speak to us."

"So soon?" Ruben turned to the girl now, and he looked as stunned as Marie-Claire did. Freya felt her skin tingle with a combination of excitement and fear.

"I need to get the static out, but I'm pretty sure I can get the voice clear enough for us to hear." Julie put the headphones over her ears. "Yes, I definitely have something to work with here."

Marie-Claire got up from her seat, and Darren rushed to her aid.

"It's never happened this fast, this house must be very active. Let me hear what you have, Julie." The girl was still fiddling, but after several minutes, she unplugged the headphones and plugged in a set of speakers. Then she turned around, her eyes wide and her face so pale that Freya felt a jolt of fear.

"It's very clear. I didn't even have to cut out too many of the background noises." She pressed a button and a voice, soft and female, sounded over the crackling noises.

'The equinox is near. You must leave. I'm getting weaker. The Angels will be free."

The same short phrases were repeated over and over in a desperate tone. The acid in Freya's stomach bubbled, and a thick, sour-tasting bile made its way from her throat to the back of her tongue before she managed to swallow it away. Every muscle in her body tensed, only relaxing when Logan rested his warm hand on her shoulder. She turned her head up to him.

"I wish I knew where Oliver was," she whispered. "This stuff is freaking me out." He nodded and slid his arm around her chest, pulling her closer.

"I need to seek out the entity that we've heard." Marie-Claire's voice rang over the recording. "The best way to go about this is if we have a one-on-one communication."

"We don't know what we're dealing with yet, *chérie*. Let's not be rash."

"There is an opportunity here and now, so I will investigate it. As I always do." Her voice was sharp.

"You said this house was different, that we had to be careful, and now you're running into the unknown without caution."

"I don't think this spirit is malevolent, Ruben."

"Marie-Claire, We don't know that."

"Please, don't argue with me."

Ruben's shoulders slumped, and Freya knew Marie-Claire was the more dominant of the two.

"At least take Pierre with you."

Marie-Claire shook her head. "It works better if I go alone."

"You wanted to record the phenomena, didn't you? Then take the *putain* kid with you." He swore under his breath in French.

"Fine, if that's what you want." The older woman's voice held its sharpness, but her face was gentle. This round was for Ruben, but it was a small victory judging by the man's sour expression. Pierre grabbed his camera, an eager expression on his face, and then he took hold of Marie-Claire's hand. They exited the kitchen together, leaving the rest of the company watching the monitors.

Chapter 27

The power of the house was so potent she could see the contours of the building. There was magic running through the very mortar holding the bricks together. Part of it came from spells, Marie-Claire knew. She could feel them, protective spells mostly, but the magic had been corrupted somehow. Yet there was something else here, something so ancient, she didn't know what she was dealing with, though she planned to find out.

A spirit had reached out to them, had called out a warning, and Marie-Claire wanted to investigate what it all meant. The warning made her a little wary, the equinox was drawing near. In fact, it would be at midnight that very night so time was running short.

Marie-Claire knew from experience that the dead possessed a sense of melodrama, yet at the same time, she wasn't the kind of woman who would take a warning lightly. It worried her that the spirit had made contact in daylight. That was unusual. Marie-Claire never knew why, but sunlight seemed to have an effect on paranormal activities.

"This is the room where the EVP was recorded." Darren's hand was clammy and hot in hers, and she heard nervous enthusiasm vibrate in his voice.

"Is there a place where I can sit?"

"There's a bed."

"Bring me to it. Then keep your distance and roll the camera."

The side of the bed pressed against her knees, and Marie-Claire felt her way down, her hands touching the mattress carefully. She took a deep breath and smelled the scent of the sheets, the wood of the bed, and a hint of cleaning fluid. Darren's footsteps retreated a few paces, and she heard the clicking of the camera. Her hands rested in her lap, she inhaled deeply and opened her mind. Around her, the room came to life, an otherworldly white canvas interrupted by violet and fuchsia rays of light. She allowed her third eye to roam around the room, to connect with the energy of the house.

"I am here if you wish to speak to me. I am open and willing, and I will listen." She spoke the words softly, repeating them a second time. She opened her thoughts to let the influences of the house inside.

A spiritual essence hit her with such force that Marie-Claire was pushed all the way across the bed to the headboard. The blankets tangled around her legs, and the impact against the wood made her teeth rattle. She could hear Darren yelp and curse, but she held her hand up to indicate that he should keep his distance. Marie-Claire struggled to get her thoughts together, as it felt as if dozens, perhaps hundreds, of eyes were suddenly upon her.

"I got your attention it seems," she muttered breathlessly. "Good, maybe now we can talk."

There were several different emotions pressing upon her psyche. She felt the fear of the spirits in the attic, their child-like minds, young and old at the same time, nudging her gently. At the same time, she felt curiosity from the lost ones, who were now part of the house but still had some sense of individuality left. And she felt the strong, hungry minds of those who resided below. They were the most interested, and they called out to her, taunted her without words. She felt their hunger, their longing. They wanted to harm her, not just kill, but to break her very essence. Marie-Claire battled the fear she felt for them, refusing to let them get the upper hand. There was something parasitic about these ones, and although she had encountered the force before in poltergeists, it was never this strong. There were so many of them, and Marie-Claire experienced a strong urge to flee the house.

"I acknowledge your presence." Her voice was breathy with exertion. "But I'm here to speak to the woman who talked to us. Can you reveal yourself? I am here to listen." The medium pushed the different minds away from hers, giving her a bit of breathing space. The hungry minds were particularly difficult to push; they were clinging to her like hooks in the mouths of fish.

"I am here to listen," Marie-Claire repeated. Something rushed at her, and she was shocked to see a woman dressed in a nun's habit. Her face was unclear, but she could sense her as a light shadow.

"What's going on, Marie-Claire? I see a really weird light near you." Darren's voice trembled.

"I see it. There is a spirit here with me."

"You must leave, before it is too late." The voice was the same from the EVP recording.

"What is your name?"

"I am Sister Agatha. I built this house almost two hundred years ago. I am the only truly free spirit left in Angel Manor."

"What is it that you want, Sister Agatha?"

"I don't have much time. The equinox weakens me, while the others grow strong. The living need to be away from the dead before it's too late."

"Too late for what?"

"The existing spells won't hold the Angels when the equinox is here. Even the power of the salt borders will be diminished. It is their time, and they must perform their unspeakable acts. They will not spare the living. They will seek them out the same way they sought out the children. Get them out."

Marie-Claire felt the spirit weaken; the house was siphoning off its energy.

"We will leave this house as soon as we can. But there are those who are tied to this house who can't physically leave. And there are spirits here that need to be released."

"No." The word was a desperate scream that filled Marie-Claire's head, and the elderly woman cringed. "You must not free the spirits of Angel Manor. If you do, you will put everyone in danger. Leave this house." The face came close now, and Marie-Claire could feel the anger within it, the bed bucking as wildly as an angry bull.

"Holy shit, are you guys seeing this?" Darren sounded terrified, and there was loud banging all around. The spirit was manipulating their surroundings, but its strength was running out. Marie-Claire watched the shadows fade as its power drained. Then it disappeared and all was quiet again. The old woman's heart hammered in her chest, and it took several minutes before she could move or speak again.

"Did you get all that?" Her voice betrayed her fatigue.

"I certainly did. That was insane."

"Good, let's go join the others."

***

Ruben played the video again, and all eyes were on Freya and Logan.

"Yes, there, I can see her clearly. It's a female figure and she's dressed as a nun." Freya looked around the surprised faces. "You can't see her?"

Ruben shook his head. "I just see light."

"I can see her too." Logan frowned and put his fingers on the bridge of his nose, massaging the flesh gently. "What does that mean?"

"It means that you're connected to the house." Marie-Claire stood in the door opening, a flustered Darren behind her. "You will be far more sensitive to what this house has to offer than the others are. And, you are right, the woman was wearing a nun's habit. Her name is Sister Agatha. I'm not sure, but I think she might be a defence mechanism of the house. She really doesn't want us to release the spirits. What she does want is for us to leave." The old woman waved her hand, her face was filled with fatigue. "I've seen this before at strong supernatural hotspots, spirits trying to protect the area from human activity. They are usually quite harmless, a lot of noise but no real fireworks."

"Did you see what she did to the doors, or the bed you were sitting on?" Ruben frowned. "She was hardly powerless. Every door in the hallway slammed open and shut, and your bed actually left the ground a few times. You know spirits like that are dangerous."

"It left her drained. I don't think she has a lot of power left. She fears the equinox, and I think that might be the perfect time to release the spirits. I might have a plan as to how to go about it. There is powerful magic in the changing of the seasons."

"The guys will return in a few hours. Will that be a problem?"

"It won't be convenient, but if they keep out of the way, it should be fine. Things might get a little intense here tonight, though." It was Ruben who answered the question. "We've dealt with onlookers before."

"If these boys are in any way connected to this house, perhaps it's for the best that they are around. You said yourself you have bonded with the house. Perhaps they've done the same?" Marie-Claire rested her white eyes on Freya, who shook her head, a pang of worry knotting in her stomach.

"I don't know. I don't think any of the guys had nose bleeds. I just don't want them to see anything scary. They don't know the house is haunted, and I want to keep it that way."

Logan stepped up next to her. "I agree with Freya. When the guys come back, I'm going to let them collect their stuff. They're going to stay in a B&B for a few days while you work your mojo. I can't take a risk with these kids. Freya and I will stay, and I hope we'll hear from Oliver too, but the rest of my group is getting out of this house." His words flooded her with a sense of relief, and her hand found his. She wrapped her fingers around his and squeezed, and he responded to the gesture.

"Very well, if you believe that's best. I don't mind either way."

"Good, then we agree."

"If you don't mind, we have a lot of things to prepare for the exorcism. We shall start the ritual at sundown. Your presence will be required, Miss Formynder, since you are the blood-link to this house."

"I'll be there. I promised the children I would help, and I will."

***

It was late when the four young men and two counsellors spilled into the house, laughing and chatting. Logan greeted them in the entrance hall.

"You came home late." He chided with a grin. "Did you guys have a good time?"

"It was awesome." Terrence smiled brightly, and Logan realised how young the boy looked. "We should have done this earlier. There were these two women—"

Logan held up his hand to stop Terrence from talking. He was too drained to listen to their stories now, too eager to say what needed to be said.

"Listen, guys. There is some stuff going on around here,

in the house, and you six need to clear out for a few days."

"Now?" Jim rubbed his gleaming scalp. "It's past half-nine, Logan."

"I really want you to leave as soon as possible." Logan hoped his friends and colleagues could see that he meant business.

"What's going on?" Jim took a step forward, cocking his head, his thick beard standing out. "You're acting very strange."

"There's been some stuff... in the house. We're trying to sort it out." Logan ran his hand across the back of his neck, and he wished he'd prepared more for this conversation.

"What kind of stuff?" John stepped forward now too, his brow low and furrowed. "What are you on about, mate?"

"I really don't know how to explain this to you, to be honest, John."

"Explain what?" John rested a hand on Logan's shoulder. "Let's talk, you and I." They stepped away from the curious stares of the others.

"What's going on, Logan?" John repeated Jim's question.

"There's a ghost hunting team here."

"Ghost hunting?" John laughed loud and deep, then his face turned serious. "You're not kidding?"

"Nope, there is something going on in this house, and it's insane."

"Ghosts? Come on now, Logan. Don't tell me you're buying this crap?"

"I saw them, John." Logan couldn't look his friend and colleague in the eyes. "We saw some dead kids in the attic, and we saw some sort of ghost nun on the camera just now."

"Ghost nun?" Jim's voice was loud and his eyes were round. "Fuck that, I hate nuns."

"I think it's best if you and the boys leave." Logan rested his hand on John's arm and squeezed lightly. "Maybe just for a little bit, or maybe forever. I don't know. I suggest you find a bed and breakfast tonight and either stay there for a few days or go back to Edinburgh."

"Logan, come on..." John shook his head, a half incredulous smile frozen on his lips. "You're not serious? Ghost nuns?"

Jim flinched again.

Logan sighed. "I'm deadly serious. I don't know what to expect, but I don't want the guys to be a part of this."

"We can leave in the morning, mate. We've had a long day, we're all tired, and we don't want to go back out again looking for a bed and breakfast."

"This is not negotiable, John. You leave tonight." Logan wasn't talking quietly now, and he looked at the four young men as he spoke the last words.

"Fine by me," Jim muttered, and then he repeated, "I hate nuns."

"No they don't." Oliver's voice cut through the entrance hall, and Logan looked at him with surprise. The figure in the doorway looked as if he'd just gone on a three week survival hunt. His clothes were torn and filthy, and his brown curls hung listlessly and greasy on his forehead. Oliver's skin was pale, and deep blue circles lined his eyes; he reminded Logan of one of the ghost children, but the difference was that Oliver Jardin was still very much alive.

"Everyone into the kitchen. I have something to tell you." He pointed with an authoritarian gesture towards the West Wing, his eyes blazing. The young men complied in shocked silence, and even Logan followed along, though he wondered why he was listening to the mad-eyed man. The scent of sour sweat, and what Logan suspected could be vomit, permeated from Oliver's every pore, and he had to do his best not to gag. There was something else he could smell too... a more disturbing scent. Oliver smelled like death. "Where were you, man?" Logan eyed the dirt on his torn clothes. The man's whole appearance was unsettling and Logan felt a nagging in his stomach. "Freya was worried sick."

"I have an important announcement."

"Are you okay?"

Oliver gave him an agitated glare. "Just go into the kitchen."

Logan sighed, but he followed Oliver's lead, partially out of curiosity and partially because the shorter man sounded so convincing.

They stumbled into the kitchen, the guys wide-eyed at the sight of all the equipment, and Florifera's crew looked up from their screens in surprise.

"Ollie?" Freya took a step towards him. "What happened to you? You look a right mess."

"I have something to say." Oliver swayed from side to side.

"Say it, mate." It was John who spoke, and though Logan couldn't see his friend's face, he heard the irritation in his tone. "I would like to know what's going on here."

"Tonight is an important night. Angel Manor has informed me that you will all be its guests for the equinox."

"Ollie, you're sounding a little mental." Freya ran her fingers through her dark hair, her nose wrinkled and her eyes round. "The house informed you?"

Oliver turned to her. "Yes, Freya... the house. Aren't you the one who is going on about hauntings?"

"I thought you didn't believe in ghosts." Freya sounded exasperated.

Logan took a step towards Freya, ready to protect her from anything he possibly could. There was sadness in her eyes, and he wanted to be her hero, but he didn't quite know how.

"Oh, there's no denying that ghosts are real, Freya. No denying it at all." Oliver shook his head slowly, a too-wide grin plastered on his face. "And the ghosts here are important. They keep the world in balance. You have no idea what we are a part of... absolutely no idea. It's so magnificent. You are all so fortunate that you can be a part of it too."

He pointed from the Chancers, who were standing together in a corner, to Florifera's crew, who were sitting behind their computers.

"Tonight the house will have fresh souls. It's been longing for them for several generations, but the children of the bloodline have been too careful, too prepared." He turned to Freya again and pointed at her. "Until you came, Freya. You broke that spell. You brought new blood into the house, and it woke up. It's hungry. The house is so very hungry. You can feel it too, can't you? As can you, Logan..."

"Dude is off his fucking tits," Terrence whispered, and someone else giggled in response. Oliver didn't seem to notice. His eyes were still on Freya. Logan had to admit there was a point to what the crazy man was saying. He could sense the hunger too, and it seemed to be growing.

"Listen, Oliver. How about you sit down, mate?" Logan lifted his hands. "I'm going to let John and Jim and the guys collect their stuff, and get them out of here. Then we'll talk about this, okay?"

"They're not going anywhere. The house has other plans for them."

"Okay, that's really nice, mate. But I don't really think

there's anything you can do to stop them from leaving."

"I can't stop them, no. But Angel Manor can. Can't you feel it? The magic? It's almost time..."

"Okay, fuck this. Come on guys. We're going to get your stuff." Logan put his hand on Freya's shoulder and squeezed it. "Are you going to be okay?" She looked at him with those big grey eyes and nodded. His stomach flipped. "Good. I'll be right back, okay?"

He jerked his head towards the door, a sign for John, Jim and the rest to follow him. Oliver remained where he stood, and for a moment, Logan was afraid that he would try to block his exit. He really didn't want to fight him, not because he was afraid, but because Oliver was obviously unstable.

"Step aside, mate. Let's not do this."

"It won't matter. The house won't let you leave."

"Step aside." Logan's voice was low and menacing, and Oliver stepped out of the doorway. Relief flooded through Logan's mind, but he remained wary of the wild-eyed man. He stayed near the door, allowing the young men to go through first, followed by the two counsellors. Oliver never moved. Logan stared straight ahead, his nerves on edge. It wouldn't surprise him one bit if Oliver turned out to have a knife hidden somewhere. As he walked by, he felt Oliver's eyes burn in the back of his neck, but there was no attack.

"What the fuck?" Terrence's cry tore him from his thoughts of Oliver, and Logan looked up perturbed. They had walked through the door, but instead of the large entrance hall, they were in a room that looked vaguely familiar to Logan.

"Where did the main hall go?" Everyone froze, and Logan made his way around the young men to inspect the room.

"Where are we?"

Logan stepped further into the room. His hand rose to his mouth. Nothing in his mind could make sense out of what he was seeing.

"This is impossible," he muttered.

"What the hell is going on?" John stood next to him. Logan was at a loss for words, and he turned back to the door to the East Wing only to see that it was gone.

"How did we get here?" Terrence stepped further into the room, but Logan's hand shot out to hold him back.

"We're in the attic." Logan's breath was heavy and his words were soft.

"That's not possible." Terrence shook his head and pushed Logan's hand away.

It wasn't possible, and yet... there they were. Logan took several deep breaths and tried to control his chaotic thoughts.

"Okay, I don't know what's happening, but we need to get out of here."

"It's too late. The house won't let you go. It has waited for this moment." The voices were sad and soft, yet they rang clearly through the attic.

"Oh shit." The boys huddled together, and they looked more lost than Logan had ever seen them.

"Are those ghosts?" It was Mason who spoke, his body shaking. "I can't deal with ghosts." He pointed at the darkness, and when Logan followed his finger, he saw the children.

Chapter 28

"All the screens just went black." Pierre looked over his shoulder, and Freya leaned forward to see what he was talking about.

"We're not having a power failure," she said, looking at the lights in the kitchen. "Everything else seems to be working."

Pierre pushed the button on his screen, but it remained black.

"Can't get mine to work either." Darren sighed and stood up, inspecting the cables. "Nothing's unplugged."

"The sun has gone down. The witching hour is upon us." Marie-Claire's voice carried despite its soft tones.

"Midnight is nearing." Oliver's tense words sounded from the entrance. "Soon the Angels will be free."

"You keep saying that." Freya couldn't keep the irritability from her voice. "Would you mind explaining what you mean by it, though? Because, frankly, you're starting to get on my nerves."

"Why do you think I let you bring these mediums into our house, Freya? I wanted more people here for when the equinox started. The more the merrier." His laughter was high and hysterical.

"Jesus, Ollie. You're starting to sound like a cartoon villain. Stop it. What the fuck is wrong with you?" Though she was looking at what was technically her best friend in the whole world, Freya barely recognised him. Even his body language was different, and she didn't know what to do.

"EVP is still working, we just have no visual." Ruben's voice broke the tension, and Freya turned to look at him. She noticed that no one else was paying attention to Oliver; they were too busy trying to get their equipment to work. Only Marie-Claire Florifera stared blindly in Oliver's direction, though Freya wasn't sure if she was paying attention to him or if it was just coincidence.

Oliver just stood in the door opening, swaying on his legs, and every so often he would look outside or to the ceiling and a dark smile would cloud his face.

"What are you looking at?"

"Nothing. Just waiting." Oliver looked at his watch. "Two and a half hours until midnight. That's when the festivities begin." He chuckled again, his eyebrows raised so far they disappeared under the matted brown curls.

"Oliver, please piss off now. I can't deal with you. This is too mental. Go to your room and stay there or something."

"Don't worry, Frey, the house has acknowledged us as its guardians. It needs us, you know? Did your aunt tell you that? She didn't, did she? She hasn't told you shit, that old bitch."

"I'm going to put you to bed. I've had enough of your shit." She gathered her courage, not wanting to admit that this new Oliver was frightening her, and grabbed him by the shoulders. For a moment, he looked as if he were going to pull loose, or perhaps even hit her, but he just stared at her from under his curls with those mad round eyes, and Freya wanted nothing more than to kick him out of the house. But she couldn't. He was bound to this place the same way she was, and no matter how much he freaked her out, she would do nothing to harm him.

"We'll be safe, Freya, but we need to let this happen. We need to help the house. It's important. We need... we need to make the sacrifice, Freya. Don't you feel it? Don't you know what it demands of us?" His eyes pleaded with her

292

now, and a little bit of spittle ran from the corner of his mouth. Freya wanted to cry, but she fought the tears.

"I'm going to take Oliver to his room, okay? I'll be right back."

"Be careful, dear." Marie-Claire reached out a hand in her direction. "The boy is under a spell, and it's a powerful one."

Every muscle in Freya's body tensed. It made sense, what the old woman said, but the thought of Oliver under a spell made her feel extremely vulnerable. If the house could get to him in this manner, it could get to all of them. Oliver was the one who didn't believe in ghosts, the one who had always been down to earth and sceptical. It seemed absurd that he would be the one in the grasp of magic.

"Can you undo it?"

"I hope that, when I find a way to release the souls from this house, it will release his spirit too. That should break the spell." The old woman frowned, her face creased. "Technically, it should break it."

"And if it doesn't?"

"Then we try something else." The old woman sighed. "I told you, dear. You are no longer alone. Now, go put that young man to bed, and stay with him. I don't want him getting in the way. I suspect he might try to sabotage any effort we're making."

"You told me that spirits couldn't harm us." A bitter taste coated her tongue, and she couldn't keep the accusatory tone from her voice.

"I said they couldn't harm you physically. I believe I mentioned they could influence our moods and minds though."

"This is more than a little influence." She pointed at her friend.

"This house is stronger than anything I've encountered before, dear. It's rather exceptional. Your friend must have been an easy target for it. Perhaps he was emotionally unstable when you moved in, or perhaps he wanted something too much. I can only guess. Whatever it was, the magic has him in its hold now, and you'd best stay with him tonight."

Tears spilled across Freya's cheeks. She wanted this night to be over. The way Oliver spoke about it made her afraid. The thought of the Angels, whoever they were, made her stomach sink to her knees. She didn't want them to roam free. In fact, she didn't even want to be in this house. She felt young and helpless.

"Please help us."

"Yes, dear. That's what I'm here for." The French accent was soothing, and something between a sigh and a sob escaped from Freya's throat as she wiped the tears from her eyes.

"Thank you."

She grabbed Oliver by the shoulders again and spun him around.

"Come on, sunshine. Let's put you to bed until the worst is over."

To her relief, Oliver let her guide him with a lamb-like docility as she steered him into the hallway. Something struck her as odd, but she couldn't put her finger on it. Only when she opened the door to Oliver's bedroom and peered inside did she understand what was bothering her.

"What the hell? How did we get here?" She looked into the dining room. It looked brand new now, its floors polished and the rug unblemished and bright. Light from the candelabra filled the room. The table was set with silver dishes, and the whole room smelled of salty roast meats. Freya's blood ran cold.

"It's starting." Oliver giggled and sat at the table, tucking in to the banquet as if he'd been starved. His hand wrapped around the leg of a large turkey, and he pulled with all his might until the meat came loose. To Freya's horror, the turkey started to bleed thick, dark red blood.

"Oliver, don't touch that." Her hand went up to warn him. Oliver turned around, the leg between his teeth, the corners of his mouth curled up behind the meat. He ripped a piece of the flesh off while the red liquid dripped down his chin, and when he smiled at her, maggots wiggled on his tongue.

"You should try some of this." A swarm of black flies flew out of his mouth, and Freya screamed.

She turned and ran, trying to find her way back to the safety of the kitchen. Somewhere in the house the old grandfather clock chimed eleven times.

***

The house was gaining strength fast, and Marie-Claire was sure the oncoming equinox was only partially to blame. There was something about this place that worried her, but she couldn't quite divine what it was. The darkness woke the house, and she could feel it fight back against her efforts to understand it. Whatever made this building had given it a twisted form of consciousness; the whole thing had a mind of its own. There was something special about this area, and it wasn't just the house. The magic ran deeper and wider than that, all the way to Lucifer Falls.

Perhaps you have bitten off more than you can chew on this one, she chided herself inwardly, though her pride refused to admit it. She heard the crew muttering over their loss of feed, but the old woman knew this wasn't about proving things to the world anymore; this was now simply about survival. She promised the girl she would help, but she hoped the sacrifice wouldn't be as great as she feared it might be. The image of the nun came to mind. "Ruben." The word came out like a command, and Ruben rushed to her side. The smell of his cologne was familiar and comforting.

"What's the matter, *Cherie*?"

She rested her head on his chest. "Do you remember that time in Taiwan? In the Bagua building?"

"The mass exorcism? How can I forget?" He patted her hair.

Marie-Claire looked up at him, frowning. "I want you to start setting it up. We're going to go ahead with it tonight."

"Just like that?" She felt his hand on her arm. "Marie-Claire, I thought you wanted to get some data first. To get some proof this time? Why the change of heart?"

"This house is more dangerous than I initially thought it was. I didn't see it before, but I do now. Let's not take risks." She patted his hand with her own. "I would like to have everything ready before midnight, so I need you to rush. There isn't much time. Set everything up in that large area just off the entrance hall. That's a nice central place in the house, and it should draw everything towards it. I would like to have things contained before these 'Angels' get loose. I don't trust them."

"This will ruin all that you have worked for. You know that, right?"

"There will be other times. Please, I don't want to take the risk. That boy is already possessed, and we don't know what else will happen."

"We've dealt with possessed people before."

"Ruben, please. Just stop arguing with me."

"Fine, but I'm taking Darren with me."

"Do so, but please be careful." She heard the sound of the clock striking eleven. *Only one hour until the equinox.*

***

"Why do we need to get stuff for a ritual? I thought Marie-Claire could show the spirits the light." Darren adjusted the lens of his camera and aimed it at Ruben, who gave him a grouchy look. The corridor was dark, and he wondered whether the lights simply hadn't been turned on, or if they didn't work. The house was in some disrepair.

"She can. We're just going to get a few little things to help her against any spiritual influences. Rock salt, sage, cedar... the usual stuff. And chalk to make a ritual circle. You'd be amazed how easy these things are. It's not even about saying the right words, though that can give the caster a bit of a benefit. Mind you, there needs to be magic behind it; these are merely tools to enhance it."

"It feels a bit hoaxy." Darren pointed his camera at the hall, his eyes fixed on the screen.

"It's effective." There was a terseness to Ruben's voice, and Darren knew he had to watch what he said next. The old man's feathers were easily ruffled. Darren didn't want to be on Ruben's bad side. He had seen the treatment Ruben gave Pierre, and he wasn't about to invite the same behaviour.

"Sure," he said, pointing the infrared camera the other way. "Wait..." Darren came to a halt. "We took a wrong turn."

"It seems so. We should have gone the other way." Darren watched Ruben turn around through the eye of his camera. The white-on-green images were more comforting than facing the darkness. Darren still felt the fresh tingle of nerves each time they visited a new haunted area, but this house was a little too intense for his liking. The others had sensed it too, Darren was sure of it. Everyone was more serious than normal.

Something moved across the screen on his camera, startling him into a soft yelp.

"What?" Ruben turned to him with an irritated glance.

"I think I saw something move."

"What?"

"I don't know... it was really fast. I can't see it now. Maybe it was just a shadow or something. I'm not sure."

"*Merde*, where are we? I can't find the kitchen anymore." Ruben cursed under his breath and turned around. "This whole corridor looks different from how it did before. I don't understand."

"Maybe we got turned around again?"

"Put that stupid camera down and help me look." Ruben put his hand on the camera and pulled it away from Darren's face. Darren sighed. He knew that the older man was irritable, and it was best to help him find his way. He looked around and realised he hadn't been through here before. Ruben spun back around and took tall strides towards the end of the corridor.

"Dead end."

"Then we should go the other way?" He posed the idea as a question, afraid to tick Ruben off even more.

"There is no other way to go, is there?" Ruben walked towards the other side, Darren in tow. But when they reached the end of the corridor, all they found was another dead end.

"This isn't right." Ruben stood still, scratching his head. "I don't understand what's going on here. How can this be another dead end? We didn't take any turns anywhere, did we?"

"I don't think so."

Behind them, they heard a loud metallic bang.

"Eh..." Darren froze to the spot and looked at Ruben.

"It came from there." Ruben pointed at a large metal door.

"What does it mean?"

"How should I know?"

"You're the ghost hunting expert. I only joined two years ago. I've never heard any sound like that before."

"I rather not find out what it means, thank you. Let's just find a way out of here. I would feel better if we could get back to Marie-Claire."

"What about the salt and stuff?"

"Fuck the salt. I think it's better that we just stick together now."

***

"There has to be an exit somewhere. I know the attic runs across the whole of the top floor. We'll go through a window if we have to." Logan eyed his young crew, who were uncharacteristically quiet. Even Terrence, who didn't easily lose his bravado, was subdued. Mason looked positively terrified. He had no idea how long they'd been in the attic, but it had to have been at least an hour. As far as he knew, they'd searched every corner, every nook and cranny, but they had yet to find a way out. The house kept changing around on them. Logan decided he had a passionate hatred for Angel Manor. If he ever got the chance to burn the house down, he would. First the bastard had to let him go, though. He didn't want to end up like that little pink-haired girl.

The ghosts were still with them, and Logan was grateful that the young men seemed less frightened of them now. After all, the spirits seemed harmless, but the frustration of being locked up in this huge, dark attic was getting to all of them. Even John and Jim, who were mostly down-to-earth fellows, were pale and silent. Somewhere in the depths of the house, Logan heard the loud chimes of a clock. With each ring, the sound seemed to grow louder. Mason Applebaum fiddled with his thick glasses and counted along with the chimes.

"Nine, ten..."

"Come on guys... we'll try this way again," Logan urged, feeling a growing unease with each chime.

"Eleven."

"Maybe we can pry open that window we saw earlier."

"Twelve."

The house trembled with a loud roar. Logan felt his ears pop, and he swallowed hard to negate the uncomfortable feeling. The attic was cloaked in silence. Not a creak or a sigh of wind... and for a moment, Logan wondered if he had gone deaf. Then... the screaming began.

Chapter 29

They all felt it. Every living person in the house felt the arrival of the equinox. The darkness spread from the very core of the ground beneath the house, stretching up like tiny black veins, painting everything in shadow. The inside of the house expanded, keeping its living victims in the centre, away from any potential escape routes. The energy of the sun and the moon breathed even more life into the house's soul, and Angel Manor woke with a hungry shudder. It knew it was time for the sacrifice, but this time would be different. This time, there would be fresh meat.

***

This was her chance. Bam felt the power of the equinox wash over her. Her ghostly form seemed to become more substantial, and power coursed through her. The house tugged at her, demanding obedience more than ever before, but she had more natural strength too. All she needed to do was to find Freya, and she could help. Angel Manor would allow her to help Freya, she just knew. It was more difficult to sense the living now that the magic was alive. Finding Freya could prove a challenge. The only benefit was that it would be more difficult for the others as well.

Where are you, Freya?

***

After the tremor, the corridor went deadly quiet. Ruben cursed himself for not knowing where they were. They had been walking up and down, opening all the doors and looking for ways out, but nothing had proved successful. In a desperate attempt to escape, he'd tried to throw one of the chairs he found through a window, but the chair just smashed and bounced off the glass. Nothing had worked, and Ruben realised that the house was more potent than anything either he or Marie-Claire had ever experienced before. There had been a few moments during his life with Marie-Claire when he had been afraid, but he had never truly feared for his life before. Not up until now. Ruben was balancing on the verge of panic, and he didn't even know why. Perhaps it was because he was lost, or because Marie-Claire wasn't with him. Perhaps it was the strange earthquake which had unsettled him, he just didn't know. All he knew was that he would rather be anywhere else than stuck in this dark wing of the house with an asshole like Darren.

Could have been worse, he told himself. *Could have been Pierre.*

Then the whole house shook. Ruben didn't need Marie-Claire's second sight to feel the supernatural phenomena building up around him. Seconds after the tremors, he heard a screeching that went straight through his very soul. Loud, high-pitched voices, more wicked than anything he had ever heard, laughed and screamed. The voices startled Darren so badly that the imbecile dropped his camera, and he took a few steps back into the room, putting his back against a wall. Ruben was about to make a snide remark when a noise in the corridor outside made the words die on his lips. It was a wet sound, like naked feet walking clumsily on marble, not one pair of feet, but many. Soft sniggering accompanied the sound, as if a dozen schoolgirls were sneaking through the house. But Ruben knew these weren't schoolgirls. The hairs on the back of his neck stood on end, and he felt cold chills run down his spine.

He had seen spirits before, in pure form and those which had possessed humans, and there was always something unsettling about seeing them. But when the door to the room opened all by itself, Ruben knew a fear he'd never before experienced. Three women stood in the opening, and all of them were stark naked. Their skin was so pale the light of the moon coloured it a grey hue.

Cobwebs of blue-black veins lay close under the skin, and they looked at the world through milky eyes, fixing their sights on Ruben. A rotund woman with a stomach that hung over her skinny legs in three fat folds stepped into the room. She had long, waxen brown hair, hanging in frizzy curls over her shoulders. Her thin lips were covered in mucus, making them look little more than a dark gash in her face. There was hunger in her expression, and with a black tongue, she licked her lips to confirm his fears.

"The master demands his sacrifice." She spoke to him not with the ethereal voice those of the afterlife possess, but with that of a living woman. Everything about her was strong, and Ruben's knees buckled. Behind him, Darren whimpered, a dark stain spreading across the front of his trousers.

"You mean to take our lives?" Ruben turned his gaze to the woman.

"That wouldn't be much of a sacrifice. One must suffer when blood is spilled." She held up a hand, a rusty pair of clippers sitting between her fat fingers. He wondered if they were real, but in his heart of hearts, he knew the answer.

The two women stepped into the room. They were the identical image of each other. Both were tall and slender with soft round breasts, and each had long honey-blonde hair falling over their pale shoulders – one wore it to the right and the other to the left. They would have been pleasant to look at if it hadn't been for the dead eyes, the blue veins and the black mouths. They turned their heads in unison towards Darren, who let out a high-pitched scream. Each sister held a long, thick spike, and took slow, jerky steps towards him.

"Ruben?" Darren's voice was tight, but Ruben didn't dare break eye contact with the woman holding the clippers to look at him.

"I don't know who you are, lady, but we're here to help

303

you. If you haven't found your rest, then we can guide you towards the light. My companion..."

"The only help you can give me is by spilling your blood on my skin." She snipped the clippers and laughed at him. "But first, you must watch." The woman lunged towards him with inhuman speed, and her plump hand gripped his wrist like a vice. She pulled him towards her, pressing his back against her soft, doughy flesh and placing her face on his shoulder. Her chin dug into the muscle at the bottom of his neck, her waxy hair tickled against his face, and he could smell a hint of almond mixed with the bitter scent of rotting meat.

A pale arm wrapped itself around his chest, and fingers pinched his chin, forcing him to look at Darren, who was retreating towards the window.

The young man pleaded with the advancing females, holding a thin silver crucifix up in the air in an attempt to ward them off. Ruben knew that was the kind of superstitious nonsense that could only work for a true believer. Unfortunately, Ruben suspected that it didn't really matter whether Darren was one or not. These ladies were nothing like the spirits he had ever encountered. These naked females seemed to be moulded from flesh and blood, the same as the living. The women closed in on Darren, who had run out of places to manoeuvre to, and they raised the metal spikes in their hands. Darren fought back, but they each grabbed one of his arms, and though Ruben could see him struggle, they held on to him as if it didn't matter. He kicked and snapped his teeth at them, but the women remained unperturbed. They pushed him into the window, pinning him under their weight, and then brought the spikes down into his closed eyes. Darren screamed, and Ruben's stomach burned with terror. He couldn't look away. The hand had his face pinned, and when he closed his eyes, the sharp points of the clippers pierced his back. The rusted metal cut through his shirt and the top layer of his skin, drawing hot blood that stuck to his clothes. He opened his eyes again and felt the metal retreat from his back.

Darren still screamed, and the two women, working with the elegance of synchronised swimmers, pulled back their spikes. Darren's eyeballs came out of their sockets, trailing spidery webs of bloody tissue along with them. Gravity became too much for the wounded man, and he sagged to the ground. The women inspected the eyeballs, each moving as the exact mirror image of the other. Thin fingers gripped the soft tissue as they pulled the eyes free. With satisfied smiles, they popped the eyeballs between their teeth and swallowed them before lifting their spikes in the air once more and clinking them together in a grotesque toast. Then they turned back to Darren, driving the spikes into his arms, torso, legs and face as they saw fit, while he desperately fought to defend himself. Thick, dark blood oozed up from deep cuts, but the spikes drove home time and again. His face was mutilated, his jaw hung slack against his neck, and his ear had been torn clean off. Ruben's knees buckled once more. The woman behind him lost her grip for a brief second, and he struggled from her grasp and ran. Her fingers touched the cloth of his shirt, but sheer terror gave him a speed he didn't know he possessed. He almost stumbled over his own feet, but he managed to regain his balance. Ruben was determined to find Marie-Claire if it was the last thing he'd ever do. His heart pounded in his throat as he made his way to the end of the corridor.

It's not going to be a dead end this time, he thought with a mixture of desperation and determination. *It's not because I won't allow it to be.* He barely noticed the horde of women walking through the corridor behind him, and he didn't allow himself to look back. The door loomed out of the darkness, and Ruben threw himself towards it. He wasn't out of the woods yet, but there was hope.

Chapter 30

She had been lost for hours when the clock struck twelve, and Freya's anxiety was building with each passing minute. Then the screams began, and the stress was too much for her body to bear. A wave of nausea hit her and the yellowish liquid she vomited splashed on the marble floor, oozing in different directions. The sight of it made her sick a second time, and the noxious pool on the floor grew. She wiped her mouth with the back of her hand and moved as far away from the mess as she could.

The house was like a maze, and it seemed alive somehow. The corridors refused to stay the same, and though she hadn't seen a single set of stairs yet, she was sure she had run through several different floors. The impossibility of what was happening was no longer relevant. Freya just needed to stay alive. The screams from below gave her renewed energy, and she knew she had to find a way out. She wasn't sure what she wanted to find more: the front door or Marie-Claire and her team. Her solitude was the most frightening of all, and she regretted running away from Oliver; he may have gone completely crazy, but at least he was another person.

Something stirred in the darkness beyond. A figure. Freya's heart leapt, and she ran towards the movement.

"I'm here," she cried. "I'm so lost. Please help me."

The figure turned, and Freya stopped in her tracks. It was a woman, old and naked. The sight of her was so unexpected and ridiculous that Freya fought to stifle a laugh.

"Who are you?" The words escaped her mouth before she realised what she was doing. "Are... are you one of the spirits?"

The woman looked too real to be a spirit. She looked alive. No... not quite alive; her skin was too pale, and the black veins that shone through it were too dark. There was something about her eyes too, and Freya wondered if the woman was blind like Florifera.

"You are the child of the blood." Her black mouth was lined with deep gashes, and the teeth inside were dull grey stumps covered in dark mucus. They reminded Freya of the substance they'd found on the walls on the first day.

"Pardon?" Freya blinked and took an involuntary step back.

"I can smell it. You are a guardian." The old woman raised her head and sniffed the air. Her grey hair hung in wet strands across her wrinkled cheeks, the ashen skin of her scalp showing between the thin roots.

"Eh... where exactly did you come from?" Her mind struggled desperately to catch up with the situation.

"Come here, child. You have a role to fulfil."

"What role would that be?"

"The master who sleeps demands sacrifices. We don't want him to wake now, do we?"

"Uhm, no?"

"He demands your blood, child. And your suffering."

Freya took another step back, and the stooped figure stepped forward, beckoning her with a gnarled hand. "Come, child. Let me bathe in your blood." The woman's hand opened and closed, but the hungry expression on her old face was enough to snap Freya out of her trance, and the girl turned and ran.

The rubber soles of her Doc Martin's made a screeching sound on the marble as she skidded across the corridor. She heard the bare footsteps of the old woman behind her, too close for comfort, and her heart leapt when she came to the end and saw a set of stairs leading upwards. She grasped the wood railing and hoisted herself forward as fast as she could, taking two steps at a time. Something grabbed her ankle, and Freya screamed.

***

The spirits in the attic were hysterical, and Logan struggled to have a clear thought. The ghostly children ran and screamed, which was bad enough by itself, but their fear affected the house somehow. Walls built up out of nowhere, and the ground beneath them cracked open in dark gaping chasms that led to the floor below yet wouldn't stay open long enough for anyone to actually jump through.

He needed to keep a level head and get his guys away from danger, but Logan couldn't think of a way how. The screaming, the chaos, and the constant changes grated on his last nerve, and he had to do his best not to break down. John and Jim were as useless as he himself felt as they each tried to guide the guys away from the shape-changing elements in the room. He felt as if he was lost in the funhouse of a freaky fucking carnival.

The deafening sound of wood cracking overtook the screams, and suddenly everything stopped. The children stood to the north wall, huddled together with fearful eyes as they stared at the centre of the floor. Something was breaking through the wood. Hands clutched the boards from below, and Logan watched as pale figures pulled themselves up from the hole. Seven women crawled from the opening like twisted spiders. The children's screaming was replaced with whimpers. The women's movements were jerky, as if they were string puppets, their limbs waving in awkward angles as they rose to their feet. When the nearest one, a tall and very skinny woman with long black hair, looked up at him, Logan urged the boys to move. She took a step in their direction, her thick bush of pubic hair looking like a cluster of spiders between her long, bony legs.

"Fuck man, that's the creepiest fucking bitch I've ever

seen."

Logan could feel Terrence tremble in his grip, and he looked like he was about to burst into tears.

"Don't look at her. Just move."

He tried to follow Jim, but the attic creaked again and a wall sprung from the ground, forcing Logan and Terrence to jump back.

They're separating us, Logan thought in horror as he tried to find a way around the wall. There wasn't one.

***

John Norris couldn't believe his eyes. This went from being a nice day out with the lads to being stuck in an attic with ghosts and crazy naked women. The ever-changing surroundings were incomprehensible, and all he could think about was getting himself and the two young men he'd firmly gripped around the arms to safety. Mason and Angus were crying, but John had no time to deal with their emotions. They ran across the floor, away from the women, away from the walls that sprang out of nowhere... just away. If he had to jump out of a window to get out of this madhouse, he knew he would risk it. He didn't even notice that he was getting further separated from Logan and Jim, and even if he had noticed, he wouldn't have cared.

He scanned the attic, looking for where the light was coming from. It was difficult to make out because he wasn't seeing things for what they really were. He blinked with the vain hope that his vision would clear, but there was more in his eyes than just dust or tears. It was like being on drugs. John pulled Mason away from a wall just as it folded in on itself, morphing into a new shape, and pushed Angus to safety from a large broken plank spearing up from the ground. He failed to see the hole beneath him, and his right foot stepped on empty air. John's automatic reaction was to cling on to the two guys as he fell backwards. Angus was the first to lose his balance, and he plummeted down the dark chasm in the wooden floorboards. Mason still stood on the edge trying to catch his balance when John turned, but the falling Angus grabbed at him, and he fell too. John moved as fast as he could and managed to wrap his hand around the guy's wrist. Down below, he saw Angus connect with the marble floor. He lay still, his eyes wide open, looking directly at John. He couldn't tell if the boy was dead or just stunned, but Mason demanded his immediate attention. The boy was slipping in his grip, and John reached out with his other arm and grabbed him by the collar, pulling him up as best he could. An ominous crackling noise filled the air, and he realized that the floor was in the midst of closing itself again. Panic struck his heart as he frantically tried to pull the struggling Mason up.

"Damn it, boy. Help me out here," he groaned, his forehead slick with sweat. There was terror in Mason's eyes, and John felt sick. For such a skinny guy, Mason weighed a ton in his arms.

"Stop panicking, Mason. I got you, son." He tried to keep his voice calm, but the floor was starting to crumple in on itself, and he was hanging half down the hole. "Come on boy, I need you to pull yourself up."

"There isn't time. You need to let me go." Mason's eyes shot to the narrowing hole. "Let me go, Mr. Philips. I'll be okay. You need to pull back."

"No, son. Come on, there's still time." The crackling intensified, and splinters of wood pushed against John's clothes.

I need to let go. If I don't...

He never got to finish his thought. The floor closed with unexpected speed, trapping John the way a predator snaps its sharp jaws around its prey. His skin tore, and hot blood soaked his shirt. The wood merged with his organs, tearing through his stomach, liver and bowels. John still held on to Mason, his blood showering the young man's face and glasses. He could hear him cry, but the sound was so far away. He was alive when his torso disconnected from his midriff and fell down to the floor below, his hand still wrapped around the boy's. He died before they hit the ground. His soul was welcomed into the depths of Angel Manor.

Chapter 31

"What's happening?"

Marie-Claire heard the fear in Julie's voice, but she herself felt oddly calm. She knew the house had some power, and she had suspected the equinox would feed it, but the magic she felt was so strong that she could see as if she had first sight. Everything in the house was clear to her third eye, and she could even see the shadows of the living as contrast against the background of the house. A darkness, not black but more purple, lined with thin veins of light, spread out before her. It was in the walls, in the floor, and all around her, spreading like cancer. *The essence of the house,* Marie-Claire thought, and she felt it tug at her consciousness. It called to her, promised her a glorious death if only she would give in to it. It asked her for a sacrifice, and it wanted those around her as well. The voice, made of wordless promises, whispered to her soul, and Marie-Claire struggled to keep her mind clear.

"The house is alive. And we must find a way to release the spirits within, or the consequences will be dire." Marie-Claire stood and faced her two remaining companions. "Whatever we do, we must stick together. I feel that the house wants to divide us. I sense its hunger and I do believe it wants us all dead."

"That's comforting." Pierre's voice was dull.

"Can we get out?" Julie's voice trembled, but Marie-Claire hardened herself to the woman's fear and banished the feelings of guilt from her mind.

"I think offence is the best defence, as the sports fanatics might say." The words came out of her mouth, but her mind remained focused on the growing purple cloud around her. It was strong, but she knew that she could be stronger. She wished Ruben would return with her supplies, but she was prepared for him not to make it back in time. She had underestimated the house, and she wasn't planning on doing it again.

"I need you to go through the kitchen cupboards. Find me as much salt as you can, and we need something to write on the floors with. We're going to fight back."

**

Freya screamed, the sound coming from the depths of her being, and she jerked her leg away from the hand.

"Freya." The familiar voice cut through her screeching, and Freya fell quiet instantly. She didn't dare to turn around. It wasn't the old woman behind her, it was something far worse, and at the same time, more comforting. Tears fell from her eyes. For a moment, she wanted to drop to the ground and lie there, holding her knees.

"I... I can't do this. Not now." She hung her head.

"Freya..." The voice was soft and pleading.

"Please, Bam. I'm so scared. I can't face you right now."

"I'm trying to help you. You need to get to safety. You need to live, Freya. Don't you understand? I... I need you to." The voice sounded so much like it had when Bam had been alive, and yet there was something hollow about it, something different. An echo of death. "The house is allowing me to save you."

"And Oliver?"

There was silence, and for the first time, Freya found the courage to turn around. She saw her friend looking so much like she had in life. Bam was even wearing the same clothes as the last time she'd seen her. But her hair looked different somehow, her eyes were darker and deeper set, and her skin looked like it had been made from a hundred molten candles.

"Oliver is with the house. He belongs to it." Bam shook her head slowly.

Freya bit her lip. "So do I."

"No... not in the same way. You... you haven't given yourself to it. You're fighting it. But you're blood. The house can't exist without you. You are an essential part of the magic."

"Is there a difference?" She furrowed her eyebrows.

Bam nodded, and Freya noticed how small and childlike her friend looked. There was a strange smell too, one she had smelled before. *Bitter almonds.*

"You need to follow me, Freya." Bam half turned, motioning with her hand.

"Will you lead me to the others?"

"No. The others will die. The house needs more souls. It hungers."

Freya took a step back, her body tense. "I need to find Logan and Marie-Claire."

"No, it's too late for them. You need to come with me. I will show you the way out." Bam reached out her hand.

Every fibre in her body wanted to give in, to follow her best friend to the exit, to get away from the house and its darkness, but the thought of leaving everyone else behind sounded like a heavy price to pay. Could she live with herself? Freya had no answer to that.

"Bam..." Her voice wavered, and she felt as if she had swallowed a golf ball. "I don't know..."

The sound of wood ripping drowned out her voice, and Freya looked up to see a large hole opening up in the ceiling. Seconds later, a young man fell through, and before she could scream, a second one followed. Someone grabbed him, and Freya stood frozen as John Norris struggled to keep the boy, Mason, from falling. For what seemed like forever, she watched them fight as the hole began to close. Then, with a snap, the floor became one again, tearing the gentle, quiet man in half. Mason fell, still holding onto John, and her hand went up to her lips to stifle a moan.

Mason landed on top of Angus, who lay so still that Freya feared the worst. A pool of blood had formed underneath his hair, and it dawned on her that she could see everything clearly. The corridor seemed to be lit with a diffuse white light, too bright for moonlight.

It wants you to see. Like a cat bringing you a dead mouse.

The spell broke, and she rushed towards the young men. Mason was curled up in a little ball on the floor. Something crunched under her foot, and when she lifted it, she saw Mason's shattered glasses. She avoided John's dismembered torso, though to her dismay, she saw that Mason's fingers were still entangled with the dead man's. They lay across Angus' chest like a macabre version of Michelangelo's *The Creation of Adam*. Only this wasn't the Sistine Chapel.

"Mason, honey?" Freya turned her head away from John as she pried Mason's hand loose from the corpse's fingers.

"Mason, are you okay?" It was a stupid thing to say, but Freya was very much at a loss for anything logical.

He groaned and started to sit up. Freya tried to detect a pulse in Angus' neck, but the back of his skull had cracked open and a gelatinous bloody mass had spilled out on the floor. She withdrew her hand and moved back a few feet.

"Come on, Mason." She didn't recognise her own voice anymore. "We should go. Where are the others?"

He didn't respond at first, then he got to his feet and stared at the body of John Philips. Freya made the mistake of following his gaze, and she couldn't pull her eyes away from the blood-soaked part where his body abruptly ended or from the torn skin just visible under the fabric. A wave of nausea hit her again, and Freya turned away to expel a wave of greenish bile. When she had nothing more to give, she wiped her mouth on her sleeve.

"Mason, we have to go."

He nodded with a lost expression on his face.

"Let me show you the way out, Freya."

She had almost forgotten about Bam, the sight of the recently dead having blocked her friend from her mind. The temptation was still there to just run, but if she did, she would feel the same guilt she'd had after leaving Bam behind. She would do her best to save as many people as she could, and if she couldn't save them all, she knew she would have to save Logan. Freya wanted him more than anything in this world, and if he died here, she would never forgive herself.

"No." Her voice sounded more resolute than she felt. "Not without Logan. And I should find Marie-Claire as well. It needs to stop."

"You don't understand The house needs to be what it is. You can't stop it. All you need to do is survive the equinox."

"Fuck that." Freya took a few steps towards the stairs. "Is Logan upstairs?" Her words were directed at Mason, and the boy seemed to snap out of his stare.

"I can't go back up there!" Tears poured down his pale cheeks, and his bottom lip trembled.

"Then wait at the top of the stairs."

"No, please... you don't know what's up there. There are these... women. They are horrible. I think they may be dead."

"I saw one of them down here too. The dead are everywhere." She pointed at Bam, but the young man just followed her finger with a blank stare. "You don't see her?"

"Who?"

She turned to Bam.

"He doesn't see you?"

"Not unless the house wants him to. My only task is to bring you to safety. I am not part of the equinox."

Freya rolled her eyes. The image of Bam didn't frighten her anymore, not after she'd seen the dead bodies. To her, this was just something that looked like Bam, not actually her friend. She was too different; everything in life that had made Bam who she was had died. The humour, the energy, the spark that she'd had, it was all gone now.

"Freya..." The hollow voice of the dead girl pleaded with her, but it lacked the emotion it needed, and Freya stubbornly made her way up the stairs. She heard Mason sob, and though she didn't want to frighten the young man, she didn't want to stand around and discuss things with him either.

What on earth do I think I can do if I find Logan? Do I think I can save him? Am I that arrogant that I think I can somehow fix this? The sound of her feet hitting the wooden steps beat in synchrony with her heart, loud and intense. At the top, she stopped, then reached out a trembling hand. She opened the door to visions of chaos. It was hard to focus on anything inside because the attic kept changing form and shape, moulding and morphing as if it were some sort of living creature. There were figures inside. Freya saw several pale women carrying horrific metal instruments of torture. She saw the children, who looked more human now, running around screaming and trying to hide. One of the women dragged a little boy away from the wardrobe he had been hiding in. In her chubby hand, she held a pair of ancient clippers, and she brought the edge of them to the child's ear and applied pressure. The child let out a high-pitched scream that cut through the sounds of terror. Freya tore her eyes away from the child and his blood-covered face, her eyes scanning the room.

Please, God... give me the strength to stop this madness. Then she spotted him, Logan, near the south part of the attic.

"Logan." The sound called attention to her, but she didn't care. Instead, she stepped forward. "Logan."

Logan saw her, and his tense face showed relief. He pulled Terrence forward, herding the boy in front of him while they made their way quickly towards her. The floor shook, and one of the walls moved with a slow but frightening motion to block off the area where Logan and Terrence were. She screamed a warning but Logan had spotted it and reacted quickly enough to manoeuvre around it, dragging the poor guy with him. The south part of the attic was closed off, and it looked like the room wasn't done changing. Logan and Terrence scrambled to keep their balance as they ran in her direction.

"Have you found an exit?" Logan was out of breath, his eyes wide and his chest moving up and down with rapid breaths. "We need to get out of here."

Freya nodded and pointed at the door.

"Where?" Logan looked where she pointed, his face filled with confusion and disappointment.

"You can't see it?" Freya flung herself at the door and yanked it open. "It's right here." She took a step through the door. "See?"

Logan's expression cleared, and without a word, he grabbed Terrence and shoved him after Freya.

"I can't find the others," Logan said as he followed them. "I lost John and Jim." He looked over his shoulder, but Freya grabbed his arm.

"John's dead. We need to go."

The look of devastation and incomprehension on his face broke her heart, but Freya knew she had to be firm if she wanted to save him.

"And Jim?"

"I don't know, but I think if we don't find that Florifera woman, we're all going to be in a lot of trouble. So let's just go, okay?"

Logan's mouth was a narrow line of determination. "Jim might need me."

"I need you."

Her words seemed to do the trick, and he nodded before following her to the stairs. Freya looked for Bam, but she'd disappeared.

Shit, I guess we're on our own.

Freya knew she had to be their guide. Logan hadn't seen the door, so perhaps there were other things that she could see but he couldn't. She took a deep breath and tried to concentrate on finding the way down. Hopefully Marie-Claire Florifera would still be in the kitchen, and Freya prayed that the old woman would know what to do.

***

She wanted to follow Freya up to the attic, to convince her to come away from the house. It was strange speaking to her friend again, and Bam realised she had changed. Freya had seen the change too. It was in her eyes. *Can the living understand the dead? And likewise, can the dead understand the living?* Bam wondered.

The hunger for Freya's warmth had been less than she'd felt before, and Bam had a faint hope that she could, indeed, break her bond with the manor.

If Freya needed to save the others, Bam would help her as much as she could. As long as Freya would then leave the house. She knew Bam was in here now, and the young American girl had no doubt she would do anything to help her. Determined to find her friend, Bam set foot on the stairs, but before she could take another step she felt a familiar presence.

"There you are, Bambi." Chuck's voice was sweet as poisoned honey. "I've been looking all over for you. How did you manage to hide from me?"

She turned slowly, her soul feeling like lead, and looked at him.

"Chuck..." The rest of the words died on her lips. Death hadn't changed her fear of him. In fact, Bambi decided, she was more afraid of him now than she ever had been in life. He had been cruel then, but in death his dark side was truly unleashed.

"Come to me, Bambi. You're mine now." He held out his hand to her, his eyebrows raised and a predatory smile spread across his lips. "The house has given you to me."

"I'm not yours, nor do I belong to the house." She fought her fear with every inch of strength she had and bolted from the stairs as fast as she could. If Chuck caught up with her she would be lost; she could feel it. He still had power over her, and all she could think about was getting away.

Bam ran.

Chapter 32

Marie-Claire stood back and looked at the circle on the floor. The symbols stood out to her second-sight as bright purple marks, a sign of strong magic. She had given them her all, for she knew the house would fight her in every way, and the equinox seemed to negate the protective spells already woven about the house. Marie-Claire knew that if she cast them right, her spells could withstand the innate magic of the house. The circle would have to keep her and the others safe in the next phase, the moment she would battle the house itself. If only she'd had more time to investigate its past, to know why these spells had been cast. She sat in the circle, her dress billowing around her, legs crossed and her hands resting gently on her knees. Then Marie-Claire opened her mind.

The house's energy hit her with the force of a bus, but the circle protected her from being overwhelmed. It couldn't quite reach her, but the force was formidable and Marie-Claire felt a drop of urine blossom in her underpants as she fought to gain control. She ran her mind's fingers across the spells woven in the house, disentangling them as she worked out their purpose. Most of them were protective spells, and to her surprise, she found they were made to keep spirits from crossing over to the light.

What monster would do this?

It took great difficulty to ignore the spirits in the house. Some of them had taken on

full physical shape, and she could almost feel their flesh in her mind.

Angels, they call themselves angels. But they are nothing of the sorts. They are made from malice.

Marie-Claire feared these creatures more than any of the spirits she had ever encountered, and she hoped they wouldn't find her until it was too late for them to stop her tampering with the spells.

The spells in themselves were not too complicated, but the years had mutated the magic, as magic often did when it wasn't maintained, and Marie-Claire wanted to be very careful with the unravelling process. She tugged gently at one of the strands, allowing her mind to wrap around it. The energy of the strand reacted immediately to her presence and coiled itself around her mind's eye like a snake. Marie-Claire fought not to panic. She had never seen anything do this before, and she wondered what the magic was feeding on. She pulled at a different strand this time, but again the magic reacted aggressively, and she was afraid it would pull her in if she continued. Not even the spell she cast around her was resistant to this much force.

"Marie-Claire?" Julie sounded on the verge of panic. "There's something outside the door." The blind woman opened her eyes. Julie was just a shadow against the light of the house, so she couldn't see the girl's features or expression, only where she stood. Her blind eyes flitted towards the door, and she could sense the creatures that scratched at the wood.

Not the Angels... but something else. Strays, spirits claimed by the house. They must have sensed our warmth. They are dangerous too; the house feeds them.

"They can't break the circle." Marie-Claire didn't want to tell the girl that she wasn't so sure they couldn't. The magic here was unlike any she had come across before, and the old woman was afraid. She needed the girl, the one whose blood was bonded to this house. Marie-Claire could only hope she could reach out to the young female; she would have the Achilles heel of Angel Manor with her. Besides the girl, she needed a considerable source of power to help her with her spell.

If only she had more time.

***

Jim saw the window first, slapping Gary against the arm and pointing. He nodded. They had been cowering beneath a large table, their eyes on the bloodbath unfolding before them. His heart went out to the little children who'd come out of nowhere and were being systematically butchered, but his main concern was to get himself and Gary to safety. The window seemed like a great option, and although he wasn't a fan of heights, he would be more than willing to risk climbing from the window just to get away from this insane place.

They scrambled away from the table, Gary in front with Jim close behind him. He prayed that they wouldn't be noticed by the thin woman with the scythe standing nearest to them, and he tried to run as quietly as he could. Gary was the first to reach the window, running his fingers across it, searching for an opening. Jim joined in to help. Somewhere behind him, he heard the swishing sound of the scythe, and panic struck his heart. They didn't have time to fiddle with the latch. They needed to get out now. He didn't dare to look back, so he pushed the young man aside and punched the glass. The pain was horrific, but he would not relent, and the window broke after the second blow, piercing his skin with glass shards. He didn't care. Behind him, something moved closer. With the speed of a desperate man, he pulled the big shards loose, praying the opening would be big enough for them to get through.

"Please, God, if we make it through, I will go to church every Sunday." He pushed himself up against the windowsill and used his jeans-covered knee to knock the last bits of glass out. The fresh air hit him, diluting the smell of rot hanging in the attic. A thin ledge ran under the window, and Jim was sure they could make it. His jeans ripped on the glass remnants, and he felt the hot sting of torn skin, but it didn't matter. He could smell freedom, feel it in the cool air. The ledge was narrow, but Jim managed to find his footing. He leaned back inside and held his arm out.

"Come on, Gary. You're next."

Gary nodded and pushed himself up while Jim pulled at him, careful not to lose his balance. The young man couldn't find his grip, and he slid back down, almost causing Jim to fall backwards.

"Come on, Gary," he urged, and his gaze slid to the woman approaching behind the young man. Her head was tilted to one side, her dark eyes glinting in the bright light of the moon, and there was an expression of curiosity on her pale, gaunt features. "Jesus, Gary, hurry up." Tears formed in Jim's eyes as he tried to pull at the boy again. "Fuck, she's right behind you... no... don't look back, just climb, Goddamn it."

Gary pushed himself off again, his eyes holding Jim's, looking for strength in his counsellor. Jim saw a shadow of movement behind Gary, and then a loud swish cut through the air. Gary's eyes widened as the tip of the scythe protruded from his mouth, thick red liquid dripping off it like syrup.

"Oh God," Jim sobbed as Gary went limp in his arms. He let him go, but the young man stayed upright, his dead eyes still locked with Jim's. Gary's head twitched and pulled back as the scythe slid from his skull, then his body slumped to the ground and Jim was face to face with the wielder. He almost lost his balance again but grabbed the windowsill just in time. The woman pulled the scythe back and brought it down on Jim's right hand, severing two of his fingers. Jim screamed and let go. Blood poured from the stumps. The woman brought the scythe down a second time, this time catching the counsellor between the eyes, and Jim felt a brief flash of pain as the sharp blade slid effortlessly through his skull and severed his brain. His world was sucked up by the darkness.

***

"Where are you, child?"

Freya looked around to see where the voice was coming from. She heard the French lilt in the tone and knew it was Florifera talking to her, but she couldn't see the old woman.

"I'm here," she called out in hopes that Marie-Claire could hear her.

"Open your mind to me, child, let me see through your eyes."

"What?" Freya looked around again, alarmed. "What do you mean?" She stopped running.

"Fuck, what's wrong with you, lady?" Terrence said as he ran into the back of her.

"Freya?" Logan stopped in his tracks and walked back to her, his body tense as he eyed their surroundings. "What's going on? Why did you stop?"

"I heard Florifera. I just..." Her mind whirled, and she felt something press against her thoughts.

"Open your mind to me. Just let go."

"I..."

She closed her eyes and let her mind relax as much as she could, and she felt the woman slip into her thoughts like a warm hand through cold water. Something in her mind woke up, and when she opened her eyes, her vision had changed. It was as if she were looking at the world through hologram eyes. There was the world the way she saw it normally, but there was an extra layer, one made of white and purple colours, and it was beautiful and terrifying at the same time.

"Holy shit, that bitch is bugging out." Terrence's voice sounded far away.

"Are you okay?" Logan touched her arms. "What's going

on with your eyes?"

She blinked and smiled at him, trying to ease the obvious worry on his face.

"It's Florifera. She's in my head somehow, seeing through my eyes. She's going to guide us to where she is. Just follow me."

***

Logan didn't like the sight of Freya's eyes. They'd turned white, like the blind woman's, and it was unsettling to see the expression on her face as well. Yet he trusted her. Not that he had much choice, because he really didn't fancy trying to navigate his way through this hell house. If there was any way he could get out, he would take it, though he felt upset that he couldn't save everyone. On the way down, he had been confronted with the severed body of his long-time friend, and it had made a deep impact. Logan now functioned on pure survival instinct. He worried a little about Mason, whose eyes were too wide for comfort and who didn't seem to blink anymore. The young man hadn't said a word; he just hugged himself with his thin, gangly arms. *Shock perhaps, I can't blame the kid.*

Freya led them through the house, more of a maze now than anything else. Sometimes she would make choices that seemed odd to Logan, and from the cursing, he could tell Terrence wasn't pleased with them either. Sometimes she would walk through a wall, or avoid places that looked like an exit, but strangely enough, she was always right. She would see changes to the house before they occurred. Freya danced through the darkness like a fairy, and Logan and the two boys followed.

The surroundings were getting more familiar as they walked on, and to his excitement, Logan noticed that they were on the bottom floor.

"This is the West Wing. I'm sure of it." He didn't say it to anyone in particular, but Terrence seemed to be the only one who responded to his voice.

"I just want to get out of here, Logan. Why isn't she leading us to an exit?"

"I don't know, Terrence, but I'll get you out of here, I promise."

The boy nodded, his face ash-grey.

"We are almost there." There was a hint of a French accent to Freya's voice. "There are problems. Spirits are in the corridor blocking our way to the kitchen. We're lucky that they aren't Angels."

"Angels? What fucking angels?" Terrence swore under his breath and ran his fingers through his short cropped hair. Logan didn't have to answer. He heard their laughter and screeching from a distance.

"Tell me those are not Angels?" Terrence shuddered and stared at Logan.

"I wouldn't be surprised," he answered. "Doubt there is anything angelic about them though."

"This place is so fucked up."

Logan felt a pang of guilt. *I should have listened to Freya and gotten the boys out of here when I still could. Now it's too fucking late. I had no idea it would get this bad.*

"The Angels are upstairs." Freya still spoke with the French lilt. "They are not down here... not yet."

The last words brought a chill to Logan's spine, and he shuddered. "And those things? Are they dangerous?" He knew he wasn't really speaking to Freya.

"Yes, they are very dangerous, but not as aggressive or clever as the Angels. There should be a way around them. Someone will need to create a distraction."

"I'll do it."

Logan turned to Terrence and shook his head. "No. I'm not going to put you at risk."

Terrence narrowed his eyes, his arms hung by his side, his fists clenching and unclenching. "I'm fast. Faster than any of you. If anyone can make a run for it, it's me. I outran so many psychos in my neighbourhood, I don't see how this would be any different."

"Well, they're not ordinary guys, for one. We don't know what we're dealing with. They could trap you. This house is constantly changing."

"And they can't get to me when you're near?" The look Terrence gave him felt like a physical blow to his stomach. "I've seen how well that worked. Mr Norris was cut in half, man. There is no way you can keep me safe."

"Terrence... I can't let you do this."

"Well, I ain't asking your permission now, am I?" He stared at Logan, holding his eyes for a few seconds. "Get them to safety and get those fuckers before they get me, okay?" Then he sprinted off in the direction of the spirits before Logan could do anything to stop him.

***

Oliver wiped the sweat off his brow and tried to collect his thoughts. Somewhere in the depth of his mind, there was still a little part left of the person he'd been before the house had claimed him, and that part was very much afraid. More afraid of what he'd become than anything else. Angel Manor had tainted him the same way it had tainted all the other spirits. Oliver had wanted the house so badly, he had given into it, and he'd felt the hunger of the house, which in turn had brought out his own bloodlust.

His fingers ran across the walls, and he was connected with it all, a multitude of voices whispering at him. He rested his head against the wall and pictured hot blood running through his fingers. Oliver knew that his turn for sacrifice would come very soon. He would experience the sweet pain the house craved for. There were some perfect victims in the house for his plan, but he knew he had to be cautious around the roaming spirits. If they got their hands on him, his safety would not be guaranteed, Anne had told him as much.

"I will need a weapon. Something to carve the succulent flesh." He smiled wickedly, while deep inside his mind the old Oliver moaned. The house pulsated with the power of the equinox, and it throbbed through him like a second heartbeat. He weaved his way through the corridors, making his way towards the kitchen to find the weapon he sought.

"This way, my love." Anne appeared several feet ahead of him, her fingers beckoning him to come hither. "I shall guide you through the house... keep you safe."

"Yes... the house, it wants to consume me." Oliver's eyes rolled in his sockets, and he could barely focus his vision. "It's so strong, my love. It's pulling at me."

"You are so important to Angel Manor. You are the first who is not of the bloodline who has loved the house like you do."

"The house is a part of me now. All that it does... that's part of me, too. I have accepted it fully into my soul." A stream of saliva ran from the corner of his mouth as he spoke, and he wiped it away with the back of his hand, smearing it across his cheek. His eyes rolled back into his head again, his muscles no longer under his control.

"We must sacrifice for the Master who sleeps. We must keep the world in balance... it is what is wanted of us." He stepped forward, following the ethereal creature.

"Yes... and we must keep the Manor pleased. We must still its hunger, and our legions must grow."

"I will make a sacrifice this very night."

Chapter 33

They almost had him. The sight of his brother standing there with some fat dead guy had nearly slipped him up. He'd skidded to a halt, and they'd turned to him in unison, like in one of those horror movies Terrence liked to watch. It was surreal to be in this situation, the idea of facing off against a bunch of undead fuckers...

The sight of Tyrell was off-putting, but Terrence told himself that this dark figure was not his brother, so he tore his eyes away before he turned around and ran... straight into Roger Mace.

"Roger?" Terrence froze to the spot. For a moment, he thought Roger had come back, that he was alive and trapped just like he was, but then he noticed the pale skin and the deep-set eyes. Roger looked the way he had in life, only different. Dead. "Shit man, what happened to you?" He glanced to the figure at his side, and he recognised Lyndon Farrow.

"It's beautiful here, Terrence. We would like you to join us."

Something snapped in Terrence, and he found his senses. He slipped between Roger and Lyndon, low and fast, feeling the air on his skin as their hands tried to grab at him. His heart pounded with adrenaline, but his mind was calm. He had been here before. True it was different, but he wasn't going to focus on who or what he was facing, just on getting away. He ducked and ran, his feet hitting the marble floor with a light tread, his hands pumping by his sides. For the briefest second, he looked back and saw the four figures behind him. They were fast, but not exceptionally so. No faster than the guys he'd run from before, and he knew that his brother couldn't outrun him for sure.

You'd better fix this Logan, he thought while he ran. *I plan on getting out of here alive.*

***

Where am I running to? Bam wondered. She had been running for what seemed like hours, and still Chuck found her. Twice, she had lost him, but her brother seemed more determined now to catch her. Bam considered going outside. She was limited to the grounds, but she might find a better hiding place out there. For a moment, it seemed like her best option, until she passed the basement door. She knew where to go. She had to go deeper down. It was a forbidden place for the spirits, and it would be the only place where the house couldn't reach her. She hesitated for a moment, but Chuck's presence forced her hand and she flung open the basement door.

In life, Bam had been afraid of the dark, but death embodied darkness, and she ran down without any fear. She felt the many deaths that had occurred in this place, the house had sucked up every last one of them. There was no evidence of their demise, and yet Bam could see them clearly. She didn't mourn their deaths, but she mourned their imprisonment.

The presence of the *other place* was almost stifling. She opened the second door in the basement and made her way to a dark hatch in the floor. Her whole spirit trembled as she opened it. Below her was a darkness that was both inviting and appalling. A distant noise startled Bam, and she wondered if Chuck had found her. She desperately wanted to go through the hole in the floor, but something wasn't letting her. *It's the house... it won't let me go.*

Bam felt Chuck's presence coming closer and started to cry.

***

When Florifera left her mind, Freya felt as if she had exhaled through her eyes rather than her mouth. Her brain

331

was cold and empty all of a sudden, as if a part of it was missing, and yet at the same time, it was a great relief to not have a second mind present. It took a minute for her vision to clear, and Logan roughly shoved her into the kitchen where Florifera and her two remaining team members sat in a circle on the ground. The circle was glowing with a purplish luminescence, and the sight of it surprised Freya.

"Come to me, child. I need you here right away." The blind woman signalled impatiently for her to come close, and Freya obeyed. The presence of Florifera within her mind had changed Freya's perspective of the woman a little; she didn't feel like a stranger anymore. It wasn't exactly that she and Marie-Claire had bonded over thoughts, but her consciousness had merged with the old woman somehow, creating a link between them.

"What do you want me to do?" She was careful where she put her feet, afraid to step directly on the illuminated symbols in fear of disrupting their magic.

"You know what we did before? How I looked through your eyes?"

"Yes?"

"That was me flowing through you. For this spell I need to do the opposite."

"What do you mean?"

"I need you to flow through me."

"I don't know how to do that."

Florifera took her hands and squeezed so hard her bones rubbed together. She pulled Freya down in front of her, the white eyes holding hers.

"You can do this. I will talk you through it and help you."

She nodded in response, but her whole body was tense.

"All of you, get into the circle. It holds a little protection against our foes in this house, but I can't know for certain how long it will last. I need everyone to be as quiet as they can. We shall need utmost concentration."

Freya looked around at the four people behind her, all standing close together, their expressions ranging from frightened to determined to utterly shocked. *Whatever we're going to do, please let this work. Please let all of us get out of here.*

"Are you ready, dear?"

"Yes," she lied. She wasn't ready at all, but she didn't want to wait; she just wanted to get this over with as soon as possible.

"Now, look into my eyes and open up your mind. Can you do that, dear?"

Freya looked into the white eyes. They weren't as white as she thought they were. Underneath the blank eyeball she saw a hint of a circle, a faint light purple colour, and in it an even darker circle. Her mind relaxed as Marie-Claire's consciousness reached out to her like invisible hand. The warmth of the other mind engulfed hers, her vision changed again, and this time it was she who could see through Marie-Claire's strange blind eyes. A new world opened up. A world of magic, portrayed in shades of darkness and light.

Every muscle in her body relaxed, and Freya fell back to the floor, her eyes still open but unable to see the world around her. Her mind roamed through the house, together with Marie-Claire's, and she saw it all: the dead, the spells, every brick and every stone. Her mind touched them as if she were running her fingertips across them. She could feel its essence, and she knew that she was connected to it, more so than anyone else. "Do you see the threads of the spells?" The disembodied voice of Marie-Claire ran through her mind. Freya looked at the long strands of energy that were shaped almost like words and symbols, woven through reality itself. She saw their ends sticking out.

"I see them. I feel I can just pull at them."

"You can. Touch the magic. I will aid you."

She reached out a hand, not a physical one but one made of ideas, memories and identity, and touched the magic. The strands curled around it, recognising her the way a dog recognises its master. The sensation tingled, almost painfully, and Freya pulled the strands apart. The house trembled, resisted, but she grabbed the next part and pulled. This time, it didn't come apart so easily, but she didn't give up, the strength of Marie-Claire backing her up.

The spells started to crack and the house moaned. It pushed at her mind, cruel and painful, taunting her with her own feelings. Freya saw the tormented face of Bam, and for a moment, she stopped what she was doing, but then she pushed on, ripping away at the spells with more determination than before.

A high-pitched, guttural scream bellowed through Angel Manor. The walls creaked and moved a few inches inwards. Cracks formed in the brickwork, deep and black, running down like snakes across the stone. A black liquid with the consistency of jelly poured forth from the cracks and drizzled down with languid speed. She felt its pain. The house cried out in betrayal – she was taking its soul, destroying its mind. Something begged her not to do this, a female voice, but it was faint and Freya ignored it. Of course the house would protest.

***

Sister Agatha felt the spells unravel before Angel Manor did. She had helped create them, and though they had changed over the years, she still felt every thread as part of her being. The equinox had left her weak, but now the house was being ripped apart. The tethers she and the other spirits had to the house were loosening, and she realised that soon they would all be free. A part of her felt an incredible sense of relief. She would be freed from this house, from this place that she had dedicated her life to, had sacrificed herself to. She would be duty bound no longer, and there would be rest for her, eternal rest.

But her sense of duty, which had become ingrained into her restless soul, screamed out. If the spells were broken, the defences for Angel Manor would be disabled. Her freedom could cost so many lives, and Sister Agatha needed to stop what was happening.

She found the girl, the one of the bloodline, but she was too weak to stop her. She shouted, but her voice was too soft. The house around her was breaking down, and there was nothing Agatha could do to stop it. Soon they would all be free.

***

Logan wanted to rush to Freya's aid. Her whole body rocked back and forth with spasms. A foamy, white liquid spilled from her lips, and her eyes rolled to the back of her head.

"Don't." Julie held his arm and looked at him with pleading eyes. "She's fine. Florifera has her."

"She looks like she's having a fit."

"I know."

A loud crash sounded in the distance, and the house groaned again. Cracks appeared in the walls, sending a light rain of dust and cement down on them, and Logan was worried that the building might collapse. He didn't know where Terrence was, or Jim or Gary, and as much as he wanted to find them, he knew it wouldn't do any good.

He decided to stay where he was for now, but if he saw any further sign of danger, he would grab Freya and Mason and run from this house - fuck the rest of them.

A smell hit him, a combination of burned rubber and ammonia, strong enough to make him gag. The house trembled with the ferocity of an earthquake, moving to the same rhythm as Freya's shaking body.

Without warning, Freya's shaking stopped, and she became as stiff as a board. Her eyes were wide open, as was her mouth, and for a moment, Logan feared she was dead. Then Freya bolted up to her feet, her body movements physically impossible. A loud scream escaped her rigid mouth, and a cloud of black smoke exploded from her pale lips and evaporated into the air. The house went dark, all the lights went out, and even the light of the moon, which had seemed so bright before, had dimmed. A hushed silence settled over Angel Manor, and Logan could hear the beating of his own heart. Freya's body relaxed and she slumped to the ground, hitting the tiles of the kitchen floor with a sickening thud. This time, Logan rushed to her side.

He picked her up in his arms, resting her back against his knees. Her eyes fluttered open, and she gave him a weak smile. The lights went on again.

"Is it over?" Her voice was hoarse, and her lips were pale and cracked.

"I... I don't know?"

"Not yet. We've only released the spirits from the house. Now we need to exorcize them." Florifera crawled to her feet and shook the dust from her shoulders and skirt. "You broke the spells though, dear. The rest is my department."

"Can we leave the house?"

"Yes, but the spirits are still dangerous. Though, admittedly, they've lost the magic of the house, which means they can't manipulate it anymore."

Freya's eyes met Logan's. "Get the kids out of here. I'll stay with Marie-Claire and her team. Get Mason to safety, and maybe you can find Terrence?"

"I can't leave you here."

"You're not leaving me; you are getting the kids out. I will join you as soon as I can."

"You took a bad fall, Freya. I should get you out. Get you to a hospital. Your head is bleeding." He looked at the nasty gash on the side of her head and the long line of red liquid running from it. Logan held the sleeve of his shirt against it until the bleeding slowed.

"I can't just leave this place, not until Marie-Claire is done."

"Marie-Claire?" Logan turned to the blind medium.

"You best go now, boy." The old woman sounded tired. "We have only won half the battle. It's time to bring these spirits to the light. And some of them will refuse to go. There is nothing you can do to help here, and the spirits have proven that they can be dangerous."

Logan looked at Freya again. She was struggling to sit up straight.

"Freya..."

"Just go. I'll be fine, I promise. I've made it through this much; I can get through the rest. You go, and meet me outside. Get in the car or something. Stay there. If something happens, you can just drive away."

"I won't just drive away."

"Go now. Take Mason."

Logan got to his feet and grabbed the young man's arm. Mason barely responded, his eyes were still wide and he seemed to have been pulled away into a little world in his mind. There was cement dust all over his hair and shoulders, and Logan patted at it with the palm of his hand. There was still no reaction, and he glanced at Freya one more time, but she didn't look back. She was too busy talking to Florifera.

"Let's go, Mason." Logan squeezed his arm and pulled

him along.

***

The house released her the moment Chuck opened the second door to the basement. Bam put one foot into the hole, finding a staircase leading downwards. There was something hidden down there. It had an even stronger impact on her than the house had, and she feared it. But, she decided, she feared Chuck more.

"Bambi... don't go down there." Chuck's voice was commanding, and for a moment, Bam froze. Then she ran.

It pulled at her, whatever it was, drowning out her own thoughts with a million screams. Yet she kept running. Behind her, Chuck followed, but Bam knew she had to keep it together. She couldn't concentrate on her fear of him. The latch fell shut, and Bam realised vaguely through the chaos in her mind that, instead of outrunning Chuck, she was now trapped in here... with him.

Chapter 34

No matter how hard he ran, they were always a few steps behind him. He could hear their footsteps, but worst of all was the smell. That ominous scent of death. It turned his stomach as much as the fear did, and Terrence understood that ghosts didn't need to rest. He might be faster now, but his body would give out. His muscles ached, and his adrenaline was starting to wear thin. The house around him shook and trembled, and there were moments when Terrence thought the roof might cave in on him, but somehow everything still stood. He had hurt his ankle when the ground shifted under his feet, leaving him with a burning pain. But his physical pain was nothing compared to the mental anguish he was currently feeling; it even blocked out the fear in his heart.

Why Tyrell? I could deal with those crazy naked bitches, but not my brother. Tears stung his eyes, and his heart drummed like a bird fluttering against the bars of a cage. As he turned towards the south corridor, his ankle collapsed without warning, and Terrence connected brutally with the marble floor. His weight landed on his arm, and it exploded with a burning pain. Panic stricken, he tried to scramble to his feet, but his arm would not support his weight and the hurricane of emotions was clouding his senses.

He's going to get me. The fucking zombie Tyrell is going to get me. He's not just going to talk to me now, I know it. He's different.

Terrence turned himself on his back and watched them approach. Tyrell walked in front with the other three close behind. They weren't exactly running. The house gave another shudder, and the walls creaked. Terrence pushed himself away from the oncoming spirits.

I don't want to die like this. Not like this. Tears ran freely now, mingling with the snot running from his nose. He knew he couldn't get away; there would be no escape.

A strong hand grabbed him, and Terrence screamed with all his might. The hand jerked, pulling him along the floor, and Terrence struggled.

"Damn it, boy. Stop that. Come here." A voice with a thick French accent barked at him. "If you don't come with me, you will be dead. They're after you."

The man was pale, and his high forehead was covered with little drops of sweat. He crouched at the top of the basement steps. Terrence pushed himself towards the opening and threw himself down the stone stairs. Each step connected heavily with his skin, and he grabbed hold of Ruben for support, sending the both of them tumbling until they reached the bottom. They lay side by side in the dimly lit basement, trying to catch their breaths. The other guy was on his feet first. He ran to the bottom of the stairs and knelt on the ground, scraping at something.

"What are you doing, man?" Terrence's voice was hoarse, and his back, arm and leg ached.

"The salt is part of the defence in this basement. I think the spells are meant to keep things in, but I'm pretty sure in this case it can keep them out as well."

"The ghosts?" Terrence sat up wild-eyed.

"Yes."

"You keep them out with salt?"

"Yes."

"Is this like fucking magical salt or something?" He fought a wave of hysteria.

"No, just salt." The man's breath was ragged.

"So we could have stopped these fucking things with a

bit of salt?" He couldn't comprehend the idea.

"I don't know. These spirits... they are unlike anything I've ever encountered. But sticking to tradition can help. Magic is strange that way. It likes ritual."

"Dude, you are making so fucking little sense to me right now." He rubbed his temples. "But if you think you can stop those things, then you are my fucking hero."

"Let's hope I get to be your hero, or we will both die quite horribly." The man massaged his arm and looked as if he were about to pass out.

A scream, not exactly human, made their eardrums ache. Around them, the walls shifted out of place, creaking and groaning, cement dust cascading down on them. A burst of energy caused the hairs on the back of Terrence's neck to stand up, all the warmth drained from the building, and the lights went out. The basement was pitch black and eerily silent.

"Mr?"

"I'm here, kid." The French accent soothed Terrence's frayed nerves.

"Do you know what just happened then?"

"Not sure, but I think it might have been the first step of the exorcism."

"There's an exorcism?"

"Yes, kid. That's why we're here, to cleanse this house."

"Oh... good."

The light flickered back on, and a mild sense of relief arose in Terrence's chest.

"Is it over?"

"No, my boy."

A loud cackling sounded above them, turning Terrence's blood to ice.

"I'm afraid it's only beginning."

***

The house looked smaller somehow, though Freya couldn't explain why. The wallpaper looked more faded, and everything appeared dusty and old. Even the brand new stairs looked forlorn in the shadowy main hall. The electric light did nothing to brighten the large room, and the marble floor reflected it dully.

The house looks dead.

She dug her fingers into the bag of salt and finished the large circle she was creating. The Angels screeched in the distance, and the sound of their voices was unsettling. They'd lost control of the house, but that didn't make them any less dangerous, and now that they were no longer bound, they were capable of leaving Angel Manor. The exorcism had to work.

The sheer thought of those naked, bloodthirsty women out in the world made Freya cringe. Footsteps sounded behind her, and she turned, her heart pounding, but it was only Marie-Claire and Julie. The younger women held Marie-Claire by the arm. Florifera looked as if she had aged ten years overnight.

"Did you find what you were looking for?" Freya raised her eyebrows and bit her lip.

"Yes. Are you done with the circle?"

"Almost."

"Hurry then. This isn't over yet, and I don't know how much longer I can distract the spirits. Once the spell I cast earlier wears off, they will be coming straight for us. We living are like beacons to the dead. They are drawn to our life energy and our warmth, and we don't know how these spirits will respond now that they are freed from the house."

Freya focused on the salt again, making sure the circle was not broken anywhere.

"Done. How are you going to exorcise the house?"

"I'm going to use a little extra magic," Marie-Claire answered with a hint of mystery in her voice.

"Extra magic?"

"I'm going to use Lucifer Falls. It's the perfect place to draw lost spirits to and give them a place to rest. It's a gate, if you will."

"Like the pearly gates."

Florifera laughed an unexpectedly young laugh. She shook her head, a strand of long, white hair loosening from the elastic band and falling across her cheek. "No child, the pearly gates are just a myth as far as I know. The gate to heaven is more abstract, I should think. Though perhaps you are not altogether wrong when you compare it to the concept of the pearly gates. Lucifer Falls will serve as a very strong light for spirits to be drawn to. I don't believe these spirits will be too willing to go, so we need an extra incentive."

"And you think Lucifer Falls will be it?"

"I do. I hope it will draw them like a moths to a flame. The problem is getting that light connected to our spirits."

"Do we have to lure them towards it or something?"

"No, it's more the other way around. We need to get the light to them."

"And you know how to do that?"

A thought crossed the woman's face, Freya could see it but couldn't make out what it was. *Hesitation?*

"In theory, I have an idea how to. This magic is stronger

than any I have ever used, so I can't tell you for sure."

"So this might not work then?" Freya's voice was soft and filled with fear. Marie-Claire didn't answer her but instead directed Pierre to get her bag. The young man ran eagerly, his eyes darting around. He obviously felt as paranoid as Freya was.

This has to work.

"I don't know how many survivors are still in the house. I felt a few when we were unravelling the spells, but I didn't have time to focus on them. I don't know where they are." Florifera sounded brittle, and she spoke an octave higher than normal. "We need to act fast if we want to save them."

Pierre handed the woman a large carpet bag, and she placed it on one of the steps. With a click, she opened the top and pushed her arm inside, rummaging around the contents. Seconds later, she pulled out four herb bunches tied together with a purple ribbon, and she held her hand to Pierre for a lighter.

"I need you three to stand in the circle like the guardians of the east, west and south. I will represent the guardian of the north." She clicked her fingers impatiently, her brow furrowed. "Please, take your places."

Freya looked at the circle, not sure what to do next, and Julie pointed her to the space where she was supposed to stand. Marie-Claire lit one of the herb bunches and handed it to her. Then the old woman lit a second and handed it to Pierre, the third she gave to Julie, while she kept the fourth for herself.

"I call upon the guardians of the north watchtower. You are the powers of the earth both generous and divine. Please protect this north gate and guard all within this circle. Thank you. I welcome you."

Marie-Claire waved her herb bundle in the air, creating fragrant smoke rings. Freya coughed slightly, the scent of the herbs making her mouth dry. When Marie-Claire was still, Julie moved her herb bundle and spoke in a loud clear voice.

"I call upon the guardians of the east watchtower. You are the powers of the air both generous and divine. Please protect this east gate and guard all within this circle. Thank you. I welcome you."

Freya felt a hint of panic; she was the next in line, and she had no idea what to say for this spell. She knew nothing of magic.

"Say the words with me, Freya." Marie-Claire spoke in soft, comforting tones, and her mind pressed against hers, causing Freya's muscles to relax. She opened her mind as she had before, and felt the consciousness slip into her, but only on the surface.

"I call upon the guardians of the south watchtower. You are the powers of the fire both generous and divine. Please protect this south gate and guard all within this circle. Thank you. I welcome you."

Her mind cleared, and Marie-Claire left her feeling empty as she retreated from her consciousness.

Pierre spoke last: "I call upon the guardians of the west watchtower. You are the powers of the water both generous and divine. Please protect this west gate and guard all within this circle. Thank you. I welcome you."

Marie-Claire stepped into the middle of the circle and spread her arms wide.

"Guardians of the watchtowers of earth, air, fire, and water, allow me your power and protection tonight. Thank you. I welcome you." The temperature changed, the air now feeling hot and dry. Some invisible force wrapped itself around her shoulders, and the blood rushed to her cheeks.

"We are now safe to cast our spell." Marie-Claire gave a curt nod at no one in particular. They extinguished their herb bundles; Julie took Freya's from her grip and placed the burned out remains beyond the circle of salt. Pierre moved near Freya, pulling her further into the middle, and he grabbed one of her hands while Julie took her other. Marie-Claire stood across from her, holding hands to close the circle.

"We summon the gates to the eternal hereafter. We call upon the light. We call upon the darkness. Reveal yourself to us, and to those who walk this plane past their welcome. We ask you to take these weary souls from this plane and let them follow the right path."

Freya watched, a little uncomfortable and unsure of what to do, while all three people around her closed their eyes and threw back their heads. The three voices spoke out in unison.

"Regna terrae, cantata Deo, psallite Cernunnos,

Regna terrae, cantata Dea psallite Aradia.

caeli Deus, Deus terrae,

Humiliter majestati gloriae tuae supplicamus."

The words meant nothing to Freya, she felt she should say something, join in, but she couldn't. Nerves tickled her stomach, and she had to suppress an anxious laugh.

"Cernunnos ipse truderit virtutem plebi Suae,

Aradia ipse fortitudinem plebi Suae.

Benedictus Deus, Gloria Patri,

Benedictus Dea, Matri Gloria."

The words rang with power, and though Freya wasn't speaking them, she could feel every intonation vibrate through her bones. She would never have even dreamed that magic was real a few short months ago. It was as if someone had removed a veil from the world and revealed its hot energetic core. Her life would never be the same after what she had seen, and Freya wondered for the briefest of moments where she would go from here.

A rush of air filled the room, hot and dry, like a desert wind, and there was a magical pull. Freya opened her eyes and looked over her shoulder. The wall behind her looked almost translucent, and a very faint light emanated from it. It was nothing like she'd expected. Freya had envisioned an actual portal or a brightly lit hole in the centre of the room, like in horror movies. This was different. At the same time, she could feel the intense magical pull of the portal, and her soul longed to pass through to the other side.

"Now we must draw the souls here and guide them to the light."

"How do we do that?"

Marie-Claire's expression hardened, showing a hint of darkness that made Freya's knees weak.

"That's the tricky part, dear. We have to lure them here."

"How?"

"Bait." It was Pierre who answered the question, and he gave her a dark grimace.

"Well, that's comforting." Freya sat down and wrapped her arms around her head. The thought of luring angry spirits made her want to give up on the whole endeavour, but then she thought of Logan and Oliver, and she knew she had no choice.

"I'll serve as bait."

"As will all of you, dear. I will be here to act as a guide."

"Tell me what I have to do."

***

He could hear them in there... chatting, chanting, whatever the fuck they were doing. He didn't care. They'd killed the house – Oliver was sure of it. They had ripped out its beating magical heart, its beautiful soul and its actual being... and they had obliterated it. He couldn't feel it anymore. The voices had stopped talking to him. A deep, unsettling emptiness had made itself master over his soul.

The house had spoken to him one last time, right before it had died. At that moment, the house had shown him everything it had ever done. Every drop of blood that had been spilled on the ground crossed Oliver's mind's eye, and he felt as if he had been there. Each murder, in a way, was committed by his hand. He had been in this house for many generations, from the very beginning, in fact. His body had been different, but his soul had been the same, he was convinced of that. The sacrifice he longed for had already been made, over and over again. He had been not only the living but the dead in the house, and everything had always come from him. He knew that now. The house and he had been merged throughout his many lives. Oliver never believed in reincarnation, but Angel Manor had given him proof.

And then it died. He had felt the house retreat from his soul, letting go of it and leaving it cold and empty. He had held Anne in his arms when her spirit was rudely torn from the magic of the house. He had seen the desolation in her eyes, and he had felt anger. She had left him then, pulling away from him as her body lost its solid form. He wanted to hold her close, to savour the metallic taste of her lips again, but he knew he couldn't. Anne's power had come from the house, and now her strength had weakened too much.

Someone would pay for this, for murdering Angel Manor, for taking Anne from him. He knew just who to get. Perhaps if he could stop them, he could restore the house once more and bring back his connection with Anne. After all, he had bonded with this house. It was his now, not Freya's... *His*.

***

Ruben felt a nagging throb in his arm, and his chest was

tight. He needed to get himself and the young man out of the basement, but his mind wasn't working clearly. His vision was blurry, and he thought he'd seen that girl... the one they'd lost in the suicide forest. *What was her name again? Marie-Claire, what was the name of that girl?* The house pulled at him, begging him to join it, but he felt it slowly dying. *I'm dying too... my heart, it can't stand what I've seen here today.* The girl stood and reached out her hand to him, and Ruben felt a moment of utter peace as he took hold of the translucent fingers. *I'm free now, I'm sorry I never got to say goodbye, Marie-Claire. How I did love you.* As Ruben's soul left his body, the house died a violent death.

***

There was a hint of light in the cooling air, the first sign of dawn. Logan opened the van with trembling hands and helped the shocked Mason inside. The boy's skin was so cold, and if it hadn't been for Terrence, Jim and Gary, he would have driven the young man straight to the hospital. But Mason's shock would probably not kill him, while the others might not be so lucky if they didn't get a chance to escape.

And then there was Freya. He knew he couldn't leave her, and in his heart of hearts, he would gladly sacrifice all others if it meant saving her, but she had explicitly forbidden it. She needed to do what she needed to do. Logan understood that, but he didn't like it one bit. He didn't want to be macho about it, but he felt very protective over Freya, even if it was out of purely selfish reasons. He wanted her. He had done ever since he'd met her, and that night in the attic had only strengthened his desire.

The winds picked up as he made his way back to the house, determined to find Terrence and maybe the others, and to be at least close to Freya. Hard gusts of warm air slammed against his body, and he fought against the elements. It surprised him that the wind was warm, hot even, and dry, unlike the winds he was used to in Scotland.

The air was charged with electricity, and for a reason he couldn't explain, Logan felt the need to look back. The moon was full, and it shone over the poppy fields by Lucifer Falls, bathing them in soft light, showing off the dark, gaping maul in their midst. Light flashed from the hole, as if there was a storm brewing underneath the earth's crust. The sight of the sharp veins of light made him breathless, and Logan watched with a growing sense of unease as the light became brighter.

A long streak of lightning shot across the valley, up into the sky in an elongated arc, and crashed into Angel Manor. Logan fought to catch his breath as he ran towards the house, his heart beating so loudly he thought it might give out at any moment. Something was happening inside, and he knew he had to get to Freya.

***

What is this place? For a moment, Bam thought she had entered the afterlife, but then she realised she was still underneath Angel Manor.

"Bambi..." Chuck sounded out of breath, which was ridiculous because he didn't need to breathe. Bam felt as if she were trying to wade her way through a room full of water. Nothing around her was clear, and the darkness was so vivid she almost mistook it for light. *Is this the light we are meant to move towards?* she wondered, but she knew it wasn't. This was no portal to the afterlife. She didn't know what this place was, but she could feel that the Manor had taken a lot of its power from here.

"Bambi..." Chuck was near her now. She turned to him and saw a dreamy expression on his face.

"You have no power over me, Chuck. Not here." She placed her fingertips on his shoulder and pushed him away gently. He staggered as if he were drunk.

"We're trapped here, Bambi." His speech was slurred. "You and I together. You have no power here either."

"I am as trapped as you are." She looked up at the ceiling. "We can't get out until someone opens that latch. But it doesn't matter because you can't hurt me. This place won't allow you to."

Her own words were as garbled as Chuck's were and her vision blurred. This place was almost too much for her. It was difficult to exist, and she wondered how long she could manage to hold herself together. She hoped it was longer than Chuck could.

***

Terrence stared up at the stairs. The figure of his brother sat at the top, leaning on his knees and staring down at him. He couldn't see the other ghosts anymore, but it was only Tyrell that mattered. Part of him had not yet accepted that his brother was dead, and he still believed in his heart of hearts that the house might be playing a trick on him. "What do you want from me, T?" He didn't even care anymore that the white guy was there; he just wanted to talk to his brother.

"I don't know anymore, bro. I thought I did. I wanted you dead, here with me. The house... it wanted you."

"It doesn't anymore?"

"No... maybe... I don't know. I don't feel the hunger I felt anymore. I just feel lost now."

"Are you really T?" Terrence hoped that the spirit would deny being his brother, that he would be able to go home and pick up his life again.

"What do you think, Terrence?" Tyrell looked up at him, his eyes sunken into their sockets. "Do you think I'm your brother?"

"No... yeah. I think I do."

"There's something about this house, bro. I told you this before. There's something else here."

Terrence felt the skin on his back erupt in little goose bumps, and his stomach dropped. He looked at the white guy, who sat with his back against the wall. If he was paying attention to the conversation with Tyrell, he didn't show it. The man had his eyes closed and he appeared to be either very deep in thought or sleeping.

"You mean like those Angels?"

"No mate, something worse. They're protecting something, those Angels. They're here for a reason, but I can't quite tell what. It's bad, though, I'm pretty sure of that."

"You're making no sense, T. I don't know what to do with this."

"I think my time here is drawing short. I hear them calling for me, little brother. And when they do, you and I will never speak again."

Tears welled up in Terrence's eyes, and he felt a painful lump in his throat.

"I don't know how to live without you." A single tear escaped from the corner of his eye, hot and salty.

"Going to have to, little brother. You got no choice." Tyrell looked over his shoulder as if someone was talking to him, and he nodded his head. "Not sure if it was such a good idea to let the spirits go, Terrence. I think your friends seriously fucked up on that one. But I'm grateful nonetheless. I'm happy that I didn't have to kill you. Take care, little brother. Don't take crap from no one." Tyrell got to his feet and brushed off his jeans. "They'll talk shit about me. Mostly about me being gay, so be prepared for that. But none of that matters. I don't care, so neither should you. Don't be a hothead about it, okay? Just know that I loved you."

He turned and walked up the stone stairs, leaving Terrence entwined in his own thoughts and emotions. The pressure of the day, the fear of death, and the thought of never seeing Tyrell again finally exploded in a sea of tears, and Terrence sagged to his knees. The white guy still hadn't moved, and when the majority of his tears had been spent, Terrence walked over to him.

"Mr?"

There was no response, and Terrence felt the familiar fear again. He knelt next to the man and pushed gently against his shoulder. He didn't move. Terrence pushed harder this time, a little too hard, and the figure slid sideways, falling to the ground.

"Fuck, man. Don't be dead. Please don't be fucking dead." He felt his skin. It was still lukewarm, but Terrence could find neither a pulse nor any evidence of breathing. "No, this isn't fucking fair. You can't just die on me, you white piece of shit." Terrence jumped to his feet, afraid and vulnerable, and kicked the man, immediately regretting it the second after. "Shit, shit, shit." The tears were flowing again and he had never felt so lost and alone before. He needed this stupid stranger; he was the one who was going to save him, and Terrence had never before in his life wanted anyone to save him. But now... he was so out of his depth. He didn't want to stay down here anymore, not with that dead guy.

Terrence inhaled deeply and took the first three steps of the stairs. He wondered if the spirits were still up there, waiting for him, but he had to take the risk. He needed to find Logan, or anyone else, and he needed to get the fuck away from this house... and whatever was still lurking here.

Chapter 35

Before they had a chance to execute their plan to lure all the spirits to the main hall, a single spirit found them. Not one of the naked females, but a pretty woman dressed in a nun's habit. Her eyes were large and dark, and they were filled with sadness.

"You mustn't." Her voice was ethereal and distant. "You must stop this."

Freya felt for the woman, and she knew she had seen her before, but couldn't remember where.

"You are putting everyone in danger." The spirit sounded so lost. The woman kept looking longingly at the portal, as if her heart yearned for it.

"I understand you have been tied to this house for a long time." Marie-Claire looked straight at the spirit, and Freya remembered how well the woman could see the supernatural through those blind eyes.

"I have to stop you. You're making a mistake."

"You need to step into the light. Feel its warmth and its welcome. You've been here on this plane too long. It is time for you to be where you belong. You can feel the call, can you not?" Marie-Claire's voice was soothing, encouraging, and doubt played on the spirit's face.

"The Angels... we kept them here for a purpose. They... they have to..."

"Was it you who cast the spell to keep everyone here?" Marie-Claire sounded surprised, her voice was a little more shrill than the soothing tones she'd used before.

"Yes, Anne... and I..." The spirit sounded confused. Her

eyes kept wandering to the portal, and she took a few tentative steps in its direction. "We had to. Otherwise we would have had to spill so much blood. It was better this way... to keep the circle unending. Sacrifice..."

"Go to the light."

"But if I do, if I leave... who will look after Angel Manor?"

"There is no need for that anymore now. The curse is broken. You can rest."

The spirit took another step towards the dim light, her hand outstretched. Then she pulled her hand away and looked at Freya with pleading eyes.

"If you release the Angels, there is nothing more I can do."

"There is nothing left for you to do here. You fulfilled your task. Now it's time for you to rest."

"I am so tired."

"The light is calling. Can you hear it?"

"I can. It promises me peace."

"Answer the call. Go to it."

The spirit of the woman looked at Freya one last time.

"I'm sorry. I tried, but it's your task now. Your responsibility." The essence of the spirit unravelled into long ribbons of light, swirling in a macabre dance. They fluttered towards the portal and faded out of sight. Freya felt inexplicably empty, as if part of her had just disappeared with the woman.

It's my responsibility now, Freya thought, *if only I knew what she meant by that.*

"We must find the other spirits." Marie-Claire's voice cut through the silence, and Freya thought she sounded a bit smug. "Bring them here. It'll be dangerous, but it needs to be done. We can't let these souls loose on the world."

"What about what that spirit said just now?" Freya felt a hint of rebellion surface.

"Spirits get lost and confused as time goes by. Their identities change if they are bound to this earth too long. They start to adapt to a purpose; hers was to protect the house. But there is no need for that now. That's why she could let go."

"What if there really is more to the house, and to those Angels?"

"Spirits can be very tricky, dear. You shouldn't take them too seriously. She's at peace now, and the others will soon be too. I am sure more will use trickery to try and tug at your heartstrings. They can only influence you if you let them."

Freya raised an eyebrow and thought of the severed corpse of John Philips.

"To be fair, these spirits can do a lot more than influence me."

"If you think it's too much for you…"

Freya shook her head, forgetting for a moment that Marie-Claire couldn't see her. She corrected herself. "No. I can do this. I… I'm just not sure that we're doing the right thing."

"Would you rather leave these spirits here? Ready to kill again?"

"No."

"Then you know what to do."

***

Freya didn't have to go far to find the Angels. A group of them were gathered in the East Wing. They looked a little lost, just standing together and staring around as if they couldn't understand what had changed. In a way, they reminded Freya of a cluster of zombies from a horror movie, their naked bodies covered in remnants of blood. It was terrifying to see them like that. She swallowed and stepped out before them, trying to remember the sentence Marie-Claire had taught her.

"The guardians of the four watchtowers command you to find the light and take your rightful place in the afterlife." Her voice cracked, and she held the sachet of herbs out in front of her as if it were a shield.

The Angels turned as one to face her, their cold, dead eyes boring into her soul. There was a moment where all they did was stare. It was brief, but felt like a lifetime. Then the front woman, whose flesh bulged out in layers, smiled. Dark mucus dribbled past the corner of her mouth and across her chin, where it fell down in a long strand like spider silk. There was a change in their body language. Where their movements had been deliberate before, they now appeared to be emptier, though not any less hungry for blood. The recognition she had encountered before, the acknowledgement that she was the blood tie to the house, was gone, and Freya knew that if the Angels caught her, she would die.

She ran.

***

Logan burst into the main hall, his head spinning with fear and adrenaline. He saw the old medium standing in the middle of a large, white circle. *Sand? No, maybe salt?*

"Freya? Is she okay?" His eyes darted around the room, but he couldn't see any other person.

"Do not disrupt our ritual. You have no place here. We sent you to safety."

"No, I'm not leaving here without Freya, and I want to find the others."

"There won't be any survivors if we don't get rid of these spirits." The old woman pointed towards the door. "Go." Her white eyes stared at him, but he folded his arms and stood his ground. "I'm not disrupting anything."

At that moment, the door burst open and Freya ran through.

"They're right behind me." Freya panted.

"Quickly, get into the circle. You too, boy. It's too late for you now so you'd better just go along with this."

They ran into the circle, and the minute they stepped inside, the doors behind them opened again. Logan counted thirteen of the naked women. To his horror, he noticed that a short, skinny blonde carried the head of the boy they had talked to in the attic. His face was a mask of terror, and strands of tissue and muscle hung bloodily from his neck. It had not been severed by a clean cut, but instead looked like it had been ripped off with brutal force.

There was something bestial about the women, something primal. Though they were shaped like humans, they were more like animals. They didn't speak; they just took slow steps in their direction. Logan felt his skin grow cold, and he hoped that something as common as salt, or sand, or whatever it was on the floor, would be enough to save their hides. Unless it was some kick-ass magic dust, but he doubted that somehow.

The old woman stepped towards the edge of the circle, her face stern and filled with determination.

"The guardians of the four watchtowers command you to find the light and take your rightful place in the afterlife." Her voice was so strong that Logan felt a physical reaction to each syllable she uttered, and when Freya's doubtful voice joined in, he felt strangely safe. He almost joined in repeating the words over and over, but he remembered the warning about not disrupting anything, so he just stood by and watched and listened.

The naked women didn't seem to budge at first, but then they turned their heads to one of the walls. The brunette stepped closer to the circle, close enough to make the old medium shuffle backwards. She sniffed the air the way a bear would sniff for prey, her eyes settling on the blind woman.

"The guardians of the four watchtowers command you to find the light and take your rightful place in the afterlife." Marie-Claire's voice was less determined now, and Logan could hear a hint of panic. The naked woman reached forward, stretching out her hand slowly but without hesitation. Something stopped her just beyond the circle, and the spirit looked surprised. She tried again without success.

Marie-Claire found the confidence in her voice again and repeated the chant, though it didn't seem to be having the effect she wanted.

"Look at the light." The old woman sounded hoarse with desperation. "All of you, look at the light and pass through it. I command you!"

The spirits looked up in unison and, for an instant, Logan thought that they were going to storm the circle and tear them apart, but then their faces turned back to the spot on the wall. They cocked their heads as if they shared a hive mind. They seemed to be listening to something. Logan closed his eyes, and he could almost hear it, a disembodied voice that was so faint it could be nothing more than the rapid beating of his heart or the rushing of blood in his ears. Whatever it was, the hive was responding to it, and they moved towards the faint light.

"That's it. Give in to the call. Be at peace."

The women threw their heads back and screamed. Invisible claws tore at their skin, and deep gashes appeared in their naked flesh. Black blood oozed from the gaping wounds, but the claws continued, tearing the flesh until it stretched and shredded, hanging in ribbons from the dead bodies. Loose flaps of skin were pulled towards the portal. Logan watched with a mixture of satisfaction and horror as an arm was ripped from an elderly spirit and pulled into the beyond. Even the spilled blood was sucked up. There was no wind, no change of temperature, and yet Logan felt the force of the opening.

The whole spectacle must have taken no more than five minutes, but every last detail of every last second was etched into Logan's brain, and he was exhausted.

No one spoke for quite a while.

"Is it over?" Logan was the first to talk, and as if on cue, the doors burst open with a loud bang. Seven more of the naked women stepped through, holding a fully dressed girl in their midst. Logan recognised Julie and gasped. The girl was not in good shape; she was conscious but barely. Her face was swollen and covered in blood, her clothing was torn, and her right leg dangled at a weird angle behind her as she was dragged. He readied himself to run to her aid, but Marie-Claire held up a hand.

"No heroics."

Logan wondered if she could read his mind, but he stayed his ground.

"Release the girl."

Two identical naked women, familiar to Logan, dragged Julie forward. Right in front of the circle.

These aren't as bestial as the others. I wonder why? They seem more lucid somehow.

They held Julie's semi-conscious face up to look at Marie-Claire. Julie seemed to come around a bit, and her eyes opened wide. Tears streamed across her chubby, freckled cheeks. The women brought their pale faces to hers, and with the tips of their black tongues, they licked the salt water from her skin. Their eyes turned towards the people in the circle.

"We have to do something," Logan said.

"If you step out of this circle, we all die."

A sense of helplessness washed over him, and Logan stood frozen to the spot as the women continued to lick the girl's face. Then they drew their heads back, their faces contorted into wicked sneers, their black teeth exposed, and they lunged simultaneously at the girl. Red blood poured from the wounds. Julie whimpered more than screamed, and her eyes rolled back into her head. Freya cried out, but like Logan, she was helpless to do anything.

"The guardians of the four watchtowers command you to find the light and take your rightful place in the afterlife." Marie-Claire screamed the words as the two women went in for another bite out of the young woman, this time from her neck, and Julie twitched, screaming louder.

"I command you!" Tears ran from the older woman's face, and she repeated the chant over and over until the two women dropped Julie. The girl wasn't quite dead yet. Logan could see her chest move, but she'd lost a lot of blood.

Like the women had done before them, the naked spirits moved to the portal, and again the invisible claws tore them apart. This time, Logan found it less difficult to watch; at least the bleeding girl on the floor had been avenged.

"How many more are there?" Logan moved towards the edge of the circle. If he could take two steps out, he could pick up Julie's fallen form and bring her to safety.

"I don't know. I sense there are more spirits, but I think we forced most of the angels to go to the other side. It's hard to see them now. The gate is obscuring my vision."

"Can I pick the girl up?" He pointed at Julie. "There is no one else here now."

"Yes. You may try."

Logan stepped from the circle. The air was much colder beyond the safety of Marie-Claire's barrier. His heart drummed in his throat as he lifted the wounded girl, the sight of her torn flesh making him gag. She was hot under his touch. Relief settled over him as he stepped back into the circle, and he placed her down on the ground before taking off his t-shirt and holding it against her wounds.

"What do we do now?" Fatigue made master of him all of a sudden, and he realised he had been running for his life the whole night. Every muscle in his body protested at once now that the adrenaline had gone, and all he wanted to do was to curl up in a ball and fall asleep. But it wasn't over yet, and he knew it.

"Now we wait for Pierre." Marie-Claire sounded as weary as he felt, and he could see that Freya too was starting to show signs of fatigue by the way she stood.

After a few minutes of watching the door, they all sat down, leaning against each other. Julie seemed to be sleeping, and other than keeping his blood-soaked t-shirt pressed against the wounds in her neck, Logan didn't know what else to do. John would have been in a better position to help the girl, but John was dead. He wondered who else had died, but he was so tired he didn't even feel the emotions anymore.

***

Terrence walked with slow, deliberate, sideways steps, keeping his back to the wall as much as he could, though chances were the spirits could walk through brickwork. He had no idea how this shit worked, and he wished the French guy was still with him. That dude seemed to know what was going on, whereas he had no fucking clue. He had made it through the whole of the South Wing, and to his relief, he saw the entrance to the main hall. He was about to step out from his hiding place in the doorway when a shadowy figure walked out of one of the doors.

Terrence froze, his heart pounding in his throat. He pressed himself against the doorframe as the figure slinked around the corridor and disappeared through another door. The figure glanced over his shoulder, and Terrence could see his face in the light of early dawn.

It was Oliver Jardin, and he was holding one of the large knives from the kitchen.

***

They sat and dozed, waiting for Pierre to make his way back from the kitchen, but losing hope he would. Once in a while, a lost spirit came in, drawn to the light of the portal. Marie-Claire guided them into the light without much trouble. Only the Angels were difficult to convince. They rarely came in alone too, and after a couple of hours, Logan was convinced that Pierre had probably met his fate with them.

Then the doors to the West Wing opened and Pierre staggered towards the circle, panting and wide eyed, his clothes covered in dust and cobwebs.

"I didn't run into any Angels in the West Wing. In fact... I didn't see a single spirit. I did find something else though. There is something underneath..." His words failed as a knife plunged into the flesh of his neck, cutting through the collar of his shirt.

A thick wave of blood spilled from Pierre's lips, pouring down his chin like a macabre waterfall, and he slumped to the ground in slow motion. Crimson spread around the collar of his striped shirt as Oliver pulled the knife free from his neck and looked at Logan, his lips tightened into a sneer.

"You took it from me, all of you. Don't you understand? It was all I had... this house... it was all I was, all I have ever been. You didn't just rid the house of its soul. You stole mine in the process. Everything here... everything it was, that was me. These were sacrifices I made, and you took them from me." Tears poured down his cheeks, and he moaned with grief. His hate-filled eyes met Logan's.

Oliver raised the knife and rushed at Logan. His shoes made a horrible sucking sound as they ran across the marble, and one of his feet slipped through the white grains on the floor, breaking the circle. Logan froze as the temperature dropped around him. He saw Oliver come at him as if all the man's movements were in slow motion, and although his mind told him he was in trouble, his body was unresponsive.

A shadow crossed the room. Oliver stopped, his mouth opened in an ugly grimace, his tongue lolled out, and a few drops of blood sprayed against his cheek. Then he fell down. Terrence stood behind him, a heavy piece of wood clutched in his hands and his brow furrowed in determination.

"I saw him come in here. He had a knife... I... I hid."

"It's okay." The sight of Terrence broke Logan from his spell. "You did good."

"You think I killed him?"

"Nah, I think he'll be all right."

"Logan?" Freya's voice sounded shaky. "Get him in the circle... something is going on with that portal thing."

Logan looked over his shoulder. The portal was growing, and the light that shone from it was getting brighter. Strands shaped like lightning bolts were spreading far and wide over the walls, the ceiling, and the floor. Despite his dislike for the unconscious man, he picked him up and carried him inside the circle, laying him next to Julie. Her face was an open-eyed death mask, her mouth a grimace of pain. Logan reached over and felt for a pulse; there was none. He suddenly remembered something.

"The circle is broken. Will it protect us?" Logan pointed at the gap that Oliver had left.

"Mend the circle!" Marie-Claire's voice was high and filled with panic.

"What's going on?" Freya yelled at the old woman. "What's the portal doing?"

"I don't know. I've never seen anything like this."

Logan sank to his knees and scraped the white grains together. *Oh God, please work.*

The building around them groaned as the hole grew bigger, engulfing everything around them. Logan pulled back from the rim of the circle as light flooded over the marble ground, and he caught a glimpse of the world beyond. He saw the end of life inside it, the light speaking to him of redemption, of eternal peace, and of letting go. Part of him yearned to step out of the safety of the circle and join the soft voices promising him bliss.

The inside of the salt circle didn't light up like the rest of the room. Instead, it stayed grounded in reality, and only when Logan felt Freya's arms around his waist, pulling him away from the rim, did he stop staring into the light. He turned to her and buried his face in her hair, knowing at that moment that he loved her more than anything, even more than death.

"Do you hear the singing?" Freya looked at him with her large, grey eyes, forcing him to see her. There were tears on her cheeks, and he suddenly felt the tickle of tears on his own. Two wet drops hung at the same level as his mouth, like pressure points, cooling quickly. He listened and realised that the voices he heard could very well be singing. It was hard to tell; he couldn't make out their words, yet he understood them as if they were talking just to him.

"I hear them." His voice was hoarse.

Freya's voice trembled. "I don't want to die yet... but at the same time I want to give in."

"Not today. We're not dying today." He wrapped his arms around her. Behind him, Terrence sobbed, and he reached out a hand to the young man, but Terrence was staring at the open doors and wouldn't budge. All four were open now and spirits poured through one by one. One of the spirits was Tyrell, and Logan was a little surprised and saddened to see the boy here. He saw Jim and John herd the guys inside, guiding them to the brightest part of the light. His heart broke when he realised they were all dead, and his stomach sank when he saw the figures of Lyndon and Roger amongst them. *This fucking house claimed so many lives.*

"I can't see Bam," Freya whispered. "There's too many of them, and I can't see her."

Logan looked around the dead, and he couldn't spot the girl either. His attention was drawn away to those he could see. He wanted to look at them one last time because he would never see them again.

The whole room was a beacon of light, drawing the spirits to it, each stepping inside and falling apart. Some would dissipate in beautiful colourful ribbons, while others were ripped apart. The voices became loud and more intense, and Logan wondered if he could ever have sane thoughts again after what he'd seen. How could he go back to his existence when he'd looked into the afterlife?

Marie-Claire swayed on her feet, commanding the spirits to embrace the light, but Logan had a suspicion the dead no longer needed the old woman's help and were finding the light just fine.

The last spirit was a red headed woman, her long hair falling past her shoulders and onto her back like liquid flames, and she wore a diaphanous nightgown. She would have been beautiful – could have been beautiful – if her face wasn't so filled with hate and her eyes weren't so harsh.

"What you have done... there is no redemption." Her

milky white eyes looked straight at Freya, and her black mouth was a thin hard line. "I am the last of the legacy. It's your responsibility now." With those words, her body began to rip itself apart. Limbs tore from their sockets as she screamed for mercy, but the gate had none.

Then the light faded and the gate shrunk with alarming speed until it had folded into itself. The house died a second time, but this time if felt final. The voices were silenced. The singing stopped. Logan felt empty to the depths of his very soul.

"Is it over?"

"There are no spirits left in this house." Marie-Claire had tears in her white eyes too. "This house is a dead cell."

"What do we do now?" The words came shakily from Freya's throat. "I mean... where do we go from here? There are so many dead. How do we explain that? We're going to get arrested or something."

"No." Logan's mouth turned into a thin line. "Just him." He pointed at Oliver's unconscious form. Freya stared at her friend's body, shock rendering her speechless. If it hadn't been for Logan, Oliver would have been swallowed by the light.

"I can't..."

Logan gathered her in his arms. "Let's not do this now. Let's just enjoy that we're alive."

"Oh, God... Logan." Freya's tears were flowing again. "I can't believe we survived this."

Chapter 36

3 months later

"Yes mom, I got your parcel. Thank you. Yes, just in time for Christmas too." Freya rolled her eyes at Logan, who was holding the cardboard parcel. "No, haven't opened it yet, but did you get the biscuits I like? Thanks." She nodded at the phone. "Yes, we're fine."

Her face pulled into a frown, and she went quiet as she listened to her mother over the phone.

"Oliver? They say his court date won't be for at least another year." She nodded at the voice on the other line again. "Yes, I have to testify against him. I know... yes. You did warn me about the house. Yes, you were right, it drives people crazy. Yes, Aunt Miriam was a nut too." She rolled her eyes again and made a duck bill with her hand, moving it to mimic her mother's words. Logan laughed softly as he used a knife to cut open the duct tape binding the cardboard box together.

"No mom, we're fine."

They were fine, Logan agreed wordlessly. Surprisingly so. It had been almost three months since they'd left Angel Manor in the bright light of the equinox day. Logan had been sure he would never be the same again, and yet he'd proved surprisingly resilient, as had Freya. They kept each other going, he had to admit. She suffered more from nightmares than he did, and they found it difficult to be away from each other. He had never been more obsessed with a girl. She was his only tether to sanity, he often thought.

Leaving Angel Manor came with some hiccups; it was impossible to walk away from a bloodbath such as that unscathed. Most of the bodies were never retrieved, just Julie's and Pierre's, and since it was proven that Oliver had killed Pierre, he was taken into custody. Oliver played the part of the insane murderer perfectly, and he confessed to crimes he hadn't even committed. It looked like they might get off the hook, though he, Terrence, Freya, Mason and Marie-Claire were warned they could not leave the country as of yet. The investigation was still going on, but Logan couldn't worry himself about that. He was alive, and that was all that mattered.

The only person they still spoke to was Terrence. He was even joining them for Christmas. Mason went back to his parents in Edinburgh, and Logan felt relieved for that. At least the young man had decent parents, unlike Terrence, who now lived with a friend in a flat in Bristol. What Florifera was doing, he didn't know. They had parted ways rather abruptly.

He pulled food from the box, Dutch biscuits called Stroopwafels, a jar of mayonnaise, and then, in the bottom of the box, he saw what looked like a notebook. Curiosity tickled his senses as he pulled it out, and he was vaguely aware of Freya's words to her mother.

"What did you send me? You had it all along?"

It was a diary, Logan realised, not just a notebook, bound in black leather. He opened it, feeling a little guilty for snooping, and pulled a large, white envelope from the first page. Curly black writing spelled 'Freya Formynder' in old-fashioned penmanship. He held the letter up for Freya to see, and she nodded at him then moved her head towards the phone to show she had to finish her conversation first.

He ran his fingers through the pages, and suddenly remembered the other diary they'd found and had never had time to decipher. The handwriting in this journal was clearer.

"*—that's when Beth built Angel Manor, to keep the*

369

souls protected." His heart skipped a beat as he read the words, and he snapped the journal shut. Freya needed to read this with him; he couldn't do it alone. The words 'Angel Manor' alone terrified him.

"I thought she was never going to stop talking." Freya exhaled a deep sigh. "Did you know she had Aunt Miriam's bloody diary this whole time? She didn't want to send it to me because it was filled with crazy talk, but after what happened at the house, she decided it might be good to send it after all."

"Why?"

"Because my mother is crazy."

"Ah, you might have mentioned that."

"I have to admit, I can't really blame the woman. I wonder how much she knew. She still won't talk to me about it." Freya shook her head and wrinkled her nose at him. There was a smile in her eyes, though. Logan had mixed feelings about the diary. He wanted to know more about it, and at the same time, he feared the can of worms it might open.

"You found it then?" Freya's voice cracked, and she ran the tips of her fingers across the black leather.

"The diary?"

"No, the Holy Grail." She made a face, and he had to stop himself from kissing her; she looked so cute when she did that.

"Yeah. It was in the bottom of the parcel. It has a letter in it, addressed to you." He handed her the letter with a bit of a flourish and looked at her with curious expectation. Her hands trembled ever so slightly when she took the envelope from between his fingers, and she stared at it with some hesitation.

"Do you want me to read it?"

"No, I'm okay." Her finger slid into the gap in the top of the envelope and she tore it open, the paper ripping with a crisp sound. She bit her lip and pulled out the letter between her thumb and forefinger. The paper fluttered as she shook it open, and she eased herself onto the candy-red sofa, drawing her legs up under her. Logan slid next to her, careful not to look over her shoulder, as she didn't like him reading along.

Freya cleared her throat and read in a soft voice.

"My Dear Freya,

"I have created a new journal which will ease you through your task as a Guardian. A lot of the old texts were lost in the fire at the convent, so what I have written down is a mixture of the stories that have been passed down for generations, the ones my parents told me, and the diary of Sister Agatha that I have placed in the attic in my grandmother's writing desk. The diary is rather incomprehensible, so I didn't want to risk you having to decipher it yourself."

Freya tapped the side of her nose.

"So that's the thing we found, Agatha's diary? I'm glad Aunt Miriam decided to decipher it for us." She lowered her eyes again and read the rest.

"Of course, it would have been better if I could have trained you myself, but your mother never gave me the chance. I think the dairy will speak for itself. I'm sorry this is your fate now, but it's a burden we must all bear. It's our family curse and our secret. Please don't neglect this duty. The fate of the world is in your hands."

Freya lowered the letter and let it rest on her lap, her eyes filled with worry.

"What?" Logan ran his hand across her jeans in what he hoped was a comforting manner. "Why the frown?"

"I just can't help that nagging feeling."

"What?"

"That we missed something. That there was a reason why those spirits were locked up in that house. I mean... why would my family take care of them for generations? Why not just have them exorcised like we did? I'm sure there are others like Florifera who could have done the same. Why go to all these lengths to be the Guardians of a house?"

"Because they were crazy?" He squeezed her thigh and was glad to get a little smile out of her, but her face turned serious again instantly.

"I think there might be more to it than that."

"Don't know, Frey. It could just be simple indoctrination, you know? If it started with ancestors, and they taught their children to be 'Keepers' or 'Guardians' or whatever, and they taught their children... that kind of behaviour can last generations. Look at the Amish, they teach their kids their lifestyles. This is not that different... it just has ghosts. I'm sure they all felt they were doing something important."

Freya squinted at him, her brow furrowed and her lips curled in a doubtful sneer.

"What if we're wrong, Logan?" Her bottom lip twitched. "What if there is something else there? What about that sleeping master thing? The spirits talked about it. What was that? We never found out."

"What do you want to do? Go back to that house?"

"No... oh God, no." Her fingers clutched the paper envelope and it folded under her touch. "I... I want to read that diary, though. At least see what she has to say about it." She shrugged, and he could see she was uncomfortable.

"Well, you got the diary, so why not?" He grabbed the journal and handed it to her. He was curious too, though he wouldn't have minded if she had burned the thing either.

Freya opened the journal and started reading.

***

"Listen to this," Freya glanced at Logan over the top of the journal. "I'm not going to read all of it to you because there's a lot about the history of the world and stuff. It talks about some sort of celestial beings, angels and demons. Not sure what to make of it all, but this is where it gets interesting. *'Four Horsemen were created, or perhaps they were already in existence. They were brought forth because of our presence. Their sole purpose was to destroy everything in existence for the great rebirth.'*" Freya rubbed her nose, and she saw that her excitement was lost on Logan. "I think these things are meant to restart the world or something."

Logan just shrugged, and Freya continued to read. *"'What stopped them was a great sacrifice, one that we still talk about in the Bible.'* It goes on to talk about Jesus, and then this: *'It was not his fate to die. He was meant to prosper, but his sacrifice saved us all. The Four Horsemen were buried deep within the earth, but the only way to keep them in their slumber was if we kept making true sacrifices.'*"

Freya stopped reading. She looked at Logan and tried to understand the expression on his face, He looked deep in thought. His brow was furrowed and his green eyes looked far away. She took a deep breath and held it before speaking again.

"According to this, Angel Manor is the tomb of one of the Four Horsemen."

"What do you make of all of this? Do you think it's true?" He looked pale, and the question brought a pang to her heart.

"I don't know. Celestial beings, the Four Horsemen? It sounds crazy, but after what we've seen, we can't take the risk."

"You want to go back to Angel Manor?"

"Want? No. But I have to." She bit her lip. "You don't have to come if you don't want to."

"Don't be daft. Of course I'll come. You don't have to do this alone." He leaned in and kissed her, and she felt safe. There was no place on this earth where she would ever feel safe again, except in Logan's arms. Their relationship had not been going long, yet there was a depth between them that she had never before experienced. Freya knew with certainty that he was the love of her life, and that she wanted to be with him for the rest of her days. The thought of him coming with her was an immense relief.

He found her mouth with his, soft at first, but then his kisses became more passionate, his tongue curling around hers, his lips massaging her mouth in a delicious rhythm. Her body sang each time he touched her and she responded to his kisses with her own, her hands stroking his neck and shoulders.

Logan froze mid-kiss, his forehead creased, and he pulled away from her. She looked at him, wide-eyed and confused.

"What's the matter?"

"That diary spoke of the solstice and the equinox. When *is* the next solstice? I mean... it's winter... has it been already?"

Freya felt her blood go cold.

"I don't know. Google it." A dreadful sense of urgency overtook her as she pointed to the laptop standing on the breakfast bar. Logan jumped up and turned it on, his hands visibly shaking. Ages passed before he could click on the browser and look up the information they needed.

"Has its own wiki page," he muttered with some amusement. His face went pale. "December 22nd this year."

"Oh goodie... so we have plenty of time then," she said miserably.

"Two days."

"Well, one really, since it's late now. Day after tomorrow. We need to go back to Scotland, back to the house as soon as we can. We really do know how to time this shit, don't we? I feel like one of those clichés with a ticking time bomb... you know, the kind with only a minute left?"

"This could just be nothing. I mean, it's a pretty farfetched story."

"As farfetched as murdering ghosts?"

"Touché. I guess we'll leave in the morning."

"Yes, but for tonight... please just hold me."

He wrapped his arms around her, and Freya wondered if she would ever get to feel this safe again.

Chapter 37

The house looked different this time. Freya suddenly remembered the first time she'd stepped out of her car, filled with expectation. She could almost hear Bam's voice ring clear across the garden, see her run up the steps towards the house. She felt Oliver's hands on her shoulders... that moment seemed a lifetime ago now. The row of twelve angels stood guard in front of the house, looking alive in the bright white light of the moon, but the friendly yellow bricks looked grey and cracked. Freya wanted nothing more than to sell this cursed house, but somehow she still felt linked to it. She had to know if her aunt was speaking the truth, if one of the Horsemen really slumbered underneath the rock and concrete. Logan could be right; it could just be some hysterical myth that was made up generations ago and grew with the telling of it. Perhaps this whole thing was founded on the plans of some crazy nuns who just looked for an excuse to torment children.

And yet...

Her pace was slow and her heart was pounding. It was late, as their journey had taken longer than they expected, and the midnight hour dawned. Each step to the front door was agony, and when she reached for the lock, the key shook in her hand.

"Where do you want to look first?"

"The basement. If there is any way down, it should be there."

"Good idea."

She pulled the police tape aside and pushed the door open. The lights still worked, and she stepped into the dimly lit main hall, Logan only a step behind her. The inside felt bigger somehow, more spacious than before... more intimidating.

The house itself is still dead.

Even the large grandfather clock did not show any signs of life. There were still traces of blood on the floor in the main hall, and evidence that the police had done their investigation. Freya was shocked that no one had bothered to clean any of it up, and that apparently she was responsible for this. She couldn't look at the blood. In the past three months, she'd often wondered where all the bodies had gone. She knew that the children had disappeared with the other spirits, but there were several human casualties of Angel Manor, and the house seemed to have devoured their physical remains somehow. The idea sent shivers down her spine.

They walked through the main hall to the West Wing, and Freya opened the door to the kitchen. Tables and chairs were overturned, and the coffee pot lay broken on the ground, surrounded by a dried up coffee stain. Freya grabbed a knife from the counter and held it to her side.

"What is that for?" Logan arched his eyebrows and gave her a crooked smile.

"I don't know, it just makes me feel safer. Who knows what's in this house now? Could be squatters or something." She shrugged, and he chuckled in response before grabbing another one of the knives.

"Better safe than sorry, right?" He winked at her, and she pushed her body against his with a smile on her face. They wandered through the West Wing, looking in all the rooms.

"We left most of our stuff behind. I guess I should really pick up Bam's and Oliver's things one day."

Logan nodded. "Let's not worry about that right now though. Let's just set your mind at ease first."

"Yeah. I guess we should head to the South Wing then. I'm pretty sure the entrance to the basement is there."

Logan nodded again, and from the expression on his face, Freya guessed he was as nervous as she was. They walked side by side, slow and careful as if they were trespassers.

Not all the lights worked, and they had to walk through the dark corridor of the South Wing carrying the torches they brought. Freya almost expected one of the Angels to come running at them, ready to tear at their flesh, but nothing came and the corridor remained deadly silent.

She needed some help with the large metal door to the basement; it was very heavy. Logan yanked it open and allowed her to pass through first. The light at the bottom of the stairs was already on, and Freya saw symbols painted on the wall as she made her way down the steps. The single light bulb didn't illuminate enough of the basement for Freya's liking, and the whole area was cast in deep shadows.

"There's a door there." She pointed at the far end. "We should try that." Then she added as an afterthought: "If I don't chicken out."

"I'm here. You'll be fine."

They made their way to the door and found a smaller room. It had another light bulb that dangled from a long black wire, and it cast a sickly yellow light in the otherwise empty room. The walls were decorated with painted symbols, similar to the ones they saw on the way down the stairs.

Spells... or at least they were. "There's a hatch. I think this might be what we're looking for."

Logan shone his torch on a wooden square in the centre of the room and Freya walked up to inspect it. "Shine your torch on it and I'll pull it open."

She nodded and took a step back. An ominous creek rang through the small room as he pushed the wood back, revealing a dark hole underneath. Freya shone her light down and saw a narrow staircase carved into the rough stone wall. The steps looked barely big enough to put her feet on.

"I'll go first." Logan took her gently by the shoulders and moved her to one side.

Freya nodded gratefully and watched Logan descend through the hole, and seconds later she followed him. There was an old smell in the air, of limestone and something rotting; Freya was sure she smelled it before in the house, only it was stronger here.

The stairs wound down into the earth, and the atmosphere below was cold and moist. Somewhere off in the distance, water dripped down in a thunderous rhythm that echoed throughout the underground cavern.

"This place is amazing," Logan whispered. "I had no idea this was down here."

"Aunt Miriam's story is starting to sound a little more credible." Her muscles tensed. "That worries me." There was a slight echo when she spoke, and their steps sounded hollow as they walked further down.

At the bottom of the stairs, her feet touched stone, and Logan held out his hand to her. She grabbed it and took comfort in its warmth. The floor angled down, making it difficult to balance, but at least there were no more stairs. A narrow stone corridor led them to a cavernous area with a large marble slab set into the centre of the floor. It reminded her of ancient churches and the resting places of saints.

"Is this it?" She shone her torch on the slab, highlighting the strange markings on it. If they were words, they were written in letters she had never seen before, though Freya was sure they weren't pictures.

"I think so. Your aunt was definitely right. There is something buried here."

"Do you think it's one of the four Horsemen?" Her voice broke as she spoke.

"I don't know how to answer that. I don't know what to think. What time is it, anyway?"

She shone the light on her watch.

"Almost twelve thirty."

"We've been here longer than I thought."

"Yeah. Funny, but somehow I half expected something horrible to happen at precisely midnight." She giggled a little, her cheeks flushed.

"You know what? Me too." He laughed.

The cavern rumbled and shook with a familiar tremor, and Freya almost dropped her torch.

Deep cracks appeared in the marble slab, and an unnatural cold spread through the whole area. Black smoke rose through the cracks, and Freya felt a fear like she had never experienced before. Not even the sight of the Angels had made her feel the way she did now. The marble exploded outward, raining tiny, sharp pebbles down on Freya and Logan, and they held each other as tightly as they could. The stone around them groaned and rumbled, and above them the cavern split. Earth and dust fell from above, though not nearly enough to justify the opening that was appearing.

Oh fuck, why did I come here? Why did I take this risk? Freya shivered.

The front legs of a horse, as pale as the moon itself and as large as an elephant, scraped across the edges of the tomb. The sound of neighing tore through her soul and hot urine trickled down her trouser leg. For a moment, fear took hold of her heart, strangling it, and part of her welcomed death.

The head of the horse slowly emerged, its thin white skin pulled tight against muscle and bone, its red eyes glaring from fiery sockets. The horse pushed itself up against the stone, and for the first time, Freya saw the rider. He was tall, at least nine feet, and he wore a long robe the colour of midnight. Under the cowl, she saw his skeletal face, eye sockets blazing with the same flames as the horse. He looked like a figure straight out of Dante's *Inferno*, only he was real. She saw the details on his bony hands, the scratches in his skull face, and she knew what true fear was. There was nothing she could do to stop this, and she felt utterly powerless.

Long lines with hooks appeared out of nowhere, attaching themselves to the rider and his horse. The horse's pale skin ripped, and black blood flowed freely. Freya looked up, and there, at the edge of the hole in the ceiling, she saw the twelve angels that stood guard outside the house.

They made their way down to the Horseman, their marble wings beating with a thunderous sound as they lowered themselves. More ropes were cast, like the web of a spider, covering the Horseman and his horse, but to no avail.

"They need a sacrifice." She wasn't sure who said it, or if it was just a thought that came to her, but she knew it was true. In order to keep the Horseman sleeping, she needed to give a sacrifice. And it would have to be a great one.

She looked at the hole in the slab; she could throw herself down there and not survive. It would be a sacrifice... *but would it be enough?* She wanted to die. More than anything at that moment, she wanted to die. *It won't be enough to sacrifice myself.*

Her heart fragmented into a thousand pieces as she turned to Logan. He looked at her, and she thought she saw something in his eyes. *Acceptance?* She didn't know, but all she could do was grip the kitchen knife tight and bring it down at him with force. His eyes widened as the blade hit his chest, and his eyes filled with betrayal. Freya knew she would never be able to rid herself of that image. She would carry it with her throughout eternity, but she pulled the knife back and stabbed again. Through tear-stained eyes, she watched him fall to his knees, and she pushed the blade into his neck this time. His flesh gripped the point of the knife, sucking it into his body. She stabbed him twelve more times. The hot spray of his blood covered her face, arms, neck and torso, but it didn't stop her. The pain she felt escaped her body through a gut wrenching cry, directed at the Horseman as he slowly sank back into his tomb. The marble realigned itself and the angels moved away with jagged motions, positioning themselves on each side of the large slab... frozen in time once more.

Freya stood and stared at the tomb. She couldn't bear to look at Logan's still body. All her love, all her safety, any chance of happiness lay dead at her feet. She wished she could have died herself, she wished she could gather Logan into her arms and kiss him, she wished... but she knew there was no more wishing. She knew that she had a task to fulfil.

She was the bloodline of the guardians.

EPILOGUE

Angel Hotel looked just the way she had hoped it would. It had taken some time and a lot of money, but the hotel was beautiful and inviting. Freya knew she would have to find a better way to make the sacrifices, to keep it inconspicuous, because the last thing she needed was the police on her back. She leaned against the entrance and sighed, rubbing her large belly. The baby had been quiet the past few days, which hopefully meant it was time. She'd passed her due date several days ago. If only Logan could have seen his baby girl. But life was cruel, and she had a duty.

A translucent hand rested on her shoulder. Freya could barely feel it, but she knew who was there.

"Our dream is almost built." Bam's voice was soft.

"Yes." Freya rubbed her belly. "I am glad you decided to stay here and help me, Bam."

Bam smiled. "I don't think you can do this without me. The living are filled with sentiment; you need me to help you keep what lies below dormant."

"I thought you'd gone, you know." Freya turned to her friend. "With the rest of them."

"If I hadn't been stuck down there, I would have. You know that." Bam looked downcast.

"I didn't know you were down there. All we did was leave the latch open... you got out by yourself."

"As did Chuck." There was a bitterness in her voice, and her eyes stared into the distance.

"But we sorted that. Chuck is trapped in the basement.

It's a good thing we got our hands on the journal... eventually. He won't get out, don't worry. You're safe."

"For now..."

"I'll keep you safe," Freya promised, and she looked down at her stomach. "I will keep both you and this little one safe." She had never been more determined in her life. Freya would train her daughter with the knowledge of the Master who Sleeps, and her bloodline would continue to keep the world safe. It wasn't an easy life but, she decided, it was a noble one.

THANK YOU FOR READING

Thank you for taking the time to read this book. We sincerely hope that you enjoyed the story and appreciate your letting us try to entertain you. We realise that your time is valuable, and without the continuing support of people such as yourself, we would not be able to do what we do.

As a thank you, we would like to offer you a free ebook from our range, in return for you signing up to our mailing list. We will never share your details with anyone and will only contact you to let you know about new releases.

You can sign up on our website

Http://www.horrifictales.co.uk

If you enjoyed this book, then please consider leaving a short review on Amazon, Goodreads or anywhere else that you, as a reader, visit to learn about new books. One of the most important parts about how well a book sells is how many positive reviews it has, so if you can spare a little more of your valuable time to share the experience with others, even if its just a line or two, then we would really appreciate it.

Thanks, and see you next time!

THE HORRIFIC TALES PUBLISHING TEAM

ABOUT THE AUTHOR

Chantal Noordeloos lives in the Netherlands, where she spends her time with her wacky, supportive husband, and outrageously cunning daughter, who is growing up to be a supervillain. When she is not busy exploring interesting new realities, or arguing with characters (aka writing), she likes to dabble in drawing.

In 1999 she graduated from the Norwich School of Art and Design, where she focused mostly on creative writing.

There are many genres that Chantal likes to explore in her writing, but her 'go to' genre will always be horror. "It helps being scared of everything; that gives me plenty of in-spiration," she says. Angel Manor is her first published full length novel, and she had to reach into the darkest parts of her mind to write it.

Chantal likes to write for all ages, and storytelling is the element of writing that she enjoys most. "Writing should be an escape from everyday life, and I like to provide people with new places to escape to, and new people to meet."

ALSO FROM HORRIFIC TALES PUBLISHING

HIGH MOOR

When John Simpson hears of a bizarre animal attack in his old home town of High Moor, it stirs memories of a long forgotten horror. John knows the truth. A werewolf stalks the town once more, and on the night of the next full moon, the killing will begin again. He should know. He survived a werewolf attack in 1986, during the worst year of his life.

It's 1986 and the town is gripped in terror after the mutilated corpse of a young boy is found in the woods. When Sergeant Steven Wilkinson begins an investigation, with the help of a specialist hunter, he soon realises that this is no ordinary animal attack. Werewolves are real, and the trail of bodies is just beginning, with young John and his friends smack in the middle of it.

Twenty years later, John returns to High Moor. The latest attack involved one of his childhood enemies, but there's more going on than meets the eye. The consequences of his past actions, the reappearance of an old flame and a dying man who will either save or damn him are the least of his problems. The night of the full moon is approaching and time is running out.

But how can he hope to stop a werewolf, when every full moon he transforms into a bloodthirsty monster himself?

If you're craving some good werewolf action with well-developed characters and a fantastic plot, skip the Hollywood films and go straight for this electrifying novel, which is far more entertaining.
- Hellnotes.com

Graeme Reynolds has written a captivating, action packed, this-should-be-a-movie werewolf novel in High Moor and if this is going to be a series of some sort, count me in for the ride. It should be a fun one. - **Horrortalk.com**

http://www.horrifictales.co.uk

Chantal Noordeloos

HIGH MOOR II
MOONSTRUCK

The people of High Moor are united in horror at the latest tragedy to befall their small town. As dawn breaks, the town is left to count the cost and mourn its dead, while breathing a collective sigh of relief. John Simpson, the apparent perpetrator of the horrific murders, is in police custody. The nightmare is over. Isn't it?

Detective Inspector Phil Fletcher and his partner, Constable Olivia Garner, have started to uncover some unsettling evidence during their investigations of John Simpson's past – evidence that supports his impossible claims: that he is a werewolf, and will transform on the next full moon to kill again.

However a new threat is now lurking in the shadows. A mysterious group have arrived in High Moor, determined to keep the existence of werewolves hidden. And they will do anything to protect their secret. Anything at all.

A reminder of why werewolves are supposed to be scary – 10/10 – **Starburst Magazine.**

A masterclass in modern action horror - **Gingernuts of Horror**

An absolute must for werewolf fans - **Hellnotes.com**

The action is explosive and relentless, the violence is gory and ferocious, yet it is far from mindless as it is underpinned by a superb and fascinating story. - **The Eloquent Page**

I don't think I can recommend this book highly enough but with the caveat that this tale is not for the faint of heart, or indeed those looking for Twilight-type lycanthropy! - **Andy Erupts.com**

http://www.horrifictales.co.uk

Angel Manor

OF A FEATHER

Socrates has a gift, a power even he doesn't fully understand.

But old Gert, who feeds the pigeons in Gustav's Park, understands. Pretty Jamie, who works at the Bird Emporium, understands. And the old Indian chief who wears a strange, two-sided bird mask, he understands too.

As does the ancient, angry spirit called the Thunderbird and about a million of Wellington County's feathered creatures...

They know what Socrates Singer really is.

And they know what he can do...

Ken Goldman continues to prove why he's one of my favorite up-and-coming authors. OF A FEATHER is a diabolical and absorbing tale that takes wing early on and pulls the reader through the darkest of skies. The journey is astonishing and the destination, unforgettable. **- Benjamin Kane Ethridge - Bram Stoker Award Winning Author of Black and Orange**

This is one of those stories that has a natural almost organic sense of momentum towards it gruesome conclusion. Peppered with some extremely intense descriptive passages, this book will keep you on the edge of the seat, right up to it's pitch perfect ending. - **Gingernuts of Horror**

A bloody horror story that will continue to haunt the reader long after they put it down. **- Books and Booze Blog.**

The pacing was almost perfect and I greedily consumed this read in two sittings. **- Horror After Dark.**

http://www.horrifictales.co.uk

Chantal Noordeloos

WHISPER

It was supposed to be a fresh start. A place for Steve & Melody Samson to begin their new life together away from the noise and crime of the city. However, their new home – an idyllic cottage nestled deep within the dense solitude of Oakwell forest-has a disturbing history, hidden for generations by the locals. There is evil in Hope House, and the cursed forest that surrounds it. Evil that has awakened after lying dormant for decades, and has terrifying plans for the young couple.

Once you hear the whispers, it may already be too late.

Michael Bray's Whisper is a solid piece of horror fiction. It's a ghost story that puts the reader in a trance. I found myself blasting through the last half of the book, wanting to know how it ended and wanting to know that very moment. That's the mark of a great story-teller. **4.5 / 5- Horrornovelreviews.com**

I was supposed to being doing chores and cooking and my poor partner did it all *grin*. I really could not put this book down. - **Saguaro Moon Reviews**

Michael Bray's writing is reminiscent of James Herbert. Intelligent and descriptive, without unnecessary rambling. The characters we encounter are colourful and very life-like, with believable reactions to the events unfolding, which is very important to me. The ending is fast paced and breath-taking, in complete contrast to the slow build at the beginning - **Readersfavourite.com**

http://www.horrifictales.co.uk

Angel Manor

Seven years have passed since the fire at Hope House. Despite surviving, the lives of Steve and Melody Samson have changed for the worse. Steve has become a virtual recluse, while Melody is consumed by guilt, and sees in their son a constant reminder of the man Steve used to be.

The town of Oakwell has become a tourist hotspot for paranormal enthusiasts, eager to learn more about the 'Hope House Haunting', becoming everything the residents of the once sleepy town fought so hard to prevent.

Ambitious town councillor, Henry Marshall has an idea to turn the unwanted attention on the town to his own advantage, by building a hotel on the site of Hope House.

As construction begins, the evil within Oakwell forest stirs. Influenced by the powerful Gogoku, Marshall becomes consumed with the need to draw Steve & Melody back to Oakwell, no matter the cost...

What a fabulous book!! **4.5/5 - Horror Web.com**

Bray's style of writing is a pleasure to read, however his subject matter is not. He manages to really make his characters real and forces emotions to the surface. **- Fluffyredfox Reviews**

http://www.horrifictales.co.uk

Chantal Noordeloos

LUCKY'S GIRL

Something has awakened on Grove Island. Something that, even in sleep, has held Elton Township in its black embrace. Something old, wise and patient. Something that walked the ancient forests and howled beneath black skies.

Kenny McCord had a good life - his own slice of the American Dream. But all of that is over, so he is heading home to the small town he left behind so many years ago. However Kenny is not the only son that has returned to Elton Township. His childhood friend, and worst enemy, has come back to settle old scores and, quite literally, raise a little hell.

If you like Horror that could give you nightmares, this could be a contender. **4.5/5 Shadowgum.com**

For dark, twisted, and an altogether messed-up horror that throws you to the wolves time and again, you really can't go far wrong with this hellish-trip of a novel. It's got more nightmares and mind-screwing horror packed into its pages than a night spent in the LSD-corrupted mind of Charles Manson at the pinnacle of his sex-crazed-power-tripping madness. **9/10 DLS Reviews**

Holloway has taken the American horror premise and woven in a dose of cult dynamics through it to create a gripping narrative – **5/6 Horror Hothouse**

http://www.horrifictales.co.uk

Angel Manor

HIGHMOOR III
BLOODMOON

The war has begun...

As the humans make their move against the werewolf threat in their midst, and civil war threatens to break the pack apart, John and Marie struggle to free the only person who can unite the werewolf factions against their common enemy: Marie's brother, Michael.

However, their efforts may be for nothing. As tensions mount, the Moonborn prepare to combat the human aggression with an assault of their own. An attack that could spell doom for both man and werewolf alike.

COMING 2015

http://www.horrifictales.co.uk

Chantal Noordeloos